CW01149301

CHANCE

A Small Town, Enemies to Lovers, Surprise Pregnancy, Protector Romance

Ghost Ops
Book 2

LYNN RAYE HARRIS

H.O.T. Publishing, LLC

For Linda Ketter. Thanks for all your help with Rory's diabetes. I did my best. Mistakes are mine.

All Rights Reserved. This book or any portion thereof
may not be reproduced or used in any manner whatsoever
without the express written permission of the publisher
except for the use of brief quotations in a book review.

This is a work of fiction. Names, characters, places, and incidents either are the products of the author's imagination or are used fictitiously. Any resemblance to actual persons, living or dead, businesses, companies, events, or locales is entirely coincidental.

The Hostile Operations Team® and Lynn Raye Harris® are trademarks of H.O.T. Publishing, LLC.

Printed in the United States of America

First Printing, 2024

For rights inquires, visit www.LynnRayeHarris.com

CHANCE
Copyright © 2024 by Lynn Raye Harris
Cover Design Copyright © 2024 Croco Designs

ISBN: 979-8-89117-040-7

Chapter One

AURORA HARPER STARED AT THE TEST STICK LIKE IT WAS A STICK OF dynamite.

This could *not* be happening.

But maybe it was. Her heart certainly felt like it was.

Staring back at her, very clearly, were two pink stripes. The little key on the handle helpfully told her that two pink stripes meant pregnant.

"Oh my God," she breathed, sinking onto the closed toilet to process the information. She couldn't be pregnant. What about her stupid birth control implant? What'd happened to it?

She didn't need this right now. Not on top of everything else in her life.

There was the Salty Dawg Tavern where she bartended six nights a week and took care of the books and ordering supplies. Her big brother, Theo, was the chef and part owner, but her skills were more suited to running the business than his were. They were doing really good after years of mismanagement by the person her grandmother had hired to oversee the business. She could almost taste the black columns on her spreadsheet, they were so close now.

Then there was this farmland and the house, forty acres of rolling green pastures and woods. She and Theo had inherited the property and the Dawg when their grandmother died a few years ago, and they'd worked hard to keep it in the family.

Sure, they could have sold off thirty-five acres or so and let the developers move in to build a subdivision, but she didn't want that. Theo didn't want it either.

He lived over the Dawg and she lived here. She felt guilty about wanting to hold onto the farm sometimes because selling the land would eliminate all their problems with the Dawg, but Theo was adamant that selling was a last resort.

Unless it got her a cure for the diabetes she'd had since childhood, which they both knew wasn't possible.

Rory looked at the pregnancy test on the counter again.

Pregnant.

She swallowed. Type 1 diabetics didn't have the risks they'd once had, but it was still more than usual. Which meant she was going to have to make an appointment with a gynecologist—or an obstetrician?—ASAP.

She was thirty-four, thirty-five in two months, and she'd all but given up any idea of having a child. She'd been planning to marry once, a little over four years ago, but the asshole had left her a couple of weeks before the wedding for one of her bridesmaids.

Humiliating didn't begin to cover it.

Mark and Tammy had gotten married and moved across the river to Decatur—thank God—where they procreated with stunning regularity. Rory tried not to look at their social media, showcasing their perfect life with their perfect kids in the historic district, but it sometimes slipped through.

They were up to two kids with another one on the way.

Ugh.

Rory blew out a breath. She had choices, she knew that, but she was running out of time and there was no potential husband on the horizon. If she was ever going to have a baby, it was now.

Except it wasn't as easy as that. She damned well knew who the father was, and he wasn't likely to be thrilled at the news.

She pictured Chance Hughes with his stunning good looks and Southern drawl. She'd known he was a player when she'd fallen into bed with him, but she'd just had a brush with death and she'd been in a huge fuck-it-all mood.

When you nearly died thanks to a madman who pretended to be someone he wasn't—not to mention pretending interest in you when you were feeling pretty lonely—then you pretty much said fuck it and did what you wanted.

At least for a few crazy days.

Hot, steamy, insanely crazy days.

Rory shuddered with the ghost of remembered orgasms. Emma Grace Sutton, her bestie in the whole world, had told her to grab Chance's ass and see where it went. She'd had no intention of doing it until he'd stormed into that tent where she'd been chained up and went all Conan the Barbarian on the place.

He'd gotten her free, cradled her against his massive body, and hadn't let go until they'd gotten to the hospital. She'd liked it more than she should have. Liked it enough that she'd pushed away her reservations about him and let herself enjoy the attention.

And when she'd gotten out of the hospital and he'd brought her home, he'd stayed by her side every moment he wasn't at work. Theo had been hospitalized too or he'd have been the one to take care of her, which meant she wouldn't be in this predicament now.

Because Chance wouldn't have been swaggering around her place with his perfect face and his fine ass and his firm muscles, and *she* wouldn't have been tempted beyond reason. She'd held out for a few days, at least.

Chance had installed an alarm system in her house, cameras on her long driveway and the barn—she'd insisted on paying for all of it even though it'd been a pretty penny—and stayed as close to her as she'd let him. He hadn't said Hotty Toddy even once.

Not that she *really* cared about him being an Ole Miss fan. Or, rather, she did care, but it wasn't a deal breaker if everything else was right.

When she'd felt recovered enough—and horny enough—she'd grabbed that fine ass, at least metaphorically, and Chance Hughes rocked her world with probably the best sex of her life.

She'd *craved* him. And she'd been terrified of him, too. Of what he could do to her if she let him mean more than she should.

So she'd ruined it between them. Not at first. She'd enjoyed him spreading her out on the bed and making every inch of her body tingle with pleasure.

She'd enjoyed his big cock, the way he groaned when he came, how he gasped when she took him in her mouth, the way he thrust into her so slowly she wanted to scream before he drove her into the mattress with powerful thrusts that blew her mind and stole her breath.

It'd been so, so good.

Too good.

That's why she'd had to tell him it'd been fun but it was over. She couldn't risk the heartache if she fell for him.

Been there, done that.

He'd frowned at her. Tilted his head like a dog that'd heard a strange noise.

Her heart had hammered in her chest as he'd studied her with those blue eyes. She'd been prepared for his anger, for him to fling insults at her.

He'd done none of those things. Instead, he'd nodded once, firmly, came over to kiss her on the forehead, and walked out of her life as if he'd been walking out of the Dawg at the end of an evening.

No big deal, see ya later.

Rory squeezed her eyes shut at the knot forming in her throat.

Dammit.

It'd been the right damn thing, so why did it still hurt to remember it?

Her phone dinged with an alert from the camera that Chance had installed on the fence post at the end of her driveway. She swiped her hand beneath her nose and reached for the phone.

A white truck with a decal on the side moved up her drive. She couldn't quite make it out, but she went to grab Liza Jane, the 20-gauge shotgun she'd inherited from Gramps. Her heart pounded a little more than it used to whenever someone came to her house unexpectedly. She slipped down the stairs to the front windows.

There was a porch running the length of the house in front and wrapping around one side. There was a swing, built by her grandfather for her grandmother, and a table, but she was sorely lacking in furniture and plants otherwise.

She kept telling herself that one day she'd make the space as pretty as Granny had, but she never seemed to have the time.

A commodity that was about to get a whole lot more scarce if she had a baby.

Oh God, what would Theo say?

Rory swallowed and watched as the truck swung into the circular drive in front of her house.

D&B Properties

A man in jeans and a cowboy hat got out of the passenger seat. The man in the driver's seat had on a ball cap with the company logo on it. He also wore jeans. He gestured to the land in front of him, to the barn, and around to the other side of the house.

Rory's blood boiled. She told herself to simmer down, that she didn't yet know what these men wanted, but she could guess.

She thought about going back upstairs and staying put until they left again, no matter how hard they knocked on her door. But instead she pumped the shotgun once and stepped out on the porch.

"Morning, gentlemen," she called.

The men turned almost in unison. Cowboy hat dude pasted on a smile as wide as Texas and marched toward her, hand out.

"Hello, ma'am. I'm Ronnie Davis of D&B Properties. How are you today?"

Rory leaned against a column and rested the shotgun across an arm. "I'm not selling, Mr. Davis. Not an acre. So no need to waste your time."

His smile didn't falter. He came to a halt at the bottom of the stairs and gazed up at her. He had a mustache with a touch of gray in it and dark eyes that seemed to bore into her. She swallowed and tightened her grip on the gun.

"I'd just like to talk to you a little bit, ma'am. Maybe offer a number that could change your mind."

"I don't want to talk, thank you. And you don't have a number that'll change my mind. This land has been in my family for five generations, and I intend to hold onto it for at least one more. So you'll forgive me for being abrupt, but I don't want to stand out here and explain it anymore than I already have."

The intensity in his dark eyes unnerved her.

"Well, now, Ms. Harper, I think that's a mighty big mistake you're making. What could you and your brother do with the one-point-seven-five million dollars I'm prepared to pay you?"

Rory stiffened. She didn't like that he knew anything about her, but of course he did. She moved the barrel of the shotgun from her arm to her palm.

"Is that all?" she said as breezily as she could manage with rage simmering in her belly. "I'm not sure after taxes and expenses, it'd be worth the hassle. Now if you'll excuse me, I have things to do."

Davis's smile had dimmed a bit, but it wasn't gone. His eyes, however, bored into her in a way that made her shiver. She thought of Simon Marsh, aka Kyle Hollis, the man who'd broken into her house, hurt her brother, and then held her and Emma Grace captive not quite two months ago now.

She made herself take a slow breath. Just because Ronnie Davis was annoyed and trying to hide it didn't make him the same as the psychopath who'd ripped her insulin pump from her body and nearly killed her by denying her insulin.

If Chance and his friends from One Shot Tactical hadn't found them when they did, she'd be dead.

"I think you're making a mistake, Ms. Harper. I'm prepared to discuss increasing my offer. But why keep all this land? Why not let other people have homes out here in this beautiful landscape? More residents equals more dollars in town. Surely you wouldn't mind more money coming into the Salty Dawg Tavern?"

Rory leveled the shotgun at him. She wouldn't shoot, not unless he tried to attack her, but the surest way to piss her off was to refuse to hear a word she'd said. It wasn't salesmanship. It was disrespect, pure and simple. He thought he was smarter than she was, thought all he had to do was keep talking and she'd change her mind.

"Off my property. Now. And don't come back."

Davis backed away, both hands lifted. The man who'd been driving the truck put his hand behind his back and she knew he was about to pull a gun.

"I wouldn't do that if I were you," Rory growled, aiming her shotgun at him instead. He was younger than Davis. The look he gave her wasn't nearly as civilized either. "You're on private property and I've asked you to leave. I'm within my rights to defend myself if you don't. You pull a weapon, I'm dropping you where you stand."

"Stand down, RJ," Davis said. "We're leaving, ma'am. No need to get hostile."

RJ lifted both hands and went around the truck to climb inside. Davis joined him. RJ stomped the gas pedal, throwing rocks toward the house before he sped down the driveway in a cloud of dust. The rocks didn't quite reach her, but gravel landed in her granny's flower beds and across the lawn. There were also two deep grooves where the truck had been parked.

Assholes.

Rory sighed and lowered the gun, her body beginning to tremble. Those men weren't dangerous, not like Simon Marsh, but they were a nuisance. She didn't think she'd seen the last of them, either. Not with the way this part of Alabama was growing.

She was tired suddenly. She slumped against the column, tears filling her eyes as she looked at the land she loved.

Why was it that every time she thought things in her life were looking up, something had to come along and remind her that she wasn't that lucky?

Chapter Two

Chance "Wraith" Hughes walked into the Salty Dawg Tavern behind Blaze "Shadow" Connolly and Emma Sutton. His gaze strayed immediately to the bar. Rory was there, golden hair pulled back in a ponytail, her white tank top clinging to her full breasts. He tried not to notice, but he was only a man.

A man who knew what she tasted like.

Her gaze was on the two men seated in front of her as she set down beers for both of them. One said something that made her laugh. Chance's heart squeezed at the sound. He'd made her laugh too, but mostly he'd made her moan.

He clamped down on that line of thought. Didn't need to remember what it'd felt like to have Rory beneath him. On top of him. Surrounding him.

He reminded himself that Rory wasn't the only woman in town. He'd find someone else to have fun with between the sheets. Eventually.

It was for the best their little fling was over.

Blaze might have gone against orders in falling for a woman, but

Chance wasn't planning to give their team leader a heart attack by being Victim Number Two to the love bug.

Poor Ghost. The one thing he'd told them back in DC when he'd recruited them for this job was that their lack of family ties was a plus. No kids or wives to worry about. No parents requiring weekly or daily phone calls. No siblings sending texts at all hours.

No one who would talk about them to the wrong person if someone showed up asking questions. And no one who would suffer if the mission went wrong and they ended up in prison. Or dead. Couldn't forget dead. It was possible.

The mission was just for a few months while the Ghost Ops team prevented a top secret national defense project from being sabotaged or the technology stolen. Once Athena was launched, Chance and his team were in the clear. They could leave Alabama, return to HOT HQ, and be reinstated in the military if they wanted.

Chance was pretty sure that's what he wanted. What they were doing in Alabama was incredibly important, and yet it wasn't the same ops tempo he was used to. He missed grabbing his gear and hitting the tarmac, piling into a C-5 Galaxy and heading overseas to rescue hostages, kick terrorist ass, or fight insurgents.

All three if he was lucky.

He'd miss his team when this was over. These men were his brothers, his family. Some of them might return to active duty with him. Not all, though.

Blaze certainly wouldn't. But Seth would. Ethan too, because he was from New York state and kept lamenting there wasn't any decent Italian food anywhere to be found.

The others were a mystery.

Chance pushed away the hint of doubt that reared up inside him whenever he thought about returning to active duty. What the hell else was he going to do if he didn't put the uniform on again? Stay in Alabama and teach gun safety and personal security to civilians as well as teaching companies how to keep their premises secure?

Hell, he didn't even know what was going to happen to One Shot Tactical, the gun range and store where they operated out of, once their mission was done anyway. It wasn't like they truly owned the property, even if they did on paper. It was part of their cover, not permanent.

What the government giveth, the government taketh away.

Especially something that had cost so much to build and maintain.

"Hey, Chance."

Chance jerked his gaze to the waitress who always flirted with him whenever he showed up. "Hey, Amber."

She was pretty, with short brown hair, dark eyes, and cleavage that wouldn't quit. She wore tight T-shirts and cut off jean shorts when she worked, and Chance couldn't help that his gaze strayed over her assets every time.

He wasn't tempted, though. Never had been, which he couldn't figure out. She'd all but told him she was his for the taking. Help get his mind off Rory, that's for sure.

"You gonna be around at closing?" she asked, shooting him a pouty look from beneath her long, fake eyelashes.

"Uh, not sure. Maybe."

She grinned. "Well, if you *are*, I need a ride home. I'd be *very* grateful."

He grinned back even though he didn't feel it. "I'll keep that in mind, darlin'."

After another flirty look and a palm skimmed over his arm, Amber jumped when Rory barked something at her.

"Gotta go," she said with an eye-roll Rory couldn't see before skittering back to the bar.

Chance looked up and made eye contact with the woman behind the bar. Rory glared daggers at him, and his gut twisted.

Nothing new about the daggers. But for fuck's sake, he hadn't done anything wrong.

He gave her a little wave and she turned away without acknowledging him. Typical Rory.

It pissed him off and wound him up at the same time. She'd been the one to break it off, not him. So why she acted like he'd done something wrong baffled him.

One thing was for sure: he wasn't ever gonna understand Aurora Harper. No point in even trying.

Chance turned away and headed over to the table where Kane "Demon" Fox and Seth "Phantom" King sat with a pitcher of beer and a basket of wings. Blaze and Emma were already there.

Emma was frowning at him as he walked up but she quickly looked away. He didn't know if that meant she felt sorry for him or what. She was Rory's best friend. For all he knew, Rory had shared everything about their fling with Emma. He ached to ask her what the hell Rory was thinking, but he knew better.

"Didn't know you were coming, Chance," Kane said as he snatched up a wing.

"I wasn't planning on it until these two dragged me over."

He'd been cleaning up at the range, planning to go to his room at the farmhouse and veg out with a cold beer, a couple of pulled pork sandwiches from the Gas-n-Go, and a Doctor Who marathon when Blaze and Emma talked him into going to the Dawg. Hadn't taken much talking, really, if he was honest about it.

It'd been at least four days since he'd lain eyes on Rory and he'd wanted to see her. Make sure she was okay. He hadn't forgotten how confused and pale she'd been when he'd found her in that tent. He'd learned everything he could about Type 1 diabetes after that. He knew it was manageable and that people lived normal lives. They just had more risks than others did.

And more to think about, like how many carbs were in a meal and whether or not they were exercising or getting hot and needed to adjust their insulin levels. It was a lot, but Rory had been doing it since she was thirteen. He'd quickly learned she didn't like anyone fussing over her or thinking she couldn't handle something because of her disease.

"I don't think it was quite dragging," Emma said, taking the seat that Blaze pulled out for her. "More like a little nudge."

"All you had to do was remind me it's meatloaf night. That's a good enough reason for anybody."

The guys enthusiastically agreed. The Dawg's meatloaf was famous in at least three counties. They served it with creamy mashed potatoes and beefy gravy, buttered corn, green beans with ham hocks, and yeast rolls or cornbread. Dessert was cobbler of some kind, probably blackberry, though peaches would be in season soon.

All of it delicious.

Blaze plunked down beside Emma and draped an arm over her chair. He was still possessive and protective after what'd happened with Simon Marsh a couple of months ago.

Chance understood the feeling. He'd felt it from the moment he'd walked into Rory's house and discovered her gone. It'd only intensified once he'd learned she was diabetic and Marsh had ripped her insulin pump from her body.

He still wasn't over it, not really, but Rory had made it perfectly clear she didn't want him in her life anymore.

"Thank you for the sex, Chance. It's been nice. But I'm done now, and I want you to leave."

That was over a month ago, and she'd shown no signs of missing a single thing between them.

So he hadn't either, even though he went to bed at night with a burning in his belly and woke up with the same. He still ate at the Dawg—maybe not quite as often as before—still flirted shamelessly with every woman that crossed his path, and pretended not to notice Rory unless she was right in front of him.

God forgive him, he'd even gone back to annoying her with football rivalries. But that was when her eyes flashed and he felt her gaze burn into him.

Part of him craved that burn, so he kept poking at her with shit talk about Alabama and their new coach. One of these days, she was going to hit him over the head with a beer mug. At least then he'd know she felt something, even if it was fury.

Chance took the seat beside Emma. She gave him a small smile and he smiled back. Yep, she definitely felt sorry for him. *Fuck.*

Now he was gonna spend the evening wondering what the hell Rory had said about him. His ego wanted to know if she'd disparaged his abilities in bed. What else would make Emma look at him like he deserved pity?

Amber came over to take their drink orders. She winked and smiled at him, sidling up so close he could feel her body heat. He winked back because, fuck it, no way was he letting Emma think he couldn't deliver in the bedroom. It'd be just like Rory to diss him that way.

"Be right back with those drinks," Amber said, skimming a hand over his biceps and through his hair as she turned to walk away.

"Looks like somebody might get laid tonight," Seth observed.

"Amber hits on everyone," Chance said dismissively. He caught Emma's frown and barreled on, despite the voice in his head telling him to shut up. "Still, she wants to take me for a ride, who am I to say no?"

Blaze was shaking his head behind Emma, mouthing the word no. Chance thought about saying something else just to make it clear he didn't care what Emma or Rory thought about him, but it was kinda hard to do when Emma had cared enough to sew him up a couple of months ago. She hadn't asked too many questions, though she'd been pissed about it at the time. She'd known he and Blaze were lying about what'd happened, but she hadn't pushed them for the truth.

And now she knew the six of them were a Special Ops team and the range wasn't their only reason for being in Alabama. More than

Chance

that, Emma was Blaze's woman. Chance wasn't going to annoy her if he could help it.

"On the other hand, I got an early morning tomorrow," he said. "Have to go do a security test in Research Park for a bunch of scientists."

Blaze nodded, looking relieved. Emma turned to tell him what she wanted for dinner and then he kissed her before she got up and headed for the bar. For Rory.

Chance reached for a wing off Kane's plate, needing something to do.

"Here." Kane pushed the ranch dressing at him so he could dip the wing in the sauce before he shoved it in his mouth.

It was the perfect kind of crispy. He hated a soggy wing.

Theo Harper was the chef at the Salty Dawg Tavern. He served up bar food every night along with homestyle lunches and dinners. Sometimes he made it up as he went along, but there were some things you could rely on.

Prime rib on Friday night.

Meatloaf.

Fried chicken.

Cajun pasta drenched in a creamy, spicy sauce and served with shrimp and garlic bread.

And of course the bar food like wings, burgers, and fries.

If the bar atmosphere was too much for anyone, Miss Mary's Diner served up breakfast, lunch, and dinner from six in the morning until nine every night. Their pies were the best around. Apple, chocolate, coconut, cherry, and fruit cobblers that made your teeth ache and your belly cheer.

"Sorry about that," Blaze said. "But Emma cares about you and Rory both. I think she holds out hope y'all will get back together. You going out with Amber would crush that hope."

Chance shrugged. "I get it, but we weren't ever really together. And I'm not going to be celibate just so Emma can feel good."

"Nope, got it. But I appreciate you letting her down easy tonight."

"I don't want her upset, brother. I just think she's got to face reality." Same as he did.

"And that is?" Blaze asked with an arched eyebrow.

"Rory isn't into me. That's all there is to it."

Which, yeah, pricked his pride. He was a fucking delight. Most women adored him.

Not Rory Harper though. She'd made that clear when she'd told him to get out.

"Never knew you to give up so easily," Blaze drawled. "The Chance I know keeps on going even when he's been told the odds are against him. Got us all out of that scrape in the jungle a few years ago because you wouldn't give up."

Chance shrugged off the needling. As much as he could anyway. "That was life or death. Not the same thing."

Blaze lifted an eyebrow as he reached for one of the wings that Kane and Seth were no longer eating.

Kane nodded. "Dude's got a point. You aren't a quitter, Chance. None of us are. Kinda why we're here."

"Not quitting," Chance snapped. "I'm not interested in Rory Harper. Been there, done that, it was okay, the end."

"Oh my."

Chance's head whipped around. Amber had just walked up with her tray and now she was giggling and looking much too pleased. "I promise you it'll be more than okay with me," she whispered in his ear as she set his beer in front of him. "Take me home tonight and find out."

Chance curled his hand around the bottle. "Thanks for the beer, Amber."

"Anytime, hot stuff." She winked and pulled out her order pad. "Now what do y'all want for dinner?"

Chapter Three

"You okay, hon?"

Rory blinked and jerked her gaze to Emma Grace, who'd come over to the bar to talk while she waited for her food to be delivered to the table she shared with the One Shot Tactical guys. Rory nodded and pasted on a smile, though her heart beat a little faster tonight and her stomach had decided to get queasy. She didn't know if that was the pregnancy hormones or her encounter with Ronnie Davis and his driver earlier.

She wished she'd been just a hair nicer to them. Then she'd know who the driver was too. But all she had was a face, some initials, and a hard look to remember him by. If she'd been a little more approachable, and a little less irritated, maybe the men would have gone away with smiles on their faces instead of carving two trenches in her driveway.

"I'm fine," she said, taking a sip of the ice water she'd poured for herself tonight.

"Blood glucose levels okay?"

Rory gave her friend an exaggerated frown. "Emma Grace, I know you're a doctor and all, but honestly, I've been living with this disease for more than twenty years at this point. I know how to keep an eye on myself."

Emma Grace looked chastened, and that wasn't what Rory intended. She reached for her friend's hand and gave it a squeeze.

"I'm sorry for snapping. I'm a little bit stressed if I'm honest, and that's spiking my blood sugars. I've adjusted for it on the pump."

"Anything I can do to help? About the stress?"

"It's just something I'm working through."

Rory loved that Emma Grace accepted her apology and moved straight into support mode. She didn't hover, didn't insist on getting all doctor-y, though Rory would let her if she truly felt sick. She wasn't stupid. She didn't like to be coddled and she'd had a lifetime of people hovering over her, getting poked by doctors, and generally being treated like she was made of glass when she just wanted to be normal.

She fought for her normal, because she was normal. Living with diabetes added extra steps, but she wasn't an invalid and she didn't need twenty-four hour supervision. She'd had to fight Theo when their grandmother died and she wanted to keep living in the farmhouse. He'd wanted her to take the other apartment above the Dawg so they'd be close to each other, but she'd gotten pissed and called him a big lug and he'd gotten pissed and called her a little ant.

He finally saw things her way when she went ballistic on him, yelling about Mark dumping her before the wedding, about her bridesmaid running off with her fiancé and getting the life she'd been supposed to have, and a bunch of other stuff about how she was never getting married or having kids so why not just let her have a small slice of happiness, for fuck's sake.

In the end, she'd promised to text him regularly and answer the phone anytime he called so he'd know she wasn't in a coma, and that had been that. It'd worked for almost five years now and it was going to keep working for many more.

Chance

Because she wasn't selling, no matter how much money Ronnie Davis came up with.

"Let me know if I can help you work through it," Emma Grace said.

Rory thought of the pregnancy test she'd stuffed back into the foil before throwing it away. Emma Grace could refer her to an obstetrician, but this wasn't the place to discuss it. Because her friend was going to want answers, and Rory wasn't prepared to give them when Chance Hughes sat ten feet away, looking like a romance novel hero with his tight polo shirt and ripped muscles, his sparkling blue eyes and dazzling smile.

Really, he was too gorgeous and he knew it. She remembered him strutting around her bedroom stark ass naked, everything on display, not a single hint of modesty about him.

She'd loved looking at him. Touching him.

Feeling his body thrusting into hers.

Amber sashayed over to the table with the tray of drinks Rory had just finished pouring. When she set Chance's down, she leaned in close and whispered in his ear.

Rory deliberately turned away. She didn't want to see Chance flirt back.

Amber, bless her, had asked Rory if she and Chance were a thing or if he was open game. Rory had told her to go for it.

Her stomach chose that minute to roil and she pressed a hand to it, willing the queasiness to subside. Emma Grace was watching and Rory decided she had a choice to make. Tell her doctor friend about the pregnancy or tell her about Ronnie Davis and his pal.

"Got a visit from a property developer today," she said, taking a sip of the club soda as Nikki strolled up to the bar with an order. "At the farm," she clarified.

"Oh yeah? What did they want?"

Rory grabbed a couple of glasses and set them beneath the taps, pulling the handle to release yeasty beer into one of the glasses. "To buy the land. I told them to get lost." She grabbed another glass and scooped ice into it, snagged the nozzle for Coke and splashed it into the glass. "I don't think they took it well, though," she said, setting the Coke on the tray along with one of the beers before pulling another one.

"What do you mean?" Emma Grace said, looking concerned. "What happened?"

Rory set the second beer on the tray and Nikki returned from where she'd been putting food orders into the system to pick it up and carry it to a waiting table.

"I mean a man named Ronnie Davis of D&B Properties offered me nearly two million bucks, then got mad when I said no. His driver peeled out and left gouges in my driveway. Scattered rock all over Granny's flower beds too."

"Oh damn, Rory. Why didn't you call me?"

Rory gave her friend the arched eyebrow. "Seriously, what were you going to do about it? Go after them with a stethoscope and a hypodermic needle?"

Emma Grace laughed, then smoothed the laughter away as if she hadn't meant to do it. She put on her serious face and gave Rory a look. "No, but I know some guys who specialize in dissuading people from doing stuff like that. Heck, they'd probably get Mr. Davis and his driver to pick up all the rocks and rake the driveway if you wanted them to. They'd also make sure that Davis and his people never bother you at the farm again."

It was a nice idea but Rory didn't need to be asking the One Shot Tactical guys for help every time she encountered a difficulty.

"I think I might have persuaded them myself," she said, leaning against the bar with her arms crossed. "I took Liza Jane out to meet them."

Emma Grace blinked in confusion.

Rory rolled her eyes. "Liza Jane? Gramps's double-barreled Browning 20-gauge?"

"Oh, that's right. I'd forgotten about the name. It's been years since I've even seen that gun. Did they piss themselves?"

"Welp, they showered the front with rocks and carved those grooves in the gravel, so maybe?" Rory shook her head. "I expect they'll be back, though they'll probably come in here."

Emma Grace smirked. "Guess they don't know that Theo's even ornerier than you are about some things."

"They'll find out, won't they?"

Amber returned with an order and Rory filled it. Her stomach was settling, which was a relief. She opened a sleeve of saltines and nibbled on them. Emma Grace twisted her wine glass back and forth, a habit Rory knew meant her friend was thinking hard about something.

"Everything okay with Mr. Romance?" Rory asked.

Emma Grace's focus snapped from the glass to Rory's face. "Sorry, I was thinking. And yes, everything is fabulous." Her face took on that dreamy expression that Rory might hate on anyone else. "He writes me notes every morning and leaves them in different places so I can find them."

"Sickening," Rory said with a grin. "Tell me more."

Emma Grace laughed. "He scoops the cat box so I don't have to."

"Oooh, romantic."

"Sure is. There's other stuff, but I don't feel right going on about my life when I'm worried about you."

Uh-oh.

Rory shrugged. "Nothing to worry about, babe. I'm fine."

Emma Grace leaned in. "I just... I want to know what happened with you and Chance. He was so protective of you, and you seemed happy about it. He was at your place all the time. Y'all were getting along so well, and now you're back to avoiding each other when you aren't sniping over stupid stuff."

Rory felt the pinch of those words in her heart. "I'll have you know that SEC football is not stupid stuff, madam."

"I love the Tide as much as anyone, Ror. You know what I mean."

Rory spread her arms wide. "It didn't work out, okay? It was all sizzle and no spark. Nothing to keep burning when the new wears off, you know?"

Emma Grace studied her. "So you *did* get that Vitamin D."

There was no point in denying it when the truth was going to come out very soon anyway. Rory glanced around to make sure nobody was listening as she popped her arms around her middle, feeling protective and somewhat uncertain of herself. "Yes, I got the D," she said quietly. "It was really, really good, too. But D isn't the same as HEA."

"H-E—what? I don't know what that stands for."

Rory shook her head. "My poor, nerdy doctor friend. You didn't read nearly enough romance novels in your life, did you?"

"I've read them," Emma Grace muttered. "I even read that reverse harem book you loaned me. Blaze says thank you very much, by the way."

Rory snorted. Nothing like a steamy romance to improve the sex life a bit. "Tell him he's welcome. I've got more. Also, the HEA is the happily ever after. It's where the heroine gets all the D she can handle along with the hero's undying love. It's when the romance is wrapped up in a nice, neat bow that never comes untied because the hero is devoted to the heroine beyond all measure." Her throat was tight. She leaned toward her friend. "It's what you have with Blaze. Devotion, love, great sex. A man who writes you little notes, looks at you with his heart in his eyes, and cleans up cat poop. For a kitten he *gave* to you, I might add."

Emma Grace's eyes were suspiciously moist. "I do have that, don't I? Wow." She sniffed and lifted her chin. "I want that for you, too. So bad, Rory."

"I know, babe." She smiled a little sadly. "I just don't think I'm the kind of person who inspires that level of devotion."

Emma Grace's expression hardened. "What did he do? Or say? I'll strangle him myself."

Rory blinked at her friend's ferocity. Then she laughed as she held up a hand. "Whoa, whoa, whoa. If you're talking about Chance, he didn't do anything. Honestly, he was great while it lasted. But it was just sex. We had our fun and now it's over. Time to move on."

Her gaze drifted over Emma Grace's shoulder to where Amber stood next to Chance. She had her hand on his shoulder, laughing at something he'd said. He put his hand on hers and Rory looked away, her eyes stinging. Damn hormones.

"Okay," Emma Grace said, sighing heavily. "If that's the way you want it. But don't tell me you aren't the sort of person who inspires devotion. You just haven't met the right guy yet, that's all."

"Maybe. You better get back to your table. Amber's bringing plates out."

Emma Grace slid off the stool. "I'll be back after I eat."

"I'll be here." Rory smiled as she watched her friend return to the table. Four sexy men looked up and smiled at her. Blaze got up to pull her chair out, his gaze lingering on her face as she sat. He pressed a kiss to her forehead and sat beside her.

Rory sighed. Emma Grace thought she just hadn't met the right man yet, but Rory knew it wasn't happening. Especially now. Single moms typically had a harder time finding a man willing to take on a baby that wasn't his. Maybe later, when the kid was a little older.

It could happen. Or not. Probably not, with her luck.

She looked over at Chance again. Amber was gone, and he stared straight at her. Rory dropped her gaze away, her heart throbbing at that simple touch of their eyes.

She picked up a saltine and nibbled on it. How in the hell was she going to tell him she was pregnant but she didn't expect anything from him? That he could keep on seeing whoever he pleased and she'd never ask him for a thing?

She didn't know, but she was going to have to figure it out. Soon.

Chapter Four

Chance sat in his truck in the parking lot behind the Salty Dawg, waiting for Rory to walk out. He gripped the wheel in both hands, clenching and unclenching his fists on it.

She'd been threatened. Two men had driven onto her property, offered her money for the land, and made a mess of her driveway when she said no.

To be fair, she'd had a gun, but that was still no excuse.

Chance thought back to the moment when Emma had told everyone at the table what'd happened. It'd taken everything he had not to get up and go over to the bar and ask Rory what the fuck she was thinking. Not only had she confronted two men alone, she hadn't even bothered to ask for help when they'd left her place in disarray.

He hadn't gone to the bar because he'd known how that would go. Rory would light him up then and there in the middle of the Dawg with half of Sutton's Creek as witnesses. The crowd would get a charge out of it, no doubt, but Chance didn't want to give her any excuse not to listen to what he had to say.

She could yell at him when it was just the two of them. And

when she finished yelling, he'd go right back to the topic until she fucking got it in her thick head that she wasn't an Amazon warrior queen. He'd installed cameras for her, shown her how to use them, as well as a basic alarm system on the house. He'd have done more, but she'd insisted on paying for everything herself.

He'd thought to lowball her and install what he wanted anyway, but he'd had to get that idea right out of his head when she'd said she wanted an itemized bill that contained everything he installed, including serial numbers and warranty information, plus a to-the-minute accounting of any labor.

He hadn't known how to fake that, especially since Rory had a business degree from the University of Alabama and knew her balance sheets backwards and forwards. If she got a suspect invoice, she'd know it.

He'd thought he could talk her into upgrading after she'd used the system for a week or two. He'd expected to be there with her, protecting her, so he hadn't worried too much about it.

Then she told him to get lost.

Chance glanced around the parking lot. There weren't too many cars left at almost eleven at night. The Dawg closed at ten on weeknights, one a.m. Friday and Saturday, and they were closed on Sunday. Since this was a Thursday, he expected her any minute now.

The glow of a cigarette caught his attention behind Colleen Wright's store. A moment later she came toward his truck. He had the window down and an arm resting on the sill. It was May in Alabama, still comfortably cool in the evenings, but growing hotter every day.

"The spirits want you to know something," Colleen said as she walked beneath the soft light of a streetlamp. Her crystal necklace caught the light, sparkling.

"Evening, Miz Wright. How you doing?"

Colleen flicked the cigarette to the ground and stepped on it. "Just peachy, dear. How about you?"

Chance shrugged. "Well enough."

"Exactly." She folded her arms over her chest, her caftan flowing around her in the evening breeze. "You need to watch that girl closely. She's in bigger trouble than she realizes. If she isn't careful, she'll lose everything."

Chance didn't like the way the hairs on his neck prickled. He didn't truly think Colleen knew anything supernatural, but it felt a little uncanny that she'd focused on Rory when she was his entire reason for being out here tonight.

Then again, Colleen could be taking a stab in the dark. He hadn't said who he was waiting for.

"Which girl?" Chance ventured. For all she knew, he was meeting Amber or Nikki once they were done closing up for the night.

Colleen scoffed. "Child, please. Aurora, of course. She's the one you can't stop thinking about."

A prickle of annoyance stabbed to life inside him as well as a healthy dose of surprise.

"What makes you think I can't stop thinking about her? I spend a lot of time not thinking about her at all."

Colleen had already pulled a fresh cigarette from somewhere and proceeded to light it. "I know things because the spirits tell me. They've told me you have a healthy obsession with Aurora Harper, and that you aren't wrong to worry about her. That's all I know, and why I walked over here."

She took a drag of the cigarette. Chance shook his head, more to himself than to her.

"If they tell you anything specific, like *why* she needs watching or *who* the threat is coming from, I'd be much obliged, ma'am."

"It doesn't work that way, but you can be sure if I get a message like that, I'll let you know about it."

"Thank you, ma'am. Appreciate it."

"You're welcome. Now can you please tell me when you boys are going to help me record my alien sightings? I asked Blaze, but he keeps telling me he doesn't have time. What about you? Can you be there in the morning at two a.m.? That's when the aliens are most active. Reba will be there, too."

Chance blinked. He vaguely recalled that Reba was Colleen's friend from Huntsville. "Can't Reba film the aliens?"

"No. She has to chant."

Chance cleared his throat. "Uh, yeah, I see. Don't think I can make it this time, Miz Wright. Gotta be to work early, and I need my beauty sleep."

She scoffed. "You're already pretty enough, but I understand. Next time I'll give you more notice."

The last thing he needed was for her to think he was ever going to stand in a cotton field at two in the morning to record aliens. "I think you need a smart phone, ma'am. If you had one, you wouldn't need us at all. The cameras on phones are pretty amazing these days. You could set it on a tripod and get everything yourself."

"Young man, I have a flip phone because it's easy to make calls. I don't have to hunt for an app or touch a screen. I have buttons and I can use those. Besides, if your average smart phone was good enough to capture the aliens, don't you think someone would have done it by now? What I need is specialized equipment, and you boys have that out there at your range."

Chance didn't know what to say to that. "Yes, ma'am, guess you're right. If it was that easy, somebody else would have captured it by now."

Somebody else would also need to be as kooky as Colleen to believe aliens were frequenting the night sky over Alabama fields on a regular basis. So far, seemed like the only other true believer was Reba.

"Glad you see my point. I'll let you know the next time we're going out. Now you keep an eye on Rory and don't let her do anything stupid."

Chance wanted to ask if Colleen knew Rory at all with a comment like that. You didn't *let* Rory do anything. She was strong-willed and fiercely independent. Best you could do was give her reasons why she shouldn't do a thing. If the reasons were good enough, she'd listen. Maybe.

Colleen strolled into the darkness, the cherry red glow of her cigarette bobbing in the air as she walked. Cigarette smoke wafted to him on the breeze and he waved it away, frowning at a memory of his mother sitting at the kitchen table, lighting a cigarette when he'd never seen her smoke before. She'd been shaking that day as she'd pulled the cylinder from the crisp pack of menthols and lit it up like she'd been smoking every day of her life.

He didn't remember a lot about that day, because he'd been thirteen and more concerned with going to the community pool with his friends, but he knew that it wasn't even twenty-four hours later that his life had changed forever.

The back door of the Dawg opened and Amber came out. Chance drew his arm into the truck so she wouldn't see him sitting there. She stopped and pulled something from her purse. A vape pen. He could see it when she tapped her phone and the screen lit her face.

Nikki came out next and Amber walked with her toward a beat-up old Chevy S-10. They got inside and Chance exhaled. Amber had found a ride home after all. Actually, she'd probably never needed one. She'd just been trying to get in his pants.

He sighed. If he hadn't met Rory, hadn't been aware of her from the first moment he'd lain eyes on her in the Dawg back in January, he'd have probably been a willing participant in Amber's scheme.

Fucking Rory. How was it out of all the pretty women he'd met since moving to Alabama, she was the one he couldn't quite get out of his head?

Nikki and Amber drove away with the windows down, singing Mötley Crüe as they drove past his truck.

When the door opened again about fifteen minutes later, Rory walked out. He wanted to get out of the truck and storm over to her, ask her what the hell she was doing walking into a dark parking lot alone, but Amber had done the same thing and he'd barely blinked.

Sutton's Creek was small and welcoming, but that didn't mean bad things couldn't happen. Fucking Kyle Hollis, aka Simon Marsh, had walked into her living room and attacked her before she'd understood what was happening. She almost hadn't survived.

Rory walked over to her truck, a 1970 Ford F-250 that'd belonged to her grandpa. The damn thing didn't have modern safety features like airbags or disc brakes, but Rory flew down the back roads like it did. Chance knew because he'd ridden with her once. The windows had been down, her hair whipping in the breeze, and she'd laughed like it was the best thing ever.

Hell, he'd laughed too. At the time, maybe it *had* been the best thing ever. The day'd been sunny, the temps were warming, he'd been deep inside her only an hour before, and life was fucking great.

Chance thought about following Rory home and confronting her there, but he didn't want to scare her by turning into the driveway behind her. If it was daylight, she'd know the truck was his. If he called to tell her he was following, she'd argue with him on the phone, then speed up her driveway and go inside to lock the doors before he could step a foot onto her porch.

Or, hell, maybe she'd threaten him with Liza Jane.

He pushed his door open and stepped out. "Rory," he called.

She turned in his direction. Then she straightened her shoulders as if preparing for battle. "What do you want, Chance?"

He strolled toward her, hands in pockets. Feigning a coolness he didn't feel.

"To talk to you."

She tossed her head, blond hair shimmering in the streetlight. "About what? And why didn't you come up to the bar if you wanted to talk?"

He went up to her and stopped a couple feet away. He was close enough to smell that damned vanilla and peach shampoo she used. Made his balls tighten with memories.

"Didn't seem like the time. Emma told us about the construction company."

Rory made a noise. "Big mouth bestie." She cocked a hip and put a hand on it. "Look, it's fine. A man came out to the house and wanted to buy it. I said no. He and his driver left in a hurry and kicked up some rocks. I'll have to pick them out of the flowerbeds and rake the grooves back into place, but that's really the end of it."

"So you were just gonna threaten two strangers with a shotgun and clean up the mess they left and not tell anyone about it?"

She popped her arms over her chest and glared. "I told Emma Grace, didn't I? And I told my brother because the land is his too."

"Oh yeah? What did Theo say?"

"Not that it's any of your business, but Theo doesn't want to sell either."

"Uh-huh. That's it?"

Because he'd learned to have a lot of respect for Theo Harper after the way he'd tried to protect his sister from Hollis. The man wasn't a warrior but he'd taken a lot of abuse trying to save her. Even when he'd gotten out of the hospital, he'd been protective of her. Theo had looked Chance in the eye and promised an ass whooping to beat all ass whoopings if he hurt Rory in any way. Not that Theo was any match for him, but hadn't stopped the man from threatening anyway.

"He might have suggested that Liza Jane was a bit too strong of a statement." Rory sniffed in disdain. "I don't agree, however."

"Jesus, Rory. You could have gotten hurt, you know."

"How? It's my land and I was defending it. They were trespassing."

"You could have called your friends. You could have called *me*."

"That's sweet of you, Chancey Pants, but a girl's got to know how to take care of herself these days. Kyle Hollis taught me that.

I'd rather go in with both barrels loaded and ready than get caught unaware ever again."

Chance raked a hand through his hair and swore. "You need to expand the alarm system. Add higher resolution cameras, a bigger hard drive to record activity. I can do that for you."

"I'd love to but I don't exactly have the budget for that right now. Maybe later."

"Rory, for fuck's sake. I'll get the equipment at cost. Labor is free. Pay me back when you have the money. This is what I *do*."

She took a step toward him, her eyes glittering in the light. Or flashing, perhaps. "Installing alarms is what you do? I thought you shot guns and taught others how to shoot them. Oh, and self-defense. You do that too, plus you put on tactical gear and rescue people from bad guys. Now you're an alarm company as well?"

Chance gritted his teeth. "I'm a security specialist. I protect people and I show them how to protect themselves. This is not news to you. As far as rescuing people, you already know how we found you and why we were there. If we hadn't tracked you and Emma, you'd both be dead. So I'm really fucking glad we knew how to do that, okay?"

He was breathing a little harder than the situation warranted, but fucking hell she annoyed the crap out of him sometimes.

"I'm glad too," she said, her voice smaller than before. "And I'm sorry for fighting with you, but I've been on my own for so many years that I know I have to rely on myself. Theo would drop everything for me, but I don't want him to. I want him to have a life of his own. Which means I have to do it myself, okay?"

"All I'm talking about is expanding your system, Rory. I'll keep it reasonable. I'll give you all the costs upfront. Except labor. Non-negotiable. And I want you to *call me* if those assholes return. I know you're a badass who can protect your own house, but it's literally my job. Let me be your back up the next time."

He thought she was about to refuse, but she huffed. "Okay, fine. I'll call you if it happens again. Which I don't expect it will. I was clear with Ronnie Davis that I'm not selling. He'll probably try again by upping his offer, but he'll call or drop by the Dawg. He knows he can't intimidate me at home anymore."

Chance thought she was probably wrong about that. Maybe Davis wasn't the type, but there were others and they were sure to come calling as property in and around Sutton's Creek became more desirable.

Still, he wasn't starting that argument with her. Let her believe what she wanted so long as she called him when she needed to.

"I'll follow you home," he said.

"What? No, you don't need to do that. I'm fine."

Yet her voice shook the tiniest bit. He wouldn't have known if he hadn't been paying attention. Or if they'd been talking at the bar while she'd been working. He wouldn't have heard it with all the noise.

"I know you are. But humor me. Let me make sure you get inside the house safely. I'll check out the grooves in the driveway, see how bad it is. And I'll figure out where to put a couple more cameras while I'm there."

"It's the Harper Farm, Chance. Not Fort Knox. I got the alert when they turned into the driveway. That's why I was ready for them." She dragged her phone from her back pocket and swiped. "You can look at the feed now if it makes you feel better. Nobody's been there. I don't have alerts set when I'm at work because I'd get one every time a deer walked across the driveway, but I check them out—"

"What is it?" he asked, everything in him going still when she didn't finish the sentence.

"There was a car an hour ago. It went to the house."

"Let me see."

She handed him the phone and he replayed the video. A dark sedan crept up her driveway toward the house. He couldn't read the license plate. Yet another reason for better cameras. He opened the feed for the camera he'd put on the porch. The car halted and a person got out. Looked like a man, tall and lean. He was dressed in black and he had a black mask over his face.

A balaclava.

Chance barely suppressed the growl crawling up his throat. The man went to the left, beneath the trees, and disappeared. Chance fast forwarded through the feed until the man was back, getting into the car again. He backed up and turned, then crept down the driveway again.

Rage, cold and dark, roared to life inside Chance. No way in hell was he letting Rory go home alone tonight.

"I'm following you home, Rory. You aren't stepping foot out of your truck until I've checked everything."

"Okay," she said, her arms wrapped around her middle. He hated that she was scared, but he was glad she wasn't arguing.

He figured that was about to change with what he said next, but he was saying it anyway. And then he was fucking doing it whether she liked it or not.

"Once I've made sure it's safe, we're going inside. And I'm staying the night."

Chapter Five

HEAT BLOSSOMED IN HER CHEST AND SPREAD THROUGH HER LIMBS when he said he was staying the night. Rory shook her head even though her heart danced at the idea.

"No, you can't stay. There's no need."

"Not up for debate, Rory. It's me, or I'm calling Theo and he'll come stay with you." He dragged his phone from his jeans pocket. "Which is it?"

She stared at him, willing her mouth to tell him to fuck off. But the words wouldn't come. Because she was scared. Because she didn't like the idea that some asshole had been creeping around her house in the dark. What had he been doing anyway?

It made all the fear from when Kyle Hollis had kidnapped her come rolling back to life like a wave heading to shore.

She could let Chance call Theo. Her brother would insist on going with her and staying overnight.

But the last time Theo had tried to save her, he'd nearly gotten himself killed. She believed with all her heart that her brother was capable of protecting her, but what if somebody got the jump on him the way Hollis had? He hadn't seen it coming because he wasn't trained for it.

Theo was a gentle soul who loved those he loved, and who liked tinkering in the kitchen and cooking up heaps of delicious food. He wasn't a warrior.

Chance was. Not that she knew she would need a warrior with her tonight, but she'd rather inconvenience Chance—and herself since this heat simmering in her blood was anything but hate—than drag Theo into another situation where he might be in over his head.

"You're staying in the guest room."

"No can do, honey. Your bedroom is on the first floor and the rest are on the second. I'll take the couch."

Rory glared. "Why don't you just check everything out and head home again? I'll lock the door. I always do now. And don't call me honey."

His militant expression softened by degrees and she knew he was thinking of why she locked the door when she never used to. "It's one night, Rory. Locking the door is good, but it's not everything. You're ten minutes from town, and twenty from me. I'll be there in case someone comes back instead of trying to race over if they do."

Her heart thrummed a rapid beat as she swallowed. Was it because he'd be in her house, steps from her bedroom door, or because her fear was spiking at the idea of the trespasser returning? It couldn't be Hollis. He was dead. So who else would want to break into her home?

"Fine, but this isn't an invitation to start another fling. Just so you know."

"Never said I wanted to."

His words stung more than they should. "Didn't say you did. Putting it out there in case there was any question in your mind."

"There isn't."

"Good." She gestured over her shoulder to her truck. "I'm going to drive home now. I'll stay in the truck until you tell me it's safe to come out."

He nodded. "I'll be right behind you."

Rory walked over to the old truck, which she'd affectionately named Clyde, and unlocked the door before swinging up into the cabin.

Dear God, how was she going to drive a baby around in this thing? The seat belts were almost an afterthought, there were no airbags, and where the hell would she buckle in a car seat? Did the truck even have crumple zones?

She slid the key into the ignition and Clyde turned over as smooth as a baby's bottom. She loved this old thing because Gramps had loved it. He'd taught her how to take care of it, how to work on it and keep it running, and she'd been doing that alone for the past several years now. Theo tried, but he was hopeless with mechanical things.

She was not.

She'd gotten rid of her Kia a long time ago and she didn't miss it. But she was going to have to find something that had a backseat and safety features. She would never get rid of Clyde, but she wouldn't get to drive it as often once the baby came.

A chill ran through her as she reversed the truck and headed for the street. Her life was going to change drastically over the next few months. Was she really prepared for it? Or was it going to be another disaster in a long line of disasters over the years?

Not that she wasn't happy with her life. She loved Sutton's Creek, loved running the Dawg with Theo, and loved living in her grandparents' farmhouse with the rolling fields and peaceful woods. She'd grown up there after her parents died, and she wanted her kid to grow up there too. She just hadn't imagined doing it alone.

She'd wanted to live there with Mark. He'd agreed it would be a wonderful place to bring up kids and she'd blissfully planned an entire future for them.

Then he ran off with Tammy and that dream had died.

When she turned off the road and headed up the drive toward the house, her heart squeezed in her chest. The lights were on in every room, because she had a hard time with the dark these days. They were on a timer so they came on about half an hour before she got home. Maybe she should light the place up like the Fourth of July every night at sunset. That way nobody would think she wasn't home.

"Who are you kidding," she muttered. Everyone in Sutton's Creek knew that Aurora Harper would be at the Dawg six days a week, standing behind the bar and slinging drinks like she had at her college job. Back then, bartending had been a way to pay for school. Who knew it'd turn into a way of life?

She liked it, though. She was an extrovert and she loved talking to people. Sure, the majority of her clientele hailed from Sutton's Creek and she'd known them forever, but they were getting more and more outsiders moving in. And more tourists passing through the quaint town that Southern Living Magazine had named one of its hidden gems in an article a couple of years ago.

Her headlights shined across the driveway. The grooves were still cut into the gravel, two deep marks that went all the way down to Alabama clay. Rory drove past and pulled to a stop beside the house, beneath the tree where Gramps had always parked his truck, and waited for Chance to do his thing. He parked beside her, then got out and walked around the front of his black truck. It was a RAM, but she wouldn't hold that against him.

She rolled the window the rest of the way down as he walked up beside her. It was a little sticky so it took a moment. Chance's expression held no softness as he looked at her. He gripped a pistol at his side and looked menacing in a way she hadn't seen since that night when he'd pulled her from the tent where Kyle Hollis had held her and Emma Grace hostage.

"I need your house key. I'll check inside first so you can go in. Then I'll scout the barn and outbuildings."

Until she'd been kidnapped she'd kept a key on the porch,

tucked away beneath the doormat. Chance had told her she couldn't do that anymore. She hated that he was right, but he was. The world wasn't the same as when Gramps and Granny had lived here.

Or maybe it wasn't the world that had changed but simply that it was getting closer to Sutton's Creek all the time. Too many developments going up nearby. Too many people moving to the area. Not that most people were bad, but the more of them you had, the more likely there'd be some bad ones in the mix.

Rory took her keys from the ignition, found the house key, and twisted it off the ring before handing it to him. His fist closed over it and he nodded.

"I'll be back soon. Roll the window up, Rory. Be ready to drive away if anything happens. Call the police when you get somewhere safe."

Her heart thumped. "You're scaring me, Chance. It was just a guy prowling around, not a fucking invasion from a foreign army."

"I never assume, sweetheart."

He was gone before she could tell him not to call her sweetheart. She grasped the handle and rolled for all she was worth until the window went up and she couldn't roll it any further. Rory took her phone from where she'd put it on the seat beside her and checked messages.

There was one from Emma Grace.

> Sorry I told the guys, but I had to. I'd expect Chance to say something about it at some point soon.

Rory sighed and tapped a reply. It was late, but her friend would see it in the morning.

> Already has. Now I'm dealing with him playing protector.

EMMA GRACE:

What? Aren't you home yet? OMG, is he with you?

First, so much for Emma Grace being asleep. Second, she'd said too much. How was she going to explain Chance's presence without mentioning the man on the camera?

She wasn't. She had to tell her friend because she didn't know when Chance would tell Blaze. If Emma Grace learned it from her man instead of her bestie, she'd be even more upset.

I'm home and Chance is here. He was waiting for me outside the Dawg. Don't flip out, but there was a man on the security camera at my house. Chance came with me to check it out.

EMMA GRACE:

WHAT?! I'm waking Blaze up. We'll be there in a few minutes.

RORY:

NO! It's fine. Chance is here, he's got a gun, and he's doing that whole superhero thing where he makes sure nobody's still around. Hell, for all we know, people always snuck out here before Chance put the cameras in. Gramps has a lot of stuff in the barns. Could be somebody looking for tools or scrap. It's not a big deal.

EMMA GRACE:

Have you ever noticed anything missing?

RORY:

> Did I mention there's a lot of stuff? It's a picker's paradise in some of those buildings. Other than the tools I use to work on the truck or repair things around here, I'm not 100% sure about everything. Gramps collected a LOT of stuff.

Stuff that her granny hadn't gotten rid of when he died. There were metal signs, scrap metal, old tools, a couple of old cars, and a bunch of other stuff in those buildings. Yet another reason Rory hadn't wanted to sell. What if Gramps had something truly valuable in there? Even if he didn't, he'd spent years collecting it all. It was almost like he was still with her if she went out there and opened one of those doors.

EMMA GRACE:

> You need to report it to Chief Vance. Maybe they can send a patrol car by once in a while.

RORY:

> I love you, girl, but you know that's not going to happen. I'm not wasting the chief's time with a trespasser. Unless Chance finds a body or something, then all bets are off. What would they arrest someone for anyway? Making off with a rusted sign or an old gas pump?

EMMA GRACE:

> It's still your stuff. And nobody has a right to steal it.

RORY:

> We don't know that's what happened. Now cuddle up to your man and stop worrying. Chance is here and he won't leave tonight. Trust me, I tried. But he won't budge. I'm safe.

EMMA GRACE:

I'll try. Tell me all about it at lunch.

RORY:

I will. G'nite.

"Hey."

Rory jumped and screamed. Chance stood next to her door, frowning. She pushed it open and glared.

"What the hell, Chance? Can't you warn a girl?"

Her heart raced and she might have peed herself a little.

"I walked out the front door and down the steps. Thought you saw me."

Rory had a hand to her heart. "Well I did *not*. Jesus. Announce yourself the next time."

"Short of singing the Star-Spangled Banner while clanging a cymbal, I don't know how I could have been any clearer in my approach."

"I was texting with Emma Grace."

"Did you tell her about the man?"

"I did. I didn't want her to hear it from Blaze if you told him before I told her. She wanted to race over here, but I put a stop to that. Unless you want Blaze's help?"

"I don't need any help," he growled. "Inside is clear. You can go in and wait for me. I'm gonna check out the barn and buildings."

Her heart thumped extra hard. "Be careful, Chance."

He grinned at her, the first time he'd smiled at her all night. She didn't like the way it made her pulse thrum or her blood heat. "Careful is my middle name."

"No, it's not. It's Henry."

"Don't remind me," he said darkly. "You getting inside or what?"

Rory pushed the door all the way open, snagged her backpack, and jumped down. "Hold your horses, stud. I'm getting there."

He waited for her to press the lock and shut the door. She'd never locked the truck until Kyle Hollis happened. Who wanted an old truck anyway? But now she locked everything.

"You first," Chance said, waving an arm for her to go ahead.

She walked up the wide front steps to the wraparound porch, feeling anxious and annoyed at the same time. Anxious because how dare someone creep around her house in the dark and annoyed for the same reason. Because it affected her life and increased her fear. Because she was grateful Chance was there instead of in his own bed far away.

But he was too tempting, and he made her nervous. Not only because her body insisted on reacting at the sight of him, but also because she had a secret that involved him.

She was no closer to figuring out how to tell him than she'd been hours ago when she'd first looked at those pink lines.

Rory opened the storm door Gramps had installed when Granny wanted to see the view outside. Chance had left the wood door open inside the storm door and light poured from her living room onto the porch outside. She turned to look at Chance, the light picking out the planes of his face and illuminating him like he was on a Hollywood set.

Really, was it fair to be so attractive without doing a damn thing to make it so? He had to work out with a body like that, but he didn't wear makeup. Probably a good thing, but still unfair considering she spent time in front of the mirror putting hers on every day before heading to the Dawg.

"Shut the door and lock it. I'll call you when I'm ready to come inside."

"Okay." She dragged her lower lip between her teeth. "Thanks, Chance. For coming out here and making sure everything's good."

"You're welcome." He cocked his head as if something was dawning on him. "That sounded like a goodbye. You better open this door when I call or I'll be forced to pick the lock."

She hadn't considered locking him out, but now her ire was rising that he could be so bossy about it. "And if I arm the system?

You'd have to explain to the police why you picked my lock and forced your way inside."

Chance frowned. "You do that to me and I'll tell everyone in town that you screamed Hotty Toddy for me when I made you come."

Her jaw dropped just a little. "You wouldn't dare. Not only that, but nobody would believe you. I'm a Roll Tide girl all the way and everyone knows it. I would *never* utter the Ole Miss cry, not even for an orgasm."

"You're welcome to test the theory. Lock me out, set the alarm, and find out. Or let me in like a reasonable woman and nobody will be the wiser."

She couldn't speak for a full ten seconds. "Now you're fucking with me, Chance Henry Hughes. It *never* happened. It never will. So don't go acting like it's a fact and you're being a gentleman by not mentioning it."

His grin was unexpected. "About time you realized I play dirty when I want something. Lock the door like a good girl and I'll be back."

Rory took great delight in shutting the door in his face. Even if it was what he'd basically ordered her to do.

Chapter Six

"Asshole," Rory muttered as she went into her bedroom and dropped the backpack on the worn Queen Anne chair sitting in one corner.

The room was large, with tall windows, original scraped pine floors, and plaster walls. She'd kept them white, because she liked how bright the room was during the day. Her bed was a four poster, inherited from her grandparents, though of course the mattress was new. She'd bought new sheets and a duvet, but the quilt was one Granny had pieced herself.

Rory's heart flipped at the memories of what she'd done with Chance on that mattress. She'd told Emma Grace she wasn't ever gonna go there with Chance, and then she had. So damned easily, in fact. She'd softened like butter left out on the counter, and she'd melted like it too.

Rory went over to her nightstand and took off her watch and earrings, dropping them into the dish she'd put there for that purpose. Then she went into the bathroom to wash her face. She figured Chance would be gone long enough for her to do that, and she was tired.

Tired and wired, but she still had to get ready for bed. She'd sleep in tomorrow because she didn't need to be to the Dawg until three. Amber was opening, and she could handle the lunch crowd. They typically didn't get too many drinkers early in the day, and those who wanted a drink usually wanted beer. There was the occasional wine or mixed drink, but those mostly came later in the day.

Rory didn't change her clothes yet, because she didn't want to put on her pajamas until after Chance was in the house and she could close the bedroom door and not see him again.

Once she'd washed her face and twisted her hair onto her head in a messy bun, she decided to forgo teeth brushing and get a small glass of wine. Her nerves were wired, and she figured a four-ounce pour would take the edge off. She could have taken a Xanax, but those typically knocked her out for hours. When she woke, she didn't feel rested at all, just more tired.

Rory went into the kitchen and took the bottle from the fridge. She was so focused on the idea someone had been creeping around her property before it hit her why she couldn't drink it.

"Dammit," she grated before putting the bottle back.

She grabbed the pitcher of sweet iced tea instead, programmed the number of carbs into her insulin pump via the app on her phone, and carried the glass to the living room. People often asked her if she should be drinking wine or sweet tea, or eating sugary desserts, breads, or pasta. So many things people thought they had a right to comment on.

The answer was that she could eat whatever in the heck she wanted so long as she accounted for it with insulin. Her life was normal. She just had the added complication of figuring her carbs manually instead of her body doing it for her like most other people.

She'd been doing it for so many years now that it was second nature. She waited a few minutes, then took her first sip of tea. She didn't make it too sweet, but it was sweet enough to make her think of summer days on the front porch with Granny, snapping beans and sipping tea while feeling put out that she had to snap beans in the first place.

What she wouldn't give to sit out there and snap beans with Granny again.

Rory picked up her phone and scrolled social media. She was starting to get worried about how long Chance was taking when her phone finally rang. She thought about not answering to screw with him for worrying her, but that would be mean after the trouble he was going to.

"Let me in, Rory," he said without preamble.

"Say please." She didn't know why she felt compelled to needle him, but she couldn't seem to help it. It gave her a little thrill inside. She didn't know what that said about her, but he was the only one she did it to. Probably a good thing.

"Please let me in," he growled. "Before I huff and puff and blow your house down."

"Ha. Ha."

She went over to the door and unlocked it. Chance looked irritated, but what was new about that? He was always irritated when he was around her. Except for those couple of weeks where she'd let herself go and stopped thinking about the future.

"Find anything?" she asked as she turned to go back to the armchair she'd been sitting in.

He closed and locked the door behind him. "Footprints in the clay that aren't yours. Too big. You have anyone out here for anything recently?"

"Nope. I mow the yard myself, and it's not time to bale hay so the guy who bales hasn't been here yet."

"If they took anything from one of those buildings, I don't know it. You'll have to look when it's light out. I didn't see anything out of place, but I'd like to get the guys out to do a more thorough sweep during the day."

Rory gaped at him. "A more thorough sweep? Chance, I'm a

woman with some desirable farmland, not a foreign country to be invaded. What do you expect to find? Landmines?"

His mouth twisted as he flopped onto the couch and leaned back against the cushions. Now why the heck did he have to look so damned handsome slouching on her sofa? He wore faded jeans that were loose but somehow molded his body in all the right places and a white T-shirt that said *"Into Fitness. Fitness Taco Into My Mouth."*

There was a picture of a taco as well. Dang, now she wanted a taco.

"No landmines, but if it's the construction company guys, hard to say what they might fuck around with. You got good insurance on this place?"

Her heart dropped. "I don't know how good it is, but I've got insurance. To replace the house, but not the barn or other buildings. It costs too much to insure everything and this is no longer a working farm. But the property is paid for. Has been for years. You don't really think anyone would do something to the house or buildings, do you?"

She envisioned a fire, because that's all she could picture, taking decades of history and memories with it.

"It's my job to think of the worst things people can do, and to prepare for them."

Rory sipped her tea and shook her head. She needed the warm burn of alcohol in her stomach right about now but this would have to do. "I could see where a fire would benefit them by leaving me without a home, thereby making their offer tempting, but I can't see where it would be worth the risk of getting caught. Arson is a felony. And it's punishable with as much as life in prison in Alabama."

"Guess it depends on how badly they want the land. Did they say what they want to do with it?"

"Not specifically, though they mentioned building homes and bringing more dollars to town. But there are other plots of land to buy. They don't need mine. They can buy somebody else's and build their subdivision there."

"No doubt they will."

"Precisely. You can see why I'm doubting that someone from D&B Properties trespassed tonight. Now somebody prowling around Gramps's stuff looking for treasure or just stealing tools? That I could believe."

"Except the guy didn't have anything on him when he returned to the car."

Rory's heart stuttered at the truth of Chance's words. But she found an explanation after a moment's thought. "Casing the place. He'll come back another night when I'm at work with a truck or something."

"Uh huh." Chance shoved a hand through his hair and yawned. The dark strands stood on spiky end and she found herself wanting to run her fingers through them. "You gonna give me a blanket and pillow for this couch or do you want me to get them from upstairs?"

The intimacy of him knowing where things were was almost too much. "You could sleep in one of the beds, you know. Sleep in mine if you want." His eyebrow arched. "My *childhood* bed," she added.

"Too short. And I'm not sleeping in Theo's room either, so forget it. The couch is fine."

Rory finished the tea and went into her room to retrieve a blanket and pillow from the linen closet. She tossed them onto the couch beside him. "You know where the bathroom is. I have to brush my teeth, but I'll be out soon."

There was only one bathroom on the first floor, and it had a door into her room and one into the hall. One day, if she had more money, she'd like to add a big ensuite and wall up the door so she wouldn't have to share with anyone who came over to visit. She'd have her own bath, with a big tub and a walk in shower, and it would be heavenly.

"You still have an extra toothbrush in the drawer?"

"Yes."

She always tossed the toothbrushes from her dental checkups in there since she used an electric toothbrush and the dentist didn't hand out refills for that.

"Okay, then. See you in the morning."

"I don't have to be to the Dawg until three, but if I'm not up when you need to go, wake me and I'll let you out."

"Or you could give me the spare key in the kitchen junk drawer."

He knew where the spare was? Of course he did. She didn't think much got by him. Or his friends. Weirdly observant, all of them. But they were former military guys, so maybe that had something to do with it.

"You don't need the spare key," she said, though it would be easier. But if she gave him a key, then what? It seemed like a step too far in the direction of relying on him.

"Suit yourself, Rory. I was trying to be nice so you could sleep in."

"I appreciate that, but I can let you out. No need to complicate things."

He stared at her for a long moment. Her pulse beat a little faster at the scrutiny.

"The only person complicating things is you, honey. You seem to have trouble accepting help. Or maybe it's just me you have trouble with. I'm not quite sure. But okay, I'll wake you up. Then I'll get out and let you be happy you got your way."

He got to his feet and she took a step back, but all he did was toss the pillow to the head of the couch and shake the blanket out. She was trying to think of how to respond when he eyed her again.

"You planning to brush your teeth first or what?"

"I'm going. Just wanted to make sure you have everything you need," she lied.

"I'm good, Rory. Don't worry yourself about me. I have to be out of here by eight, so you'd better get to bed and get some sleep."

"Okay. Good night then."

He didn't look at her. "Night."

She went into the bathroom, closed the door behind her and leaned against it. She couldn't even talk to him about basic things without problems cropping up between them. How in the hell was she going to tell him she was pregnant?

Chapter Seven

Chance woke a little before six. The sky was already lightening and sunrise was imminent. He lay on the couch, listening to the sounds of the house and the birds chirping outside.

It was peaceful in the country. That was one of the things he liked about living at the range with the guys. The range was on an old farm, much like this one, and there were two farmhouses on the property, one smaller than the other. They'd planned to live three and three, but Blaze had wanted to live in town so Chance shared the bigger house with Ghost and Seth while Kane and Ethan lived in the smaller one.

He'd miss the quiet and the slower living when the mission was over and he was gone. Not completely, but part of him would. Missions could be quiet too when they were somewhere remote, before they'd made contact with their enemies.

It wasn't the same thing at all, but it was funny how two different situations could share the same peaceful feeling for a brief time. Typical missions were anything but peaceful, though. This one wasn't typical, but he didn't mind it.

Chance sat up and yawned. He knew from experience he

wouldn't go back to sleep, so he might as well get up and shower, fix coffee, and wait to wake Rory until he had to. He could always take the key and leave her a note, but he wasn't sure it was worth the fight that would follow.

Rory didn't want to pursue a relationship with him, physical or otherwise, and he wasn't the kind of man who stuck around where he wasn't wanted. He wasn't going to take her key and let her think he was determined to be in her life.

He thought of Colleen saying he was obsessed with Rory and his gut burned. Not obsessed. *Concerned.*

There was a difference.

But yeah, he didn't understand how she couldn't want more of the kind of sex they'd been having, though maybe he was the only one with an endless appetite for it.

He went upstairs as quietly as possible to shower there. He didn't want to wake Rory by using the bathroom next to her room. The pipes for the upstairs bath went down a different wall than her bedroom so she wouldn't hear the water running. He turned on the shower and stripped out of his clothes, frowning as he sniffed the underarm area of his T-shirt.

He had a One Shot Tactical polo hanging in his truck so at least he wouldn't show up at the client's today smelling like he'd been to the gym. Not to mention the questionable professionalism of wearing a shirt that had a taco on it to a business meeting.

Even if the object of the business meeting was to test their security and see where the vulnerabilities lay. Yet another way in which the Ghost Ops team was infiltrating the local scientific and Department of Defense contractor community. It seemed like nearly every company in Huntsville, from big to microscopic, had something to do with the nation's defense. Most of them weren't involved in the Athena Project, but it was still a lot of ground to cover before the system was live.

Aside from the mission to infiltrate Royal Shipping and destroy the microprocessors they'd discovered, things had been quiet.

There'd been no more covert infiltrations of companies since then, but they were plenty active in other ways. Their security training and testing was a big way they were involved in keeping tabs on the organizations involved.

The range was thriving now, and they'd hired an assistant to take care of scheduling and front desk duties. Daphne Bryant was perfect for the job. He didn't know how they'd done it without her for the first few months.

She lived in the Sutton building, same as Blaze and Emma, and often rode to work with Blaze since her car had crapped out last month. Kane had taken it upon himself to find her a good used car she could afford. He was still looking as of yesterday. Chance didn't know what the situation was there, but Kane had taken it upon himself to treat Daphne like the little sister he never had. She didn't seem to mind it, though sometimes she appeared more annoyed than thrilled with his interference in her life.

Chance finished his shower and dried off in front of the half-window with a view of the woods and hills. Alabama was hilly in the north of the state and flat in the south. Sutton's Creek, and Huntsville in general, were situated in the Tennessee River Valley, but they were also part of the Cumberland Plateau, which made for beautiful rolling countryside.

He could understand why Rory was partial to her home when he stood here and watched the sun rising over the hill to the east. A herd of deer grazed there, just outside the tree line, and there was patchy fog that rose off the grass. He cast an eye over the ground he'd covered last night and saw nothing out of the ordinary.

The barn was visible through the trees, though he couldn't see the smaller buildings where her grandfather had kept his collections. Chance had opened those doors and peered in. If somebody had stolen something, it'd be hard to tell. Chance would have called it hoarding, but he knew the politer term was collecting. At least the old man had kept it in sheds away from the house.

He pulled on his clothes, except the shirt, and went downstairs to the kitchen. He knew where the coffee was and how many scoops to measure into the basket. He even knew if there were no eggs on the counter he could go to the coop and find fresh ones there.

Theo had a garden plot for growing fresh produce for the Dawg, and he and Rory had rebuilt their grandmother's chicken coop. There was a big run that was fully enclosed, though not roofed, and motion lights to help keep predators at bay. A neighbor came over at sunset on the days Rory worked and closed the coop so the chickens were protected at night.

In fact, Chance figured he should probably go out there after starting the coffee and open the coop so the girls could get out to peck and scratch. He could scatter the feed for them too. He'd done it while Rory had been recovering so why not?

She was determined not to need anyone, but he could take care of the chickens for her and make this day easier at least. He poured water into the pot, flipped the switch, and headed out the back door. The chickens were happy to see him, assuming chickens were ever happy. He scattered feed, collected eggs, and locked the enclosure, thinking how different his life was from how it'd been growing up. Once his parents were gone, he'd endured a revolving door of foster homes until he'd ended up in juvenile detention.

He'd been an angry kid, rebellious, and there were people who'd thought he'd be dead before he reached twenty-five. He'd thought so too, until a military recruiter mentored him and taught him about personal responsibility and being an asset to his country. Sergeant Major Thomas was gone now, but he'd probably never have pictured Chance on a farm feeding chickens.

It was enough to make him smile as he walked back to the house. He set the basket of eggs on the counter and poured coffee for himself. The house was quiet so Rory wasn't up yet. He still needed to get his shirt from the truck, but he'd might as well take the trash out for her while he was at it.

Look at him being all domestic and shit.

He went over to the can and lifted the lid to get the bag. There was a flattened box on top of the trash. A pink box. He wouldn't have paid any attention to it if not for the giant words that leapt out at him.

Pregnancy Test

Chance lifted it in two fingers, staring at it as a riot of emotion began to boil inside him. He told himself there could be a simple explanation. He couldn't imagine what it was though. Rory was the only person living here, and there was a pregnancy test in her house.

And they'd been having sex just a few weeks ago.

The floor creaked in Rory's room, which meant she was up. The bathroom door opened a moment later. Chance went into the hallway and stood there with his heart hammering in his chest, wondering what the fuck he was going to say to her.

Then he heard the sound of retching.

Fear and fury rolled over him in equal measure. He was still telling himself there was a simple explanation, but the animal part of his brain didn't believe it. He thought back to all the times he'd been inside Rory. They'd used condoms at first, and then they hadn't when she'd told him she had an implant.

He'd loved going bare inside her. Best damn feeling in the world.

Had she lied about the implant? Or had it failed?

He didn't know, but he was about to find out.

Because he wasn't fucking leaving this house until he had the truth.

Chapter Eight

Rory rinsed her mouth and patted her face with cool water. How the hell was she going to survive months of this?

Though maybe it wouldn't be months. She needed to read up on morning sickness and pregnancy in general. Hell, she still needed an obstetrician. Probably needed to talk to Emma Grace about that *today*.

And then she needed to tell her brother. After him, probably had to tell Chance.

Though maybe she had that backwards and she should tell Chance first.

Dear God, Chance. He was on her couch. Except, no, he was up because she smelled coffee. She just hoped he hadn't heard her be sick. How would she explain it if he had?

She could say it was something she'd eaten if he asked. Or maybe something was going around and she'd caught it. That would work too. Just until she could figure out how to tell him.

She finished her business in the bathroom, then went back into her bedroom and put on a bra beneath the T-shirt she usually slept in and some yoga pants. Mornings were still cool, but by June she'd be wearing shorts in the morning.

Rory twisted her hair up and clipped it, then sucked in a breath and prepared to go greet Chance since she was up. She could send him on his way and climb back in bed if she wanted. Or she could go poke around Gramps's sheds and see if anything was obviously out of place.

Rory opened the bedroom door and gasped at the sight of Chance in the hall. He leaned against the doorjamb coming from the living room, arms folded, as if he'd been waiting for her. He wasn't wearing a shirt, and his jeans hung low on his hips. Her eyes greedily roamed all that tanned skin, her fingers itching to follow.

She'd never been with a man as fit at Chance before, and it'd been every wet dream come true to explore all that hard muscle and sinew. She still dreamed about it sometimes.

He stared at her and she stared back. Maybe she should say something. Before she could, he unfolded himself from his lazy slouch against the door. Then he unfolded his arms. A pink box appeared, and her heart sank.

"Care to tell me about this?"

"I, um…."

Rory's knees were suddenly liquid. She caught herself on the door frame before she could fall. But Chance was there, swooping her into his arms the way he had in the tent. She barely had time to appreciate the feel of his bare skin before he deposited her on the couch and stood.

"Do you need anything? Water? Something to eat? Are your blood sugars okay?"

"I'm fine."

But misery exploded inside her head and heart. Being pregnant seemed so overwhelming suddenly. And this certainly wasn't how she'd wanted him to find out. She hadn't buried the box in the trash. She hadn't thought of it because she hadn't expected Chance to be there.

Chance disappeared for a second and returned with water. He set the glass on the side table, then sank onto the chair across from her, leaning forward with his elbows on his knees and his hands hanging down.

Seriously, the man was too handsome. Why he'd been interested in her she'd never know, but she knew it couldn't last with someone like him. Too pretty, too capable of having any woman he wanted. Why would he want a neurotic mess of a woman nearly past her prime who had a serious medical condition that wasn't ever going away?

Not that she wasn't healthy, because she was, but diabetes had the potential for complications as you got older. She didn't know for certain that she wouldn't experience any of them. It was a lot to take on. *She* was a lot.

"Are you pregnant, Rory?"

She picked up the water because she needed something to do. "Yes," she said without looking at him.

A breath exploded from him. "Jesus. How the fuck?"

Anger flared to life. "Oh, I don't know, maybe the fact we fucked repeatedly for two weeks had something to do with it?"

"I meant *how* when you told me you had an implant. Or was that a lie?"

She wanted to throw the glass at him but she refrained. "It wasn't a lie," she grated. "Birth control isn't a guarantee, apparently. And *I'm* the one who's pregnant here, so I get to be even more pissed off at the manufacturer than you do."

"Jesus," he repeated, shoving a hand through his hair. "This can't be happening. I can't be this stupid."

Hurt and anger warred inside her. "It's not your problem, Chance. You don't have to do a damned thing, okay? I'm keeping the baby and I don't want anything from you. I definitely don't want you to change your life and be pissed off about it for the next eighteen years or more." She flicked a hand at him. "So you just go and do whatever it is you want to do and I'll deal with this, okay?"

"Not my problem?" he growled. "Not my fucking problem? You're pregnant with my kid. If you think I'm not going to be involved in that, you're delusional. I'm in this as much as you are. You don't want anything from me? Too fucking bad. You're getting it. You're getting so much of me in your life you're going to get sick of the sight of me."

"I'm already sick of the sight of you," she clapped back. It wasn't as true as she wanted it to be, but that little demon over her shoulder that always had to fight with him was right there, spoiling for it.

Her CGM beeped to alert her that her blood sugar was getting low. Chance was on his feet instantly.

"What do you need?"

"Breakfast, but I'll take some apple juice to start."

He was back with a glass and she drank it down before setting the glass on the table. "If it's still low in fifteen minutes, I'll need more of that."

He sat again. "Why does that happen?"

She looked at him. "Honestly? Stress. It can affect blood sugar quickly. That's why I tipped over into ketoacidocis so quickly when Kyle Hollis kidnapped us. I can't control it, unfortunately. And this situation is stressful."

"But ketoacidosis is caused by high blood sugar, right? This is low blood sugar."

She wasn't upset that he wanted to understand. "That's right. I have too much insulin in my system and not enough sugar. Stress can make the numbers go either way, unfortunately. That's why I have to pay attention. It's early. If this was happening later in the day, it'd probably too high rather than too low."

He rubbed his hands along both sides of his head and then folded them over the back of it as he leaned forward and stared down at the floor. Her heart thumped.

"Is it even safe, Rory?"

She blinked. "What? Being pregnant?"

He nodded without looking up. She sighed.

"Not as safe as if I didn't have diabetes, but it's manageable. Type 1 diabetics used to be encouraged not to get pregnant, but that's not the case anymore. I'll be considered high-risk and I'll have to be monitored more often, but I should be okay."

"Have you seen a doctor yet?"

"No. I just took the test yesterday. I was planning to ask Emma Grace for an obstetrician recommendation. I'll need one who specializes in high-risk pregnancies. I'll need to talk to my endocrinologist too."

His mouth was a flat line when he looked at her. "This changes everything. You realize that, right?"

Her heart thumped. "My life is changing. I know that. I've thought about it, and I'm ready for it. This is what I want."

"No, babe. Not your life. *Our* lives. I'm in this now, and you aren't cutting me out. Like it or not, you're going to have to learn to deal with me without losing your shit every time you try and talk to me."

"I don't lose my shit every time I talk to you," she snapped. "But you don't automatically get to start bossing me around just because you knocked me up."

His eyes flashed. "I'm going to boss you around about some shit, like it or not. Like those high res cameras and the hard drive. You're fucking getting them and you aren't paying for it. Second thing you aren't going to like, but I'm not taking no for an answer. You ready for it?"

"I doubt it but go ahead." He stood, towering over her so she had to crane her neck back to look up at him.

"I'm moving in."

Chapter Nine

As expected, she lost her shit. Chance folded his arms over his chest and let her rant about how there was no way in hell he was moving in, she didn't need his help, didn't want him in her space, and had no intentions of letting it happen. She'd bar the door with Liza Jane if it came down to it.

"Not afraid, Rory," he said when she sputtered out of things to say. "You can threaten me with that gun all you want, but you're too smart to shoot me."

"Wanna bet?"

Her head was tipped back, her hazel eyes fiery, her blonde hair clipped on her head in a messy knot. Her skin was flushed, and her chest heaved beneath the thin T-shirt she wore. She'd said that stress affected her blood sugar. He knew he couldn't stop her from stressing, but he was damned sure going to be ready to get more apple juice, or whatever she needed.

That's why he'd stood in the first place, but now he appreciated the dominant vantage point as he stared down at her and watched her cycle through a range of emotions. She didn't stand, maybe because she was too shaky—which he didn't like—but his was the position of authority and she was damned well going to listen to him.

"When do you plan to tell the kid you shot his or her father, huh?"

Just saying those words boiled up a whole lot of emotion inside, but he kept a lid on it. Rory was lashing out because she was angry and maybe a bit scared. She wasn't truly violent, not even when she'd punched him in the arm that day. She wasn't like his mother.

Charity Hughes had always been a bit broken inside, so when she'd shot and killed his father that awful day, it wasn't as much a surprise to most people as it had been to him. She'd been stonily silent when the police found her, stonily silent during her trial. Not that he'd been allowed to go to the trial, but he'd read about it when he'd gotten older.

Guilty. Life in prison.

Rory wasn't that kind of person, no matter how she blustered. Her cheeks were red as she dropped her gaze.

"You play dirty, Chance."

"Told you that last night, didn't I?"

Her chin lifted. "I'm not going to shoot you, but you still aren't moving in."

"Wanna bet?"

She glared at him. He glared back. "It's been fifteen minutes," he said softly. "Check your sugar."

She picked up her phone to read the monitor. "Another glass of apple juice, please."

He went to get it, fuming inside and frustrated that she seemed to despise him so much. She hadn't for at least a couple of weeks. He'd preferred that relationship over this one. Hell, he'd just like a smile when she saw him instead of a frown. That would be enough for a while.

Chance poured the juice and returned to her. She drank it, frowning the whole time.

He wanted to tell her to calm down, but he knew how that would go. Like tossing a match onto jet fuel.

"Thank you," she said when she finished. "I'll check again in fifteen."

Chance looked at his watch. He needed to be on the way to Research Park if he was going to make the client meeting at Griffin Research Labs, but he didn't want to leave her. Not when she was like this. And not when some asshole had been creeping around her property last night. Could be someone after her grandfather's stuff like she said, but it could be the construction company too.

He didn't know which possibility he liked least. Neither one was safe, especially when she lived alone.

Chance took out his phone and sent a text to Seth. A few seconds later, the reply pinged back.

SETH:
Yeah, I can do it. Everything okay?

CHANCE:
I'm fine. But somebody was at Rory's place last night and I'm concerned it was the construction guys. She's having low blood sugar issues too. Says stress causes it.

SETH:
Damn. Good you're staying with her. I'll let the boss know I'm taking your place.

CHANCE:
Thanks. I'll call him soon. Is the range covered for the day?

SETH:
It's handled. Daphne continues to amaze with her organizational skills.

CHANCE:
Kane still denying he's hovering like a big brother?

SETH:
Oh yeah. Denial is his middle name these days.

Chance couldn't figure it out. Kane was one of the most womanizing dudes he knew, always dating a new lady, always flirting, always soaking in the female adulation. But for some reason, he didn't flirt with Daphne. He didn't try to charm her. He literally hovered over her like a protective big brother and denied he was doing it.

Whatever. Wasn't Chance's problem.

He turned to look at Rory, who was scrolling through her phone instead of haranguing him about moving in. He knew the conversation wasn't over, but if ignoring it helped her blood sugar normalize, then he was all for it.

"Seth's going to take my client in Research Park today, and the range is covered. I can do a more thorough sweep of the buildings now that it's light, and I can fix breakfast. I let the chickens out and fed them. Collected the eggs. Anything else you need done?"

She looked up, her eyes tired instead of angry for a change. "Thank you, but you don't have to stay with me today. Everything will be fine soon. I was planning to do some laundry and I need to cut the grass before I head over to the Dawg later."

"Too late, Rory. I'll cut the grass for you."

She arched an eyebrow. "Will you now?"

Damn he loved her spirit, even if she pissed him off with it sometimes. "If you prefer to do it, I'll do laundry. Just tell me which one."

Because he knew insisting wasn't the way. Give her a choice, let her make the decision.

She sniffed. "I don't trust you with my laundry."

"Afraid I'll steal a pair of panties and sleep with 'em under my pillow?"

She blinked. "No. I was more afraid you'd wash my Alabama sweatshirt with bleach or something."

He snorted. "I wouldn't. But it's a good idea. Filing that one away for the future. Just in case."

"In case what?"

"In case you try to hide the Ole Miss gear from our kid."

Her eyes widened for a moment. "Oh my God. If you think for one second my child is wearing Ole Miss colors, you've lost your marbles."

"We'll come up with a schedule. Some days are Ole Miss, others are Alabama."

"I think whoever's won the most national championships should be the primary. The *only*, in fact."

She said it primly. Made him laugh. "Wonder why you think that?"

"Seems fair to me."

"It would."

"So you admit Alabama is superior?"

"I admit no such thing, Aurora. But I'll consider it."

"Can't deny the truth, Chancy Pants." She grinned then and it was like watching the sun come out. In that moment, he didn't want to deny anything if it kept her smiling at him.

"You feeling better?"

She checked the numbers on her phone. "Yes. All is normal again."

He couldn't help but frown. "I don't like how fast that happened, Rory. If you were here alone, then what?"

There went the smile. "I've been living alone for close to five years. Think I got it."

"You nearly fainted. How would you have made it to the kitchen and poured juice if that happened?"

She looked uncomfortable. "That was because of you. I didn't expect you to know about the pregnancy yet. I wasn't prepared for it."

He didn't think that was entirely true but he wasn't going to argue with her. "Okay, but you have to acknowledge that you don't yet know what being pregnant is going to do to your body and your blood sugar. Maybe having somebody around for a while is a good idea."

She arched an eyebrow. "I know what you're doing. You're trying to convince me you need to move in here and take care of me instead of insisting you're going to do it anyway."

"Is it working?"

She growled. "I don't like you. I don't want you here."

That pricked his pride. "You liked me well enough to make a baby. Were you even planning to tell me?"

"I liked your dick and your mouth and the way you use them when you aren't saying things that piss me off. I didn't know we'd get a baby out of it. Definitely wasn't my plan. And yes, I was going to tell you. I just hadn't figured out how yet."

"It's your plan to keep the baby, so that means you keep me in your life too. Can't have it both ways, Rory."

She closed her eyes. "I know. Dammit!"

Really, he was trying not to let her dislike of him hurt, but it did. He wasn't a bad guy. Sure, he liked women and he'd flirted with a lot of them in the Dawg in plain sight of her. But since the first moment he'd seen her standing behind that bar, he hadn't taken a single one of them home. Hell, he hadn't even gotten laid since he set foot in Alabama other than the two weeks he'd spent with her.

"I'm gonna make this easy for you, babe. I'm staying, at least until we know who was creeping around here and why. Maybe by then you'll have your doctors in place and you'll know what you have to do to keep your blood sugar stable. You can argue with me, but I'll be at the Dawg tonight, telling everyone who'll listen about how sweetly you sound screaming Hotty Toddy in my ear."

Her eyebrows arrowed down. "That worked last night but it's not working today. First of all, nobody will believe it. Second of all, even if they do, why should I care? I'm a grown-ass woman, not a girl desperately trying to fit into her high school. And finally, you may be a badass who can take down evil guys John Wick style, but Theo is my big brother and he's going to clock you for daring to speak so crassly about me in public. And you'll let him because you know you're wrong."

Well, fuck. He was impressed with her logic because it was pretty much spot on. Still wasn't deterring him, though.

"Okay, you got me there. But I'm staying for the glaring reason that I'm the father of that kid you're carrying and keeping you both safe is my responsibility. There's nothing I wouldn't do to protect you both, you hear me? If I go back to my place and something happens to you, either because your sugar crashed or because some jack-off breaks in here again and hurts you and our kid, I'd never get over it." His blood was boiling, his temples pounding, and he had to work to keep his voice steady. "I know what it's like to lose people, Rory. Suddenly, unexpectedly, and violently. I won't let it happen again."

She stared at him, her eyes wide. He thought she might argue, because that's what she usually did, but then she swallowed and clasped her hands in her lap, her gaze dropping.

"I'm really sorry you lost someone like that," she said, her voice barely more than a whisper. "Is that why you moved to Sutton's Creek?"

"No. I was thirteen when it happened. Even if I'd known it was going to happen, there was nothing I could have done. I didn't know how. But I do now. And I won't hesitate to kill anyone who tries to hurt you."

She shuddered, and he wondered if he'd gone too far. He was a warrior, he did what he had to do, but she wasn't used to it. Maybe stating it so firmly was a mistake. She'd see him as a monster instead of a protector, and that wasn't what he wanted.

"Okay, Chance. You win. Guess you're staying. But only for a little bit, you hear me?"

It was enough for now. "Heard, understood, and acknowledged."

Chapter Ten

Chance fixed scrambled eggs and toast and Rory ate more than she would have thought she could just an hour ago. Her stomach wasn't queasy at the moment and it went down well. She spent breakfast wanting to ask him who he'd lost at thirteen, and how, but she couldn't imagine a way to do it that wasn't intrusive.

He'd been emotional, or as emotional as she'd ever seen him. He hadn't looked it, but she'd heard it in his voice. It was the reason she'd given in. That and the fact she knew he wasn't lying. He really would step between her and anyone who tried to harm her.

Ordinarily she'd rely on Liza Jane for self-defense, but she had to be honest with herself and admit that wasn't the wisest idea right now. She was subject to random bouts of morning sickness, and she was more tired than usual. She wasn't completely on her game, but she had no doubt she'd get back to herself soon enough. Just had to get used to these pregnancy hormones and keep her blood sugar under control.

After breakfast, she showered and dressed and started to drag the laundry down to the basement. Chance stopped her with a frown as he was coming out of the kitchen. Without a word, he hefted the wicker basket into an arm and carried it down for her.

The stairs were steep but it was light in the basement because she'd hung bright LED shop lights to replace the incandescent bulbs her grandma had used for so long.

"You could break your neck coming down those stairs," Chance grumbled when he dropped the basket by the washer.

"Haven't yet."

"You need a laundry room on the ground floor."

"No kidding, Sherlock." She dropped the last item into the washer. "But until I win the lottery or inherit millions from a rich aunt I didn't know I had, I've got to save up to build what I want. At the rate I'm going, probably get there in about five years."

Maybe. And that was if she did some of the work herself.

"This isn't going to be easy when you're a few months pregnant." He frowned as he looked around the laundry room. "The stairs are steep, and you'll basically be carrying a bowling ball and a laundry basket."

She started the washer and turned to him, irritation flaring. She was already feeling off kilter and he wasn't helping. "I'll figure it out. I assume you know where the mower is?"

He ground his teeth. "Saw it in the barn last night."

"There's a gas can on the shelf if it needs any."

"Saw that too. Might want to start locking the gas up. Just until we know if that guy's coming back again."

"Let's see if there's any left when you're done and we can talk about it then."

"Honey, there's a lot we need to talk about. And don't think we aren't gonna do it, either."

"Never said we weren't." She gave him the sweetest smile she could manage, but they both knew it was fake. She was torn between wanting to hug him hard for the loss he'd suffered and wanting to wrap her hands around his neck for being bossy and annoying.

"After you," he said, motioning to the stairs.

Rory went up in front of him, trying very hard not to think about him watching her ass as she walked. When they got to the top, she went to the little nook at the front of the living room that housed her computer. It wasn't until she heard the screen door shut at the rear of the house that she could breathe again.

Being around Chance was like being around an electrical current. She buzzed with energy when he was near. Energy that made her jump and twist and ache deep inside.

Rory fired up her computer and sat down to work on some of the figures for the Dawg. She could have called Emma Grace to ask about that referral, but she decided it was a conversation best had in person.

The buzzing of the mower in the background had her looking out the window from time to time, watching Chance drive up and down on the zero turn mower that was ancient by current standards but still worked well enough for her purposes.

He wore a ball cap and he'd removed his shirt because of course he had. There was a pulse that throbbed low in her belly as she watched him. Finally, she shook her head and got back to the books. By the time he was done with the yard and the edges of the driveway down to the road, she'd moved the clothes to the dryer and fixed lunch.

It was simple, just a couple of turkey sandwiches with tomato, mayo, and cheese, and a few potato chips. She didn't eat them often, but occasionally she indulged. Today felt like an indulgence day.

Chance walked over to the sink and turned it on, then splashed his face and dried it with a couple of paper towels. His hair was damp, his skin tanned, and she found herself wondering what it'd be like to have him there every day. To count on him.

Her stomach twisted as he sat down and drank half his water before looking at her. She picked up a chip and nibbled on it.

"Thanks for lunch."

"You're welcome."

"I'll fix the grooves in the driveway and pick the rocks out of the beds after I eat. And I'll get some groceries later if you tell me what you want."

"You don't have to do that," she said, a stone forming in her belly. It wasn't that she didn't appreciate the offer, because she did, but it reminded her too keenly of the days when she'd thought Mark was the perfect man for her. He'd taken care of everything, taken care of her, and promised he always would.

She'd trusted him, relied on him, and he'd broken every promise he'd made. It wasn't that she couldn't take care of herself, because she damned well could and she'd proved it, but she grew up with Gramps and Granny and she'd seen how it could be when two people were truly committed for a lifetime.

She'd thought she'd had that, but she'd been wrong. In retrospect, the signs had always been there. She'd just been too blind—and too hopeful—to see them. And she wasn't ever letting it happen again.

Chance sighed. "I'm eating your groceries, Rory, so it's only right I buy some. As for the driveway and the beds, I'm getting it because I'm already dirty and I might as well. Unless you want to get sweaty before you go to work?"

She hated it when he made sense. "Fine. But get what you like at the store. I don't care."

"Hoo-ah."

"What?"

"Heard, understood, and acknowledged. I got you, Rory. You don't care what I buy and you'll begrudgingly accept my help outside because it's one less thing to worry about since you don't know when or if you're going to feel bad again."

There was a knot in her throat. She sounded like such a bitch when he put it that way. And maybe she was, but self-protection was more important than niceties. And she needed all the self-protection she could get with him.

He made her want things, and that was dangerous. She pushed

back from the table. "You know, I think I'll head into town early. I want to see Emma Grace before I have to start my shift."

His gaze dropped to her sandwich. "You only ate half."

Her heart was throbbing as she stood. "I'm not all that hungry. I'll take it with me."

"You took insulin based on what you were about to eat, right? Don't you have to do something about that?"

"I'll eat it on the way."

He stared at her. Then he unfolded himself until he towered over her. "Shit, Rory, if you don't want my company while you're eating, just say so. You don't have to run off with half a sandwich and eat it on the way so you don't have an episode. For fuck's sake, just tell me you want to be alone. I'm staying to protect you, but I don't expect to spend every waking moment in your company. Especially not if my presence makes you this fucking uncomfortable."

Rory closed her eyes and swallowed the fear. What the hell was wrong with her? She could handle this. She wasn't a naïve Regency miss from one of her novels. She could handle the company of a full-grown alpha male. Even one who'd been inside her not all that long ago.

"I'm sorry."

He stared at her. "For what? Hating me?"

She dragged in a breath. "I don't hate you, Chance. I just... I can't *like* you. I can't let you in. It's not personal. It's me."

"Honey, I say this with no malice whatsoever, but you can't close the barn door after the horses escaped. We're in this together. I'm in, like it or not. You still don't have to like me, but you aren't going to run away every time I walk into a room. It's going to make raising a kid damn hard if we can't even be in the same room, don't you think?"

She sagged against the counter where she'd gone to get a baggie for the sandwich. "Honestly, Chance? I'm still working out the next few months in my head. I don't have space for the next few years yet. The idea that we're raising a kid together? I haven't wrapped my mind around it. I'm still working on how to get through the next few days when I have to tell my best friend and my brother what's going on."

He closed his eyes for a moment and shook his head. When he opened them again, she was struck by how blue they were. Like the Emerald Coast of Alabama and Florida, where the water was so pretty and turquoise that it took your breath away. She'd gone to Dauphin Island with Emma Grace and her parents for several summers when she was a kid. The water there wasn't that color, but when Emma Grace's parents would take them on a drive to Orange Beach, Perdido Key, and Pensacola Beach, the change was stunningly beautiful.

That was Chance's eyes. Stunningly turquoise.

"Eat your sandwich, Rory. I'll take mine outside and get back to work. We've got time to figure this out."

Her heart throbbed as he took his plate and headed for the front door. She should stop him, but she couldn't find the words.

"What the fuck is wrong with you?" she muttered to herself. Her issues weren't his fault. And yet she panicked when he was near. She could feel those shields shoot up from the floor of her heart and surround it whenever he walked into the room.

She got stupid. Stupid and mean, and she didn't like herself when she did those things.

Rory retrieved her plate and finished the sandwich, then decided to head into town. She grabbed her backpack and keys. Chance was busy tossing rocks from Granny's flowerbeds back onto the driveway when she stepped onto the front porch. His plate sat on the porch near the steps, the sandwich and chips gone.

He looked up as she approached. The shirt was gone again, and she swallowed hard.

"You headed out?"

"Um, yes. I thought I'd see if I could get a minute with Emma Grace. I could call and tell her, but I think this is an in-person conversation."

He leaned on the rake handle he'd been using. "If you could ask her not to tell Blaze just yet, I'd appreciate it. I want to tell my guys myself."

"I don't think she'll have a problem with that. I'm not technically her patient, but I'm sure she respects patient confidentiality too much to blab my news to anyone else."

He looked thoughtful for a second. "Think you're probably right. If I don't get over to the Dawg for dinner today, I'll be waiting for you at quitting time."

"You don't have to do that, Chance."

"Yeah, but I'll be there anyway. Drive safe, Rory."

"I will."

She didn't argue with him about meeting her after work because it was pointless. He'd be there, even though he had a job and usually started early each day.

She stepped off the porch and headed for Clyde. She unlocked the truck and climbed inside, then rolled down the windows and started him up. The engine roared to life with a guttural purr that she loved. Especially since she was the one who kept it that way.

Rory made it to town in ten minutes, as usual, and parked behind the Dawg. She waved at the regulars as she climbed the stairs to her office on the second floor. Theo's apartment was at the front of the building while the office was at the back. She knew she wouldn't run into her brother because he was in the kitchen, going through supplies in the walk-in and making sure everything was in good shape.

Theo had always wanted to go to culinary school, but he'd never managed it. He'd worked in restaurant kitchens since he was a teenager though, first at the Dawg and then at a few different upscale restaurants in Huntsville. He'd learned the business the hard way, but he was a damned fine chef even if he didn't have a degree in it.

Rory's heart thumped as she thought about telling him her news. He was going to hit the roof. Not because he thought she wasn't entitled to her own choices in life, but because of the diabetes and the potential complications.

Hell, he'd be glad that Chance was staying with her. Rory frowned as she remembered Chance the way he'd been when she opened her bedroom door that morning, shirtless and bossy, looking so damned fine she'd wanted to jump his bones. Then he'd lifted that box and her stomach had cratered.

He'd been super pissed, but he'd gotten it under control. And, truthfully, though it wasn't the way she'd wanted him to find out about the baby, she was glad it was over.

Even if he'd gone all alpha caveman on her. She had to admit, if only to herself, that having him tell her he'd do anything to protect her and the baby turned her into a puddle of mush. It wasn't a proper reaction for an independent woman, but nobody ever said she didn't love the idea of a hot alpha male who was infatuated with her.

Not that Chance would ever be that guy, but it was a fun fantasy.

Rory unlocked the office and went inside. It was spacious, with antique furniture and comfy chairs. The walls featured old advertisements and photos that dated back to the late nineteenth and early twentieth centuries. The building had been a hardware store at one time, but that'd been at least eighty years ago.

The desk was an old roll top that sat unlocked and open. She went over invoices and orders there, and she updated the spreadsheets she kept in the cloud so she could also work on them at home. Instead of sitting at the desk, she sat in one of the old armchairs by the window and took out her phone to send a text to Emma Grace.

RORY:
I need to talk to you in person sometime today. I can come over there before 2:30, or you know where to find me starting at 3:00.

It took a few minutes, but a reply pinged her phone.

Chance

> EMMA GRACE:
> Just finished with a patient. I'll come to you. Need to pick up a coffee at Kiss My Grits anyway. Want anything while I'm there?

Rory sighed. She would flipping *love* a coffee but more than two small cups a day was out according to the internet. The slight twinge of a headache tickling her brain didn't appreciate the news, that's for sure.

> RORY:
> No thanks. See you soon.

Twenty minutes later, she got a text from Emma Grace.

> I'm walking into the Dawg.

> RORY:
> I'm in the office.

> EMMA GRACE:
> Be right there.

The door opened and Emma Grace walked in with her coffee and a bag. "Wendy just took some lemon blueberry scones out of the oven. I couldn't resist. I got enough for you if you want one."

Rory's stomach rebelled at the idea of lemons right now. Must be a pregnancy thing, because she usually loved lemon anything.

"Thanks, but I'm good."

Emma Grace frowned as she took a seat and studied Rory. "Looks serious, babe. What's wrong? Did Chance say something I need to make him regret?"

Rory shook her head as a well of emotion crested inside. What the hell was wrong with her? Was this a hormone thing? Because she was *not* a fan.

"I, um, I need some help, Idgy."

When they were kids, Rory had given her friend the nickname

Idgy from running together her initials. EG. Ee-gee. It'd morphed into Idgy over time. She'd only started using it again when Emma Grace moved back to town, and usually only when she was feeling particularly sentimental or emotional.

"Honey," Emma Grace said, taking Rory's hand and squeezing it. "What's wrong?"

Rory reached for the box of tissues and swiped a couple, pressing them beneath her eyes to stop the flood. Emma Grace rubbed circles on the back of her hand, waiting patiently while she got herself under control.

"Sorry," she said, giving her friend a quivering smile. "It must be the hormones."

Emma Grace's gaze sharpened. Not much got past her. "Hormones? You aren't saying…?"

Rory gave an exaggerated nod. "Yes. I'm p-pregnant."

Emma Grace's eyes were a little wide. "How do you feel about that, Ror?"

"I feel a lot of things. Happy. Scared. Worried. Doubtful. I'm not sure I can handle it, and yet I want to. I want to keep the baby." Her eyes filled again. "When will I ever get another chance?"

"Oh, honey. I understand. Completely. If this is what you want, you know I'm going to support you. I'll help you find a high-risk obstetrician."

"Thank you. That's what I hoped you'd do."

"So, uh, what about the father? How does he feel? Or have you told him yet?"

Rory snorted at how hesitant her friend suddenly was. "Listen to you being all polite and professional, madam doctor. You know damn well who the father is. And yes, he knows. He found the pregnancy test box, and he's decided he's moving in and bossing me around whether I like it or not."

"Oh, my. How do you feel about that?"

"Angry. Annoyed." She put her forehead in her palm. "He fed the chickens and collected eggs, then he mowed all the grass. He was picking the rocks out of Granny's flowerbeds when I left, and I'm going to bet I won't see even the hint of a groove in the driveway tonight. It's nice to have help. But Idgy, it's *Chance*. He's not the staying kind."

Emma Grace sighed. "I don't think you really know that, honey. He wants to be there with you, right? That says something, don't you think?"

"He's not staying for long. I let him do it because of the man who was at the farm last night, and because of how angry the construction guys got when I said no. It's not permanent."

"Did he find anything?"

"No." Rory told her friend about her low sugar episode that morning and about Chance taking off work and how he planned to poke around again in the daylight. She also told her about the upgraded cameras and the hard drive he wanted to install.

Emma Grace nodded. "I think that's a good idea. It's dark out there and you've got a lot of ground to cover, plus you aren't there most evenings. You need to know who's poking around in the dark."

"It's someone looking to steal copper or parts from the sheds, that's all. But if it makes him feel better, then fine. I can't stop him anyway." She bit down on the inside of her lip to stop herself from getting emotional again. "D-do you think I'm making a mistake keeping this baby? With the diabetes, and being a single mom— what if I'm biting off more than I can chew? What if something happens to me and I'm not there for this kid while they're growing up?"

Emma Grace was at Rory's side in a heartbeat, wrapping her in her arms. "Honey, I think a *lot* of women wonder if they're ready for such a step, diabetic or not. What you're feeling is normal, but it's understandable you're even more concerned because of your condition." Emma Grace let her go and knelt at her side, brushing a strand of hair off her cheek and tucking it behind her ear. "Honestly, something could happen to you. It could happen to *anyone*. We aren't guaranteed tomorrow. If you start down the path of all the what-ifs, you'll make yourself crazy. If you want to keep this baby, then yes, your life is going to get even more complicated. But you've got me and Blaze, you've got Theo, and you've got more friends than you realize. My mother is going to show up armed with cake samples for your shower and fabric samples for the nursery when you tell everyone the news. She's probably going to volunteer to babysit, and she won't be the only one. You aren't going to be in this alone."

Rory closed her eyes and nodded. "Thank you. I needed to hear that."

"You're welcome." She took her seat again, picked up her coffee, and sipped it. "Now tell me which room you're planning to turn into the nursery. Auntie Idgy needs to know how big it is so she can buy the biggest stuffed bear ev-ah."

Rory laughed. "You aren't buying a giant stuffed bear. Now make it a giant pony, we can talk."

"How about a real pony?"

"Oh Lord, you're going to be that kind of aunt, aren't you?"

Emma Grace's eyes twinkled with mischief. "What are aunts for if not to spoil their nieces and nephews silly?"

"I want you to remember that if you and Blaze decide to have a kid. The road goes both ways, girlfriend."

"I know it does, Ror." She glanced down at her smart watch. "Crap, I have to get back to the office. My next patient will be there in a few minutes. I'm prescribing you some prenatal vitamins and anti-nausea meds, by the way, so get over to Beadle's and pick them up this afternoon. I'll do some research and have an obstetrician for you by the end of the day. You'll want to make an appointment with your endocrinologist and your primary care doc, too."

"Aye, aye, Captain." If Mr. Beadle was still the pharmacist, she wouldn't be caught dead buying prenatal vitamins in fear Mrs. Beadle would blab it all over town. But Mr. Beadle died a couple of years ago, and the new pharmacist didn't gossip about patients. Thank God.

Emma Grace was on her feet. "Not kidding, Ror. Call those two *today*."

"I will." Rory stood and hugged her friend. "Chance asked that you not tell Blaze yet. He wants to do it."

"I won't say a word. And babe?"

"Yes?"

"If Chance wants to help, you need to find a way to make it easier for the both of you. Not saying you have to get married or have a romantic relationship, but you *do* need to have a relationship with him. Try to make it a friendly one."

Rory swallowed the knot in her throat. "I hear you. And I'm trying."

"I know you are. But he's not Mark. He's Chance. Try to remember that."

Chapter Eleven

"Okay, Chance, you called this meeting. What do you want to say? Is Rory okay?"

Alex "Ghost" Bishop sat at the head of the oval table in the SCIF, which had been built especially for this mission. It was made from a shipping container and held state of the art electronics and communication equipment. The facility was small but secure. It had to be since the president herself sometimes briefed them from Washington.

It was fully contained inside the building that housed the range, and accessed from Ghost's office. There were two doors, one that required a code and one that required a palm print scan. To anyone looking at the entry door from the outside, it looked like storage.

Chance swallowed. It was after six and they were closed for the day. Daphne had locked up and gotten a ride home, and it was just his team. His brothers.

Chance let his gaze slide across five expectant faces. His heart thumped a little harder than usual. Telling these guys he'd gotten Rory pregnant wouldn't be a big deal if it weren't for the mission.

Ghost Ops. Six men with no family ties, no connections. All they had to do was fly under the radar and make sure the Athena project stayed on track by any means necessary. They were supposed to be operators with nothing to lose, men who could disappear if they had to. Men who could follow orders and get the job done, no matter what it took.

They weren't supposed to build permanent ties to the community, and they definitely weren't supposed to get anyone pregnant. They were ghosts because they had to be, and they were expendable if the mission went wrong. They all knew it, all signed up for it.

But now he was expecting a kid with a woman who deserved the best he could give her, no matter what she thought about him.

Blaze had made it work with Emma, but Ghost had been pissed when Blaze got involved with her. They lived together, but it wasn't technically a relationship and they weren't supposed to do anything that hinted at commitment until this mission was finished.

Even though everyone here knew they were committed.

"Uh, Rory is fine. I couldn't find any evidence her intruder was the construction company guys, and if anything's missing from those sheds of her grandfather's, nobody would know it."

"You need us to do anything?" Seth asked.

"I need to change out the cameras for the higher res when they come in, and install the hard drive for the system, but I can do that myself. Though I'd like a couple of you to come go over the grounds, see if I missed anything."

"I can do it," Kane said.

"Me too," Seth added. "Can help with the cameras as well. It'll go faster with more than one person."

The other guys offered as well.

"Thanks. I appreciate it. And could you check out D&B Properties when you get a chance? Just want to know a little bit about them."

"Yep," Seth said, scribbling the name on a notepad.

Chance rubbed his hand across the back of his neck. He was fucking sweating. He'd been as cool as you please striding into terrorist cells the world over. He'd taken out drug dealers and terrorists, fought his way out of more shitty situations than he could count, and this is what threatened to undo him.

Because he didn't want to disappoint the man at the end of the table. A man with more commendations than anyone Chance knew other than General John "Viper" Mendez, the commander of the Hostile Operations Team. Ghost had single-handedly saved HOT from annihilation when he'd run ops from the basement of a residential house in order to clear Mendez's name a few years ago. Ghost was legendary.

"Just spit it out, man," Ghost said. "You want to tell me you've got the hots for a Southern girl same as Blaze here? Fine, shack up with her, but I don't want to know if you've pledged your hearts and gotten matching tattoos, okay?"

Oh Jesus. He was in so much fucking trouble.

"Uh, it's a bit more complicated than that, sir."

Ghost groaned. "I'm not gonna like this, am I? What'd you do, Wraith? Bad news doesn't get better with time."

Chance met the man's gaze. Swallowed. "Rory's pregnant."

Ghost stared. The room was dead silent. Jaws dropped a little. Blaze was the first one up, clapping an arm around his shoulders and squeezing. "Man, congratulations. That's fucking awesome."

Ghost banged his forehead against the table while the other guys jumped up and joined Blaze in congratulating him.

"Are you assholes trying to get me removed from this command? What'd I ever do to any of you other than drag you away from the military and get you sent to Sutton's Creek, Alabama, where there's a psychic who sees aliens and a bunch of friendly locals? You've got a town quainter than anything Hollywood could dream up, Southern cooking, and you get to spend your days teaching self-defense to people who aren't actively trying to kill you. It's a fucking Hallmark movie here, without the snow."

"Sorry, boss," Chance said sheepishly.

"I'm gonna be scraping chewing gum from under tables at a fast food restaurant in Bumfuck, USA, before this is over. Hell, maybe I should just call the president and resign now, make it easier on her. Then she can send somebody down here who can maintain control and keep you jerks laser-focused on the mission. Did I mention national security is at stake? Millions of people's lives? Ring any bells?"

Heat crept up Chance's throat. He wanted to tug his collar but didn't. The other guys looked chastened as they took their seats again. Chance sank into his chair as well. He'd stood to address them, but now he joined them around the table.

"The situation is complicated, boss, but I don't think it's all bad. I'm not technically in a relationship."

"Explain."

He cleared his throat. Man, it was gonna hurt to say it aloud, but what choice did he have?

"Rory and I had a brief fling but she doesn't like me. Told me so just today, in fact. I think she's as shocked about this pregnancy as I am, maybe more so since she's a diabetic and there could be complications. We *were* careful, but it wasn't enough. She's not asking me to marry her, and even though I would because it'd be the right thing to do, I'm not offering because it isn't what she wants. She intends to keep the baby, and I intend to be there to help her out. But we aren't in a relationship. She's made that clear."

Nobody said anything. Chance sighed as he shoved a hand through his hair.

"It's okay. Really. We've never gotten along, other than briefly after she and Emma were taken, so it's not like there's a lot of emotions involved. We had a fling. It was fun. Thought it was over, but now there are consequences. I'm not abandoning her or my kid. I intend to be there for them both, and I'm staying at the farm for now because we don't know who's been trespassing or why. It's not permanent."

Ghost eyed him. "This going to affect your work?"

"No, sir. My head's in the game. Rory's health concerns me, but she's getting a doctor who can monitor her during her pregnancy. I intend to keep her safe from assholes who want to harass her over her property, but that's not going to stop me from doing my job here. Nothing's changing other than I'm having a kid."

Which meant everything was changing, but he couldn't wrap his head around that yet. Could he still return to HOT and active ops when this mission was over? Did he want to?

Ghost sighed as he leaned back in his chair. "All right. We'll go with that for now. But you ever feel like you aren't in this the way you should be, I need to know. I can't have you endangering the mission because you're distracted. It's too important."

"Understood. But I'm committed. I know what we're doing means my kid will grow up safe. If we fail, that doesn't happen—and I won't be the reason it fails."

"I believe you," Ghost said. "Nothing like a baby on the way to make you more determined to succeed."

A sense of relief flooded him. He tipped his chin at Seth. "Thanks for taking my place today."

"No problem, man."

Ghost sat up and tapped his pen on the table. "All right, let's hear the report then. What happened at Griffin Research Labs?"

Seth's expression was grave. "Talked my way past security with a fake badge and some technical talk. Walked all over the facility. Some of the labs require codes to get in, but others I opened the door and walked through them with a clipboard, pretending to make notes. When I'd seen enough, I went straight into the CEO's office and took a seat in front of his desk while he looked mildly confused. Then I pointed a finger gun at him and told him if I'd been an intruder, he'd be dead."

"I'm guessing he didn't like that," Kane said with a chuckle.

"Not a bit. He called an emergency meeting of his security team and we went in there together. He proceeded to chew their asses over their negligence. I explained to him that anyone could have made the mistake to let me in, that it was a matter of training and strict adherence to protocol even when you recognize the person you're demanding credentials from. Then there was the matter of the labs where nobody questioned me. He fired the security manager on the spot and threatened the rest of the team."

"He called me when you were done," Ghost said. "We've got a contract to train their people and advise them on security."

"Which means we've got a way in," Ethan said. "This is good."

"Damn right it's good," Ghost replied. "We still don't know who coordinated that shipment of fake microprocessors we destroyed or how they knew the real ones would also be passing through Royal Shipping. It's either an insider at Griffin Labs or someone in the government who knows the project's inner workings. Considering how important this project is, it's fucking ridiculous Phantom got as far as he did. Hopefully nobody else has breached the labs yet, though it's possible."

"The area where they're working on the command and control system is off limits to most. I wasn't able to get into it, though if I'd had more time I think I could have hacked the entry code."

"Not encouraging at all," Ghost said, "but we'll know more about their operations after we spend some time going over their employee records and security procedures. Which we will start to do on Monday. Good job, Phantom."

"Thank you, sir," Seth replied.

"If nobody's got anything else, let's get over to the Dawg and grab dinner."

"It's Friday," Kane said. "Been thinking about that prime rib all day."

"Is Daphne joining us?" Ethan asked as chairs scraped back from the table.

"How would I know?" Kane replied. "She doesn't tell me what her plans are."

Chance exchanged a look with Seth. Seth smirked.

"Somebody call her," Seth said. "Or maybe Blaze can knock on her door."

"Think she had a date tonight," Blaze said mildly.

Kane didn't react in any obvious way, but Chance would have sworn the temperature in the room went down several degrees. Kane's look was pure frost as he glared at Blaze.

"When did she tell you that?"

Blaze shrugged, seemingly oblivious. "I don't know. Might have been yesterday when I drove her to work. Or the day before. Some guy she met at the Piggly Wiggly. Think she said he was in the chess club at the library. Hell, maybe that's where she met him. But he works at the Pig. I can't fucking remember. Why are you asking me? You want to know, ask Daphne."

"I don't care," Kane scoffed. "Just wondering why she didn't tell all of us."

"Hell if I know. Maybe because you've been a grumpy bastard lately? Think you need to call Lainey or one of those other women you're teaching self-defense and get laid. Might sweeten you up."

"Now kids," Ghost said. "No fighting or you won't get any dinner."

"Not fighting," Kane grumbled. "And not grumpy."

"Me neither," Blaze said, palms facing out. "Just stating some facts. I'll call Emma on the way and ask her to go upstairs and see if Daph's free tonight."

"Problem solved," Ghost said to nobody in particular. "You fuckers ready?"

"Hell, yeah. Let's eat!"

Chapter Twelve

Rory yawned behind the bar as she pulled beers from taps and thought about how much her life had changed in twenty-four hours.

The anti-nausea meds were helping. But they also made her sleepy. Maybe that would get better when she got used to them. She hoped so.

When she finished with the beers, she set them on Nikki's tray and sagged against the bar. She really needed a nap, but she wasn't going to get it. It was Friday night and the Dawg was hopping. Prime rib night wasn't to be missed, and neither was the band that came on later.

She thought of being here until nearly two in the morning and wanted to cry. Wouldn't normally bother her, but if she didn't stop yawning soon, she *would* cry.

She'd had a text from Emma Grace that the guys were coming and Chance had told them the news. It made her squirm a little inside to know all those big, hunky men knew her personal business, but it wouldn't be long before everyone in Sutton's Creek knew.

She'd told Theo. It hadn't gone well. He'd hit the roof, threatened to beat the shit out of Chance—which she'd pointed out wasn't really likely considering what Chance did for a living—and demanded she move into the other apartment above the Dawg.

He'd only calmed down when she'd said that Chance was staying out at the farm with her. She didn't tell him it was temporary.

Theo wasn't a caveman and didn't expect her to get married to the father of her baby and quit work, but she knew it made him feel better to know that Chance wanted to be involved.

Her brother worried about her. Always had. It was stifling sometimes, but she understood where it came from. They'd lost their parents at a young age and though they'd had their grandparents, Theo had always been sensitive to the idea that he could suddenly lose the people he loved. When she'd been diagnosed with diabetes at thirteen, he'd worried more than any fifteen-year-old should. It'd taken time for him to get used to it, and time for her.

When she'd gotten teased by the other kids for passing out because her sugar was low, Theo stood up for her. He always stood up for her.

Because of that, she'd given him a bit of grace today. He'd ranted and raved but then he'd hugged her tight and pledged to do whatever she needed him to do for her and the baby. She'd teared up in his arms, which she didn't typically do, but she blamed the hormones.

He was in the kitchen now, deep in dinner service, but he'd made her swear not to overdo it. And she wasn't overdoing it. It was the damned meds. She'd had a choice between being nauseous or being tired and she'd taken tired.

She was kinda regretting it, especially since more caffeine was out for the day.

Jimmy Turton pulled out a barstool and sat. The Turtons had land adjoining hers and they'd always been friendly with her grandparents. But Jimmy's dad had died a year ago, and now the operations fell to Jimmy and Billy. Their mother, Gail, still lived on the farm and regularly took produce to the farmer's market while her sons did the big planting like corn and cotton.

"Hey, Jimmy. What can I get for you?"

"Hey, Rory. Bud Light, please."

Rory grabbed a frosted mug and put it under the tap. "How's your mama?"

"She's good. Corn's planted and she's got tomatoes and okra in. Planning to expand the flower garden and let folks come cut their own."

"That sounds good."

"Might do a pumpkin patch this year in addition to the corn maze. Hear those do real well up in Huntsville." He eyed her. "You ever think about doing anything like that with your land?"

Rory set the beer in front of him and slid over a bowl of pretzel sticks. "Nope. No time."

"Mmm," he said, taking a sip of the beer.

"Hey, you get a visit from a construction company recently?"

"Yeah, they came by. Made a good offer, too. But Mama doesn't want to sell, and she still owns the land. What about you?"

"They made an offer but I turned it down. Theo agrees."

Jimmy took a handful of pretzels. "Might be nice to get out from under the responsibility though, huh? Farming is hard work. But you don't have to farm for a living like we do, so I guess there's that."

She didn't like the way his words pricked her conscience. "My grandparents farmed for years. And I spent a lot of time in those fields, helping."

"I know you did. But you don't have to now." He let his gaze slide over the brick interior of the Dawg. "You've got this place. You and Theo. Has to pay some of the bills."

"We're getting there. I'm still not selling though. I like living on the farm and waking up to the birds singing and the deer grazing in the pasture near the tree line."

"I wouldn't know. I'm up before dawn most days and in bed by eight."

She thought he sounded a bit resentful, but maybe she was reading too much into it. "What brings you out tonight?"

"Mama's book club. I dropped her off at Celia Lincoln's house and thought I'd come in for dinner before I have to pick her up again."

"That was nice of you."

"She doesn't see so well in the dark these days." He pursed his lips as if thinking. "Not gonna lie, Rory. I'd be happy if she'd sell. Get herself a little house in town. Me and Billy could go to work at the Polaris plant, or maybe Mazda-Toyota. Get some benefits, make good money. Billy's got child support payments. It'd help him a lot."

"I'm sorry, Jimmy. I hope she changes her mind if that's what would benefit your family most."

He nodded. "I do too. But they want all of it, Rory. Yours, ours, the Coombs land. Together, we've got about five hundred acres. They'd make a mixed use development like Clift Farms over in Madison. Apartments, houses, retail shops, restaurants. Imagine what that'd do for this town."

Rory's stomach tightened. "I've only got forty acres. It's not enough to make a difference. But you and the Coombses have the majority. They could do all those things with both of y'alls. They don't need mine."

Jimmy scratched the back of his neck. "Maybe not, but your land's between ours. Without yours, it's two separate tracts. Thought if we were all on the same page, maybe we could get more money out of them, too. Make it worthwhile for all of us. Mama wouldn't refuse if the offer were big enough."

"I'm sorry, Jimmy, but I'm not selling. Doesn't mean they won't come up on the offer for your place, though." She cocked her head. "Does Carter Coombs want to sell?"

"Last I heard, he was thinking about it. Dolly Coombs had

cancer last year, so I think they offer him enough money, he'll take it."

"Probably right."

"Think about it, Rory. Think about what we could all do with that money. Make life a lot easier. You wouldn't have to be out there alone, selling hay for extra money and taking care of all those old buildings. The house needs work too, right?"

Rory's belly churned. She didn't like the way he said those things, what he knew about her life. Hell, everyone knew it, but she still didn't like it.

"I like working on the house, and the hay is easy money. Carl Hoffman cuts and bails it and pays me for the privilege. But I'll think about it." She wouldn't, but it was easier to say she would so he'd stop talking about it. "Hey, you want to order that prime rib?"

"Yeah, and give me a double helping of mashed potatoes, please."

"Sure. You want extra gravy on the side, too?"

"Sounds good."

Rory took the order and passed it to Amber as she headed for the kitchen. She went about her business mixing drinks and taking new orders from people who sat at the bar, but she couldn't shake the sound of Jimmy's voice when he'd been talking about selling and pushing her to do the same.

There'd been *fervor* in it. She understood his reasons, but it unsettled her to hear him talk about everything the development company wanted to do as if it was the greatest thing ever. Maybe bringing all that development to Sutton's Creek was a good thing— but that didn't change her plan to raise her kid on land that'd been in her family for generations. So long as she had the woods bordering her property, maybe she wouldn't notice all those apartment buildings and stores.

Or so she hoped.

The front doors opened and a group of people walked in. Her gaze went to one man like he was a magnet.

Chance Hughes. Her heart thumped at the sight. He was knee-weakeningly tall, unfairly handsome, and utterly lickable.

Great. Now these pregnancy hormones were making her horny.

Just what she needed with Chance living in her house for the next couple of weeks.

Amber strutted over to the group in her tight jean shorts and fitted T-shirt, and Rory wanted to growl. She really needed to discuss a new dress code with Theo. Maybe black pants and white shirts like an upscale restaurant. A part of her knew that was silly, not to mention sexist, but dang it, she didn't need Amber being all sexy right now.

Emma Grace waved and Rory waved back as they crowded around a big table and Amber passed out menus. All six One Shot Tactical guys, Emma Grace, Daphne the receptionist, and scrawny Warren Trigg from the Piggly Wiggly were there.

Warren did not look comfortable but that was probably because Kane Fox kept glaring at him. Daphne glared back, but it didn't help.

Amber put her hand on the back of Chance's neck and played with his hair. Rory's belly clenched as she watched. Chance reached up and took Amber's hand, pulling it away. He didn't let go, however, and that made Rory want to march over there and dump a pitcher of ice water over his head.

Soon after, Amber arrived at the bar with their drink order.

"You're getting awfully handsy with the customers, aren't you?" Rory asked as she grabbed glasses and started to fill them.

Amber blinked. "I thought you didn't care if I went out with Chance."

Crap. She had said that, but she hadn't known she was pregnant then. Not that it mattered.

It didn't matter. Really.

"Did I say I cared *now*? I just think you shouldn't be putting your hands on him when you're meant to take orders. Get the orders, deliver them to me and the kitchen, and save the flirting for after work."

Amber's expression hardened. "I got the drink order, didn't I? I didn't dally. And since when do you care what I do? You've never said a word before. You told me he was fair game. And he said he wasn't interested in you. Said he'd been there, done that, and it was just okay. So why are you giving me a hard time?"

Rory went still. "He said what?"

Amber's cheeks were suddenly pink. "He said he wasn't interested in you. You said you weren't interested in him. Why is this even an issue?"

"It's not an issue," Rory said coolly. "Not at all. Forget I said *any*thing."

Chapter Thirteen

CHANCE FOLLOWED RORY HOME AFTER THE DAWG WAS CLOSED FOR the night. He'd stayed all evening, playing pool, listening to the band, laughing with his teammates—the ones who didn't go home—and deflecting Amber, who'd gotten strangely more aggressive as the night went on.

Rory had barely spoken to him when she'd walked out the back door and found him leaning on her truck. He'd let her get away with it because they'd be at her house before too long.

She flipped on her blinker and went up the drive, him following right behind her. The grooves in the gravel in front of her house were gone, and he'd gotten nearly all the rocks out of her flowerbeds. Might be a few stragglers, but he'd look again tomorrow.

She parked and jumped out before he'd even turned off his truck. Alarm shot through him. He had a feeling—a bone deep feeling—that if he didn't get up to that door before she was inside, she'd lock him out.

Cussing a blue streak, he shoved the truck in park and went after her, reaching her side just as she inserted the key in the lock.

Chance

All the lights were on inside, and the front porch was bathed in a warm glow. Rory's face was pink and her forehead creased in thought.

She twisted the key and the door opened. He followed her inside and gripped her elbow before she could escape.

Because she was definitely bent on escape.

Rory whirled, her hazel eyes flashing, those impossibly long lashes making her look at lot more angelic than she in fact was.

"What the hell's gotten into you?" he said.

She cocked a hip and folded her arms over her chest—after jerking her elbow free of his grip. "Oh, I don't know. Maybe it was hearing from Amber that you said you'd been there, done that, and it was just okay."

Chance winced. "That was last night."

"Oh, and that makes it better?"

"No, but in fairness you were glaring at me from the bar and Blaze was telling me Emma wanted us to get back together, and I was trying to explain how there was no us and Emma didn't need to get her hopes up. Amber wasn't meant to hear it."

"Oh, right, sure. I feel better now. Thank you for clarifying."

He eyed her. The words were right, but the tone was wrong. "Rory, for fuck's sake, what was I supposed to say? The sex was hot and you were a wet dream? You want me to talk that way about you to my guys?"

She still looked mad, but maybe she'd softened a little.

Maybe.

"Was it?"

"What? Hot? You know it was. And yeah, I've jerked off to memories of your tits bouncing as you rode me. None of those facts are things I'm telling anyone besides you."

Her face got a little redder. She thrust her chin out and glared.

"Amber wants to date you. I want you to know I don't care if you do. This pregnancy doesn't change anything. You're free to have a personal life, and so am I."

He was going to strangle her. Put his hands around her neck and fucking squeeze. "I don't want to date Amber," he growled. "And maybe you could hold off on the dating until after you have our baby, huh?"

Not that he wanted her dating then either. He simply didn't want to think about it. Pissed him the fuck off to imagine her going on a date, either right now or when she had a baby at home to take care of. Not that a woman couldn't have a baby and date, but he was still planning to be in the picture so why couldn't she just date *him*?

"We'll see. I might meet someone."

Chance closed his eyes. "Rory, I swear to God."

"Well, you shouldn't. God doesn't approve and there will be no swearing when we have a kid around."

He could only gape at her. She sounded so prim, but he already knew she could swear like a sailor. And some of the dirty things that had come out of her mouth during sex….

"I think we'll be safe for the first few months or so. The kid isn't going to repeat anything we say. Did you get an obstetrician from Emma?"

"Yes, she found one with a stellar reputation. I have to go to Huntsville, though."

"I'll take you. When is the appointment?"

"Tuesday morning. And I'll take myself. I can still drive."

"I know you can, but that truck doesn't need to be on the interstate. Nor does it need to be in Huntsville traffic."

"Clyde was driving to Huntsville before you were even a gleam of interest in your daddy's eye. I think he still knows the way."

He found it cute the way she named things in her life. Clyde the truck. Liza Jane the shotgun. She'd even named some of the deer who grazed in the fields. He knew that because he'd stood on the porch with her early one morning and she'd told him.

Buck, Bambi, Jack, Flame, Shadow, Marie, and Delaney. Delaney, of all things!

There were things about Rory that were endearing, and other things that exasperated him no end. He didn't know what to do with her most of the time. Didn't know how to breach that mantle of dislike she donned especially for him.

"I understand that, honey, but Clyde is probably a little tired of dealing with sports cars and speed demons at his age. Plus he doesn't have airbags or ABS. I'd feel better if you let me take you. Or, if you refuse, at least take my truck and I'll take Clyde to the range."

Her expression had definitely softened. "I'll think about it. Thanks."

He knew better than to argue with her. If you pushed Rory, you got pushed back. If you let her turn it over in her head for a while, she'd come to the right conclusion.

He didn't know what made her that way, but he knew that she and Theo had also lost their parents early in life. They'd been raised by loving grandparents according to everything she'd told him, and everything he knew from Emma. Maybe it was that, or maybe it was something else. Whatever it was, Rory hated to be managed.

But there were some things he wasn't accepting. Like the idea she might meet someone else. Not if he could help it. He was going to be so present in her life that any other man would definitely think twice before getting involved.

He didn't care to examine what that said about his future plans at this moment. He was just trying to get through each day, do the job, and protect his country. Not only his country, but his child and its mother.

"I'm going outside to get my duffel bag from the truck. You lock that door on me, I'll pick it. If I can't pick it, I'll kick the fucker in."

Her jaw flexed.

"I mean it Rory. I know you've had a shitty day, but I've had one too. I'm tired and I need to do a perimeter check before I can go to sleep. So first I'm getting that duffel and bringing it in, and then I'm walking out to the barn and checking things there."

One of the cameras was out and he needed to see if the battery had died prematurely. There hadn't been any visitors to the property tonight, other than the neighbor who closed the chickens in. He knew because he'd installed the app to his phone so he'd get alerts too. Not that he was telling her right now. That was yet another thing she'd get pissed about.

Rory sighed and rubbed her forehead. "You know where the spare key is. Take it. I'm tired too, and I want to go to bed. Just don't do anything to make Gramps's stuff collapse on your head. I won't know about it until morning, and that'll be too late to save you."

"Honey, I've tiptoed through minefields and survived. Don't worry about me."

She blinked and he gritted his teeth for saying too much.

"Real minefields? Where?"

"I was in the military, Rory. We went places where people wanted to protect things like drug operations. Mines are an effective way to do that. But with the right equipment and tools, you can avoid getting blown up."

"Nothing in the sheds will blow up, but it might topple. So be careful. That's all I was trying to say."

He grinned at her because he knew it would annoy her. Especially combined with what he said next. "Careful or I'll think you like me."

Her expression went blank. "Not at all, Chancey Pants. I just don't want to have to explain your demise to the police."

He tapped a fist to his chest. "You're all heart, honey. Do what you gotta do and don't wait up. I'll be fine."

CHANCE RETRIEVED the duffel and set it by the couch. He could hear the water running in the bathroom and he stopped for a second, listened. He heard movement so he knew she was fine.

"Paranoid," he muttered as he went into the kitchen to grab the spare key from the drawer. But with her diabetes and this pregnancy being new, he worried about her having another episode like she'd had this morning. He hated to think about her being alone if she did.

Still, hovering over her wasn't going to do a damned thing except piss her off.

Chance slipped out the back door and headed for the barn. He'd ordered the new cameras and hard drive he needed to beef up the surveillance on this place. It hadn't been cheap, but he'd already decided he was giving Rory a bill that didn't reflect the true cost. He had to charge her something, because she'd get pissed if he didn't, but it wasn't going to be accurate.

And he wasn't caving in to her demands for invoices. Last time he'd done it because he'd been involved with her, thinking maybe they had something that could be good for them both, and he hadn't wanted to rock the boat.

This time he didn't give two shits what she thought.

It was dark tonight, but the sky was clear and the stars shone brightly. He walked toward the barn, listening for any sounds that weren't right. Coyotes yipped in the woods, and a barn owl screeched. There was also the call of a chuck-will's-widow, which was similar to a whippoorwill's call. He'd heard both growing up in Mississippi and learned to distinguish them in hunting trips with his dad.

His gut tightened at the thought of his dad. He'd been a big man, handsome and strong, and he'd taught Chance to hunt and fish. They took weekend trips together with his dad's hunting buddies, all converging on a cabin in the woods to hunt game. He'd loved those trips with his dad.

His mother was a different story. She was mercurial. Sometimes she was happy and full of life and other times she had a hard time getting out of bed. Chance hadn't understood about depression back then. All he'd known was he couldn't count on her to do anything she promised she'd do. Sometimes she did, but most of the time she didn't.

The ball of anger and guilt in his stomach weighed on him heavily, even after all these years. What had happened wasn't his fault, even if it still felt like it. He'd had enough counseling to know he wasn't to blame, but he still felt like he'd lit the match.

He shook the memories away and stalked the path between the house and the barn. The chicken coop was quiet as he passed. He stopped to listen for the rustling of feathers. When he finally heard it, he kept going.

The barn was a big, weathered structure that used to be red but was now sun-washed and faded. It had a gambrel roof with a bright square of red, white, and blue painted in a block design on the loft doors above the breezeway entrance. He'd asked what it was and Rory told him it was a barn quilt. Apparently, there were hundreds of barns in Alabama with these squares, all different, and there was even a barn quilt trail complete with a website and a map. People drove around looking at them from the road, which he found odd, but whatever.

Chance listened for sounds out of the ordinary, but there was nothing. He took out his flashlight when he reached the structure and ran it over the building and the entry way. He was looking for things that didn't belong, wires or signs of activity. The camera he'd installed was beneath the quilt and accessed from the loft.

But it wasn't there. The base was, but the camera was gone.

He shined the light around the entrance. Something flashed in the grass and he went to examine it. The camera had been shattered where a large projectile had pierced it. A chill rolled over him as he gingerly picked up the biggest chunk and turned it over. He knew what had shattered the casing, knew he'd probably find the bullet buried in the wood where the camera had been.

Some asshole had shot the camera down, but why this one? They'd been careful about it, too. Hadn't gotten into its field of view before disabling it. He knew because he'd looked at the feed up until it went dead to see if anyone had sabotaged it on purpose.

They had, but they hadn't left visual evidence.

He went through the barn, looking at the empty stalls where cows and pigs had once lived. Then he climbed up to the loft, which wasn't empty as he'd originally thought when he'd first come out here. It was one of the repositories of Rory's grandfather's junk. There were old bicycle frames, old glass bottles, signs, and pieces of farm equipment and other tools and implements. It was almost like a museum, except without the care and cleaning to display the pieces properly.

There was nothing out of place that he could tell. Still as junky and musty as ever. He opened one of the loft doors and shined the light across the ground, over toward the coop and then sweeping back in the other direction. Whoever'd shot the camera had done it from over there.

But that wasn't the worst of what they'd done. He knew why they'd disabled the camera.

"Shit," he breathed as he looked over the destruction.

The garden where Theo and Rory grew produce and herbs for the Dawg was fenced to keep deer out, but the fence didn't matter now.

The plants had been cut to the ground. Everything was gone.

Chapter Fourteen

Rory woke earlier than she wanted to because she had to pee, but she didn't feel more than mildly queasy. Thank you, modern medicine. She'd waited to hear Chance returning to the house last night, but at some point she fell asleep anyway. It'd been nearly two in the morning and she'd been completely done in.

The clock said it was seven-thirty. She experienced a current of mild panic as she wondered if he'd made it back inside, or if he'd been crushed beneath a pile of Gramps's stuff out there. She snatched her phone up as she headed for the bathroom and opened the alarm app.

It'd taken her time to get used to having a house alarm, but she liked it now. She could check everything with her phone, arm and disarm the system, and see what times she came and went since there was a record for each time the alarm was set or turned off.

Her pulse slowed when she saw the system was armed. Unless he'd armed it when he left the house last night and he hadn't come back after all? She'd been too tired to notice.

Rory rushed through brushing her teeth and dragged on a pair of yoga pants beneath her T-shirt, then opened the door into the hallway. She crept toward the living room, but of course there was no such thing as creeping in a house as old as hers because the floor creaked.

When she rounded the corner, Chance was on the couch, one arm thrown over his head, the blanket twisted around his feet. He was wearing boxer briefs and no shirt, and Rory's pulse hummed as her eyes greedily slid over his body. She could see that every day and never get tired of the view.

Rory frowned. No. No, she did *not* want to see Chance Hughes in all his glory sprawling over her couch every single morning and evening.

"You done staring?"

Rory squeaked as she jumped. "What the hell, Chance?"

He cracked an eyelid. "Thought we weren't supposed to swear. The kid and all."

The muscles in his sinful abdomen tightened as he pulled himself up with those puppies until he was sitting, looking at her while he yawned and dragged a hand over his scalp.

"You scared me. Plus it's a work in progress. Not gonna stop using my favorite emphasis words overnight."

"Good to know. You feeling okay?"

"Yes. I was just, um, thinking about making some coffee. Decaf." Did she even have any decaf? She didn't think so since she'd had no need for it before. Not that she couldn't have a little bit of caffeine, but if she wanted to drink more than two small cups, she needed decaf.

"I grabbed some yesterday. Noticed you didn't have any."

And now she was going to melt into a puddle. Damn him for being perfect and wrong for her at the same time.

"Oh. Thank you. Guess I'm still getting used to what I can and can't have."

" 'S'okay, Rory. When I was stationed at Fort Bragg, had a teammate whose wife was pregnant. He got, uh, injured at work and we all helped out with some things. I learned what to shop for because she gave me a list."

Her heart beat a little harder. "You remember what was on her list?"

"Not really, but I know she couldn't have very much caffeine, no unpasteurized cheeses like brie or goat cheese, and certain lunch meats were off limits. Oh, and tuna was okay, but in moderation."

"Emma Grace sent me a list. I haven't memorized it yet, but I will." She hesitated. "I'm sorry I didn't wait up last night."

"It was late and you were tired. I could tell by looking at you."

She was still tired, but she'd been worried something had happened to him so she'd had to check. And now she was committed to fixing coffee. "Seems like being extra tired is one of the symptoms. Yay. But it'll get better as the pregnancy goes along."

He unfolded his gorgeous body from the couch and stretched. Rory looked away, heat pooling in her belly and groin. "Put some clothes on. Jeez."

He chuckled. "You've seen it all, babe. Had your tongue on a lot of it, too. Why so shy now?"

"I'm not shy." She turned her head to look at him as if to prove the point. "But we aren't going there again so I see no point in strutting around in the buff like we are."

This time his chuckle was a snort. "Damn, you sure make me laugh. You call this the buff? I'm wearing boxers."

"Boxer *briefs*, my dude. They show everything. If I get any closer, I'll see your pulse."

He snorted again. "Fine, I'll put on some shorts. Then I'm fixing the coffee while you sit down. I can fix half-caff if you don't want to go cold turkey."

She hadn't thought of that. "I can fix coffee, Chance. I don't need you to do it."

He slipped into his gym shorts while she watched. Really, it was no better than before. He was still a sexy, sexy man with a body that made her ache like she'd endured a porn marathon without relief.

"I know you don't *need* me to, but you said being extra tired is a symptom so let me do this for you so you can sit down, okay? It's no trouble."

She hated when he made sense. "Okay, I'll sit. But I'm going to the porch and sitting in the fresh air."

Because watching this man fix coffee without a shirt was a sure way to perdition.

He frowned and her skin prickled with warning. "What? Did you find something last night?"

She rushed toward the back door as a horrifying thought occurred. If someone had hurt her chickens…

Chance caught her arm. His touch was gentle but firm and she whirled around to glare at him.

"I was going to tell you when you were sitting down with your coffee. But since you want to sit on the porch, you're gonna see it if you walk around to the side."

"The chickens?"

Her voice cracked. She couldn't stand it if someone had hurt her girls.

Chance tugged her into his arms. "Not the chickens. I'm sorry I didn't make that clear from the beginning."

His embrace was gentle and her heart slowed. His chin rested on her head and she found herself wrapping her arms around his waist, seeking the warm comfort of his body. Seeking safety.

"It's the garden, Rory. Somebody hacked it all down. There's nothing left standing."

Shock flooded her, followed by anger. Bone deep anger. How *dare* anyone destroy what her brother had worked so hard to create? She'd worked on it too, but that was for him. It was his baby, his source of fresh produce for some of his dishes. He was proud of his garden, and somebody had destroyed it.

"Who did it? Did you see them?"

"No. Whoever it was damaged the camera beneath the barn

quilt. That was the closest one. The ones on the house aren't at the right angle, and the garden is too far."

"Dammit," she growled, feeling angry and tired and defeated all at once.

"That's why I'm putting up better cameras, Rory. Wouldn't have stopped them from shooting it down, but the others would catch them."

She tilted her head back to look up at him. "They shot the camera down?"

"Yes. Somebody destroyed it with a .22 shot. Not a powerful gun, but a lightweight and accurate one. A bullet can travel up to a mile, but it'd take some skill to do it, even with a starlight scope. I don't think they were that far out, but I've looked around and there are ATV tracks that lead from the woods to the garden. Whoever it was came through the woods, set up so they could kill the camera, and then drove over to the garden. Once they were done, they went back the way they came."

"Which direction?"

"West."

Her mind raced. "That's Coombs land over there. But I can't see Carter or his kids doing such a thing. I don't see the Turtons doing it either, though Jimmy said last night he wanted to sell and he thought the Coombses did too."

"When was that?"

"He sat at the bar and ate dinner. Talked to me about it then, but he didn't press the point. Just said he wished we'd all sell because he wanted his mother to move to town and he wanted a job with benefits. But his mother owns the farm and doesn't want to sell, so it doesn't matter. He was there when you arrived, and he left about an hour later."

"Is he capable of something like this?"

Rory shook her head. "I've known Jimmy since we were in elementary school together. He's not mean. And what would be the

Chance

point in tearing up the garden anyway? It's his mama he needs to convince, not me."

"Mmm." He sounded distracted.

That was when she noticed the insistent rise of his cock as it pressed into her abdomen. She told herself she needed to take a step back, but she didn't want to. She gazed up at him, her limbs going weak, while his eyes roamed her face. When they focused on her mouth, a shiver rolled through her at the intensity of his look.

All she had to do was lean into him and he'd kiss her. Lean in, let her hands slide down to his perfect ass, and she'd be on her back with his face between her legs, taking her to heaven, before the next ten minutes were up.

It'd been weeks, and she hadn't forgotten how thoroughly he'd owned her body. How amazing it'd been with him.

Which is *why* she'd put an end to it. Before her heart forgot it was just sex and fell for him.

He took a step back, breaking the contact between them. "Sorry. Lost my head for a minute."

Disappointment throbbed in her veins. "It's fine. Nothing happened."

Even though she'd wanted it to. Rory closed her eyes for a second. *No, you did not.*

There, she'd told herself, hadn't she?

Meanwhile, Chance backed up another step as if he could hear the argument in her head. "I'm gonna fix that coffee. Need you to sit while I do it. We'll go over to the garden together once we've got the coffee."

Rory hugged herself, belatedly realizing she hadn't put on a bra. Embarrassment flared in her belly. She'd been ribbing him about his briefs and all the while her girls were swinging free beneath her T-shirt. Which he had surely noticed.

"I should, um, call Theo, tell him what happened. He'll want to see it for himself."

"You do that," Chance said. "And you tell him I'm gonna find out who did it and make them wish they hadn't."

Chapter Fifteen

"Who would do this?" Theo waved his hand over the field, looking about as lost as a man could look when confronted with senseless destruction.

Chance didn't say that it was far better they were only talking about plants and not people. He might have encountered the kind of destruction in his life and career that was far worse than a field of plants, but for Theo Harper, having someone destroy all his hard work was a blow he couldn't yet wrap his head around.

"Somebody who either hates you, or me, or wants us to sell this farm," Rory said. "That's about all I can figure."

"You think it's the guys from D&B Properties?" Theo asked, his gaze bouncing between Chance and Rory.

"Could be," Rory said.

"But we don't know for sure," Chance added, because he had to consider every possibility. "You piss anyone off lately? Break up with anybody?"

Theo shook his head. "Don't think so. Haven't dated much since all that shit went down."

Chance knew which shit. The shit where Kyle Hollis nearly killed him and left him for dead.

"But you have been out with someone?"

"Yeah. Tera, Julia, and Poppy."

"At the same time?" Rory asked, her eyes widening a little.

"No, Ror, not at the same time," her brother said. Chance could hear the eye roll in his voice.

"Good, because that'd probably be grounds for some garden destruction right there. Tera and Poppy aren't exactly friendly. In fact, one of them could have tore up your garden out of spite because you dated the other one. Which one was first?"

"Poppy. But she's on a business trip to California. It wasn't her."

"I doubt it was any of them," Chance said. "Whoever did this shot out the camera first, and that took a good bit of skill. Tera and Julia have both been at the range for our ladies' beginner shooting, and I don't remember either of them even getting close to the center of the target."

Rory put her arm around her brother. "I'm sorry, Theo. You worked so hard on it."

"You helped. And now we're gonna have to buy more produce for the restaurant. I know that's not what you budgeted for."

"It's fine. We're doing well these days. It'll just take a little longer to pay off the debt, but we've been on the right track for so long that this is merely a hiccup."

"You're right. It'll be fine."

Rory punched him playfully in the arm. "Just think, we've got a one-point-seven-five-million offer for this place. All else fails, we'll sell up and have plenty of money to take care of the Dawg and whatever else we want."

Theo's eyes hardened. "No. We aren't selling. This is our heritage, and you're going to raise your kids here. One of these days, I might join you and do the same."

Rory teared up. Chance could see the sheen in her eyes. "I think that'd be great, big bro. But first you gotta stop dating all those women and settle down with one."

"And there's the hitch in my plan," Theo said with a laugh. He sobered quickly as he surveyed the destruction. "I can replant, but it'll take time. I started these from seeds. If I get bigger plants it'll go faster, but that'll cost a few hundred dollars."

"Get the plants, Theo," Rory said. "What's a few more dollars at this point?"

Theo eyed her. "I don't know, Ror. We have to think about the future, and about your kid."

He cut his gaze to Chance, who didn't blink at the scrutiny. "I intend to provide for my kid. It's not all gonna be on your sister."

"Glad to hear it."

Chance felt like there was more to say so he said it, Rory's opinion be damned. "I'm gonna be here for her, Theo, whether she wants me to or not. I'm not a deadbeat, and I don't skip out on my responsibilities. As much as she'll let me take care of her, I'm gonna be here doing just that. And sometimes, even when she doesn't want me to, I'm gonna be in her life telling her when she's got shit ideas and needs to pull her head out of her ass."

Theo blinked and then snorted. "I can respect that, man."

Rory popped both hands on her hips and glared. "Seriously, is this *Little House on the Prairie*? Are you two menfolk deciding what to do with the poor, helpless, pregnant lady when I'm standing right here and have my own thoughts about my life?"

"Not at all, babe," Chance said with a grin. "I'm just telling Theo the facts, and those are that you aren't getting rid of me no matter how much you might try."

"But why would you try?" Theo asked, looking genuinely puzzled. "Chance has more integrity than the asshole you nearly married. Why not give him a little more credit?"

She'd nearly married? This was news to Chance. She'd never said a word. Neither had Emma or Blaze. Either Emma hadn't told Blaze about it, or she'd told him to keep it to himself. Interesting.

Rory's face was red as she turned that glare on her brother. Chance couldn't help but think she was cute. She'd clipped her long blonde hair in one of those big banana clips on her head, and she'd slipped into a flowy dress that clung to her full breasts before dropping to skim her ankles. The dress was ivory with little pink flowers sprinkled across the fabric.

She was feminine and adorable and he wanted to pull her close and simply feel her lithe body against his. Not even for sex, though he wouldn't say no, but just to hold the body of the woman who was carrying his child inside her.

Rory wasn't in a holding mood, though. She held up her right hand and mimed snapping his mouth shut. "Shut it, Theo. None of your business. And don't be blabbing my business either, you hear me?"

Theo's gaze traveled between them for a second. "Wait… you didn't tell him about Mark?"

"Swear to God I'm going to kill you," Rory growled.

"No," Chance said. "Never heard of Mark. Rory doesn't tell me much of anything, if I'm honest. She doesn't actually like me, if you haven't noticed."

"Liked you well enough at some point," Theo said mildly.

"I think she'd tell you she was temporarily insane during that time."

"Oh my God, are you two going to keep talking over me and around me like I'm not here?"

"Rory, babe, trust me when I tell you that nobody could ever pretend you weren't here," Chance said. "I'm just filling Theo in on the things you might not have told him, considering you never mentioned this Mark character to me."

"It wasn't important." Rory folded her arms beneath her breasts, emphasizing their roundness. "You didn't tell me your life story during that time, did you? Of course not, which means you weren't entitled to mine either. Mark is nobody anymore and not important."

Chance

"Okay, babe. I'll respect you don't want to talk about it, but one of these days you're gonna have to."

Rory turned back to her brother. "We need a plan for cleaning this up and replanting. What do you want to do?"

Theo frowned. "It's Saturday. Gonna be too busy at the Dawg to get plants today, but I'll rake the big stuff out then get the tractor and plow it under before I gotta go to work. The nursery is closed tomorrow, but I'll get over there early Monday. I'll have Chris work the kitchen for lunch, and I'll get everything in over the next week."

"I'll help you rake," Rory said. "And I can plow it under. You worry about getting over to the Dawg and prepping for the day."

Chance pulled out his phone and made a call. Ghost answered on the second ring. "What's up?"

"Got an incident at Rory's place." He told Ghost the story. "Need some help cleaning up the destruction and prepping the field for new plants." He shot a look at Rory and Theo, who were watching him. "Might need to do some planting, too."

"We've got a light day. I'll head over that way with Kane and Seth after I wrap up a couple of things. Ethan and Blaze can handle the range."

Chance's chest was tight. "Thanks, boss. Appreciate it."

"You didn't have to do that," Theo said when Chance put the phone away. "But I'd be lying if I said I wasn't grateful as hell."

"It's a lot of work, brother. And we're gonna be family in a way, which means we're supposed to take care of each other. But even if that wasn't the case, Sutton's Creek is home and the Dawg is a favorite haunt for my guys. We'd help you anyway. If you think you can get those plants this morning while we clean up, we'll help put them in the ground tomorrow when the Dawg is closed so you can make sure we do it right."

Theo nodded. "I can do that. Thanks, Chance."

He held out a hand and Chance took it. They shook. Chance didn't miss the sheen of moisture in Theo's eyes before he pulled away again and cleared his throat. He seemed to be searching for something else to say, but Chance filled the gap instead.

"Why don't you head for the nursery? I think we got this. And if we don't, Rory will set us straight."

"Okay." Theo's gaze moved between them. "I feel kinda bad taking off, but if you're sure."

"I'm sure. Get the plants and we'll take care of the ground."

Theo hugged his sister and gave her a kiss on the forehead, shook Chance's hand again, and headed for his vehicle.

"Point me to the rakes," Chance said when Theo backed out and headed down the drive.

Rory turned to him, tears shimmering on her lashes. It gutted him to see her cry. His beautiful, brave, prickly-as-hell Rory.

No, not his. He had to remember that, no matter how much it confused him that she didn't want to be his.

"Thank you for doing that. For calling your guys. Theo would have done it all alone, bitching at me for trying to help him the whole time. He'd have worked too hard and wore himself out, but he'd have still worked at the Dawg all afternoon and evening. Then he'd have come back too early tomorrow to continue prepping the ground, and he'd have driven himself every day until it was done...."

She seemed to have run out of things to say. Chance put an arm around her shoulders and hugged her to his side. She didn't resist, same as she hadn't back in the house when he'd nearly kissed her.

"Rory, we'd have helped anyway, like I said, but if you think for one minute that I'm not gonna do everything it takes to keep you safe and happy, and by extension your brother, then you don't know a thing about me. Your happiness is my priority."

"That doesn't make any sense." He could tell she was trying to be prickly but it was an act. She was on the verge of sobbing in his arms.

He gave her another squeeze as he pressed a kiss to her sun-warmed hair, inhaling the peaches and vanilla scent. "Get used to it, honey. Because this is how I roll. Now let's get those rakes."

She sniffed. "Yes, let's. I have to get the keys to Betty Ann, too."

Chance couldn't help but smile. "Betty Ann?"

"The tractor."

"Oh, right. Of course."

"Why are you grinning like that?" she demanded.

He put a thumb to his chest. "Who, me?"

"Yes, you. Twerp."

"I think it's cute how you name everything."

"It's just a name, Chancey Pants. Don't get excited," she grumbled. But her cheeks were pinker as she turned on her heel and started for the barn.

He followed, grinning the whole way.

Chapter Sixteen

Rory sat in a chair beneath the tree and watched the men make quick work of the garden, removing most of the dead plants and piling them up a distance away so they could dry out and be burned.

There hadn't even been any produce to salvage. Whoever had done this smashed everything—tomatoes, zucchini, melons. Even the green beans had been mostly bruised and smashed, the potatoes dug up and destroyed, and the herbs trampled to bits. Someone had driven a four-wheeler over the garden repeatedly. What they hadn't mowed down, they tore out.

Rory hated to see the destruction, but she wasn't focused on it right now. She was focused on the Chippendale-worthy show of four men without shirts working up a sweat.

Sure, it was like a very hot, sexy version of Farmers Only dot com—one she could read about in a reverse harem romance novel where all these amazingly sexy men were in love with her and lived to please her—but it wasn't the sight of four gorgeous, sweaty, muscled men raking the garden that had her heart beating harder.

It was Chance Hughes. And not because he was every sex

fantasy she'd ever had come to life, but because he'd stood beside the garden with her and Theo, heard the devastation in her brother's voice, and done something about it. Theo really would have half-killed himself to fix the mess and get the garden planted again, and she'd have worried herself silly because of it.

But Chance stepped up. He called his friends and they rode in like the cavalry and started raking and cleaning as if they'd been farming their whole lives. They'd brought a cooler filled with water, and beer for after, and they'd gotten to work.

She'd showed Chance how to start Betty Ann—she was old and temperamental—and they'd hooked up the plow. The equipment wasn't modern, but it still worked. Gramps had bought Betty Ann in 1975 and he'd kept her going even when he'd finally caved and gotten a proper tractor with a closed in cab and air-conditioning. Granny had sold all the farm equipment after Gramps died, but not Betty Ann. She was eternal.

Chance teased her about naming things, but hell, Betty Ann, Liza Jane, and Clyde were old. They'd been in the family longer than she had. They deserved names. She'd named the chickens, too. And the deer. When her grandparents still had cows and pigs, she'd named them as well. She'd been a kid then, but the habit apparently stuck.

She wondered what Chance would think about Gus the Glamorous and had to suppress a giggle. Gus had lived in her bedside drawer until she'd hidden him in the closet when Chance came to stay with her the first time. He was still there, too. Maybe she needed to get him out again, take care of this itch she felt whenever she looked at Chance's body glistening with sweat as he worked.

It wouldn't help this emotional attachment that insisted on growing inside her, but it'd sure fix the physical ache. Wasn't that half the battle anyway?

When the men had the garden cleared, Chance strolled over to where she sat. Her mouth went dry as he walked toward her but she refused to look away. She tried to affect a bored look but she wasn't sure it was successful.

At least her tongue wasn't hanging out.

"You doin' okay sitting here?"

She lifted her glass of iced tea. "I'm fine. Blood sugar is good, it's cool beneath the tree, and I'm enjoying the view."

She let her gaze drift past him to the others before landing on his face again. His expression had hardened a fraction. Oh ho, Chance didn't like it when she admired his friends.

"It's a very inspiring view, I might add."

"Is it? I wouldn't know."

"It's like the novel I'm reading. Five hot guys—I realize y'all are only four—are running a farm. Did I mention they're brothers? Anyway, they find this poor woman in the woods who doesn't know how she got there or what her name is. And they all fall for her. They all want her. And she wants them. Every one of them, maybe all of them, at once." Rory sipped her tea. "It's very illuminating to read all the ways in which five hot guys can pleasure one woman."

His eyes glittered hotter than before as he stared at her. "If you need pleasure, I've got you covered, honey. Just let me know. I know what you like and I'm plenty capable. Don't need five men, just need me."

Her pulse tapped a quick beat. "I can take care of that myself. But thanks. What did you want anyway?"

"Just wanted to see how you were. You don't have to watch us. I'm gonna fire up the tractor—"

"Betty Ann."

"Betty Ann. Gonna fire her up and plow the garden." He closed his eyes. "Jesus, why the fuck does that sound dirty all of a sudden?"

Rory laughed. "Because you have a dirty mind, Chancey Pants."

"Honey, I'm thinking it's you who has the dirty mind and now you've got me thinking about it too."

"Oh sure, blame me. I've had provocation with the Chippendale's show going on in front of me. What would you do if four topless women were doing yard work in front of you?"

"Point taken."

"Exactly."

Her phone rang then. "Hey, Theo, you get those plants?"

"Yeah, I got the plants. But Rory, we have a bigger problem."

Her stomach tightened. "What's wrong?"

"We've got a busted pipe at the Dawg. The kitchen is flooded and I don't know how much damage there is yet. We might not be able to open tonight."

―――

RORY SAT in Chance's truck as he drove them into town, her stomach churning with anger and confusion. The burst pipe couldn't be deliberate, and yet it was one more thing in a list of shitty things that'd happened lately. It'd all started with the pregnancy test, though she didn't count that as a shitty thing.

But right after she'd gotten her results, Ronnie Davis and his jerk-off driver came up to the house, then left deep grooves in her drive. Somebody crept onto her property late at night when she wasn't home. Her sugar levels were unpredictable with the pregnancy and she had moments of dizziness, not to mention the tiredness. Jimmy Turton wanted her to sell in hopes his mother would, too. Somebody destroyed Theo's garden.

And now the pipe had burst and the Dawg was flooded.

"Do you think this is related?" she asked.

Chance glanced over at her. His expression had been grim since she'd told him the news. He'd left the guys to do the plowing and insisted he was driving her to the Dawg. She didn't argue.

"Maybe. But the Dawg is an old building. Could be a coincidence. We'll find out more when we get there."

Rory rubbed her temple. "The building is insured, but it's old, like you say. Repairs cost more. If we're closed for a day or two, we'll still be fine. Longer than that, and the expenses start to pile up. Not to mention the food will spoil and we'll be out for that, too. If the Dawg doesn't open, we aren't making money. If we aren't making money, we're losing money. I could see someone thinking that'd make selling the farm more appealing as a way to save the business."

"Possible. But let's not jump to conclusions yet, okay?"

She swallowed the lump in her throat. "Okay."

Chance pulled into a slot behind the Dawg and she hopped out before he shifted into park, ignoring the cursing as she did so. She jerked the door to the tavern open, stepping into the kitchen—

And one hell of a mess.

"Oh my God, Theo."

Her brother looked up, his expression one of misery. "Yeah."

Water dripped from a light fixture, coated one wall, and stood an inch deep on the floor. Thankfully the entire first floor was made of concrete so the only wood floors they had to worry about were over their heads. The open shelves where Theo kept supplies were dripping as well. His herbs and spices, the flour and salt, all of it was wet and likely ruined if it wasn't inside glass or plastic. She was still taking it all in when she felt Chance's presence at her back.

"Hola, Rory." A man peeked out from beneath the sink and waved. "Hola, Chance."

"Hola, Diego," Chance said.

"Hey, Diego. Whatcha got?" Rory asked.

"Water, amiga."

"I see that. Where did it come from?"

"Theo's apartment. Burst pipe beneath the kitchen sink. It's probably been going for a few hours."

"Oh, Theo. Your apartment."

Her brother looked sick. "Yeah. I'll have to stay in the other one until mine is cleaned. It was fine when I left this morning and now this."

He spread his arms to encompass the kitchen.

"We'll get it taken care of. Did you call anyone for clean up?"

"Diego has a friend who cleans up water damage. They're on the way."

"They'll extract the water and assess the structure," Diego said, getting to his feet. "Since much of this building is brick, it might not be as bad as if it were made of mostly wood and drywall. But the drywall upstairs in the kitchen will probably have to come down where it's been soaked through. Once the water has been removed, you're gonna have some industrial fans and dehumidifiers to dry the place out as quickly as possible. It'll take time, but you should be open in a couple of days."

Rory's stomach tightened. "A couple of days. Okay, that's not too bad. Theo?"

"I know, but I still don't like it. I was doing pork chops tonight with an apple brandy reduction. Garlic smashed potatoes. Cauliflower charred over a flame. It was gonna be epic."

"Dang, dude, you makin' me hungry," Diego said.

"You can still do that in two days," Rory said. "Unless the refrigerators and the freezers crap out too."

Theo's eyes closed. "Please don't say that, Ror. I beg you."

"I'm just frustrated. Sorry. But it won't happen. They're not that old and everything will be fine."

"It will be," Theo said firmly.

"I'd like to see upstairs," Chance said. "Get a look at your kitchen."

"Sure. Rory, will you take him up? Door's open."

Rory led the way to the second floor and pushed Theo's door open. The living room looked fine, but the kitchen, when they went through the door, was clearly wet. The water had spewed from the pipe, coated the floor, and leaked down through the light fixtures and walls below.

Chance went over to the sink and knelt to look at it. Rory followed, standing behind him and trying to peer at what he was doing. When he stood again, his expression was hard.

"What is it?"

"The pipe looks like it burst, but the hole is too neat."

"Too neat?"

"Like somebody drilled through it. Does Theo leave the door unlocked often?"

A chill shuddered through her. "When he's downstairs, yes. But he would have locked up before he left to come to the farm earlier."

Chance stalked to the front door and tugged it open. Then he examined the lock, tracing his finger over parts of it.

"Well?" she asked when he didn't say anything.

"Looks like it's been picked. Whoever did it was subtle, which means they have some skill. Either somebody's targeting your brother for reasons of their own, or it's exactly what you thought and they're targeting your income source to make selling the land more appealing. We need to call the cops, make a report to get it on the record."

Fear rolled through her, followed by a healthy dose of anger. "It has to be the developer. I don't think Jimmy is capable of lock picking, and I doubt Carter Coombs did it. I don't actually know he's selling anyway. All I have is Jimmy's speculation. I can ask him though. I'd like to know."

"If you do, don't mention any of what's happened. Best to keep it to yourself, see if whoever's doing this gets bolder. They might make a mistake, give us a chance to catch them at it."

"I'm not sure I can handle any bolder, Chance. What's next? Burning the tavern down? Or burning the farmhouse down? What they've done so far is small potatoes, but what happens when we don't sell? They'll escalate, and I hate to think how."

"I'm not going to let that happen."

"How can you stop them?" she cried as frustration hammered her. "You can't be everywhere at once. You have a job, and I do too. And even when I'm home, I have to sleep sometime. I can't watch the farm twenty-four hours a day."

"Honey, you don't have to. The police can patrol the area more often, at least until we solve this. I'll get the new cameras installed, we'll add motion sensor lights in key places, and I'll put a couple of cameras here at the Dawg as well. The hallway, the entry and exit. We're gonna make it harder on whoever it is to come and go without detection."

What he was saying made sense. She knew he intended to keep her and the baby and Theo safe. But she was still scared, which wasn't typical for her. If it was just her and Theo, maybe she wouldn't be so worried. They could handle adversity.

But she had a baby to think about now. A small, helpless being whose life depended on her. She couldn't charge into situations the way she once had, couldn't bluster her way through hardship with sass and grit. She had to be smart, had to think about more than her own wants and needs.

And maybe that started with trusting Chance to do what he said he would do. To be there for her and the baby.

"Let's call the police," he said gently. "Get them over here to see this. Somebody might have seen something suspicious, which the cops'll find out when they start asking questions."

Rory pulled in a deep breath, let it out again. "Okay, yes, let's do it."

Because he was right, and he *would* protect her.

It was time she let him in, even if it terrified her.

Chapter Seventeen

Rory was quiet on the ride back to the farm, which was unlike her, but a lot had happened in a short amount of time. After he'd convinced her they needed to call the police, they'd gone back downstairs to find Diego's friends had arrived and had the situation in hand. Theo had already written a sign and put it on the front door saying that the Dawg would be closed tonight. He'd also posted to their Facebook page.

Chance told Theo what he'd found. The other man's eyes grew wide, and then his expression hardened. "Fucking assholes," he'd muttered.

The police arrived soon after. Chance and Rory took them upstairs to show them the pipe and the door while Theo stayed to help move things in the kitchen downstairs. The officers—Kendrick and Bass—examined the scene, took notes, and asked questions. Then they returned downstairs to ask Theo a few questions. Once they had their report, they advised Theo and Rory to call if anything further happened.

After the police were gone, Rory had wanted to pitch in and help move things around so the guys could suction up the water, but

Chance

Theo took her by the shoulders and told her he needed her to go back to the farm. She hadn't wanted to do it, but he explained that he'd picked out his plants and they were supposed to be delivered within the hour.

Somebody needed to be there to make sure nothing happened to them once they were dropped off. Any other time and the plants could have been left beneath the tree until they were put in the ground the next day.

There really wasn't anything to guarantee someone wouldn't come during the night and destroy the new plants, but Chance intended to make it a lot less appealing for them to do so. The new equipment wouldn't arrive until next week, but he swung by the local hardware store and picked up motion sensor lights to install this afternoon. Rory already had them on the chicken coop, but that was to protect the chickens by scaring predators.

More were needed. Wasn't foolproof, but it was something. Whoever'd had the foresight to shoot down the camera could do the same for lights, but the more obstacles Chance put up for them, the more risk of being seen.

He wanted answers and he wanted them fast, but he'd been a special operator long enough to know that sometimes things happened slowly. You just had to be prepared so you could catch your target and put an end to the battle.

Seth had done some research into D&B Properties last night. What he had so far was nothing special. They were a property development company based in Texas. Owners were Ronald Davis, Sr. and Darryl Benson. Benson was at the home office in Houston while Davis was in Alabama, working on the deal that would bring a multi-million dollar mixed use development to the outskirts of Sutton's Creek. It was a big deal, requiring a huge amount of cash, but Davis and Benson seemed to have the investors.

Didn't make sense they'd resort to sabotage to get their way when there was so much developable property within close proximity to Huntsville. Sutton's Creek was the prime location because of the river. Giving up on the sites they'd scouted to start over probably wasn't ideal, but surely it wasn't worth risking jail time by breaking and entering and causing deliberate damage. Then again, people had been known to commit crimes for lesser reasons. There was a lot of money at stake in a development of this size. Who else had reason to want to force Rory and Theo to sell?

The Turtons and the Coombses notwithstanding.

"What do you think about throwing something on the grill for dinner?" Chance asked as the ride stretched silently on.

Rory stared out the window. Thinking about what, he didn't know. She swiveled to look at him and his gut twisted at how beautiful she was. What was it about this one particular woman—a woman who'd made it plain she didn't like him—that had him tied up in knots inside?

He'd never been the forever type. Never really believed it was a thing, no matter how often people tried to pretend it was. His parents had been married for fifteen years and then one day his mother lost her shit.

Chance's life had changed drastically that day. He'd gone from a normal teenage boy to an angry, sad, withdrawn foster kid in the space of a heartbeat.

His dad's heartbeat.

Christ.

"That sounds nice. What did you have in mind?"

Chance blinked. Was Rory being cooperative without arguing first? "I bought steaks when I went shopping. You've got potatoes, and I saw cucumbers and tomatoes, too. We could roast the potatoes and throw the cukes and tomatoes together with some red onion, vinegar, and sugar."

She folded her arms beneath her breasts. He really liked the way it made everything squeeze together for his enjoyment. "Do you even cook or is that the menu you'd like me to fix?"

"I cook, Rory. Which you should know because I fixed stuff for you when you got out of the hospital."

One corner of her mouth quirked. Was that a grin? "Sandwiches. Soup from a can. Grilled cheese. Not quite the same thing."

"Okay, so you got me there. I can grill a steak, though. I know how to roast potatoes in an oven, and I've got a recipe saved on my phone for cukes and tomatoes. I'm not Theo, but you won't starve and you won't gag either."

"You won't gag. Now that's high praise if I ever heard it. I may need to order shirts to sell at the Dawg."

"Very funny. What were you thinking about so intently anyway?"

"I think you can guess. I'm pissed off that someone would do these things to us. It makes me want to dig in even harder, but then I have to think about the fact I'm pregnant and I can't risk the baby's life because I'm mad."

"You aren't thinking about selling, are you?"

She shook her head. "Hell, no. I'm not selling. I just… I have to be smart about what I say and do. That's all."

"I'm glad to hear you say it. And I agree it's time to be smart."

The glare she flashed him told him he was journeying into the danger zone. He didn't know why, but he knew he needed to get out quick.

"Hey, you wanna invite Blaze and Emma over to join us?"

Nothing like derailing the train of thought before it got too far from the station.

"That'd be nice. Do we have enough?"

We. He liked the sound of that. "We do. I bought two packs of three."

"I feel like I owe your friends for their hard work today. I was gonna comp them dinner at the Dawg tonight, but maybe we could grab a few more steaks and have them all over?"

"You really want to do that?"

"Well, yeah. Invite them all. I'm used to standing behind the bar and talking to people all night, plus waiting tables when I'm needed, so the thought of a quiet Saturday night is kind of weird. And since

Diego and the guys at George's Restoration insist they don't need help with the cleanup, what else is there to do?"

He could think of some things, but none of them were going to be anything she wanted to participate in. The fact she was being nice and not prickly was a big leap forward, though, so why not do what she wanted? He'd said it was his mission to make her happy, and he meant it.

"You aren't too tired for all that company?"

"I'm tired, but I'm not going to be doing the cooking. Well, maybe a side dish. But I haven't had people over for dinner in years and I kind of like the idea of there being laughter and fellowship at the farm again. Granny used to love a party. Her and Gramps would throw big cookouts and it seemed like the whole town would come over and bring food. I'd kind of like a happy memory for today instead of sadness and anger."

He heard the wistfulness in her voice. "Okay, honey, we'll swing by the store and pick up more steaks and any other ingredients we need."

"I'm buying."

"You aren't. I've got the steaks because it was my idea. You can buy whatever you want for sides."

"I feel like I should explain that comping dinner at the Dawg meant the cost was on me and Theo, so I should buy the rest of the steaks. But I also feel like you won't agree."

"Got it in one, kitten. You inviting your brother?"

"Kitten?"

"Cute, but feisty and unpredictable."

Rory laughed. "Okay, whatever. I'd like to ask Theo to come, but I guess that depends on you. He will absolutely tell you how to cook the steak. He might even take over. If you don't want that, then I won't ask him."

He was touched she considered his feelings. It was laughable that he'd be upset, but she didn't know that.

"Babe, invite your brother. If he wants to cook the whole meal,

I'll be his sous chef. And if he doesn't, then I'll do what I said I was gonna do. It's about everybody getting together and having a good time, right?"

"Yes."

"Then that's what we're gonna do."

Chapter Eighteen

Chance flipped steaks and gazed out at the side yard where he and Rory had set up tables and dragged out folding chairs from the barn. The big oak tree shaded the tables, and birds chirped from high up in the branches. There was a light breeze that blew across the yard and ruffled his hair.

He could hear Emma and Rory inside, laughing about something. Rory's laugh was like sunshine, and he knew she was happy in that moment. He wished he knew how to make her happy all the time because he'd do it just to hear that laugh of pure joy.

The guys were at the tables, drinking beer and talking about range shit. They'd invited Daphne, but she'd gone out with Warren again. Chance didn't see that pairing at all, but Daphne seemed to like the guy.

She was a knockout in a quiet way, and Warren was the quintessential nerd, but stranger things had happened.

Kane's interest/lack of in Daphne was one of those strange things, in his opinion. Chance told his friend to just ask the girl out for fuck's sake, but Kane's eyes got big and he'd denied even wanting to do so.

"Just looking out for her, man. I don't want to date her."

Chance didn't believe that for a second. But considering Daphne worked at the range and they needed her to keep doing so, it was probably a good thing Kane didn't go there. Last thing they needed was Daphne quitting because Kane pissed her off or broke her heart. She was too good at keeping things running smoothly to lose her.

And Kane was too good at breaking hearts to trust him not to break hers.

Seth got up and made his way over to Chance. "How they coming?"

"Be done soon."

He took a drink of his beer and gazed across the fields. "It's nice out here. Peaceful."

"Yeah, I think so."

"I know we aren't supposed to get involved with anyone while working this assignment, but it seems to be working for Blaze."

"And you're saying this why?"

Seth shrugged. "You said Rory doesn't want anything from you. I'm just telling you that if I were you, I'd fight like hell to change her mind."

Chance felt the words like a blow. He also got a tight feeling in his chest from the way Seth talked about Rory. "Wait, are you telling me you have the hots for my woman?"

Seth arched an eyebrow. "Seriously, that's what you took from what I just said?"

Chance squirmed. "Well, yeah. What was I supposed to think?"

"You're supposed to think that maybe you need to fight for what you want and not accept this bullshit about her not liking you or not wanting you in her life. I get that's an easy thing to tell Ghost, especially when you believe it's true, but you made a baby together. You're going to be in each other's lives for the rest of yours, so maybe try to build something instead of believing there's no foundation and it's useless to try."

"Wow, who died and made you a philosopher?"

"I dunno. Maybe I've been where you are now. Maybe I didn't fight. Maybe I lost everything because of it." He took a swig of beer and shrugged again. "Or maybe I've got no reason except common sense and I'm trying to sprinkle some of it on you."

Chance stared at his friend. Seth wasn't a talker and what he'd just said was a lot. It also made Chance think. Had his friend really lost someone he loved because he didn't fight? Or was he making it up so Chance would fight harder to win Rory?

"Thanks, I guess. I'm not giving up, but Rory's not someone you push too hard. Makes her shut down."

Seth arched an eyebrow. "See, just the fact you know that says something."

"Everybody knows that. Rory's not hard to read."

Seth snorted. "Dude, she's a woman. You have to study her to know what she's thinking, and even then you'll be wrong the majority of the time."

Now he was really curious. "You got any particular woman you're studying these days?"

"Nope, not me. Keeping my head down as ordered. I plan to save the world and head back to DC where I'll shake off the red clay of Alabama for good."

"You don't like it here?"

"I like it just fine. People are nice. Town is cute. But it's too small for me. Everybody knows everybody else, and knows their business too. Can't throw a rock without Colleen Wright watching. Worse, she'll tell you that you threw it clean through a ghost and you need to apologize."

Chance laughed. "Or you hit an alien spacecraft and you *really* need to apologize before they suck you up and use the anal probe."

"God, that woman. Asked me last week if I'd come and record her and Reba communing with the aliens in the field."

"She asked me, too. I told her she needed to get a smartphone

Chance

and record it herself. She lectured me on the advantages of flip phones." He was thoughtful a moment. "She also told me that Rory was in trouble, and she wasn't wrong about that."

"That's because she's nosy and observant. Hell, maybe we should hire her to do surveillance."

They both cracked up at that. Colleen would notice everything, but she'd also be unable to keep her mouth shut. Everyone would know what she'd observed and the whole town would be talking.

Chance took a drink of his beer. "What do you think about all this shit with the plants and the drilled pipe?"

Seth shook his head. "Seems like it'd be related. Also seems like somebody wants revenge against Theo specifically. Could be a pissed off woman he dated a while ago. Doesn't have to be recent."

"That's true. Maybe she held a grudge and bided her time."

"Also seems like the kind of thing somebody might do who wanted to cost them a lot of money and put the farm into play."

Chance's gut tightened. "Yep, thought of that too. Rory mentioned her neighbor wanted her to sell but she insists he's not capable of doing something like this. Makes me wonder why he would anyway. All he had was an idea they might get more money if they all agreed to sell. Unless Davis told him they'd pay more for all three properties together. Davis didn't tell Rory that, though. Not that she gave him a chance when she went to meet him with a shotgun."

"Doesn't make a lot of sense the neighbor would do it, unless the offer is significantly more."

"Could be. But Rory also said the mother isn't inclined to sell, so maybe if Rory and Theo were onboard, her son could talk her into it. Which means he and his brother could get jobs with benefits and stop working the farm. I imagine they'd get some cash to split, too. On the other hand, Ronnie Davis's driver had no issues tearing up her driveway when they peeled out of here on Thursday. A little extra destruction might not bother them at all."

"Especially if they were pissed she met them with a gun and refused to consider the offer. Lotta men in this world can't take it when a woman knows what she wants and won't accept their shit."

"Truth, brother."

The back door opened with a creak and then the screen slammed shut. Chance turned as Rory and Emma walked toward them, carrying dishes. Rory was still in the sundress, still looking like summer sunshine and happiness in his mind. His belly twisted and his heart thumped as he watched her approach. She was smiling, and the smile didn't dim when she locked gazes with him.

That was nice. It wasn't often that Rory smiled at him. Smiled at everyone else a whole lot more than she did him. He didn't know what'd caused it this time, but he wasn't looking away. Couldn't look away.

Something shifted deep inside him the longer he stared. It wasn't lust, though he certainly felt that. It was something else.

Home, his brain whispered. *You're home.*

Jesus God. His body braced as truth bombs dropped on him.

Rory was home to him. He could stand at this grill and watch her walk toward him every day of his life and he'd be a happy man. He wanted to go to sleep with her in his arms, wake up with her wrapped around him.

He'd crawl across hot coals for one of her smiles. He'd throw himself in front of a bullet to keep her safe. He'd never let anyone harm a hair on her head for as long as he lived. The idea someone had tried made a knot form in his gut.

Jesus God.

This was it. The big L word. Something he'd never felt before, never thought would happen to him.

He was in love with Aurora Harper. Bone deep, world shaking, life changing love.

And there was no way he could tell her. He wanted to, desperately.

But he knew how that would go. She'd scoff or tell him to get lost or flat out say he was lying.

Worse, she'd tell him she didn't feel the same way. Which he already knew, but he didn't want to hear her say it.

Nope, no way could he tell her. He'd have to prove it to her. And he'd have to win her.

Challenge accepted.

Chapter Nineteen

"You okay, Chancey Pants?"

He'd been quiet all evening. Not just quiet, but pensive. Rory'd noticed it after they sat down to steaks, roasted potatoes, mac and cheese, cucumbers and tomatoes, and a cake that Emma Grace had picked up from the Kiss My Grits Café. Wendy Cochran's strawberry cake was just the thing for a cookout and the guys had devoured it.

Theo had come late, because he'd refused to leave the Dawg while George's guys were suctioning water and dragging out fans and dehumidifiers, which meant he didn't hang around the grill or the stove or tell anyone how to do anything. He'd complimented the steaks, told Rory she'd gotten Granny's mac and cheese just right, and remarked that nobody made cake like Wendy. But then she should have expected no less because Theo had been raised by Granny, same as she had, and Granny hadn't tolerated bad manners.

"Yeah, I'm fine. You?"

Rory nodded. "Fine. It was a nice evening."

"It was."

Everyone was gone now and they were alone on the porch. The tables and chairs had all been put away, the dishes done, and everything put back where it belonged. The plants were under the tree waiting for tomorrow, and Chance and his buddies had installed battery-powered motion lights on the barn, the big oak, a tall post they'd erected in the garden earlier, and the front and back of the house.

There were already lights on the house, but she had to flip a switch for them so it was nice to have something that would come on whenever anyone or anything crossed in front of the sensor.

She was the one who'd wanted to sit on the porch and Chance had indulged her. She'd lit a candle and brought a blanket because it got cool at night, and she'd made herself a tall glass of iced tea with Stevia to sweeten it because she'd already had enough sugar for the day. Stevia wasn't quite the same, but it worked.

She'd taken the porch swing and Chance had unfolded a lawn chair. He'd been nursing a beer for a while now. He also hadn't said much.

"I like your friends. They're really sweet to pitch in and help out the way they did."

"They're good guys. I've known them a long time."

She picked at a thread on the blanket she'd put over her lap as she slowly swung back and forth. "You were in the military together."

"Yeah. We served in the same unit for a long time, had each other's asses when we deployed overseas."

"And all of you left the military to buy a range in Alabama?"

"Not quite, but yeah. We decided it was time to pursue that crazy dream we always had to run a business together somewhere. This part of Alabama made sense because it's growing, and there's a shit ton of military and government around here. If we were going to offer security training as part of our business, can't find a better place than this one."

The swing creaked rhythmically in the darkness, a comforting sound. "No, not really. Gramps worked with the German scientists on Redstone Arsenal in the fifties, when he was still a young man and thought he didn't want to farm. I say worked with, but I really mean he worked on the Arsenal and sometimes at the test stand where they tested the rockets that eventually went to space."

"That's pretty cool, really."

"I always thought so. He met Granny, who was from Hazel Green—that's north of Huntsville—and when they got married, he brought her home to Sutton's Creek and they moved in with his parents here at the farm. Which I'm sure thrilled Granny to no end, but I never heard her say a bad word about living with her in-laws. They had three kids, one of which was my dad."

Good grief she was talking a lot tonight. But it was kind of comforting to sit in the dark and tell someone about her family. They were on her mind a lot lately, even before she'd found out she was pregnant.

"Your parents died when you were young, right?"

"Yep. Hit head on by a drunk driver coming back from a concert in Nashville. Mama always wanted to see Loretta Lynn at the Ryman, so that's where they'd gone. I was eight and Theo was ten. We were staying at the farm that night, so this is where I was when the news came."

Tears pricked her eyes. It was so long ago, but sometimes the pain was as fresh as yesterday.

"I'm really sorry, Rory. That's hard."

"It was, but we dealt with it."

"Did you get the Dawg from your grandparents, too?"

"My parents owned the Dawg. The building had been in my mother's family for three generations then. Her siblings didn't want it, so she and my dad bought them out and opened the tavern. It was a strain on my grandparents to keep it, I think, but they did it for us." She blew out a sigh. "I guess that's why it's all so important to me. The Dawg was my parents' dream, and the farm is where my memories are. It's all important, and I don't want to lose any of it. I know it'd be so easy to let this place go—or even most of it while keeping the house and barn, but I don't want to. I walk into the woods, and I know my dad played there as a kid. His initials are in a tree out there. And there's the remnants of a treehouse he and his brothers built. They're gone too. One was an alcoholic who drank himself to death, and the other drowned a few years ago. There are cousins, but they live in Florida. I've seen them once in my life, right after my parents died and they came to the funeral."

"I take it they didn't inherit a piece of the property?"

"Nope." She popped the P. "My uncle and his wife divorced when the kids were teenagers, and they weren't close to him after that. It's just me and Theo."

"Who's Mark?"

Rory stiffened at the mention of her asshole ex. The betrayal still hurt, even after all this time. Even if a part of her was glad she hadn't married him.

"Mark is nobody anymore. But he was my fiancé. Three weeks before the wedding, I caught him screwing one of my bridesmaids."

It was still humiliating.

"Ouch."

"Yep, ouch. He married her and they moved to Decatur. He's a lawyer there, they bought a house in the historic district, and Tammy loves to post pictures of her perfect house and perfect kids. She's the president of the Junior League, and she's one of the hosts for the upcoming Diner en Blanc—that's a fancy picnic at a secret location where absolutely everything you bring and wear *must* be white. She posts about the dinner endlessly. She has what it takes to be a lawyer's wife, apparently, because I did not. Which Mark told me to my face before he called me too country. He could have saved us both a lot of trouble if he'd been clear about that from the beginning."

"Rory. Babe."

His voice was gentle, and she almost hated it. Because it meant he felt sorry for her, and she hated anyone feeling sorry for her. Her whole life, people had felt sorry for her. Her parents died, she got diabetes, and her man ran off with one of her friends. She was sure there were plenty of other things they felt sorry for her over, but she didn't want to enumerate them.

Rory swiped a thumb beneath her eyes. Stupid tears. She'd never told anyone, not even Emma Grace, what Mark had said to her. It was too embarrassing. And he was right. She wasn't cut out to be a society wife. She didn't care about hobnobbing with community leaders, didn't care about making an impression, and she certainly wasn't participating in a top secret outdoor picnic every year.

"I'm okay. I should block both of them, but I didn't want them to think I cared. I *don't* care, and I don't look for her posts on purpose. But they show up often enough I know what's happening in their lives. Baby number three is on the way, and they've only been married about four years. They flew to Hawaii and got married there. It was supposed to be *my* honeymoon, but she went instead."

The porch creaked and then Chance settled beside her, scooting her over to make room. He wrapped an arm around her shoulders and she turned to burrow her face into his chest. She really shouldn't, but he was warm and solid and it felt right to be close to him.

He ran his fingers along her arm, over and over, soothing her. "I'm sorry people did that to you. But I hope you know they're the ones who've got something wrong with them, not you. I know it had to hurt, probably still hurts, but that man didn't deserve you. Neither did she. Nobody needs a friend like that, and you damn sure didn't need a husband who doesn't worship the ground you walk on. He should have thanked his lucky stars every single day that you chose him out of all the men you could have picked."

Rory couldn't help but giggle. She lifted her head and gazed up at him. His eyes were dead serious, which she appreciated. "Thank you, but I didn't exactly have them lined up down the street."

He brushed a lock of hair from her cheek, tucked it behind her ear. "Only because you scared them shitless with that glare of yours."

"You're laying it on a little thick," she said, yet her heart hammered. "But I appreciate it."

"Not laying it on thick, babe. You're a beautiful, fiery, kickass sprite of a woman and I can't imagine there weren't men tripping over themselves to be in your life."

He made her feel lighter than air. He scared her, too. She couldn't like him too much. She'd already determined she had to let him in for the baby's sake, and that meant not snapping his head off every time she had a feeling she couldn't cope with, but the urge to push him away with a smart assed remark was strong.

"I've decided to like you, Chancey Pants, but don't push your luck trying to butter me up. You're still on thin ice here."

His grin was unexpected. "Like I said, fiery."

She settled against him again. The swing creaked gently. "What about you? Any shitty exes in the past?"

"No." He sighed. "I traveled a lot in the military. Didn't ever really have time to get involved with anyone for more than a few months here or there."

"Wow. No lost loves? Unrequited loves?"

"No lost loves. One unrequited, but that happens sometimes."

She pushed away again. "Really? Tell me about her? It *is* a her, right?"

He snorted. "I forgot to mention you were also funny, didn't I? Yes, it's a her. I'm not interested in any dicks but my own."

"It's a nice dick," she said just to tease him.

"Nice? How about incredible and amazing?"

She laughed. "Well, my experience with it was brief, but it did manage to be those things."

"Not to make this awkward, but I know for a fact it wouldn't mind doing those things again."

Her pussy throbbed. "You're changing the subject here. I'm interested in the unrequited love."

"If I tell you about it, will you soothe my pain?"

"If it involves getting naked with you, no. If you want me to pat you on the back and say 'there, there, big fella', I can do that."

"I'm rather partial to that first option."

"Not tonight. Maybe not ever. Best I can do."

He skimmed those fingers over her arm again and she had to suppress a shiver. "I'll take that deal."

"Now tell me about her."

"Not much to tell. I fell hard for her. Didn't expect to. She doesn't feel the same."

"Doesn't? That sounds recent. Is it someone in Sutton's Creek?"

"No, no one in Sutton's Creek."

"Did it happen recently?"

"No. I shoulda said she *didn't* feel the same."

She searched his gaze. She didn't know what she expected to find, but he didn't crack. Rory sighed. "Sorry, Chance. I know it had to hurt. I'm sure you'll get over her eventually."

"Already over it." She wasn't sure she believed him. "How long did it take you?"

It was a valid question and yet she didn't really have a valid answer. Because while she was over Mark, she wasn't over what he'd done. Would never be over it. On the outside, she projected bravado and confidence, but deep down, she didn't believe it. Didn't believe she was worthy of devotion or loyalty.

"A while," was all she said. "You know, I think I'm ready to head in. It's been a long day and I'm beat."

Because this conversation was getting too deep, and it made her uncomfortable to expose so much of herself. Especially when she realized he hadn't exposed anything personal about himself. One unrequited love he claimed to be over but didn't tell her about wasn't all that personal, really.

He held out a hand and helped her stand, then got to his feet beside her. He was at the door first, opening it for her. She skimmed past him, her heart quickening at the sweetness of the gesture.

She turned to face him, wanting to know more about the mystery woman but knowing he wasn't going to tell her. And what would he think if she kept asking? That she was jealous? She absolutely couldn't give him that impression.

"You don't have to keep sleeping on the couch, Chance. Take one of the rooms upstairs. You've got this place wired six ways to Sunday. If anyone breaks in or trips a motion light, you'll take care of it. You should at least sleep in a bed when you aren't protecting us from evil."

"Gonna stay on the couch for now, babe. But thank you."

"Aren't you worried you'll get a kink in your back?"

"Nope. I've slept in worse places, believe me. The couch is big and the cushions aren't too squishy. It's fine."

She had a crazy urge to ask him to sleep beside her. Just sleep. Her bed was more comfortable, and she had a feeling she'd sleep even better with him there. Her fears, the ones she couldn't seem to shake since learning she was pregnant, weren't as prominent when he was near. Simply sitting next to him on the swing had infused her with calm.

But asking him such a thing was impossible. She'd just learned he'd been in love with someone, maybe still was even though he'd said he was over it. The idea that he loved another woman knotted her belly, hollowed her heart.

Which was ridiculous. What she'd had with Chance had been about sex, nothing more. A baby wasn't going to change that.

"If you're sure," she said, twisting her hands in front of her, feeling awkward and unsure.

"I'm sure. Goodnight, Rory."

"Night, Chance."

It wasn't until she was in bed with the lights out, staring up at the ceiling, that she gave in to frustrated tears. She didn't even know why she was crying.

Chapter Twenty

THE RANGE OPENED AT TEN ON MONDAY MORNING BUT CHANCE AND the guys had to get there early for a meeting. Chance tried not to wake Rory, but she emerged from her bedroom anyway, looking disheveled and sleepy. And so fucking adorable he wanted to drag her into his arms and hold her.

He'd already learned that Morning Rory wasn't precisely cuddly, though. She growled and frowned and gnashed her teeth. Then you gave her coffee and she was better. Now that she was drinking mostly decaf, he wasn't sure how that'd go. He fixed her a half-caff and took it to her where she sat on the front porch, watching the fog that lingered on the fields. There were deer near the tree line.

"Which ones are they?"

She accepted the coffee with a thanks. "Delaney and Marie."

"How can you tell?"

Rory shrugged. "Marie is smaller than the rest. Delaney is the bold one. She's always there first. The others are probably right behind the trees."

He didn't know why she named the deer, but it was one of the things he adored about her. For the longest time he'd thought Rory was simply prickly, but in fact she had a soft heart. She was often prickly to protect herself, though sometimes she just didn't like someone.

Like him, though maybe that tide was turning now. He hoped so. After the way she'd leaned into him on the swing Saturday night after telling him about her ex, he'd thought she might be beginning to trust him. She hadn't been stiff or uncomfortable when he'd moved her over and pulled her to him. She'd melted against him like it was something they did every day.

He wanted more of that. More of her. He'd do whatever it took to make that happen. Like gentling a baby horse or getting one of those deer to trust him, it took time and patience.

He hated that someone had hurt her so badly. Mark wasn't worthy of the dirt on the bottom of her shoe, but it seemed like she was still working through what he'd done to her. Not just what he'd done, but also a friend she'd trusted. What kind of person fucked your fiancé behind your back and then married him on what should have been your honeymoon? And what kind of man did that to the woman he'd been planning to spend his life with?

Neither one of them were good enough for Rory in Chance's opinion. He hoped he never crossed paths with either of them because he wasn't going to be polite. Wasn't capable of it.

"Garden looks good," Rory said, sipping her coffee.

He dragged his thoughts back from revenge against the people who'd done her wrong. "Does."

The garden was in, thanks to his guys and Rory, Emma, Daphne, and Theo, too. They'd worked on it all day Sunday, and while the plants weren't as tall as they'd been before, and weren't yet producing vegetables, Theo would have fresh produce in a matter of weeks.

The farm had been quiet the last two nights. The only alerts he'd gotten had been for nocturnal animals who'd been big enough to trip the light sensors. He didn't kid himself the danger was over yet. Somebody had crept onto her property and cased the place Thursday night. Friday night, the garden destruction happened and sometime Saturday morning, somebody had drilled a hole into Theo's kitchen pipe. The two incidents might not be related, but sometimes when it walked like a duck and quacked like a duck, it was a duck.

Could literally be somebody targeting Theo specifically, but Chance didn't believe it. No matter that he'd told Rory not to jump the gun with assumptions, his gut told him it was about the land. He was gonna find Ronnie Davis and have a chat one of these days.

Chance started down the front steps, coffee in hand. "Gonna let the chickens out and collect eggs. I'll cook breakfast when I get back."

"I won't say no to that. But you don't have to. I can go to the coop after I finish this cup."

"Already got it. You relax."

Chance liked collecting the eggs. It was calming in a way he wouldn't have thought possible to find them in the hay, waiting for him. When he returned, he fixed eggs and toast and took it outside on a tray.

"Wow," she said. "Are you trying to butter me up for something?"

"Nope." He sat on the lawn chair he'd left open and took his plate, digging his fork into the eggs. "I just like it out here."

Her smile reached her eyes. "Me too. Thanks, Chance."

"You're welcome."

He could imagine filling the porch with more chairs, a couple of tables, and plants. It was already a perfect spot to greet the day and that would only make it better.

As soon as he had those thoughts, he wondered what the hell was wrong with him. Since when did he give two shits about decorating? Or plants? Not only that, but he needed to be careful before he built a future with Rory in his head. She wasn't glaring at him, but that was a far cry from actually wanting him around.

And though he was impatient as fuck for her to see what was staring her in the face, he wasn't gonna push. Pushing Rory was bad news because she dug in like a tick and didn't give up.

"Gotta head to the range, babe," he told her once they'd finished breakfast and he'd cleared up the dishes. "You gonna be okay?"

She turned those pretty hazel eyes on him. "I'm good, Chance. You don't have to hover."

"Not tryin' to. Just not sure how the pregnancy is affecting you."

"Right now, it's making me tired, but my glucose monitor says all is normal. My insulin pump is working as it should, and nothing feels weird. I promise you that if I feel weird, I'll take care of things first and foremost and then I'll call someone."

"Someone?" He wanted her to call him but he had to admit there could be times when he wasn't able to answer, which didn't make him the best choice. Didn't stop him from wanting to be first, though.

"Emma Grace is first because she's a doctor. Theo is second. You're third."

"And 911?"

Her eyes narrowed. "It's an option, but I'd have to be feeling pretty badly for that. Not everything that happens to me requires the ER."

He swallowed the fear and nodded. This was new for him, but he had to remember she was an expert at taking care of herself. "Of course not. Just asking. Call me if you want me to pick up anything for you. If those asshat developers return, definitely call me."

"I have Liza Jane. I don't need to call you."

"Please, Rory. Not because you can't take care of yourself, but because I want to see them, get a feel for what kind of men they are. And though I know this is gonna piss you off, they'll be more likely to think twice about harassing you if they know you've got a man like me around."

She arched an eyebrow. "My, my, aren't we suffering from a case of the big head this morning?"

"Just stating a fact, kitten. Those men will think nothing of doing shit like they did the other day, but if I'm here with you, different story. Because I'm big and I look mean when I need to. They won't fuck with you if I'm around."

"I'll keep it in mind, Conan."

"Call me, Ror. Promise."

She rolled her eyes. "Yes, Mr. Big Strong Manly Man, I will call you if Ronnie and RJ return. I will stall them for the twenty-plus minutes it'll take you to get here by offering sweet tea and batting my eyelashes. I'll offer to show them the property and then walk slowly until I hear you roaring up the drive in your macho wagon."

Chance shook his head and laughed. "Good enough. See you tonight."

She put her wrist to her forehead and tipped her head back. "Whatever shall I do without you, Sir Chancey Pants? My poor feeble lady brain just doesn't know how I'm going to endure the hours."

He wanted to kiss her. Just walk over, gather her in his arms, and bend her backwards until all she could do was cling to him. Then he'd kiss the hell out of her. He didn't though.

"Bye, kitten. Behave."

"Bye, Chancey Pants. Thanks for coffee and breakfast. And don't forget that cats have claws."

"I wouldn't dare."

He grabbed his range bag and headed for his truck. When he was backing up to turn around, he looked over at the porch where she stood with her arms wrapped around herself. He thought she might flip him off, because that was a Rory thing to do, but she lifted her fingers and waved. He waved back, his heart filling his chest with emotion. Then he put the truck in gear and headed down the driveway.

Chance

It was twenty minutes to the range, and he felt every mile he put between him and the woman he loved.

Chapter Twenty-One

Daphne was already at the front desk when Chance walked in. "Morning," she said with a smile. "Coffee's made and I'm telling everyone to gather in Alex's office."

"Morning, Daphne. Thanks."

"You're welcome."

"Hey, is that your car outside?"

Daphne rolled her eyes. "No. Kane's still looking. Warren loaned me his other car for the time being, so at least I don't have to beg for rides. But I don't want to take advantage of his kindness, so if Kane doesn't find anything this week, I'm doing it myself."

"Good plan."

"I know," she said with a grin, standing up to go get something from the printer. Her red hair was in a sleek ponytail today and she wore a white button down and jeans with high heels that clicked as she walked. She'd really blossomed since the night Blaze, Kane, and Seth found her squatting in one of the unfinished apartments in the Sutton building.

She'd been scared and quiet then, but she had confidence these days. She ran the One Shot Tactical schedule with efficiency and she didn't ask questions about things outside her scope of duties.

She knew they had a secure meeting room, because their security consulting business had taken off and they needed a place to discuss proprietary information, but what happened inside that room, she didn't know. And she didn't ask. She was truly the perfect assistant.

Chance stopped and grabbed coffee before finding his way to Ghost's office. Everyone but Blaze was already there. Easy to do when the rest of them lived on the premises.

"Morning, sunshine," Kane said. "Plants still in the ground?"

Chance leaned against a cabinet and crossed his legs. "Yep. No incursions, no suspicious activity. Nothing but a couple of raccoons, some deer, and a possum last night. None of them got close to the garden. The motion lights startled them for now. Well, all but the raccoons. Those little shits don't care. They were foraging through the garden waste pile and taking whatever they could find there."

Ethan snorted. "Isn't it funny to think just a few months ago we were gearing up, hopping onto a military transport, and disappearing for weeks at a time into foreign countries? Now we're talking gardens and farming."

"Not to mention actual gardening," Ghost said. "That shit's hard on the back no matter how good a shape you're in."

"Yeah, got a kink right between my shoulders," Kane said. "Who knew it'd be that bad?"

"Farmers," Seth deadpanned.

"Yeah, but they've got modern equipment. It's that small garden shit that'll kill you," Kane grumbled.

"So just get one of your ladies to do some hardcore massaging of your back before she massages your dick," Ethan said. "Problem solved."

"Excuse me," Daphne said from the door.

Kane's face rolled through a range of emotions before he got control of himself and glared at Ethan.

"What's up, Daphne?" Ghost asked.

"Sorry, I didn't mean to interrupt the man talk." Her voice dripped honey, which Chance found amusing. Kane, however, looked annoyed. "But Special Agent Diana Corbin is out front. She's asking for you, Alex."

"Jesus H. Christ on a cracker," Ghost said, rubbing a hand down his face. "Okay. Be right there."

Chance exchanged lifted eyebrows with the guys as Ghost strode out the door. "Wonder what she wants this time."

"Haven't seen much of her since she took over the Kyle Hollis case," Seth mused.

"Yeah, but don't think she hasn't been a thorn in the boss's side," Ethan said. "She's been at the Dawg sometimes."

"Hey, all I know is she hasn't bothered us anymore, and that's a good thing," Kane added. "Besides, it's a free country. She can go to the Dawg if she wants."

Blaze rolled in a few minutes later. He apologized for being late as he dropped his range bag and took a swig of coffee. "Emma couldn't find Sassy anywhere. Then she started to panic, thinking maybe she'd accidentally let Sassy out of the apartment when she'd gone down to grab something from the office earlier. I couldn't leave her that way. Went out into the hall and started to look, went upstairs, downstairs. No cat. Then I heard Emma calling me. She found Sassy asleep in a box in the pantry." He shoved a hand through his hair and shook his head. "Took a year off my life looking for that animal and praying she hadn't gotten out. Emma would be a wreck if something happened to her. So what's up with Diana Corbin? Kinda shocked to see her when I came in."

"Don't know," Chance said. "She asked to see Ghost, he left. Guess we'll find out soon enough."

When Ghost returned, he didn't keep them in suspense. "She's being reassigned to a field office in Kentucky. Not much else to say, but at least she won't be breathing down our necks anymore."

"So why'd she come tell you about it?"

His hands were in his pockets and his eyes gleamed. "Because she's angry and she thinks I had something to do with it."

"Did you?"

Ghost shrugged. "Probably. Not my problem though. She's leaving and I can't be upset about it. We ready to head into the SCIF? Got some things to discuss."

They went through the security checks to enter the secure room, closed it up behind them, and took their seats at the conference table. There was video feed from the range entry and store as well as from inside the range itself. There was also video from the exterior —parking lot, storage units, sides and rear of the building.

The cameras they'd used were high grade, not the typical home security cameras that were great for that kind of use but didn't have the sharpness or range the commercial ones did. The new system he'd ordered for Rory wasn't cheap, but there was no price he wouldn't pay to keep her and his kid safe.

"This week we start evaluating the security protocol and procedures at Griffin Research Labs," Ghost said. "The objective is to get inside the secure lab and monitor what's going on in there. Obviously, we want a full list of who has access to the building, procedures for admitting guests, and we want a look at the logs. I don't expect them to give us access to everything, but we're gonna need to get it anyway. You prepared for that, Phantom?"

"Yes, sir," Seth said. "I've got tools to gain access to their internal network. Not a problem."

"Need Wraith and Demon on the inside as well. You two fuckers are the most charming we've got, so I need you there keeping people happy and unaware of what's going on beneath their noses."

"Copy," Kane said.

Chance echoed him, his belly tightening. Being on the inside at Griffin Research Labs meant he'd have to spend long hours away from Sutton's Creek during the day while they dug into the company's records. If Rory needed him, he wouldn't be there for her.

But he'd said he could still do the job he'd been sent here to do, and he damned well could.

Ghost Ops might feel routine these days, though it was anything but. They hadn't had the excitement of any further incursions into warehouses in the middle of the night, and they hadn't been tasked with blowing anything up. But that didn't mean they were clear of those activities or that the mission was coasting. If anything, it was growing more dangerous as Athena's launch date approached.

Ghost flipped open his computer and the overhead screens powered up. Two men were pictured.

"The FBI picked these guys up last night. They were working at a restaurant in Huntsville, and both had falsified passports. Wilhelm Olkowicz and Cyril Dyka, which aren't their real names. They arrived from Poland via Frankfurt eight months ago to attend classes at the University of Alabama, Huntsville. Both are taking engineering classes—and both went to work at Rocket City Pasta & Pizza in the Redstone Gateway shopping center two weeks after arrival."

"Griffin Research Labs is in the Redstone Gateway complex," Seth said.

"Bingo," Ghost replied. "The restaurant is a regular stop for many of the people who work at the companies located in the Gateway. Doesn't mean these guys know about Athena, but they're most certainly observing, listening, and reporting what they hear back to someone."

They all knew that even the most innocuous information, when carefully pieced together from plentiful sources, could yield dividends. Servers were invisible when they wanted to be, especially when alcohol was involved. People talked even when they shouldn't.

"Or they could be well aware of Athena and meeting someone who passes them information," Chance added, studying the sallow complexions and angry expressions of the two men.

"That too," Ghost replied. "Somebody *inside* Griffin is either talking too much, or they're actively working against the objective.

There's also the fact that someone was planning to exchange the legit shipment of processors with the bogus shipment. The supervisor who was paid to do the deed at Royal Shipping claims he never met the person behind the instructions. He got phone calls and money, and once he was in, threats were made against his wife and children if he didn't go through with the exchange."

"They'd have killed him once it was done," Ethan said. "That's the only way to keep the plan secret."

"He probably realized that once it was too late," Ghost said. "And now he and his family are in protective custody."

"Crime doesn't always pay," Blaze drawled. "Better to be on the right side of things from the beginning."

"Amen, brother," Kane said.

"We need to get inside Griffin Labs and go over that fucker with a fine-toothed comb. I want to see inside everything they've got. I want to know who's coding that command and control system and what the safeguards are. How many people are working on it? What are their qualifications? Who are they and who do they owe money to? Who do the people they love owe money to? This is good old-fashioned espionage, boys," Ghost said. "I don't care what rules you break to get that information because the enemy will do the same if given the opportunity. For all we know, they already have it. But we aren't going to let them use it. We're going to protect this system and get it over the finish line. After that, it's up to the Missile Defense Agency and the FBI to keep it safe."

"Since the government already knows who's working the project, who's doing the coding, etcetera, it'd be nice if they'd just share the files with us," Seth grumbled. "The scientists and engineers had to get clearances. There were background investigations, paperwork. Why make us go through all this back door bullshit to get the information when it's already there?"

Seth only said what the rest of them were thinking.

"I asked," Ghost said. "Straight up asked POTUS's chief of staff. He shot me down."

Ronnie Auerbach was a tight ass son of a bitch. He disapproved of Ghost Ops on some level, but he also knew the president needed it. He was determined to keep Marla Willis smelling like a rose and that meant he could be difficult to work with.

Ghost sighed and spread his fingers on the desk. "The way I see it, there are two versions of what's going on inside the company. First is the official version. That's the one with the paperwork and the protocols. The unofficial version is what we're here to find out. That's where shit's vulnerable and people are potentially going rogue. It *is* possible to pass a government background check, be squeaky clean, have good intentions, and then take the bribe anyway. Happens all the time. If it didn't, what would the CIA do with their time? They're out there busily recruiting foreign agents, knowing people have a price at which they'll betray their government. That's as true here as it is anywhere. People can be bought if the price is right."

"Still be helpful if they'd let us know who they think can be bought," Seth said.

"I know, brother," Ghost replied. "But it's up to us. Now let's go find out what's going on over there before some asshole sells the information to a rogue state or programs a back door into the control system."

The shiver of dread that traveled down his spine was a new sensation for Chance. It wasn't for himself, or even for his friends. Hell, it wasn't even for the entire fucking country, though he knew it would be bad if somebody else got control of Athena. They could take over the system, redirect the shields to cover their own ass, and launch a nuclear strike at the US.

Obliterate the entire nation, or most of it anyway.

But none of that was what made his heart fill with dread. It was the idea that Rory and their child would die in an attack. That his kid would never take a first breath, and that Chance would never get to hold him or her. That they would just be gone. All of them.

He'd never thought much about dying, even when he was actively engaged in battles that could have ended him. But now?

Now he wanted to live. For Rory. For their kid. For the life they could have together if she'd let it happen.

But first he had to get over to Griffin Research Labs and find out who the motherfucker was that was willing to sell out their country and kill everyone in it. Then he'd make sure they were locked away so deep in a government prison they never saw the light of day again.

Chapter Twenty-Two

"How's it looking?"

Rory stood inside the kitchen of the Dawg with Theo and George, Diego's friend who was in the water restoration business. George had his right elbow propped in his left hand, gripping his chin with two fingers as he frowned and walked around the room.

"Down here is fine. It's the ceiling above our heads, specifically the wood. It's drying out. Not as quickly as I'd hoped, but we'll bring in more fans. Should be dry in a day or two. You will have to call a mold remediation specialist, though."

Rory's belly sunk. The building was old, and it always had a whiff of mustiness in lesser used spaces. But this smell was stronger. It was probably just the age, and the fact the wood had gotten wet, but even the word mold had her seeing dollar signs.

"Will we need to replace the wood floors upstairs?" Theo asked. He looked worried. Not that they wouldn't do what they had to do, but the building was historic and finding the same kind of hand-scraped hardwoods would either be impossible or crazy expensive.

"I didn't see any warping. The dehumidifiers are helping and the wood is resilient. I'm worried your problem is between the floor upstairs and the tin on the ceiling down here. Might need to pull some panels down and have a look."

"So we can't open tomorrow like we thought," Theo said, frowning at her.

"Maybe we can," she replied. "Need to call the mold person and get it looked at ASAP. It might be nothing other than the age of the building."

While Theo and George talked, Rory went up to her office to reconcile invoices and make sure there were no outstanding bills that needed paying immediately. The papers blurred as she stared at them and she grabbed a tissue to swipe away the tears. What the hell was wrong with her? Why did she start to tear up at the drop of a hat these days?

Was this what being pregnant was going to do to her? Make her weepy and queasy and sentimental and so many other things she couldn't quite keep track of them all?

Because it was *exhausting*. How did women do it? How did Tammy pop out two kids, get pregnant a third time, and keep on doing her Junior League and fancy picnic shit?

Rory clamped down on that thought. She did *not* want to think of Tammy as her example of a pregnant woman because that was just going to make her feel even more inadequate.

Theo came upstairs and trudged into her office. He looked morose. "Mold specialist will be here later this afternoon."

"Nothing from the police yet?"

"Nothing but a call to say they had nothing. No witnesses who saw anything out of the ordinary."

Rory leaned back in her chair. "Of all the days for Colleen *not* to be nosy."

"She was probably sleeping off a seance. Or an evening trying to contact the aliens." He nodded at her desk. "We okay?"

"For now. We've got cash in reserve and we can probably handle a month of expenses without income, but we sure couldn't face any other disasters or we'd have to get another loan to pay our suppliers. We'd be fresh out of cash at that point."

Theo looked tired. "Then we need to pray there's no mold and we can open again soon. I'm sorry, Rory. This isn't what you need right now."

"That's life. Disasters happen. They'll happen whether I'm pregnant or not."

"I know, but I don't have to like it. You do so much to keep this place running while I get caught up in what kind of food I can serve. I feel guilty sometimes."

"Seriously? It's the food that keeps them coming back. I think it's fantastic you experiment and make things people want more of. If all we did was get frozen premade shit from the grocery service and drop it into a deep fryer, we'd be no different than the other bars that are indistinguishable from each other. Why drive all the way to Sutton's Creek when you can just drop into your local bar and get wings and fries and jalapeño poppers there?"

Theo smiled at her and she smiled back. "Thanks, Ror. Now enough about this shit. How are you feeling? I worry about you even though you told me not to."

She snorted. "I knew you wouldn't stop worrying. I just don't want to constantly *hear* it. I feel great, mostly. More tired than usual, but Emma Grace says that's normal. The nausea is mostly under control with meds. My glucose dips and soars a bit unpredictably, but I'm keeping a very close eye on it. Chance fixes breakfast and bugs me about my numbers, so you can be pleased someone is acting like a mother hen in your place."

"I like him, Ror. I mean I'm pissed he knocked you up, but I like him."

Rory bristled. "Seriously, Theo? It takes two and this isn't 1950."

"I know." He frowned. "But I'm your big brother and I sometimes feel like I do a shit job of taking care of you. Meanwhile you make sure this place is going great so I can do what I love. When do you get to do what you love?"

She blinked. "I *am* doing what I love. Being an entrepreneur, running a business, living at the farm and waking up every day in the house we grew up in. I love all of it." She put a hand over her abdomen. "And now I'm gonna be a mom, and I honestly thought my chance was gone. I'm gonna raise this kid to love the Harper Farm and the Dawg as much as I do."

"Chance says he's gonna be there for you and the kid. Do you believe him?"

Her stomach tightened a fraction. "I believe he means it right now. But after this kid is born and he realizes what a commitment it is for the long haul? Not so sure he'll stick around."

Theo shook his head. "I understand why you feel that way. I know you're protecting yourself."

"I have no choice, Theo. If I let him in and he abandons us like Mark did when he ran off with Tammy, it'll be more than just my heart that's broken."

"I know, honey. But don't you think if everybody felt that way, nobody'd ever choose to be a family? Families are messy and emotional, and they don't always work out, but that doesn't mean you shouldn't try."

Rory's heart was ice. "I love you, Theo, but you need to hush up. You're no better than I am. We both lost our parents, and you've let that color your whole life as much as I have. More. At least I almost got married. You've never had a relationship last long enough for an engagement. So maybe take a hard look at your own house of cards before criticizing mine, okay?"

He blew out a breath. "Okay, Pixie. I won't say it again. But I love you and I want you to be happy."

"No fair calling me Gramps and Granny's nickname for me," she said, her throat tight. "And I want you to be happy, too. Now before we start sobbing or something, I'm going over to Kiss My Grits and getting a latte. You want anything?"

"I can get it. You stay here," Theo said, standing.

"Thanks but I'm going. I want to walk over there, get some air.

It's a pretty day out. You know we're gonna have stifling heat soon as Memorial Day hits so I want to enjoy it now before my clothes stick to me and I'm cussing because Clyde's AC is on the fritz again."

"You really gotta get something besides Clyde if you're going to put your child in it. That thing is a tank, but it doesn't have ABS or airbags."

"You sound like Chance," she said as they walked down the hall together.

"Good. He's a sensible man then."

"Last chance, Theo. You want a coffee or not before I walk out this door?"

"Yeah, bring me an Americano. Large."

"Banana bread?"

He put a hand over his belly. "I shouldn't. But I will."

Rory was still laughing as she went out the front door of the Dawg and walked down the block. The trees had all leafed out, and hanging baskets planted with petunias and geraniums hung from poles stationed along the sidewalk. In the center of the town square, Jacob Sutton's statue stood sentinel over the town. Two little girls with blond pig tails screamed and chased each other while their mom sat on a bench and watched, rocking a baby in a carrier as she did so.

Rory observed the little family as she walked. She'd made peace with the fact she probably wasn't going to get married or have kids after Mark, but now she was pregnant. She pictured herself with a toddler, enjoying the park. And though she didn't want to, she pictured Chance there with her, laughing as their child did something utterly cute and adorable.

There were other people in the park, sitting on benches, taking pictures. One couple was having a picnic lunch beneath a shade tree. Would Chance want to picnic with her and their child? Rory imagined them there, her big strong man holding a little baby while Rory dished out chicken salad onto plates.

Not her man. Chance. Chance Hughes, annoyingly handsome Ole Miss fan who'd gotten her pregnant after two weeks of hot, dirty, creative sex. The baby daddy.

Yes, that's how she would think of him. The Baby Daddy.

Rory slowed as she walked past Little Blooms, a store with baby clothes and accessories. There was a white crib in the window decked out with a blue blanket and a pillow with little sailboats embroidered on them.

She wanted to go in, but she wasn't comfortable doing it yet.

Rory rolled her eyes. Like anybody would see Aurora Harper going into Little Blooms and assume she was pregnant. No, they'd assume she was shopping for a gift or stopping to chat with Miriam McClinton, the proprietor. Miriam was a few years younger than she was, but Miriam had grown up in Sutton's Creek and her brother was a grade behind Rory and Emma Grace. No reason why Rory wouldn't stop for a chat.

But she didn't. She kept on walking until she reached Kiss My Grits. She was just about to put her hand on the door when it flew open. She was so startled she jumped back a step.

A man looked at her in annoyance, then sneered when recognition dawned. "Hello, Rory. Get your driveway sorted?"

Rory's heart knocked her ribcage. "Sure did. How about you? Figure out how to drive yet, RJ?"

The man was tall and muscled in a way that said he worked out regularly. If he wasn't an asshole, he'd fit right in with the One Shot Tactical men. Maybe.

"Nothing wrong with my driving, little girl."

Rory clenched a fist at her side. Nothing in this world pissed her off so much as men patronizing her. Dismissing her for her gender, her size, her love of simplicity rather than the latest fashions and society. She wanted to haul off and punch him, and probably would have if not for the voice ringing alarm bells in her head. She was *pregnant*. She couldn't go getting into brawls with meathead enforcers for the property development company.

"Oh, well, if you say so," she said, seething inside even as she pasted on a smile. "I'll be sending a bill to D&B Properties for the landscaper I had to hire to clean everything up and fix the driveway."

"You do that, doll."

He brushed past her and she had to step aside at the last minute so he didn't plow her down. "Have a nice day, asshole," she called out as he walked away.

His only answer was a middle finger held over his head. Rory growled as she turned and stomped into the café. There was a line so she got in it and glared at the cases with the muffins, breads, scones, and cakes. She was so busy staring at the display and calming herself down that she didn't notice the man who stopped beside her until he spoke.

"How you doin', Ms Harper?"

Rory's gaze snapped to Ronnie Davis's face. He wasn't wearing a cowboy hat today. Instead, he had on a Houston Texans ball cap. His bushy mustache still pissed her off, and the look in his eyes didn't help. Oh, he looked at her politely, even tipped his cap when her gaze met his, but that wasn't what his eyes said. They said she was a bug needing squashed.

"I'm just dandy, Mr. Davis. How about you? Enjoying Wendy's baked goods and coffee?"

"Yes, ma'am. She makes a mighty fine blueberry muffin. Coffee's good too."

On that they agreed. "Sure is. Well, you have a nice day now, you hear?"

Dear God, was she a caricature of a Southern woman or what? If only she had some pearls to press her hand against while batting her eyelashes.

"Planning on it, Miss Harper. You think anymore about my offer?"

"No, sir. Not even a bit."

She smiled big. His eyes narrowed.

"I'm disappointed to hear it, young lady. It's a fair offer. Your neighbors seem mighty interested, I have to say."

"Do they? Well, shucks, I guess I'll just have to be bordered on two sides by subdivisions, won't I?"

"Guess so. Unless you see reason and accept my offer. I'm prepared to increase it if that helps."

Her heart thumped. She thought of the Dawg and the potential mold issue, how long they could be shut down without cash coming in. She thought of her baby and the long future that stretched ahead. There would be expenses, and there would be college. A car. Clothes and cell phones and all the other things a kid needed to keep up with their peers.

And then there was the thought she didn't often let creep into her brain, but which made her tremble when she did. If something happened to her—her disease, an accident, whatever—how would she provide for her child's future?

She could sell everything but a couple of acres, keep her house and the barns. Theo could have his garden and the chickens would still be there. And why not? She wasn't planning to start farming. She wasn't planting crops, or raising cattle, or anything else that would take her away from the Dawg.

But as soon as the thought started to take root, she cut it out of her head. She didn't need to farm. She didn't need to do anything except let Carl Hoffman, or some other farmer, harvest the hay. She just needed to enjoy the beauty of her land and pass it on to the next generation for whatever they decided to do with it.

"Not interested, Mr. Davis. But thank you anyway."

"Okay. If that's what you want."

"It is."

He took a sip of his coffee. "Ahh, so good. Nice talking to you, Ms Harper."

"You too." She definitely didn't mean it.

He took a step, then turned back to her. "Just one last thing, Ms

Harper. I'm prepared to offer more right now, but I won't be so generous if you find that you have to sell."

Her stomach bottomed out. "And why would I *have* to?"

He shrugged. "Things happen. Circumstances change. Financial obligations erode equity and create opportunity for those who have money. If you decided to sell because you need the capital to sink into your bar, for example, then I might see that as an opportunity to offer you less money because you need it rather than want it."

"I'll keep that in mind," she grated. "And Mr. Davis?"

"Yes?"

"You tell that asshole driver of yours that he's a rude piece of shit."

Davis laughed. "You mean Ronnie Junior? He gets that from his mama's side of the family, I'm afraid. But I'll pass the message. Think about what I said, Ms Harper. The clock is ticking and the price can go down just as easily as up."

Chapter Twenty-Three

"Feels weird not to be heading to the Salty Dawg," Seth said. "I could use a beer and a burger. Or doesn't Theo make that shrimp thing on Mondays? I could really tear into that."

"Yep, Monday is the Cajun shrimp pasta," Chance said. They were in Kane's Yukon, riding back from Research Park and the Redstone Gateway. It'd been a long day of boring paperwork for the most part. Before they got to the exciting stuff, they had to make a show of going over the company's security procedures and manuals. For special operators used to the excitement of combat, it was boring as fuck.

Chance reminded himself it was still combat, though. Just a different kind. Find the traitor, stop Armageddon. If that wasn't battle, then he didn't know what was.

"Does feel weird," Kane replied. "I was looking forward to a burger and some of those rosemary fries."

"Hopefully they'll be open again tomorrow," Chance said. He hadn't heard anything from Rory, but that was no surprise. Woman made a big deal out of not needing anyone. Last thing she'd do was text him to tell him anything about the Dawg or how things were going.

"Wonder if Clarence still has barbecue?" Seth mused. "Gotta pass the Gas-n-Go heading toward the range."

"We can stop," Kane said.

Chance didn't want to stop because he wanted to get home to Rory. But he couldn't say no. Maybe he'd take some barbecue home with him. If Rory hadn't eaten, she might like it. If she had, then he'd put it in the fridge and she could have some tomorrow.

It took another half hour to stop at the Gas-n-Go, pick out their food, and get back to the range. It was after six when they arrived so the range was closed. Tomorrow they'd brief the team on what they'd done so far.

"See y'all in the morning," Chance said, boots crunching across the pavement as he headed for his truck, tossed in the food, and started it up.

Twenty minutes later, he was turning into the driveway. Clyde was parked in his usual spot, but his hood was up and Rory was bent over the engine bay, tinkering with something. Chance's belly tightened. He didn't like her working on the truck alone. Didn't like that heavy old hood propped up with a thin metal rod and Rory bent over the frame.

He parked carefully so as not to startle her, in case she had headphones in, and grabbed the bag of food before walking over to Clyde. Rory's perfect ass was in the air as she stood on the bumper and leaned into the engine bay.

He took a moment to admire the roundness of her ass in overalls. Then he took a moment to remember gazing down at it while he gripped her hips and fucked her from behind. Rory didn't like straight missionary because her insulin pump and glucose monitor were usually on her abdomen and it was uncomfortable. He could get on his knees between her legs, or hold himself up on his forearms, but there was no skin to skin from shoulder to hip happening.

Didn't bother him. Just being inside her and feeling how

fantastic it was to be there was enough for him. That and her perfectly porny moans, not to mention the dirty words of encouragement.

"*Fuck me, Chance. Harder. Right there. Oh yes, mama likes it just like that…*"

Jesus. He reached down to adjust his swelling dick, getting it done just before she straightened. She turned to watch him approach, and his heart kicked his ribcage at the sight of her beautiful face. He wanted her, but more than that, he wanted her happy. *He* wanted to make her happy.

"Is that food?"

"Yup. Pulled pork, some ribs, collards, beans, and buns."

"Oh yum. Is there enough for me?"

"Of course there's enough for you. What kind of guy do you think I am?"

She grinned. There was a grease spot on her cheek and her blond hair was about to tumble out of its knot. "The kind who'd bring a woman dinner."

"Is that all?"

"What more do you want, Chancey Pants? An essay about your fabulosity?"

"If you've got one in you, sure."

She stepped off the bumper and dropped to the ground. "Not especially. But I am happy you brought dinner. I'll pay you."

"You fucking won't," he growled.

She picked up a rag and wiped her hands. "Suit yourself. I'm just about done here."

"What are you doing?"

"Checking the belts and fluids. Thought I heard a whine coming home. Wanted to make sure things were good."

"Are they?"

"Little bit of an oil leak. But Clyde's got plenty of life left in him."

"You think about getting another vehicle once the baby comes?"

He really meant *have you thought about getting one ASAP* because he didn't want her climbing in and out of Clyde when she swelled with his child. He knew better than to say it, though. Slow and steady, slow and steady.

"I've thought about it."

"You think anymore about tomorrow?"

"I have, and I'll borrow your truck if the offer is still good."

"It is. I'm also happy to drive you there." He'd have to take a couple of hours off but Seth and Kane could handle it.

"I want to go alone. But thanks."

His gut churned. "You ever plan to let me go with you?"

Her eyes glittered with a flash of temper. "Yes, I do. I just want to go alone the first time, okay? I want to process what the doctor tells me, what the risks are, on my own. I don't want to have to worry about your reactions too."

"It's your body, Rory, and I get that. You're the one who has to go through this, but I want to be involved, and I want to help in any way I can."

She dropped her rag and came over to pat him on the arm. "I know. I'm trying, okay? I'm not used to having anyone around. I've got my brother trained to do his hovering at a distance, mostly. I need to process things on my own. It's how I'm wired."

He swallowed hard. It wasn't what he wanted, but he appreciated that she was being honest. It was more than he'd expected from her at this stage.

"All right. But will you tell me what she says? Everything she says?"

A look of confusion passed over her face for a moment. "I'll tell you everything I can. Some things might be private."

"Rory. I care about what happens to you."

"I—I'll do my best, Chance. I promise."

It was the most he was going to get out of her. "All right, kitten. I appreciate it."

"Are you really going to keep calling me kitten?"

He grinned. "Think I am."

She heaved a dramatic sigh. "Fine. But I'm going to keep calling you Chancey Pants, just so you know."

"Wouldn't want it any other way."

"I gotta close up Clyde and then I'll meet you inside."

His heart squeezed. "Here. You take the food in and I'll close him up."

She frowned. "Is this because I'm a small, helpless female who needs your help?"

"Honestly?" She nodded. "No, it's because I'm a protective alpha male who needs to do things for my woman."

"*Your* woman? What are we, cave people?"

He took a step into her space. She didn't back away. Heat flashed between them, sizzling like lightning. "No, but you're still mine. Mine because I choose you. I'll be yours if you choose me. That's all you gotta do, kitten. Choose me."

Her breath hitched in. He could see the pulse in her throat, fluttering like a butterfly. "I can't."

He skimmed a finger along her jaw. She shuddered beneath his touch. "Why not?"

"You know why. I won't go through it again. I can't."

Chance caressed her cheek, tucked a stray lock of hair behind her ear. Then he dropped his hand. It was the hardest thing he'd ever done. "Okay, honey. I understand. Go inside. I'll be right behind you."

She stared at him. "That's it? You'll just accept what I said about not going through it again without argument?"

"Do you want me to argue?"

Her eyes clouded a moment. "Of course not. I'm just amazed that you aren't. We've argued since I've known you. This is a new side to you."

"It's not a new side. We argued because you took one look at me and decided you didn't like me."

She scoffed. "Did not."

"Did too. First time I walked in the Dawg. I went to the bar to order drinks, complimented you, and you let me have it."

Her face reddened. "To be fair, lots of men compliment me at the bar and I shoot most of them down. It's like I have a sign on me that says since I'm working in a bar, I'm fair game. I've learned to be defensive and shut that shit down quick."

"Okay, but you kept shutting me down every time you saw me."

"And you kept poking at me whenever you saw me."

He couldn't deny it. "Guess we got off on the wrong foot and stayed there. And you're right, working in a bar doesn't make you fair game. I'm sorry I made you feel that way. I really wanted to know you, Rory, and I fucked it up by rushing it and falling back on the usual pickup lines. Shoulda took my time and got to know you before I expressed any interest."

"Wow. And here I thought I was the only one affected by pregnancy hormones. Look at you getting all insightful and sensitive."

She cracked him up. Rory was one of a kind. Maybe he'd fucked it up in the beginning, but he couldn't regret where they were now. He'd do anything for this woman. She wasn't aware of it yet, but she would be.

"Guess I'm evolving."

"Maybe not completely." She held her hand out for the food. "I'll go set the table like a good little woman while you shut the big bad hood of my truck so I don't have to strain myself."

She flashed him a grin then and he handed over the bag. "You're fun, kitten. And while I love that we're not at each other's throats all the time, I gotta say I enjoy your smart mouth a helluva lot."

Her grin turned into a smile but she didn't move.

"What?" he asked.

"I was waiting for the punchline."

"What punchline?"

"The part where you say you enjoy my smart mouth even more when it's on your body."

"Oh, I definitely do. But I'm being sensitive here. Don't ruin it."

She turned and headed for the house, laughing. "Hurry up, Mr. Sensitive. I'm starved."

So was he. But not for dinner.

Chapter Twenty-Four

Rory got plates, napkins, forks, and knives, and set them on the kitchen table. The food smelled delicious and her belly growled. Since Emma Grace had given her the anti-nausea meds, she wasn't having too terrible of a time with food. Chance came inside and went over to the sink to wash his hands. She eyed him as she got glasses from the cabinet and set them on the table along with the pitcher of tea, her heart beating just a little bit harder at the sight of him standing at her kitchen sink like he belonged there.

He dried his hands and came over to join her. She dished out her food and handed him the containers so he could do the same.

"Any news about the Dawg?" he asked when she took a bite of her pork sandwich. She bugged her eyes at him and he laughed. "Sorry, didn't meant to ask when your mouth was full."

"We had to call a mold remediation specialist," she said after she'd swallowed her food. "There isn't any mold yet, but we'll have to be really careful because we're in the danger zone when it can start growing. George has added a couple extra fans and another dehumidifier."

"And if it does grow?"

"If it does, we're looking at a lot of money to fix it. We're also looking at having to shut down while it's done. Could take a few days. Maybe even a week."

"Assuming everything dries out without mold becoming a problem, when can you open?"

"I hope Wednesday. We have to have a health inspector out to make sure everything is good." She wasn't happy about that, but there was nothing she could do. She just had to hope everything worked out so they could open and get back to serving customers and earning an income. "The police questioned people in the vicinity, but nobody saw anything suspicious."

"Not even Colleen?"

"Nope, she didn't see anything either. Theo said she must have been sleeping off a seance or a night with the aliens."

"The one fucking time you want her to be nosy," Chance grumbled as he picked up a rib and tore a chunk off with perfect white teeth. "Damn these ribs are good."

Rory peeled off a strip and popped it in her mouth. "Oh yeah, Clarence knows his way around a pig. Speaking of pigs," she said, and then told him about running into Ronnie Davis and Ronnie-fucking-Junior.

Chance had gone still, his eyes glowing like hot coals. "He said that to you?"

"Which part, Chancey Pants? Ronnie telling me the offer could go down if I have to sell the farm to save the Dawg or RJ calling me a little girl and flipping me off?"

"All of it," he growled.

"Yes, that's pretty much word for word. They're rude assholes, both of them."

It felt kind of nice to have a man other than her brother angry on her behalf. Especially a man like Chance. Big, strong, and trained to defend.

He'd said all she had to do was choose him and he'd be hers. Longing rocked her body. She was tired of being alone, tired of fighting to keep things going by herself. Not that Theo wasn't there for her, but it wasn't the same thing. She wanted what Emma Grace had.

She wanted a man who adored her, who looked at her like she was the center of the universe, and who'd take care of her when she needed it same as she'd take care of him. Her throat grew tight. It wasn't the same for her as for other people. She potentially could need a *lot* of care at some point. She might need a kidney transplant, or her vision might fail. Diabetes had a high cost sometimes. Whenever she'd tried to talk to Mark about the future, he'd told her she needed to be positive, not negative. That it was borrowing trouble to discuss it.

She should have realized he was avoiding the issue because he actually didn't want to deal with her being incapacitated in any way. Maybe that was why he'd started the affair with Tammy. Because the reality of Rory's health was too much for him and he didn't have the balls to tell her so.

"I'll put a stop to it. And if they approach you again, I'm gonna make them wish they hadn't."

His expression made her stomach clench, but in a good way. Good grief, what did it say about her that she actually got a little turned on by a man intimating he'd commit violence on her behalf?

"You don't have to do that." Because somebody had to be reasonable here. Much as she loved the idea of him kicking asses for her, it wouldn't be a good idea. Chief Vance was sure to disapprove. Then there was Chance's business with his friends. Couldn't have that suffer because he got into trouble for assaulting assholes who deserved it.

"I don't have to, but I will."

She reached out and put her hand on top of his. His eyes snapped to hers. Heat and need throbbed inside her bones, her blood. Was it the same for him? She pulled her hand away and smiled. "I don't want you getting into trouble for me, Chance. All they're doing is running their mouths. Now if they're the ones who tore up the garden and drilled the pipe, then I'd really love to see them nailed to the wall."

"Kitten, if I go after them, nobody's gonna know it was me. Promise you that."

A shiver dropped through her. "I will."

He gave her a look. "Nah, you only think you will. I was in the military. I know how to hide the bodies."

"Chance."

"I'm kidding, Rory. Mostly." He stabbed some greens with his fork. "Nobody threatens you and gets away with it. All I'm gonna do is make that known. They want to play after that, shit's on them because I'm not kidding around. I'll mop the fucking floor with them both."

She stared at him, her heart hammering in her chest. Her body was a mess of emotion, enhanced by hormones, and she didn't actually know what was going to happen next. So it really shouldn't have been a surprise when she started to cry.

Chance's face went pale. He dropped his fork and slid his chair to her side. "Babe," he said, tugging her close.

She turned her face into his shoulder and sniffled. "I'm sorry. I'm not upset. It's just these stupid damned hormones. *Everything* is emotional." She waved her hand at her plate. "The food makes me cry. I'm not at work tonight and I should be. I have to go to the doctor tomorrow, and I don't know what she's going to say."

Rory hitched in a breath and tried to stop the tears from flowing, but they dripped down her cheeks like she was the most helpless creature to ever draw breath. Really, she did *not* do this kind of thing. She bucked up and got on with it.

"Sorry," she sniffled. "Sorry."

Chance leaned back in his chair and dragged her across his lap, cradling her against his chest. She shouldn't have allowed it, but she was powerless to stop it. She didn't *want* to stop it. Being in his arms felt good, and though it was the surest way to the danger zone, she wanted the comfort more than she wanted to erect the walls around her heart at the moment.

"Don't apologize. You've been through a lot, and you've just had a life-changing event that scares you. I get it. Hell, I'm scared too. I don't know what kind of dad I'll be, if I even know how it's done."

She lifted her head to gaze at him. "I don't know, Chance, but if you can manage to comfort me when I burst into tears over pork, then I think you may have some kind of instincts in the right direction."

He brushed her hair from her face. The gesture was so tender, his expression so wistful, that she found herself wanting to kiss him and make it go away. Or maybe it was just herself she wanted to soothe. She didn't know, and that was yet another thing that worried her.

"I think it was a little more than pulled pork that did it." His voice was soft, gentle. Like she was one of the barn cats that she wanted to pet when she was little. Her mother had told her to speak softly and not make any sudden moves so they'd come to her.

It'd worked, but it took a lot of patience. Something she didn't always have.

That was Chance right now. Patient and kind.

"Maybe it wasn't just the pork." She sniffed. "Why did you say that? About being a dad?"

He sighed and closed his eyes for a second. The pain in them when he looked at her again made her heart pinch.

"I had a great dad until I was thirteen. He took me hunting, came to my games, wanted me to go to Ole Miss and play football like he did. But he and my mom…"

Rory ached for him. She didn't know what he was about to say, but she knew what it was like to lose a parent. She put her fingers on his cheek, turned his face so he was looking at her. She tried to tell him she understood, but the words didn't come.

He seemed to hear them anyway.

"My mom suffered from depression. She might have been schizophrenic, but I don't actually know. She thought my dad was having an affair. She took a pistol from his gun safe, and when he came home one night, she shot him."

Shock jolted through her. "Chance. My God. I'm so sorry."

He wrapped her hand in his, lifted it to his mouth and kissed the back of it. "I know you are. Thank you. She never uttered another word. They took her to jail, put her on trial, and locked her up. She died in a mental facility, of cancer, a few years later, having never spoken again. I went into foster care because there was no family to take me. Aged out of the system at eighteen and joined the military at twenty. The military saved me, or I would have been a punk. I was on the way there. Rebellious, angry, destructive. I hung out with the wrong crowd, did things that could have gotten me killed or jailed. So when I say I don't know how to be a great dad, I'm not lying." He blew out a breath. "Shit, didn't mean to make this about me. I just wanted you to know I understand your fear."

She couldn't help but give him a watery smile. "Chancey Pants, you're a good guy. You didn't make it about you. You distracted me and made me curious. Which I've been since you said you lost people violently when you were thirteen. I'm so, so sorry, honey. If I could change it for you, I would."

Her heart hurt for the boy he'd been. He'd had a home, parents, a dad who wanted him to go to Ole Miss, and then it'd all been taken away. He'd gone into foster care, gotten angry, and had a completely different life than he'd expected to have.

"Thanks, kitten."

He still looked troubled and she squeezed his hand, took a deep breath. "I'm scared. Not of being pregnant, though that too. But I'm scared of you. Because you say you want to be here to help me, to help with our kid, but do you really know what you'd be getting into? I don't mean the kid, because that's a lot of work for everybody. I mean *me*. I'm diabetic, Chance. It's incurable. I'll never get better. I can only manage what I've got, but there are things that could happen to me."

"I know that, Aurora. I did my research. You could need a transplant at some point. You might have vision issues. Neuropathy. Hearing impairment. There are a lot of potential things that *could* happen. Doesn't mean they will."

"Doesn't mean they won't."

He put a gentle finger over her mouth. "Shut it, babe. I know what could happen. You know, too. So if it happens, we deal with it."

Her body shook. He was like Mark, putting her off, not wanting to talk about it. She needed to get away from him, stop letting him get inside her heart and her head. The panic swelled, but she didn't move. Because another part of her brain, the logical part, told her to just fucking *listen* to what he was saying.

He didn't say to stop thinking about it or talking about it. He said they would deal with it *if* it happened.

"If I wanted to talk about a plan for *if* something happened to me, would you do that? Or would you tell me to stop being negative?"

He looked horrified. "Why the fuck would I think you were being negative? This is something you've lived with for years. I imagine you've thought of what could happen a lot."

Relief flooded her. "I have. I'm not inviting it or willing it into existence, but I feel like I need some kind of plan so the people I love aren't stuck either figuring it out or supporting me while I fall apart."

"Makes sense to me. Was it the ex who told you not to be negative?"

She nodded. "He never wanted to talk about it. Another red flag I missed. How can you contemplate a future with someone who might have serious medical issues down the road without ever discussing it?"

"Maybe he was scared. Not making an excuse for him, but some people can't handle thinking about things before they happen."

"Can you?

"My job in the military involved thinking of the absolute worst thing that could happen to me and my team and planning for it. So yes, I can."

She wanted to believe him. So much. "You can see why I don't take getting involved with someone lightly. There's too much at stake, and I don't want to go all in like I did before only to end up alone when I really need that person in my corner. I'd rather be alone now than end up devastated later."

"Babe, I say this with understanding for what you've been through, but you need to realize that's a bullshit excuse. You can't control the future. You can't control if something happens to you, and you damned sure can't control what happens to another person. Whether it's me or some other man, you don't know that we won't get hit by a bus or have a heart attack or get mauled by a bear. You don't fucking know, Rory. You can't know. The future is a gamble whether you build it with another person or go it alone."

Her eyes stung. Her heart hammered. Her body trembled. He was right. He was fucking right, and it scared her to pieces. She couldn't insulate herself from heartache by being alone. She was going to have a kid, and she didn't know that something wouldn't happen to that child either. You couldn't disaster proof your life by staying disconnected.

"I know," she whispered, her voice tight. "But that doesn't make it easy to trust someone. To trust you."

"I get that. But you gotta start somewhere. Start with believing me when I tell you I know what could happen with your diabetes. I'll discuss the plan with you as often as you want, and I'll be here for you and our kid. I'm not going anywhere, Rory. You can try your best to chase me away, but it's not happening."

He looked fierce, but she still doubted. It made no sense that he'd want to stick around. He was gorgeous and fit. He could have anyone he wanted. Sure, he was honorable and wanted to take care of his kid, but that didn't mean he had to *choose* her. He could choose anyone and still be a dad for their child.

"But why? Why would you want to stay? I'm a mess, Chance. I'm not easy to deal with, and it'll probably get worse when I have this baby. You can't really want *me*. And you don't have to. I won't keep you from seeing your child. Just be honest with me. Don't make promises you might regret later."

He gripped her chin in his fingers. Gently but firmly. His blue eyes speared into hers, and her heart skipped a beat.

"You really don't get it, do you? I *want* to be with you. You make me laugh and you frustrate the hell out of me. I'm in love with you, Aurora Harper. I know you don't feel the same way about me and that's okay. I'm gonna get you there, one way or the other. And I'm gonna be right here in your life, keeping you safe and making you as happy as I can. You aren't running me off because you can't. You understand me? You fucking can't."

Chapter Twenty-Five

He'd said too much. Chance knew it as soon as the words were out of his mouth, but dammit, he couldn't just sit there and let her tell him she wasn't worthy of devotion. He couldn't let her believe all the bullshit she'd told herself for so long was true. He had his own problems to deal with, his own guilt, but dammit, Rory was worthy of everything. He needed her to know it.

Her eyes widened as she stared back at him. Hope roared through him. But then she closed her eyes and shook her head and he knew he'd lost the battle.

"Don't say that. You don't have to say that."

"I know I don't have to," he growled.

Her eyes snapped open again and she cradled his face in both her hands. Her touch set off a chain reaction inside him. Need, want, desire. All those things and more.

"Chance. I know you think you mean it now. I appreciate it more than you know. But you can't love me. You barely know me. We had sex—great sex—and now we're gonna have a kid. But that's not love. Love takes time. It grows and builds, like a pearl inside an oyster shell. You're in shock over the pregnancy. And I get it because I am too. But please don't confuse the issue."

He gaped at her. "Seriously, you think I'm confused? You think I just put my heart on my sleeve because I'm suffering from shock?"

"It's understandable."

Good lord, he wanted to bend her over this table and kiss the daylights out of her. Then he wanted to take her to bed and worship her with his hands and mouth until she fucking knew he meant business. He wanted her to believe she was worthy of the deepest kind of love.

"Is that what happens in those novels you read? People get confused and don't know how they feel?"

Her cheeks turned pink. "That's different. It's fiction. Not real. Five men and one woman, remember? Not even close to realistic."

"Not sharing you with anyone, kitten. You said we were free to date other people, but I'm telling you right now that's not happening. I won't share you with another man, and I damn sure don't need another woman when I have you."

"You're crazy, Chance Hughes. Just crazy."

But her voice was little more than a whisper and her eyes were wide. Plus she was still on his lap. He took that as a positive sign.

"Maybe I am. But I'm also crazy about you. Are you seriously telling me you read books about love and don't believe in it?"

"I didn't say that. What I said was that it's fiction. Real life is messy, and I don't think people fall in love at first sight or anything like that. Takes time to build."

"You know what I think? I think it's like anything else. There's no single experience for everything. You don't fall in love one particular way and that's the only way it ever happens for everyone on this planet. It's different for all of us."

"Maybe so, but I still don't think you look at someone and boom, that's it."

"How was it with Mark then?"

He felt her stiffen slightly. "It wasn't love at first sight for either

Chance

of us. But he kept pursuing me, and I finally said yes to a date. It grew from there. We were together for two years before he decided Tammy was more suited to his lifestyle."

Chance tightened his arms around her for a second. "Already said so, but he's an idiot."

"I think you mean he's a douchebag."

"That, too."

"What about your unrequited love? Did that happen right away or did it take time?"

He'd nearly forgotten he'd told her that. "Took a little time. Not as much as you seem to think it does. I saw her standing behind the bar of the Dawg and wanted to know her, but she didn't like me. Then she liked me for about two weeks. Best two weeks of my life. But no, I didn't realize how I felt until I saw her walking toward me with a pan of mac and cheese and knew that she made me feel like I'd found home."

"Oh." She sounded surprised. "You meant me."

"Had no plans to tell you how I felt anytime soon, but then you wanted to know why I'd choose you of all people, and I had no choice. Need you to know how perfect you are. Anybody who couldn't appreciate you the way you deserve is a douchebag."

"Stop before you make me cry again." She swiped her eyes. "I could do without this hormonal crap, I gotta say."

He could hold her all night, but things needed doing. "Better finish your dinner, kitten. You dialed in those carbs and you don't want to be under."

Her smile trembled at the corners. "You really did research diabetes didn't you?"

"Yes, ma'am. I want to know everything about you. Diabetes is part of you, and it's not going away. Plan to know everything I can."

Her brows arrowed down. "I appreciate you wanting to know more, but please don't ever start thinking you know what's best for me. I won't be treated like I'm fragile by you or anyone. I've been navigating this reality for over twenty years now, and I know what I need to do."

"I hear you, honey. I'm not saying I won't ever do it, because I expect I will. Not worried you won't let me know, though. You're gonna chew my ass good if I do. It's not in you to be silent when you're pissed off."

"Nope. That is most definitely not me."

She got back into her chair and he slid his plate over rather than move away from her. She arched an eyebrow at him and he shrugged. "I like being close to you. No need to pretend I don't now that you know."

She picked up her sandwich but she didn't tell him to move. "I appreciate that you think you love me, Chancey Pants. I'm all kinds of awesome, after all. And you knocked me up, which makes you feel responsible toward me. But I don't believe you really love me. I think you believe it, though. But you'll come to your senses. I have no doubt."

"I was rather hoping you'd come to yours."

"And that right there is why we are not meant to be. Can't even agree on the basic stuff like I'm right and you're wrong."

He knew she was making a joke because she was uncomfortable, so he let it ride. But she was wrong. Dead wrong. And he was going to prove it to her.

Chapter Twenty-Six

CHANCE SLEPT BETTER THAT NIGHT THAN HE HAD IN A LONG TIME, even though it was on Rory's couch instead of by her side. When they'd gotten ready for bed, she'd hesitated in the cased entry to the living room. He'd thought she was going to ask him to sleep in the same bed with her. He'd understood it would be just sleep, and he'd still wanted it. Wanted to hold her against him while she slept and know she was safe.

But she hesitated too long, then said good night and left him alone on the couch. Despite that, he'd still fallen asleep soon after he'd heard her get into bed. When he woke, he went upstairs to shower, made coffee, and went outside on the front porch to watch the sun rise over the fog-laden hills and fields.

The Harper farm was beautiful, and he understood why Rory felt connected to it. Why she wanted to keep it.

Rory didn't wake before he had to leave, but he opened the bedroom door to check on her. She was sleeping, her chest rising and falling evenly. It killed him to leave her, but he had a job to do. He left her a note and his keys by the coffee pot where she could see them and headed out to start up Clyde.

The old truck rumbled along the roads pretty smoothly for as old as it was. Chance rolled the window down and put his elbow on the sill. He almost felt like he was in a country music video.

He drove through town on his way to the range. When he spotted the D&B Properties truck at Miss Mary's Diner, he whipped Clyde into a parking space and went inside. Ronnie Davis and Ronnie Junior were in a booth by the window, chowing down on what looked like a massive order of pancakes, eggs, and bacon. He knew it was them because he'd seen their faces on the security cameras at Rory's place. It'd taken everything he had not to find them before now.

He glanced around. Miss Mary's wasn't too busy yet, but there were a few people at the tables and counter, drinking coffee and eating breakfast.

Miss Mary was a large woman with a smile as welcoming as the world was big. "Dining in today, Chance?"

"No, ma'am. But I'll take one of those breakfast burritos to go, if you don't mind. Just gonna head over there and talk to my friends."

The Davises weren't his friends, but he didn't want to alarm Miss Mary. Still, she arched an eyebrow and he knew she wasn't fooled.

"No bloodshed in my restaurant, young man. I know those men have been going around to the farmers and making offers, and I heard all about what Rory said in Kiss My Grits yesterday. So if you think you're going to cause a scene, think again."

Chance held up both hands. "Ma'am, on my honor, I'm not. Just want to make it clear they need to be more respectful when speaking to my lady."

Miss Mary's eyebrows shot upward. "Your lady? Oh my."

Rory was going to kill him when the Sutton's Creek rumor mill got started, but fuck it, they'd all learn soon enough that she was pregnant and he was the father. If they thought he and Rory were a couple now, so what?

Chance

"Yes, ma'am. And that's why I can't let those men harass her. You can understand that, I hope."

"I do indeed." She pointed at him. "But like I said, no bloodshed. Say what you gotta say and leave those men to eat their breakfast, you hear me?"

"Yes, ma'am."

"One breakfast burrito coming up with sour cream and extra salsa, just the way you like it. You want a go cup of coffee?"

"Please."

Order made, Chance strolled over to where the Davis men sat in their booth, eating and talking about who they needed to visit that day. They both looked up as Chance loomed. He dragged a chair from a nearby table and plopped it down, straddling it with his arms folded across the back.

"Howdy, gentlemen."

Ronnie Davis was a florid man with a bushy mustache and gray hair. His son just looked mean. Junior was thin on top and clean shaven. He was also muscled in a way that said he worked out regular.

"Who are you?" Ronnie asked.

Chance pointed at the logo on his polo shirt. "Chance Hughes, One Shot Tactical. You might've seen the range and training facility outside of town. We offer twelve shooting bays, an outdoor range, and we provide personal security training as well as security evaluations and services."

"That's nice to know, son. We'll keep it in mind if we need some range time, but right now we're talking business."

"Oh, I know. But let me tell you a little about me. I was in the Army, did some time in special forces—that means I've seen combat. I've dropped behind enemy lines and survived to tell the tale. I've been shot, stabbed, and beaten. Even been a prisoner of war, though it was only for a week. Not as long as some of our military have endured, but not fun."

Ronnie Davis was looking irritated. Junior was interested but also wary as if he knew there was a punchline coming.

Ronnie was the one who spoke. "We thank you for your service. I'm sure we'll see you at the range soon. Helluva pitch you've got, but a bit long if I'm honest here."

Chance smiled, though it wasn't friendly. "I'm almost done. I've seen and done a lot of shit in the military. I'm just a civilian now, running a company with my Army buddies. But I still know how to do all those things, and even better, I can make you hurt in ways you haven't imagined without leaving a mark. So when I tell you that Aurora and Theo Harper are off limits, you need to realize that I'm not kidding around. You don't talk to Rory. You don't look at Rory. I catch either one of you harassing her ever again, I'm gonna show you some of those skills I mentioned."

Ronnie spluttered. "I don't think you know who you're talking to."

"I know enough. You're a rich man who thinks what you want takes priority over what people with less money and power than you want. I'm here to tell you it's not true. Something else you need to know about me—you ever harm Rory to get what you want, I don't care what happens to me. I will end you and smile during the trial when they ask me where the body is. We clear?"

Chance unfolded himself until he towered over the two men. Ronnie had the good sense to look frightened. Junior, however, looked like he wanted to tangle. But until Daddy let him off the leash, he wasn't going to do it. Chance knew that without a word being said.

"I'm reporting this conversation to the police," Ronnie told him. "See how it goes for you then."

Chance picked up a piece of bacon from the pile on the plate in the center of the table. "Be my guest. I won't deny it if they come calling. But you should know somebody destroyed a garden at the Harper farm and the water leak in the Salty Dawg was deliberate. The cops are still looking for suspects and I'm sure they'd love to have a chat with you after what you said to Rory yesterday about the price going down if she needs to sell the farm to save the tavern."

"You accusing me of something, Mr. Hughes?"

"Not at all. Just giving you an FYI." He ripped off a piece of bacon with his teeth. "Y'all have a blessed day, you hear?"

He half expected Junior to come after him, but there was no movement behind him as he strolled over to the counter. Miss Mary handed him his coffee and a plastic bag with his order, her smile almost gleeful. "I hope I don't ever get called to witness at a trial because you've committed violence against those men, because the good Lord won't let me lie to save you, but I also enjoyed that mightily. Darned Texans coming in here thinking they know what's best for this town and harassing folks to sell their land. It's not right."

"It's not," Chance agreed as he plunked cash on the counter. "Fine if people want to sell once an offer's made, but when they tell you no, you can either raise the offer to a price they agree on or you can accept it's not happening and move along. Just wanted to clarify that for them."

"I think you did. You staying with Rory out at the farm now?" she asked as she put the cash in the till.

Chance nearly choked on his coffee. Miss Mary shook her head like he was daft.

"I can see the road from here. Know which way you came from. Not to mention you're driving her grandpappy's old truck." She nodded toward the picture window where Clyde was clearly visible in the parking lot. "It's good Rory has someone staying with her. She can't be too careful with her diabetes. I know Theo has always worried about her out there alone."

And that was the point at which Chance needed to extract himself. "Rory knows how to take care of herself. She's been diabetic since she was thirteen. Learned a thing or two by now, I expect."

"I expect you're right. Doesn't stop folks from worrying though."

"No, ma'am, sure doesn't. But she's got it handled. Thanks for breakfast. Gotta get to the range."

Chance went to his truck and started it up. When he looked at the restaurant, Ronnie Junior was watching him through the window. He didn't look scared, though. He looked furious.

Chance laughed. "Bring it on, my man. Bring it on."

So long as Junior and his asshat dad focused on Chance and not Rory, he didn't care what they tried to do to him. He'd be ready.

Chapter Twenty-Seven

I︎t was late afternoon when Rory walked into the Dawg. She'd just left her obstetrics appointment and she was still reeling as she surveyed the kitchen. It looked remarkably normal, like they could open at any moment. Except for the fact there wasn't any food being prepped.

When she'd left the obstetrician's office, she wished she'd brought Chance along for moral support. She'd known she would have to be careful, that her blood glucose would have to be monitored closely, but she hadn't expected to be so overwhelmed with the potential problems that could occur.

Her obstetrician was a warm, friendly woman who assured her they would handle anything that came along, that she would have the best treatment possible. And she'd assured Rory that knowing the risks and being prepared for them didn't mean she was going to experience problems. She was healthy and her blood glucose was well under control with her CGM and insulin pump.

Still, it was scary to consider how different her pregnancy might be from someone without diabetes. Not that other women didn't have problems, because they did, but everything in Rory's life was always magnified by her condition. It was frustrating and disheartening if she let it be. Mostly she gritted her teeth and got on with it.

She hadn't called anyone during the ride back to Sutton's Creek. She'd wanted to process everything she'd been told. She was still processing it, but it was going to be okay. She had her friends. She had Chance, if only for right now. He'd help her through this, and even if he left her, she'd be okay.

She was always okay.

He said he loved her, but he was emotional about the baby. She understood. She was pretty emotional about that, too. Part of her wanted it to be true that he was in love with her, but the sensible part wasn't letting her believe it for a moment. Belief lowered guards, which was a recipe for disaster.

The door from the dining area opened and Theo walked in. "Whoa."

She lifted her chin. "What?"

"You look extremely serious. Did everything go okay at the appointment?"

She nodded. "Fine. As you might expect, there are things to be aware of, but I'll have a good team taking care of me. You'll get a kick out of this, though. Because I'll be thirty-five soon, this is considered a geriatric pregnancy. Geriatric, Theo. Like Granny was having this baby, not me."

Theo snorted as he came over to put an arm around her and squeeze. "Sorry, Pixie. I know that had to sting. Plus it's kinda ridiculous. Geriatric? Couldn't they think of another term?"

"You'd think," she grumbled. "What's been going on? Are we clear to open again?"

"Everything is dry and no sign of mold, thank God. The work upstairs will take a few more days, but nothing to be done about that. Just waiting for the county health inspector to tell us we can open. He'll be here in the morning."

"That's good. Fingers crossed it goes well."

"For sure. Soooo," Theo began.

"What?"

"You haven't been in town until just now, right?"

"Nope, why?"

"Apparently your man had a throw down with the Davises at Miss Mary's this morning. Told them if they didn't stay away from you, they'd be getting a personal demonstration of his military skills. He was a Navy SEAL, which you never mentioned."

Rory's heart was hammering. Chance had done that? For her? Adorable idiot.

"Chance was in the Army. Navy SEALs are in the Navy. Who told you the story?"

"Heard it in at the Gas-n-Go earlier. Chance parked Clyde in front of Miss Mary's, went inside and ordered a burrito, then sat down with the two men while he waited, ate their bacon, and explained why it was a bad idea to harass you. Then he left. Guess there were a few folks who saw the whole thing so it's been making the rounds. Oh, and everyone knows he's staying at the farm. I expect Emma Grace's mama to start inquiring about the wedding anytime now. Since Emma Grace and Blaze seem to be taking their time getting hitched, she might want to plan yours in the meantime."

Rory growled. "We are *not* getting married."

Theo only grinned. "Wait until everybody learns you're pregnant."

"Oh for heaven's sake. This is not 1950. Women can be pregnant and have babies on their own. We don't have to get married. It's not like they're gonna run me out of town for being an unwed mother."

"No, definitely not. But they're gonna have a lot of fun speculating why you and Chance aren't getting married when you clearly have a baby on the way."

Rory shook her head. "They can speculate all they want. It's my business, not theirs."

"Hey, y'all."

Rory turned to see Emma Grace coming through the back door. She looked pretty and happy, like she got great sex on the regular and had no doubts that her man loved her. Rory was envious.

"Hey, Idgy. What's up?"

"I've finished with my patients for the day and I saw you drive up when I was upstairs changing, so I thought I'd come see how the appointment went."

"Plus you heard that Chance threatened the Davises on my behalf."

Emma Grace laughed. "Well, that too. I doubt he really said he was a ninja, though that's what Celia Lincoln told my mother."

Rory blew out a breath. "Good grief. Better come on up to the office and I'll tell you about the appointment."

"I'm headed over to Kiss My Grits for coffee," Theo said. "Y'all want me to bring you anything?"

"Oooh, a chai latte and banana bread. Let me give you my card," Emma Grace said, starting to unzip the crossbody bag she was carrying.

"Nope, I got it. Pix?"

Rory rolled her eyes. "Now that you've trotted out that nickname again, you aren't going to stop, are you?"

Theo grinned. "Nope. You want anything or not?"

"Decaf double espresso with stevia, please. No baked goods. I have to watch the sugar even more than usual."

"You got it, hon. Be back in a few."

Rory and Emma Grace went into the dining room and up the stairs behind the bar to the office. They sat in the old leather armchairs by the window. Her parents had picked out these chairs from an antique store in Huntsville and placed them here so they could chat about the business at the end of the day with a beverage and the day's receipts.

Rory caressed one leather arm absently as she told Emma Grace about her appointment. All the things she had to look out for, like preeclampsia, eye and kidney problems, plus the greater risk of miscarriage, stillbirth, and birth defects.

"It's a lot," Emma Grace said. "But it's manageable. You workout regularly, you're fit, and your blood glucose is well-controlled. If you have any doubts about anything at any point, you know you can call me. Don't be stubborn about it. I don't care how minor you think the issue is, or what time it is, call me."

Emotion welled in her chest. "Thank you. I don't want to be needy, but I'd be lying if I said I wasn't scared about some of this stuff."

Emma Grace reached for her hand. "Honey, I know. We're going to get you through this and you're going to have a sweet little baby coming in January. Have you told Chance about your appointment yet?"

"No. I will. I promised him I would." Rory worried the inside of her lip. "He thinks he loves me."

Emma Grace broke out in a huge grin. "Oh my God, that's awesome! Of course he does. You're terrific, Ror. He'd be crazy not to. How do you feel about him?"

Rory's belly clenched. She'd been thinking about it since the moment he'd said something. It felt like there was a huge bubble of something wanting to break through the walls she'd erected, but she couldn't let it. If she did, she'd be right back in that pit where she'd landed after Mark left her for Tammy.

"I like him, Idgy. But I don't believe he really loves me. I think he's overwhelmed with the baby, like I am, and he's mixed up. He'll sort it out in a few weeks when things get into a routine."

Emma Grace shook her head. "Oh, honey. For someone who reads all those romance novels, you really are a skeptic. Do you honestly think the man doesn't know his own mind?"

"I think finding out you're going to be a father is an emotional event and maybe a bit overwhelming. I think he's projecting those feelings onto me. It's not that he doesn't know his own mind, it's that this is new territory for us both and maybe he's put a name to something when it's not the right name. He's going to wake up one of these days and realize he doesn't want to tie himself down, that he wants to go back to flirting with all the women and having his choice of who to take home each night."

The idea of Chance taking anyone home made her stomach turn over. She couldn't imagine him touching someone else the way he'd touched her. She'd told Amber he was fair game, but if she saw him with Amber now, she'd probably act like a total fool and lose her shit.

"Okay, I get it. But I think Chance has a lot more honor than Mark ever did. Can you picture Mark striding into Miss Mary's and threatening two men with bodily harm if they bother you again?"

"Well, no, but Mark's an attorney. He'd have considered the repercussions of his actions."

"Exactly. He would have thought about himself and how he might get into trouble, not about protecting you. Big difference."

Rory made a face. "That's not a fair comparison and you know it. Being sensible about making threats that can come back to bite you in the ass, and therefore your livelihood, isn't a terrible thing. Maybe Chance is the one who's wrong. Maybe it's a hotheaded thing to do and he shouldn't have done it."

Except she did love that he'd gone all badass warrior dude on her behalf. She really did, even if she shouldn't.

Emma Grace held up both hands. "Okay, you win. Just saying that Chance isn't Mark and I'd rather have a man who's willing to inflict bodily harm on my behalf—not that I approve of such things, mind you—should it prove necessary."

Theo arrived with the coffees then and the subject of Chance blessedly came to an end. Not that Rory could think of much else now that they'd been talking about it except the way he'd looked when he'd told her he was in love with her. Her heart had skipped and then hammered and she'd wanted to press her mouth to his and get lost in his kiss.

She'd wanted that lightning sizzling through her again, wanted to feel the incredible way her body responded to his touch. She'd almost said to hell with it and let him take her to bed last night, but she'd held on to the shreds of her control right up until she'd closed her bedroom door and left him to sleep on the couch.

Then she'd taken care of business with her fingers, his name a whisper on her lips the moment she'd shattered.

Chapter Twenty-Eight

"What have we got, gentlemen?" Ghost asked the assembled team.

They were in the SCIF after a long day at Griffin Research Labs going over records and training their security personnel. It was six-thirty and the range was closed for the day. Daphne was currently cleaning up the shooting bays. She had her headphones in and she was dancing with the broom from time to time.

Kane kept glancing at the screen where she was visible which is the only reason Chance knew she was dancing because he'd looked to see what was going on.

Seth flipped open his laptop and projected a file on the overhead screen. "These are the people who work in software engineering. It's a small group. The one who stands out is Caroline Crowell. She's only been on the team a few months, moved here from Virginia, and her finances are strained. She leased a small farm near Sutton's Creek when she arrived. She has a younger sister, still in high school, who she cares for. The kid rides horses and competes in jumping competitions. They have one horse at the farm, and one in training at a barn in Madison. The kid takes lessons there."

"Wait. You think this lady would take a bribe so her sister could keep riding horses?" Ethan asked.

"The parents died in a skiing accident a year ago. The kid's whole life changed. Yeah, I think Ms. Crowell might be tempted by easy money if it meant her sister's life didn't get ripped apart even further than it already has been."

"Yikes," Blaze said. "That's rough."

"What else makes you suspicious of her?" Ghost asked. Because they all knew there had to be more.

Seth clicked over to another screen. This one had a picture of Caroline Crowell. She was pretty, with brown hair, pale skin, and green eyes. She wasn't smiling. Her credentials were listed on the page beside her picture. Seth zoomed in.

Languages: English, Polish, Russian

"Ms. Crowell spent a year in Poland, working for the US Army Corps of Engineers. She worked in plans and software development, and instructed Polish soldiers in those areas. She's traveled extensively throughout the region over the past decade, and some of her mother's family still lives in Gdansk."

"Wilhelm Olkowicz and Cyril Dyka," Ghost said, naming the two men who'd been detained recently. "We need to find out if she had any contact with either of them, either here or in Poland."

"That's what I was thinking."

"Excellent work, Phantom. I'll send inquiries on Caroline Crowell's time in Poland. See what you can find during her time here."

"Roger that."

"Where are we on secure lab access?"

"Tomorrow or Thursday," Chance said. "I'm working on the protocols for all lab access and testing for weaknesses. I'll get inside the secure lab soon and then I'll exchange the cables for wifi cables so we can access the network."

"Great work, gentleman. I want in their systems by the weekend so I can report to the president. She's heading to Europe for the G7 summit next week and I think she'd like to know we're making progress on keeping Athena secure and discovering who the traitors are." Ghost let his gaze slide across everyone present before settling on Chance again. "So, Wraith, when did you become a ninja assassin?"

"What?" Chance asked.

Blaze and Ethan were snickering. Seth and Kane looked as confused as Chance felt.

"Went to grab lunch at the Gas-n-Go and heard that kid from the book store telling Clarence that you were a ninja assassin who vowed retribution if the property developers said another word to Rory again."

Chance scrubbed his hand over his head. "For fuck's sake, that's not at all what happened."

Ghost looked amused. "Didn't think so. So what did happen?"

Chance recounted the story to his teammates.

"You ate the man's bacon?" Blaze asked. "Savage."

"I took *one* piece of bacon. It looked good. Junior was pretty pissed, but his daddy seemed to get the message."

"Try not to do any ninja assassin bullshit," Ghost said. "The fact Blaze is shacked up and you've got a baby on the way is enough to land me in a river of shit if the powers that be get wind of it. Just need you boys to stay out of trouble for a few more months, m'kay? Then you can dance in the town square naked beneath a full moon with Colleen chanting to the aliens and I won't give two fucks. I'll be happily retired on an island somewhere, sipping an umbrella drink with my toes in the sand."

Chance blinked. This was the first any of them had heard about Ghost's plans post-Ghost Ops. "You're retiring at the end of this? Not going back to full-time ops?"

"Can't."

They all exchanged bewildered looks.

"That was part of the deal for me. This is over, I'm done. You boys can go back though."

"You would really retire to an island?" Kane asked.

"Maybe. Or maybe I'll pull an Ian Black and start my own operation."

"If you do, I want to work for you," Seth said.

"Appreciate that, Phantom. I'd love to have any of you who wanted to come with me, assuming we're all still standing at the end of this. And assuming I don't chuck it all and go fishing. Maybe I'll be like that Jack Reacher character and be a professional vagrant with mad skills. Who knows?"

Chance didn't picture Ghost as a loner traveling the country on busses and meting out vigilante justice when the situation required it, but he supposed anything was possible.

They wrapped up the meeting and left the SCIF. When Chance retrieved his phone from the box where they had to store them before they entered the room, he had an unread text. Shocked the shit out of him that it was from Rory.

> RORY:
>
> When are you coming home? I forgot to buy whole wheat bread while I was out and I'm craving a grilled cheese sandwich. If you can stop at the Pig, that'd be great.

Chance grinned at her message. Just like Rory to get straight to the matter without a lot of bullshit. Also like her not to send him a big text about her appointment. She was going to make him ask her about it.

He typed an answer.

> Sorry, been in a meeting. Leaving now. Anything else you need from the store?

A few moments later, a reply pinged in.

> Nah, I don't think so. Unless there's something you want. Fair warning though, you bring home any manner of potato chips and I will make you eat them outside on the porch. Maybe the barn. I don't need the temptation.

CHANCE:
> HUA

RORY:
> Is that ninja assassin speak?

Chance rolled his eyes. Jesus. Should have known Rory would have heard the rumor.

CHANCE:
> Sure is. It's code for heard, understood, acknowledged. I told you that was an Army thing before, but I lied. It's the secret language of my lethal ninja sect. Don't tell anyone I told you or I'll have to kill you.

He was sitting behind the wheel in Clyde, engine rumbling, when he got her one word reply.

> Goofball.

Chapter Twenty-Nine

Rory groaned as she slapped the novel she was reading closed and dropped it on the swing beside her. If she had to read another word about slick folds and tongues teasing body parts, she was going to die. All it did was make her think of the last time a tongue had explored her slick folds. Nearly two months ago, when Chance had rocked her world with the most spectacular sex she'd ever had.

Damn him.

She frowned, thinking hard. Was it *really* the most spectacular sex she'd ever had? Or was it the fact she'd been in a pretty intense drought by the time he came along that had skewed her memory?

After Mark left with Tammy, she'd retreated into herself and hadn't wanted anything to do with men. When she finally came out of her shell a few months later, she'd made some bad decisions. There had been a period where she'd had a lot of sex because she didn't stay with any one man for more than a month.

None of them were all that memorable. Simply itch scratching. After a while, Gus the Glamorous became her itch scratcher.

Until Chance Hughes swaggered into her house and made her so horny looking at him that she'd been helpless to resist his charm.

And here she was, thinking about it again. What she needed was to get Gus out of the closet and stick him in the bedside drawer again. Then she could turn to him and to heck with Chance.

Though Chance's gorgeous body would figure heavily in the fantasy, she had to admit.

Her phone beeped with an alert but she didn't need to look at it to know Chance was home. He'd just turned into the driveway and Clyde was rumbling toward the house, his headlights shining in the dusky gloom. Her heart ratcheted up a couple notches.

She pushed the swing to and fro, pretending she wasn't lighting up inside like the Fourth of July at the prospect of seeing Chance. He drove up beside where she'd parked his truck and pulled to a stop. Then the door shut with that heavy sound that Clyde had and Chance came walking around the truck, grocery bag in hand.

He stepped up onto the porch, looking fine in his dark jeans and One Shot Tactical polo. The shirt was fitted and clung to hard muscles like a second skin. Chance didn't have a muffin top, or even a hint of a fat roll anywhere on that shirt. His jeans hugged his hips like a lover. Could a person be jealous of jeans? Was that crazy?

"Hey, baby," he said softly. "Got your bread."

"Thank you."

"You want me to fix your grilled cheese?"

"Would you?"

He came closer, bent down and pressed a kiss to her forehead. She felt the tingle of his lips all the way to her core.

"I will. Anything special you want with it? Anything I need to know about how you like it?"

Oh my, those words set her to tingling again. She had a lot to say about how she liked it, but she didn't mean a grilled cheese. "No. Just butter and provolone. I know how many carbs to estimate if you do it like that."

"Coming right up." His gaze strayed to the novel at her side. "Is that a bull on the cover?"

Rory turned the book over. "Uh, yeah. It's a minotaur romance. Very good."

Very sexy, but she didn't add that part.

"Huh, had no idea such a thing existed."

"The romance genre is very broad. If you can imagine it, there's probably a book. This would be a paranormal romance, monster sub-genre."

"I see." The hint of a grin quirked at the corners of his mouth.

Heat flared in her cheeks. "You don't see. You're making fun of me."

"I'm really not, babe. What I think's kinda funny is how you go from the five hot dudes with one woman to a monster romance. You ever read any with boring couples? Two people, no monsters in sight?"

"Sometimes. I don't find them very realistic though."

He scratched the back of his neck. "But minotaurs are?"

"Not at all. But I don't find myself questioning the romance when it's a fantasy world."

"Got it. You staying out here while I fix that sandwich? Or coming inside to talk to me?"

She picked up the book and stood. "I'll come inside." She followed him to the kitchen and leaned against the counter while Chance got to work. "Heard you threatened Ronnie and RJ today."

He looked up from buttering bread. "Did you hear I'm a ninja warrior assassin too?"

She couldn't help but grin. "Heard that. Also, Theo wanted to know why I didn't tell him you were a Navy SEAL."

"For fuck's sake," he muttered. "Shoulda kept my voice down when telling those two assholes what I was gonna do to them. Then nobody could have blown it out of proportion the way they obviously have."

"Oh, trust me, they could. You didn't have to do it, you know. I can take care of myself, handle my own problems. Those two are no match for Liza Jane if it comes down to it."

His gaze snapped to hers, harder than she'd seen it before. "Kitten, last thing I want is you shooting anyone. It's messy and complicated, and you don't need that shit. There are repercussions to taking a life, even when it's justified. Trust me."

Her heart hammered. "I know that."

Emma Grace had killed Kyle Hollis before he could kill them, but she'd suffered from it too. She'd been honest about some of her struggles when they'd talked about what'd happened to them. Mostly, with the love of a good man and the promise of a great life, she was healing from it.

"If you know, then it's not something you're gonna want to do unless there's no other choice."

"Hu-ah, Chancey Pants. Just saying that I've been taking care of myself for a very long time and I can continue to do so. You don't have to fight my fights for me."

"I don't have to, but I'm going to. Because you're my woman and that's my kid, and nobody threatens what's mine."

She ought to correct his caveman-like possession, but the part of her that'd been reading about possessive minotaurs rather liked it. She sniffed and settled for changing the subject.

"Do you want to hear about my doctor appointment or not?"

"Yes, I most definitely want to hear about the appointment."

Rory put her palms on the counter behind her and hopped up on it. She programmed her carbs for the sandwich into the insulin pump and then she told him everything, sparing absolutely nothing about the potential complications. He flipped the sandwiches in the pan and kept his attention focused on her, asking questions when he didn't understand something.

She had to admit it was easier to tell him than she'd thought it would be. She'd shared with Emma Grace, but Idgy was a doctor. Chance wasn't, but if anything he heard scared him, he didn't let it show. He was a rock and she found herself wanting to lean on him for support. Which she should not do, but maybe it was okay for right now. Tomorrow, she'd go back to being an island.

"How do you feel about it?" he asked when she finished.

"Honestly? Fearful, but also determined. I'm going to do everything right and give this baby the best chance he or she can have. But even doing everything right, I could still have problems with high blood sugar. I'm going to have to watch it carefully and get seen if anything is even remotely wonky."

"What do you need from me?"

Rory blinked. She hadn't expected that question. "I guess I need you to help me if I ask for it. There's not much else you can do, really."

He turned off the stove and slid the sandwiches onto plates. Then he set hers beside her and put a hand on either side of her thighs, caging her in. Blue eyes bored into hers.

"Not helpful, Aurora. I can shop for groceries, prepare food, take you to appointments, keep records of what you eat or what your blood sugars are. I can pick up your medicine, and I can take care of mowing the grass and dealing with any outdoor projects around here that maybe you shouldn't have to worry about right now. I can stand between you and anyone who upsets you or pisses you off. I can hold you close if you need a shoulder and I can listen if you need an ear. Whatever you need, baby, I'm here for it."

Oh my.

Before she could say anything stupid, like what about a Vitamin D injection—his D specifically—he removed the cage of his arms. "You should eat while it's warm."

Then he left her on the counter while he retreated to his own sandwich and took a bite out of it.

Rory followed suit, closing her eyes at the warm, buttery, cheesy goodness. Nothing like a good grilled cheese to make a woman happy.

"Maybe add making grilled cheese to that list of things you can do," she said when she'd swallowed the first bite.

"It's there. Whenever you want it."

"Fantastic."

"Any news about reopening?"

She licked butter off her finger. Chance's eyes smoldered when she looked at him again. Her belly clenched and her panties grew a little wetter. What the book hadn't done for her, Chance did. All he'd have to do is slide his fingers over her and she'd probably fly apart instantly.

"Um, a little. Health inspector comes tomorrow so hopefully we'll be opening tomorrow evening. Everything is dry, no mold, but we need to keep an eye on it. George and crew are working on Theo's place, but that won't affect the Dawg. If we can just get up and running again, we'll replenish the cash we've had to spend on repairs and renewing the garden."

Chance finished his sandwich and put the plate in the sink. "Can I ask why you've never borrowed against the farm to clear the debt against the Dawg? You said before there was mismanagement by the person your grandparents hired."

She nodded. "Yes. Somebody they trusted who stole from them and nearly bankrupted the business. It was a long time ago, but when Theo and I took over, we determined to make it work on its own. Borrowing against the farm was only a last resort. And we did try at one point when things looked especially bleak, but a few years ago the bank wouldn't take that bet. Land around Sutton's Creek only started rising in value within the past couple of years. If we wanted to borrow against it today, they'd trip over themselves to loan us money. But not back then."

"So the fact the Davises have come calling with money to burn is no surprise."

"Nope. And I don't blame Jimmy Turton for wanting to sell. Or Carter Coombs either. They're still farming the land, and it can be a hard life in some ways. Dolly Coombs has been battling cancer, and the Turton boys just want regular jobs with benefits and to see their mama settled in town. I'll hate it when it happens, because I'll see those housing developments and stores whenever I drive past what used to be woods and fields, but that's progress for you. It doesn't stop because some of us want things never to change."

"Sometimes change is good. The trick is knowing which things need to change and being willing to go there."

"Look at you getting all sage-y and wise on me. Personally, I've found it easier to just stick with what I know. Easier in the long run."

"Maybe so. But sometimes you miss the best parts of life that way."

Chapter Thirty

Rory wasn't used to having anyone in the house with her for days on end, but she and Chance had almost slipped into a routine. After dinner, he cleaned up the dishes and then went outside to make sure the chickens were closed into the coop and to check on the barn and the garden.

They often watched television, which wasn't typically something she got to do in the evenings since she was almost always at the Dawg. She was going to have to figure that out after the baby came. Maybe Emma Grace would babysit sometimes. She was fairly certain that Ellen Sutton would leap at the chance, especially since Mrs. Sutton was the closest thing her baby would have to a grandmother.

There was time to figure it out. It did not have to be tonight.

Chance returned inside just as Rory emerged from her bedroom, comfy pajama pants and sweatshirt donned for the evening. Her belly fluttered as Chance turned from the door. He was still wearing that darn form-fitting polo and dark jeans, and his dark hair made him look like one of her vampire romance heroes.

Well, maybe not really, but a girl could fantasize. Maybe she could get him to wear a cape. Hmm…

"Do you want to watch TV?" she blurted. The last thing she needed was to go back to her minotaur romance, and she really didn't want to think about vampires either. Television was a good distraction. A necessary one.

It was either that or go to her room and lock the door, which she didn't really want to do.

"Yeah, sure. Let me put on something more comfortable."

"Of course."

When he lifted the edge of the polo, she squeaked. "Whoa, there. What are you doing?"

"Changing."

"Chance. There's a bathroom for heaven's sake. Or one of the bedrooms I keep offering you."

He tugged the shirt off anyway, revealing his gorgeously muscled chest. Minotaurs were nothing compared to this man. Rory swallowed her tongue for a second.

"Nah," he told her as he unbuttoned his jeans and slid them down his hips. "You've seen it all. I got nothing to hide."

"Oh for fuck's sake," she muttered, turning her head.

Chance chuckled. "Well, sure, we can if you like."

"That was *not* what I said."

"Can't blame a guy for trying."

She heard him rustling through his duffel bag. The sound of a T-shirt going on, then something she sincerely hoped was shorts or sweatpants.

"I'm decent now, kitten. You can look without blushing."

"I was *not* blushing." She turned her head and nearly choked. "Where did you get that?"

Chance grinned as he flourished a hand over the T-shirt that had a picture of a chicken in silhouette. An egg was dropping from the back end. The caption read *Chickens. The pet that poops breakfast.*

"Babe, you can get anything on the internet."

"Apparently."

"Want anything from the kitchen before I sit down?"

"No, I'm good. Thanks." She sat on one of the armchairs and curled her legs under her.

Chance went into the kitchen and returned with a beer. He sank onto the cushion at the end of the couch where he usually lay his head, then frowned at her. "Think you ought to sit beside me."

"Why?"

"Why not?" He took a sip of the beer and waited.

She let her gaze slide to that ridiculous shirt and then back up to his eyes. He made no move to turn on the television. Rory made a show of sighing and then got up and went to sit beside him. He put an arm around her and tugged her in close.

"That's better."

She was stiff for a moment, but he was right, it *was* better. Chance was warm and solid, and her body tingled with energy when he was near like he was now. She lay her head against his shoulder and told herself it didn't mean anything. They were friends, that's all. Because she was a mature woman who could be friends with the man who'd planted a baby inside her. She could even be fond of him. Was fondness the soft, warm feeling flooding her right before the sizzle of attraction took over?

"What do you want to watch," he asked, his breath ruffling her hair.

"Something good. A murder mystery. British, because I like those best."

"Need to narrow it down, honey. That's a lot of options to choose from."

"Okay, I want to watch *The Brokenwood Mysteries*. It's on Prime."

Chance navigated to the series and chose the next one in the queue. "Wait a minute," he said as the show started. "That's not a British accent."

"New Zealand. Close enough."

Chance snorted. "Yeah, I hear they're really close neighbors what with those adjoining borders and all."

Rory pinched him. Not hard because he laughed. "Hush up, I need to hear what Mike and Kristin are up to. And just wait until you meet Gina. She's a hoot."

At some point, Rory's eyes started to droop. She tried to keep them open, but it wasn't happening. She fell asleep against Chance, her body melting into his. So long as he was here, she knew she was safe.

Sometimes change is good…

When she woke with a gasp sometime later, it was quiet and Chance was moving. She blinked up at him, trying to recall what'd happened on the show, but it was blank. She'd fallen asleep long before the mystery was solved. But maybe the show was what'd caused her dream? A shadowy man had been chasing her through the woods. She'd stumbled and fallen and he'd nearly been on her when she snapped awake.

"What time is it?" she asked, her voice raspy with sleep.

"Bedtime."

That's when she realized Chance was carrying her. He toed open her bedroom door and walked over to the bed. When he set her down on it and tugged back the covers on one side, she reached for him again.

"Don't leave me."

Chance stilled. "I'm not leaving, Rory. I'm right outside the door, on the couch. If you need me, I'll be here in an instant."

It was reasonable and logical to let him leave her to go to sleep. But the dream was still too recent and her heart tapped a quick beat in response.

"I—I was being chased. In my dream. I know it's not real, but… I don't want to be alone."

Chance pushed her hair behind her ear and kissed her forehead. A feeling of calm rippled through her.

"Okay, baby. I'll stay with you. Don't worry, I know this isn't an invitation for sex. Told you I'd be here for you and I meant it."

He slid in beside her and she turned on her side away from him so he could wrap himself around her. He tugged her close, her ass nestling against his crotch. Then he skimmed a hand down her hip and back up, resting it on the mattress beside her. Rory let out a sigh. She'd missed this.

"Good night, Chance," she whispered.

"Night, kitten."

Chapter Thirty-One

SLEEPING WITH RORY WAS GOING TO BE THE DEATH OF HIM. CHANCE woke three times with a hard-on caused by her cute little ass pressing into his groin. Each time, he shifted away to break the contact and hefted a sigh while he pictured things guaranteed to make him lose the erection.

Wasn't easy, though.

He wanted her, and lying beside her with her body snuggled up to his only brought the need home that much more.

It was more than need, though. He wanted to protect her, keep her safe, and not just from the dickhead Davises. He shivered as he thought of all the things she'd told him about what could happen during this pregnancy. She already had diabetes, but apparently gestational diabetes was also a thing. It happened to a lot of women —and it was even more frightening if it happened to Rory. Her body already had a problem with sugar. Last thing she needed was more blood sugar.

It could lead to preeclampsia, which was dangerous for her. Dangerous in general, but more so for Rory and the baby. He planned to do everything he could to keep her comfortable and be there for her while her body changed and grew heavy with their child. He couldn't prevent everything, but he could be right here to watch for trouble and help her.

By the time six a.m. rolled around, he was more than ready to get out of bed. He left Rory sleeping soundly and went to shower, then headed outside to let the chickens out and collect eggs. The girls were happy to see him, or as happy as chickens can be, clucking up a storm as he scattered feed.

He checked the barn, the outbuildings, and the garden and all was as it should be. Still needed those high-res cameras to arrive so he could install them, but he was glad nobody'd been back since the garden had been torn up. Maybe Theo had pissed off a woman, but Chance's gut told him otherwise.

After his encounter with the Davises, he wouldn't be surprised if they were behind it. Junior would do it out of sheer meanness, though his daddy might have a plan to drive Rory and Theo toward a sale by chipping away at their business and causing them expensive problems.

The morning was cool, but the weather was headed for hot in the next few weeks. The thing about summer in the South was that it teased you in May with balmy days and slightly cooler nights before squatting over the region with a vengeance from June through mid-September, sometimes even into October. When summer hit, it hit hard with temps reaching close to one-hundred degrees during the day and humidity that had you ready for a change of clothes after walking to your car some days.

The farmhouse had window AC units. They worked, but maybe he needed to look into getting a proper system installed with ductwork. That'd cost a pretty penny, but he had money. Years of being single, combat and hazardous duty pay, as well as being frugal with a dollar had given him a sizable investment account.

Not that Rory would ever let him do such a thing. She had a real hang up about accepting help from anyone. Something he was going to have to work on.

Chance

He went inside and fixed coffee, then took his cup to the front porch and sat on the swing. After a while, he went for another cup. There was a small crash inside the bedroom that had him racing for the door. He yanked it open, his heart in his throat.

Rory stood just inside the closet door, a handful of boxes on the floor inside where they'd clearly fallen. She had a step stool where she'd climbed up to retrieve something from the shelf.

And in her hand was a glittery purple dong. She squeaked and thrust it behind her back.

"Knock for heaven's sake," she cried. "What do you want?"

Chance went hot and cold inside. Then he was hot again. He'd thought she'd fallen and his heart had squeezed so tight he'd felt like he couldn't breathe. But no, his woman was getting a giant purple dong from her closet.

He stalked over to where she stood, her chest heaving, and reached behind her. She gripped the dong tightly but then let go when he insisted. He held it up and her cheeks went crimson.

"What the hell, kitten? You don't need this when you've got the real thing right here."

He gripped his crotch for emphasis. She made a strangled sound.

"First of all, who said I needed it? I was looking for something and it fell out of the closet. Forgot it was even there."

He moved closer, dropped the dong on the dresser, and yanked her against his body. "Did you now? What were you looking for, baby?"

Her hands went to his chest, but she didn't push him away. Her fingers curled into his polo shirt. His dick grew harder than stone as her hips flexed into him. "Just, um, a pair of shoes. I thought they were in a box. On the shelf."

He dipped his head to press his lips to the tender skin beneath her ear. She inhaled sharply.

"Need me to search for you?"

"N-no. Not important. I must have donated them."

He licked the shell of her ear. "Baby, it's okay. You can be horny. God knows I'm horny as fuck after sleeping next to you all night. But you don't need a fake dong to get you there when you got me. I know all the things you like. How hard, how soft, how deep, how rough. I know you love it when you ride me and I tease my finger around your backside, skimming you there. Then when you come and I insert just the tip of my finger, you fucking lose your mind."

"Chance," she said, and he wasn't sure if it was a gasp or a moan.

"You like it when I fuck you from behind and lightly slap that pretty ass of yours, too. And you really like it when I tongue your clit until you sob my name." He pushed her against the door jamb, pressing his hips to hers so she got the message. "I'm here for you, kitten. Ready to do anything you want me to do. You just gotta say the word."

"You're really annoying, you know that?" she asked, her eyes flashing as she glared up at him. But those fingers were still curled in his shirt, and her body was soft against him, not stiff with outrage or denial.

"I know."

She appeared to be at war with herself. But then she curled a hand around the back of his neck and tugged him down to her. "I expect to see stars, Chancey Pants. If I don't, then you don't get another shot."

Before he could tell her she was going to see the entire fucking universe before he was done, she slammed her mouth into his and thrust her tongue between his lips.

Game on. Thank fuck.

Chapter Thirty-Two

Rory's entire body was like a dry piece of tinder. The moment her lips met Chance's, everything ignited. She needed his touch. Craved it. Everything he'd said, every little memory of the things he'd done to her, exploded inside her head until she'd had to kiss him or lose her mind.

She'd slept soundly beside him all night but she'd awakened with an ache between her legs that her fingers weren't going to ease. Not that she'd intended on using Gus while Chance was still in the house. No, she'd been planning to wait until he left for the range before she took care of business. So why the hell she'd decided she needed to retrieve him from the closet right that minute, she'd never know.

All she'd intended was to tuck him away in his drawer, but the boxes came crashing down and Chance came bursting in, and now she was about to get laid because she'd realized Gus wasn't ever going to fill the chasm of need that Chance could.

"Baby," he said against her lips. "I've missed you so much."

She couldn't respond, not with words. Instead, she went for his belt, tugging it open and attacking his zipper. She wanted his smooth cock in her hands, wanted to feel the velvety skin over the hardened steel. She wanted to cup his balls in her hand and slide him in her mouth the way she'd done before.

More than that, she wanted him deep inside her, stroking the emptiness away, filling her with his heat. He reached down and cupped her ass, lifting her until she had to wrap her legs around him. She growled that he'd taken her fun away with his cock, but it didn't last because he was walking her over to the bed, his tongue in her mouth, his fingers squeezing her ass before he skimmed a thumb over her center. Even with pajama pants blocking the way, she shuddered at his touch.

He lowered her and ripped her sleep shirt off, revealing her breasts. Her insulin pump and glucose monitor were on opposite sides of her abdomen. They sometimes made her shy with a man, but she wasn't shy with Chance. Even with the morning light streaming through the curtains and brightening the room, she wasn't worried about what he might think. Not about her body or her medical devices.

Chance had always made her feel like she was the most beautiful woman on earth when he was with her. She'd told herself that was his player gene, the one that could make any woman drop her panties and feel privileged to do so. And maybe it was, but if the result was her feeling like a million bucks naked, then she'd take it.

She went for his jeans again, intending to shove them down his hips, but he stopped her by dropping to his knees and tugging her to his mouth. He latched onto a nipple and sucked, and Rory's knees nearly buckled. She moaned as she dropped her hands onto his shoulders and held on. He worked one nipple and then the other, releasing the first with a soft pop. It'd hardened into a tight little point, wet from his mouth.

Chance dragged her pajama bottoms down until they fell into a puddle at her ankles. Then his fingers were between her legs, skimming her sex as she gasped.

Chance

"Christ you're wet for me. Need to taste you. Hop up on the bed."

She did as he told her, leaving her pajama pants in a heap on the floor. She was utterly naked and he was still clothed, though his fly was open. He came to the edge of the bed on his knees, then tugged her to him until her pussy was in his face. She let her legs fall open, her heart hammering in her chest.

She shouldn't be doing this. She should have waited to retrieve Gus, then soothed the ache with his rubbery purple goodness. He vibrated. Chance did not vibrate. She wasn't in danger of falling for Gus either. Chance, however…

"Get ready for the stars, kitten," he said, and then he licked into her core and she bowed up off the bed.

There was no buildup. No gentle climb towards a shattering orgasm. One second he fastened his mouth over her clit and the next she was arching her back and rubbing against his face as her orgasm exploded through her.

Chance didn't back off, though. He slid two fingers inside her and she gripped him tight as he worked them in and out, drawing her climax to greater heights. When she'd had too much, when she was too sensitive to take another moment, she pushed at his shoulders. He stopped what he was doing, kissing his way along her inner thigh instead.

When he looked up and their eyes met, her heart squeezed a little bit tighter. Then he got to his feet and ripped his shirt over his head, revealing acres of smooth muscle and tanned skin. He had scars, not many, but interesting ones that she'd asked about before.

He'd been stabbed and shot in the military, and it made her frantic to think someone had hurt him. That he'd put himself in danger willingly. Then there was the narrow scar on his arm that had come from a tangle with some barbed wire. The place where she'd punched him in the arm when he had stitches. She hated that she'd done that to him, but she hadn't known he was injured. Still didn't stop that pang of guilt that hit her every time her gaze landed on that scar.

"Stop thinking about my arm, kitten."

Her belly clenched as her eyes snapped to his. How did he know?

"Think about this instead." He shoved his jeans down and kicked them off, then palmed his cock as his gaze probed her from head to toe.

"You are one sexy beast, Chancey Pants," she said, trying to keep it light between them. Trying to push away the heavy, emotional cloud that sat just below the horizon inside her. The one that was bringing a storm that'd change everything if she let it happen.

"Need you now, Rory. I've been hard for you since I moved in."

He stroked his cock and she shuddered with the strength of her answering need.

"I need you, too."

"How do you want it, baby? You want to ride me? Want me behind you?"

She loved that he asked. Wearing her medical devices on her abdomen meant she couldn't take the full weight of a man on top of her, but instead of making a decision about how he was going to take her, he asked what she wanted. She could move them sometime, and would, but that's where they were right now. And Chance knew and cared.

She dropped her legs open and scooted up on the mattress. "I want you here. I want to watch your face when you come."

He knew what she meant. He put a knee on the bed and then another before he gripped her legs and tugged her to him. She was spread wide as he knelt there, looking like every perfect romance novel hero she'd ever read about.

Well, maybe not the minotaurs. Chance was better than a minotaur.

He pressed the head of his cock to her entrance, then stopped to meet her gaze. "You have to tell me if something isn't right, baby. I don't know how much you can take right now, or how careful I have to be."

That bubble in her chest was happiness. "I'm pregnant, Chance. Not broken. The hormones are making me hornier than I've ever been in my life, so I think I can take one little bitty cock."

His eyes widened and then he snorted. "Smart mouth. One of the things I fucking love about you."

Before she could respond, he thrust forward, filling her to the breaking point. Rory's gasp ended on a moan as her body stretched to accommodate him.

"You okay?"

"Oh my God," she whispered. "Better than okay. Please, Chance. Don't make me wait another second."

He levered himself over top of her, supporting the weight of his body on his elbows, and thrust into the heart of her again.

"Damn, that's good," she moaned. "Kiss me."

His mouth found hers, his tongue spearing inside. He moved slowly, deliberately, rocking into her with the kind of thoroughness that said he knew precisely what he was doing and how to draw out her pleasure.

Rory skimmed her fingernails down his back, not too hard, knowing he liked that little bit of pain as he rode her. When his movements intensified, the sounds of their bodies slapping together drove her even wilder. She widened her legs, tried to take him deeper, reached around to cup his heavy sack. It was wet with her juices and he groaned as she tugged and squeezed just enough to make him crazy.

She couldn't keep doing it, though. Her monitors got in the way of bending that far for long so she lay back and settled for running her hands up his arms and over his chest as Chance's big dick stroked into her. He bent to her breasts and sucked a nipple into his mouth, tugging deep.

"More," she said. "Need more."

He sucked harder, almost to the point of pain, and she gripped his head in both her hands and held him there while he tugged and nibbled and sucked deep in turns. Her body answered with more desire, more need. He abandoned one breast and did the same to the other until she was a quivering mass of nerve endings waiting for the right spark.

When he levered upward, breaking the contact with her breast, she could only stare into the depths of those blue eyes as he thrust harder and deeper than before. Her body stretched, sensation caught like a match, and her mouth fell open as she watched Chance's face.

"Come for me, Aurora," he commanded her.

That was all it took. The flame ignited, her body shook, and her orgasm rippled from her core to the farthest reaches of her limbs. "Chance," she cried as everything disappeared but him.

There was nothing on this earth but the two of them. Nothing more she needed. Why had she resisted for so long?

"That's it, honey," he growled, thrusting faster now, moving her across the bed with the power of his body slamming into hers.

She took him all while she shattered around him. Took him and wanted even more. When he stiffened and shouted, she knew his climax was every bit as good as hers. His seed erupted inside her, a warm flood that coated her walls and seeped from her body even as he was still coming.

"Holy shit, honey," he moaned in her ear as he collapsed beside her. "That was worth the wait."

Chapter Thirty-Three

She'd destroyed him. Chance lay on his back, breathing hard as he stared up at the ceiling. Rory slowly folded herself over until she was lying on his chest, her breathing as hard as his.

It had taken precisely ten minutes to recover from the first time, for him, but she'd been ready to go again almost immediately. She'd pushed him onto his back and rode him until her body started to tremble and her eyes fluttered closed as she threw her head back and squeezed him with her inner muscles.

He'd come hard when she did that, gasping with the force of it. Rory'd smiled as she'd lowered herself onto his chest. He loved those smiles.

He caressed the small of her back, slid his hand down and over one perfectly round cheek. Then he squeezed it, imagining himself biting it later.

"You've got a great ass, babe," he said.

"Mmm, and you have a great dick. And a great chest. Pretty much everything about you is pretty to look at."

He laughed softly. "Pretty, huh?"

"Nothing wrong with pretty."

"Nope." He squeezed her ass again. "Everything about you turns me on. Pretty doesn't begin to cover it."

She lifted her head. "Are you trying to one up me?"

"Telling the God's honest truth, kitten. You turn me on and you're more than pretty. Fucking gorgeous springs to mind."

The light in her eyes dimmed a little and he knew she was having trouble believing him. He hated that for her. Fucking Mark-the-Dick.

"You already got laid. Twice. No need to pile on the flattery."

"You think what you like, Rory, but I know what my truth is." Her CGM beeped and his entire body went on alert. "What do you need?"

She picked up her phone to check it. "Sugar's low. I need to get some juice and then I need to eat breakfast."

Chance bounded from the bed. He didn't even bother to grab pants as he headed for the kitchen. He poured juice and brought it back. Rory was propped against the headboard, waiting. He handed her the glass and climbed into bed beside her, dropping an arm around her just because he wanted to feel the warmth of her next to him.

He didn't panic, because he knew she was taking care of her needs, but deep inside a part of him wanted to scream that it wasn't fair she had to deal with this. Rory was an amazing person. She'd been through so much in her life, but she kept on fighting. And now she was pregnant with his kid and the risks to her health were even greater than before.

It chilled him to think about what could happen, but he'd told himself repeatedly since she'd informed him about the appointment that all he could do was be there for her. He couldn't rewind time and he couldn't undo what'd been done. She'd clearly thought about the risks and accepted them and he had to as well.

Diabetic women had babies. It happened. Rory would be fine. If he said it enough, it would be true.

Chance

"Tell me about the giant purple dong over there," he said, bumping her shoulder gently.

"Oh God," she groaned. "I was hoping you'd forgotten that."

"Hard to forget it. It's standing straight up on your dresser, babe."

She looked over to where it stood straight and tall and thick. It was seriously lifelike, other than being purple.

"That's Gus," she said, and he nearly choked on his own tongue. She'd fucking named the dong. "Gus the Glamorous. He vibrates. He's also very, *very* good at taking care of business if you know what I mean."

"Looks like he might do a decent job. Doesn't have a tongue, though."

Rory bumped him back. "Nope, no tongue. I was thinking of getting one of those petal things though."

"Petal things?"

She sighed. "It looks like a rose and it, uh, simulates oral sex. Just hadn't gotten around to it yet."

He was gonna get hard again thinking of Rory using sex toys to get herself off. "Don't need it, babe. You've got me. You don't need Gus either."

"I don't know, Chance. This isn't supposed to be permanent. I might need those things when you leave."

He tipped her chin up with his fingers and forced her to look at him. "Not leaving, Rory. And I'm not sleeping on the couch anymore, either. You can't put the whipped cream back in the can."

He thought she might argue but she giggled instead. "Did you just compare yourself to whipped cream?"

"If it makes you laugh, then yes, I damn sure did."

She reached over to caress his dick. It was still half hard but the second she touched it, it started to swell. "Mmm, I want to lick this like it was covered in whipped cream. Think you can handle that?"

He took her hand gently and pulled it up to kiss her fingers.

"Babe, I want nothing more. But we gotta get your blood sugar up and I have to get to work."

"Go ahead and point that out, why don't you," she grumbled.

"Somebody has to be the adult around here. Now what do you want for breakfast? I collected eight eggs, by the way."

"Mmm, eggs. How about scrambled eggs with toast?"

"Want cheese on those eggs?"

"Yes, please."

"Okay, baby. Whatever you want. Let's see if you need more juice first."

When her blood sugar was stable, she went to take a shower while Chance dragged on his clothes and headed for the kitchen. He got to work cracking eggs and whipping them together, grating cheese, and getting out the toaster. By the time Rory walked in, her damp hair a golden tangle down her back, he nearly had everything ready to go.

She wore jeans with work boots and a flannel shirt over a tank top today. Chance thought there was probably nothing his woman wouldn't look amazing in. She looked country, but he liked that. Sexy country, because Rory was a girly girl and loved makeup and glossy hair.

"You ready for me to make the toast and scramble the eggs?"

"Yep. I took my bolus insulin and I'm ready to eat."

Chance popped the toaster on and poured the eggs into the pan he'd started heating when he heard her walk across the bedroom floor after her shower. When it was ready, he took everything to the table, poured fresh coffee, and sat down to eat with her.

When he'd stayed before, she hadn't shared as much about her insulin pump or the way it worked as she had this time. Mostly, they'd had sex and talked and had more sex. Neither one of them had talked about the truly personal stuff.

It'd been about the kinds of things they liked—TV shows, foods, bands—and disliked. They'd acted more like a dating couple getting to know each other. Now it was more intimate. He liked it that way.

Chance

Didn't feel temporary, no matter what she'd said about it not being permanent.

Was to him. And it was gonna be permanent to her too. She just didn't know it yet.

Her phone pinged with a text. She picked it up to look. He knew from the way her expression changed that something wasn't right.

"What is it?"

"It's Carl Hoffman. He's been baling the hay and buying it off us for his cows at a reduced price for the past eight years." She turned the phone so he could look but whipped it back around before he'd finished reading and read it aloud instead. "*Sorry, can't do the hay this time. Found a better price over in Madison and I have to go where I can afford to get it. Hope you understand. Carl.*"

She put her head in her hands. "Not what I needed today. Eight years of baling and taking the hay and now this? There's no way he's getting that hay cheaper. No way."

"Can you get somebody else?"

She lifted her head. "This late? I don't know who. We don't have the baler anymore. Granny sold it when Gramps died. We weren't going to bale anymore, and it seemed like a good decision, especially with Carl being willing to bale and buy. It's worked well for years. The grass gets cut and we make some money from it. Thing is, with the damage at the Dawg and the temporary closure, we could use the cash. If the health inspector doesn't let us open today…"

She didn't finish her thought, but he knew what she was thinking. If the hits kept piling up, then the situation was going to get worse quickly. They would need to borrow against the farm to cover the debt, which Rory didn't want to do, but at least it was an option when it hadn't been before.

Chance pictured Ronnie Davis and his son sitting in that booth at Miss Mary's, listening to him make his speech. Junior's was the more interesting reaction, but Chance would bet his right nut it was Ronnie Davis who was behind Carl Hoffman pulling out of his agreement with Rory. Man like that had money and liked to throw it around in order to get his way.

"Do you think Carl Hoffman would sell his land if Davis Properties offered for it?"

Rory's eyes went wide. "That son of a bitch." Her chair scraped back but Chance caught her wrist, held her.

"No, baby. No going off half-cocked on a theory. And definitely not right now when you've got to worry about your health more than usual, okay?"

Her cheeks were red but she nodded. "You're right. But I can't let them get away with this. I don't know that Carl would sell, or even that they'd want his land. It's not connected to the Turtons or Coombses like mine is. He's on the other side of town, closer to the refuge. Davis Properties can't want to start dealing with federal regulations regarding protected land just to spite me. But they *could* give Carl enough cash to make it worth his while to buy hay elsewhere this year. Maybe for a couple of years. Assholes." Her gaze was troubled. "What are we going to do about it, Chance?"

His belly tightened and his heart squeezed. She'd asked him what they were going to do. She was trusting him to help figure it out, to make things right. She wasn't trying to go it completely alone for a change.

"I don't know. Yet," he emphasized, squeezing her hand. "This isn't a simple matter of knocking heads together, kitten. But give me some time, okay? You worry about what you need to do for your health. I'll see what more I can learn about the situation."

"No offense, Chancey Pants, but I've lived in Sutton's Creek a lot longer than you have. I don't think you're going to learn anything I couldn't with a phone call or two."

"I don't doubt that, babe, but who said I was limiting my search to Sutton's Creek?"

He got to his feet and kissed her forehead before tipping her head back to kiss her lips. One touch and he wanted to take her back to bed. He broke the kiss and caressed her cheek.

"I have to get to work. But you can trust me to take care of this for you. I'll tell you what I learn, and we'll go from there."

"Okay," she said, her voice barely more than a whisper. "I'm trusting you. Just so you know, this is not easy for me."

"I know. Now finish your eggs, baby. I'm trusting you to do that while I head out. Taking Clyde, by the way. You can have my truck today."

She stuck out her lip. "Who says I want your mangy old truck? It's a tin can compared to Clyde."

He laughed. "Honey, everything's a tin can compared to Clyde. But Clyde doesn't have crumple zones and my truck does. I'd feel better if you took it."

"Fine," she huffed. "What's his name?"

"Uh, Ram truck?"

"No, that's the brand. Never mind, if I have to drive him again, I'll name him. You'll be informed when I figure it out."

Chapter Thirty-Four

CHANCE'S TRUCK WAS NAMED CHUCK NORRIS. RORY KNEW AFTER her drive to town. Chuck was badass. It was the only name that fit for a big truck that chewed up the pavement and had all the bells and whistles, which Chuck did. He had a huge screen in his center console that could show a map. It could also show all her podcasts in one place, or her playlists—pretty much whatever she wanted to display. Chuck was also powerful, which she enjoyed as she pressed the accelerator and flew down country roads.

She'd finished breakfast, cleaned up the dishes, and decided to head to the Dawg. The health inspector was supposed to arrive by eleven, though she didn't plan on holding her breath. In her experience, any estimation of when an inspector would be around was more of a guideline.

Maybe they'd get lucky today. She certainly hoped so.

But the knot in the pit of her stomach wouldn't ease. She'd texted Carl back, said she was sorry to hear he couldn't cut the hay and could she perhaps offer him a discount. Of course he hadn't responded. She really hadn't expected he would. If Ronnie Davis had offered him money to go elsewhere, then Carl wasn't going to want her hay no matter what kind of deal she offered him.

It hurt that someone she'd known since she was a little girl could betray her that way. On the other hand, Carl had been raising cows for decades and anything that made life a little easier was bound to be welcome. Going to Madison to buy hay wasn't a betrayal in his book. It was very likely business and knowing the value of a dollar.

Rory parked Chuck, gathered her backpack and her giant steel cup of water, and opened the door. Colleen had the hatchback to her Volkswagen open. She looked up as Rory alighted on the pavement.

"Morning, Rory."

"Morning, Colleen. What've you got there?"

Colleen was hefting a black duffel bag that clanked as it shifted. "Oh, these are my new chains. For the exorcism chair."

"Uh, okay. Do you do many of those?"

"Not too many, but enough. You have to get new chains every few cycles. The demons are hell on steel."

"I did not know."

"Most people don't." Colleen shrugged. "It's only important for those of us who guard the portals and keep humanity safe."

"Well, thank you. For your service, I mean."

"You're welcome. I've been called to serve by the Almighty, so I do."

"How do the aliens fit into it?" Rory asked. Because she really wanted to know. As long as she could remember, Colleen had been either seeing aliens or relieving people of demonic possession. In between, she did seances, told fortunes, sold crystals, and gave ghost tours of Sutton's Creek. She was a busy woman with all her enterprises.

"They don't fit. They are simply aliens." Colleen blinked like this was sufficient.

"Oh, okay. I didn't realize."

"Again, most people don't." Colleen frowned. "I'm getting a message from my spirit guide…." There was some quiet chanting, or mumbling, before she spoke again. "It's time for you to be very careful, Aurora. There are forces out there that would do you harm."

Rory shivered from the chill that slid down her spine. It was May, not October, but it seemed that Colleen could be spooky whenever she liked.

"I'm always careful. I don't trust anybody."

Colleen's expression turned solemn. "You will have to make a choice very soon, I think."

The chains clanked again and Rory jumped. Then she was mad at herself for doing it.

"Well, better get going. Work to do. Have a good day, Mrs. Wright."

"Thank you, dear. You too."

Rory headed through the back door to find Theo at work in the kitchen, prepping his ingredients for the lunch service. "Do you know something I don't?" she asked, still trying to shake off the chill of what Colleen had said. A choice? What the heck was she talking about?

As if Colleen was an oracle. Rory nearly rolled her eyes. Kooky old woman. That's all it was. All it'd ever been.

He looked up and grinned. "Nope. It's the power of positive thinking at work. Besides, if they don't let us open up, we need to use this stuff anyway. I'll pull out the grill and have a cookout in the parking lot. We'll give it all away but I'll put up a tip jar for those who want to donate. Maybe it'll help us with expenses."

Rory blinked. "I wouldn't have thought of that. Since you aren't selling the food, I don't know why it wouldn't fly. Good plan."

He shrugged. "Thanks. Guess we'll find out soon enough." His gaze narrowed as he studied her. "Something's different about you."

Rory felt herself coloring. "Nothing's different. I'm pregnant. Hormones are a thing, you know."

"Then why are you blushing?"

"I am *not* blushing. Stop being annoying." She cleared her throat. "Here's what's different, though it's not about me. Carl's getting hay in Madison. He won't be cutting and baling for us."

Theo looked as shocked as she'd felt. "You're kidding. He's been doing it since before Gramps died, when Gramps no longer could."

"I know."

"Fuck. It's the farm, isn't it? They want to buy it and they're doing whatever they can to squeeze us. They got to Carl."

"I wouldn't be surprised. But we don't know for sure, so we can't go confronting anyone about it. We have to be cool and stay in our lane and hope, if it's them, they do something that gets them caught."

Theo's eyebrows climbed his forehead. "Wow, listen to you being all reasonable. What happened to my firecracker sister who charges into situations breathing fire and ready to knock heads together?"

"Pretty sure it's hormones. And maybe Chance. He says he'll come up with a plan. I'm trusting him to do it."

Theo put down his knife and came around to hug her. Rory hugged back, laughing. "What's this for?"

"Congratulations, Pix. Never thought you'd fall for a guy again, but I guess I was wrong."

"Who said I've fallen for anybody?" Her heart started to thrum. "He's in the security business and I trust him. That's all it is."

Theo let her go, laughing as he went back to his chopping. "Sure, you tell yourself that. But I've never known you to let anyone tell you what you needed to do and then for you to actually do it. You don't let people take care of things for you. Never have. This is new."

Rory's blush was a full on fire. "I'm an adult. I'm not unreasonable. This is his area of expertise, not mine, and I intend to take his advice. That's all it is. Now if you're done analyzing everything I say, I'm going to the office. Let me know when the inspector arrives."

"And now you're running away because you know I'm right," he called out.

Rory held up her middle finger and kept on walking. Theo's laughter followed her up the stairs.

Chapter Thirty-Five

Chance entered some numbers on the keypad and then he was inside the secure lab where GRL scientists and engineers were working on components and software for the Athena Project. He'd secured the access codes and breezed in while most everyone was on lunch break. One lone woman sat a desk with a computer screen in front of her. She lifted her head and blinked at him like he was a unicorn riding into her lab on a rainbow cloud, trailing glitter.

"You aren't supposed to be in here," she said, her brows drawing together once she'd composed herself.

Chance glanced at the name on her lab coat. *Crowell.*

Caroline Crowell. Interesting. He flipped a page on his clipboard and made a check mark. Not for any reason other than to make her wonder.

"Well, Ms. Crowell, I am in fact supposed to be here. Chance Hughes with One Shot Tactical and Security." He held out his hand. She took it, but she wasn't pleased about it. As soon as she could, she let go. "We're testing the security procedures for Griffin Research. I'm here to make sure the system is operating as it should."

Her expression didn't change, but he could sense her nervousness. "The system?"

"The security system."

"Oh, yes, of course."

"I don't want to keep you, ma'am. I'm just going to do a random check and then be on my way."

Caroline nodded. "Fine with me."

She bent to her work again and Chance made a circuit of the lab. He made sure Caroline wasn't watching him, exchanged a couple of charging cables with the ones that Seth had given him, pocketed the real cables, and made his way to the door.

He wasn't worried about Caroline reporting him. If she did, then Griffin Research Labs' security personnel would likely be called to the carpet again. Not his problem.

Seth and Kane were waiting in the conference room where they'd set up their own little HQ. There was a question in Seth's eyes as Chance walked in. He took the real cables from his pocket and set them in front of Seth who picked them up and examined the ends.

"You did it," he said, a grin breaking over his face.

"You doubted?"

"Hell no. Anybody there when you went in?"

"In fact, yes. Caroline Crowell. She seemed intent on her computer screen. Once I explained I was authorized to be there, she went back to work."

"Huh. Not a crime to work through lunch," Kane said.

"Nope." Seth opened his laptop. "Let me just check we have connectivity."

"That's scary, dude," Kane said. "A USB cable with built-in WiFi and a keystroke logger? Who the fuck knew?"

"Yep, sure is. Leave it to hackers to figure out how to steal your shit. And yep, we're connected."

They weren't worried about anyone listening to their conversation because Seth had deployed an audio jammer. Not the level of security they'd need to talk to anyone outside this room, but enough they could talk a bit more openly than they otherwise would while hanging out in their target's building.

"I still don't get how this is gonna work," Kane said. "It's not hooked to her computer. It's hooked to a random terminal."

"Doesn't matter. The system in that room is interconnected with the secure internal system the company uses. It's all accessible now."

"How do we know somebody else—the Russians, for instance—don't already have access?" Chance asked. "What if someone inside that room already swapped in one of these cables? How would anyone know?"

Because he couldn't stop thinking about the danger. This was end of the world shit, and he was finally in a place where he cared too much about living. He wanted to make love to Rory, hold his child the day it was born, talk Rory into marrying him, and maybe learn how to bale hay and renovate an old farmhouse in his off time.

He wanted to live and grow old in Sutton's Creek more than he'd wanted anything in his life. Even more than he'd wanted to rewind the clock the day his dad died and stop his mother from shooting. That'd been an angry, lonely child's fantasy. It had never been possible. Living life with Rory *was*.

But first they had to complete their mission and keep Athena safe.

"They wouldn't know," Seth said. "That's the problem. And yeah, it's possible. All we can do is follow the trail and hope we get there first. But even if we don't, we'll know what their plan is. Then we'll stop it before Athena can be used against us."

Chance wanted to march back down to that secure lab and pull Caroline Crowell up by her lapels. Then he wanted answers. But what if she didn't know the answers? What if she was exactly what she said she was, a software engineer who spoke Polish and Russian and was trying to take care of her sister after a tragedy?

Ghost Ops didn't operate on assumptions. The mission was too critical. Get it wrong and the consequences would be catastrophic.

"Hey, man," Kane said. "How's it going with Rory? She still hate your guts?"

Chance's gaze jerked to his teammate. Kane was watching him with an arched eyebrow. Chance understood that his friend was trying to distract him from dark thoughts.

"I think it's mild dislike now," he said. "I'm growing on her."

"Dude, when you told us she was pregnant, I thought Ghost was going to stick his boot up your ass before ripping out your guts with his bare hands."

Chance snorted. "Yeah, he took it a whole lot better than I thought he would. Thank God."

Kane looked thoughtful. "I think she's a good woman who's afraid of getting hurt. Somebody must have done her wrong in the past."

Chance wasn't going to talk about Rory's business to anyone else, but Kane was perceptive. "Maybe so."

"I told him he needs to fight for her," Seth said. "Make her see he's good for her. Because the woman's pregnant and they're gonna be around each other for the rest of their lives. Why not give it a go?"

"Good advice," Kane said, tipping his head at Seth. "Can't say it's not."

Chance put his feet on the table and picked up the sandwich he'd ordered for lunch. "What about you, Kane? You've got the hots for Daphne so why not just ask her out?"

Kane started shaking his head like he'd been told a bee had landed on him. "I do *not* have the hots for Daphne Bryant. Why do you guys keep saying that? She's too young for one thing. And she's not my type for another. I'm protective because of the way we found her. She was legit scared to death. Bothered me, and I don't want her to feel like that again. I want her to know she's okay with us, that's all."

Seth glanced at him. "So you're fine with her going out with Warren Trigg?"

Kane's frown grew. "She could do better. That dude is creepy. Always staring at her. Holding her hand. Talking too soft. She needs somebody who can protect her. He's the kind who'll piss his pants and cry at the first sign of trouble."

"Maybe not," Chance said. "Still waters run deep and all that. Dude might be a badass when it counts."

Kane snorted. "Doubt that. So long as he doesn't hurt Daphne, nothing I can say about it. She picked him. Must be something about him she likes. Can't see what that might be though."

"He loaned her a car, for one thing. You might want to get off your ass and help her find one of her own so she doesn't feel obligated to him. Not good for a woman to feel like she owes a man something."

"I'm already on it," Kane said. "Taking her to look at something after work tomorrow. I don't want her driving his car any longer than she has to."

Chance figured Daphne had probably accepted the loan of the car to get Kane to act. Not that she couldn't go on her own, but she'd admitted early on that she didn't know anything about cars. Kane did. He'd worked as a mechanic before he'd joined the military, which was why he was the logical choice to help her find a used car that wasn't a lemon.

"Your new camera system's in," Seth said, looking up from his computer. "Just got the delivery notice. Now you can count Ronnie Davis's nose hairs from a hundred yards away if you want."

"Good. Gonna install them after work. I wouldn't say no to some help if y'all are inclined." He could install them himself but it'd go faster with more people.

"I got nothing else going," Seth said.

"Me neither. You think the Dawg'll be open today? I really need some fried chicken soon."

"Health inspector was coming this morning. Unless the Davises are bribing government employees, I think they've got a good shot at opening."

Kane's look was not friendly. "If those assholes are bribing health inspectors and I don't get Theo's fried chicken because of it, I'm gonna make your little speech to those two jerks look like a friendly visit from the Sutton's Creek welcoming committee."

Chance couldn't have agreed more.

Chapter Thirty-Six

It was five o'clock and the Salty Dawg Tavern was officially open for business. Rory filled glasses and mixed drinks while Amber, Nikki, Perry, Susan, and Jen waited tables. Yes, they'd had to call everyone in, even the part-timers, but everyone had answered the call.

In the kitchen, Theo was as happy as a pig in mud, fixing dinner plates, frying burgers and wings, and directing his kitchen staff to chop, dice, plate, garnish, and watch timers.

It was chaos, but it was the kind of chaos Rory loved.

Mostly, since she was still more tired than usual. She was also a little bit sore in areas that hadn't been used in a couple of months, but she liked the feel. Every time she moved, she was reminded of Chance thrusting into her body and taking her to nirvana.

When the One Shot Tactical team strolled into the restaurant around seven, Rory's heart thumped and her mouth went dry. Amber was waiting for the last drink on the tray when it happened. She turned to look at Chance and then fixed her gaze on Rory again. Her mouth was a flat line.

"I can tell by that look there's more going on with you and

Chance than you let on. I wish you'd told me that from the beginning. I'm not the kind of person who'd poach on another woman's territory."

Rory flushed as she set the last beer on the tray. "You're right and I'm sorry. I thought it was over, intended it to be, but apparently we aren't done."

Amber's smile was back as if it'd never been gone. "Honey, I don't see how you could be done with a man that fine. Ride him for all he's worth, girl. If you decide to throw him back, I won't go there. You're my boss and my friend and you mean too much to me. In case you didn't know."

Rory blinked in shock. Her heart revved a little higher and heat prickled her skin. "I… Thank you, Amber. I appreciate it more than you know."

Amber hefted the tray. "Do you think I'd ever forget what that lying bitch Tammy did with your fiancé? Now she's over there in Decatur, thinking she's better than all of us when she used to wait tables here every night. She's not, though. You can dress up dog shit with glitter and douse it with perfume, but everybody knows it's still dog shit."

Rory watched Amber stride away, her eyes stinging with tears. Chance broke away from the group and strode over to her like a man on a mission. The concern in his eyes nearly undid her, but she sniffed her tears back and pasted on a semi-watery smile.

"Babe, you okay?"

He reached across the bar and cupped her cheek, a blatant act of possession that ought to be stomped back down, but she liked it too much. Who cared what people thought anyway? They already thought Chance was a warrior monk who'd taken a vow of chastity, but had broken it for her. The latest rumor she'd been asked about that'd left her slack-jawed.

She'd literally gaped at Miriam McClinton for nearly a full minute when the woman had told her that one. Then she'd laughed and said that Chance was definitely not a monk and never had been. Nor was he ninja or a SEAL. He was just Chance, a man with a military background who didn't take kindly to strangers threatening her and Theo.

"Yes, I'm fine. How about you?"

Blue eyes searched her face. Her heart ached at the concern she saw there. "So long as you're okay, I'm good."

"I am."

He tugged her toward him, leaned across the bar, and planted his lips on hers. She vaguely thought she shouldn't let this happen in front of God and everybody. But again, she liked it too much. Her mouth parted, his tongue slipped inside, and she shivered with delight and anticipation as Chance Hughes kissed the fire out of her in front of the entire Salty Dawg Tavern.

"Damn," he said against her mouth when he broke the kiss. "I have a new fantasy about laying you out on this bar and feasting on you while you writhe beneath my tongue."

"Don't say stuff like that," she begged. "It's too long until quitting time."

He stepped back with a grin. That was when she noticed all the eyes on them. Heat rushed to her cheeks, but really, did she give a crap? Let the fine women of Sutton's Creek envy the stuffing out of her for bagging a hot, protective alpha male who really oughta be on romance novel covers with those smoldering good looks.

"Guess so, but the minute we walk through that door tonight, I'm taking what's mine."

"Not if Gus gets there first," she teased, thankful they were still close enough she could say it without anyone hearing her.

He laughed. "Think I'm gonna dropkick that thing into the Tennessee River one of these days soon."

"Don't you dare."

"We'll see. Glad the inspection went well, baby. Kane's been jonesing for fried chicken and threatening to put a hurting on the Davises if he didn't get it."

"The inspector was late. In fact, the first inspector didn't make it at all. I called to ask for an update and found out he was out sick. So they sent somebody else. I thought he was going to deny us at first, because he was super picky, but he signed off and here we are. Thank God."

Chance nodded. "You got this, babe. You and Theo will make up the ground you lost. You've got enough for the staff, right?"

"Yes, but it woulda been close if we'd been closed any longer."

He leaned over and kissed her again. "You aren't, though. Care to tell me what you and Amber were talking about that made you teary?"

"You noticed that?"

"I notice everything about you, Rory."

Warmth flooded her. "I was apologizing for not being honest about you and me being a thing, and she was telling me that even if I break up with you tomorrow, she won't go there. You're persona non grata to her now."

"Thank God. I've never wanted Amber. I've only wanted you."

"Amber's pretty sexy with those tight shirts and shorts."

"She is, but she doesn't do it for me. You do."

Happiness filled her though she tried to temper it. She had to be sensible about this. Not let her head stay in the clouds. But when he said things like that, it made her feel lighter than air.

Jen strolled up to the bar with a tray and an order. Rory nodded at her. "Gotta get to work, Chancey Pants. Stop distracting me."

He winked and grinned and her insides lit up like fireworks on a summer night. "I'll distract you later. With my tongue."

"No doubt you will. Get lost, warrior monk."

His eyes widened a fraction. "That's the rumor now?"

"Yep, and I'd say you just confirmed for the entire bar that you broke your vow of chastity for little ol' me."

"Good grief, this town."

"Maybe next time you'll think twice about telling off the Texans in public, huh?"

"Not if they're harassing you. I don't care what people say so long as those assholes leave my woman alone."

There it was again, that shiver of excitement whenever he called her *his* woman. "Caveman," she said, but she couldn't hide the affection in her voice.

He took a step back. "Pretty sure you like cavemen, kitten. Or minotaurs."

"Beat it, Conan."

"Gone, babe. But not too far."

He turned and strolled into the crowd, Rory watching his fine ass in those jeans as he walked. Jen was grinning when Rory finally dragged her attention over to her.

"I mean I get why you'd stare," Jen said. "I stared too, just so you know."

"Who wouldn't?" Rory said. "That is one amazing ass in jeans."

"And out of them?"

"None of your business," Rory said with a smile. "Now what do you need?"

———

THE CROWD LIGHTENED a bit as the evening went on. Everyone came over to chat with Rory about the closure, to sympathize over the mold scare, and to offer help if she and Theo needed it.

It was the offers of help that affected her most of all. These people she'd known her whole life were willing to step up if she needed them to. She felt a little like George Bailey on Christmas Eve when the whole town turned out to dump money onto the table in front of him. If she and Theo needed any cash to get them through a rough spot, the town would be there. If they needed labor or favors or grace, the town would be there.

She would never ask them for it. Theo wouldn't either. But knowing that so many people were willing to pitch in with cash or services was enough to make her want to cry.

Chance came over to talk to her from time to time, and Emma Grace did too until she and Blaze left to go spend the evening together with Sassy. Rory envied Emma Grace her easy relationship with Blaze, but the envy wasn't as strong as it'd once been.

Sure, she didn't know what to make of Chance's declaration of love, not really, and she wasn't ready to believe it was a real thing that wouldn't change whenever he got tired of dealing with her medical issues, but she was enjoying the attention he lavished on her for now. It was nice.

A few minutes after nine, Jimmy Turton slid onto a barstool and made eye contact. Rory smiled. "Hey, Jimmy, what'll you have?"

"Bud Light. Bottle, please."

Rory retrieved the bottle and set it in front of him. Jimmy looked tired. More than that, he looked pensive.

"You doing okay, Jimmy?"

"Yeah, yeah, just fine." He took a swig of the beer and rolled the bottle between his hands. "Nice to see you open again."

"Happy to be open."

"Heard it might not happen what with the mold and all."

Rory stiffened. Of course people would have speculated. "There is no mold. We had the building thoroughly inspected and the flooded areas treated."

Jimmy nodded. "You were lucky. Old buildings like this don't always behave so well. Might not the next time."

"The next time?"

He shrugged. "Don't mean nothing by it. Just observing that y'all were lucky and the building is old."

"It is and we were. Any other observations?"

"Yeah." He rolled the bottle again as if gathering his courage. "Don't know how to say it so I'm just gonna. Mama's willing to sell if you do. Billy and I need this, Rory. We need Mama to sell up and get that house in town, and we need to get out from under the land. Mr. Davis is offering a lot of money. Money that could change our

Chance

lives. Yours and Theo's too. If we don't do it now, we might never get another chance."

Rory's stomach bottomed out. "Jimmy. I'm really sorry, but I don't think that's fair. You can't lay that on me. If y'all want to sell, then do it. But don't make me selling a condition of you doing so."

Jimmy's eyes flashed as he glared at her. She nearly took a step back. He'd never looked at her like that before. Not ever. It was anger and frustration and maybe, just maybe, a little bit of hate all rolled into one.

"You don't get it, do you?" he growled. "They won't buy the land unless all three of us sell. It's five-hundred acres and your puny farm is in the middle. You can't build the kind of development they want to build with two parcels separated by forty acres. If we don't all sell—all of us—they'll take their money somewhere else. You can't want to see the rest of us suffer because you're stubborn. It's not fair and it's not right. Take the money. Hell, use some of it to buy a smaller plot and move your grandparents' house, but for God's sake, don't make us all suffer for your selfishness."

Shock froze her to the spot. She would normally have a comeback for that kind of accusation, but she couldn't think of a thing to say to Jimmy that would make it better. The Davises wanted all the land and wouldn't buy any of it if they couldn't get it all. But how was that her fault?

It wasn't, but they were damned sure making it hers. First the garden, then the pipe and the hay, none of which she could prove they'd done. And now this. If they couldn't push her out financially, were they planning to try and guilt her out?

"I'm sorry," she said. "I don't know what to say."

"Say you'll sell the goddamn farm, Rory. Sign on the dotted line and think about more than just you and your brother for a change. Christ, you two take the cake. You don't even want to farm, but you keep it anyway when you have this."

He waved his hand around above his head before slapping it on the bar again. Rory jumped at the violence of the sound. She

253

opened her mouth to say something, though she didn't know what, but Chance was suddenly there, looming large and angry next to Jimmy.

"You'd better not be threatening Rory," he growled.

Jimmy glared at Chance. "Or what, big man? You gonna beat me up and leave me for dead like you threatened to do to the Davises?"

"Something like that," Chance said, his voice milder than was safe for anyone. Not that Jimmy seemed to realize it with the way he got off the bar stool and faced off with his hands clenched into fists at his sides. Like he had a shot in hell of besting Chance at anything resembling a fight.

"You're no better than she is," Jimmy spat. "Aurora Harper, always too good for everyone, seeking attention back in middle and high school with her episodes—" He used finger quotes on the word episodes. "—lording it over the rest of us with her land and her thriving business. And now she has a guard dog to threaten decent folk who only want to improve this town? How does she pay you, Fido? With cash or pussy? Or maybe it's both."

Rory squeaked as Chance moved. She thought for sure Jimmy was a dead man but Chance did something that had Jimmy facing the door, marching toward it with Chance behind him, holding his arms and pushing him forward until the two of them disappeared outside.

Customers ran for the door, spilling out onto the street to watch the fight. But there was no fight because Chance was back moments later, followed by grumbling people as they returned to the Dawg and went back to their tables. It was worth noting that the One Shot guys who were still there—Kane, Ethan, and Seth—hadn't even gotten up from their table.

"What did you do?" Rory whispered, her throat tight as Chance stalked over, looking angrier than a cat that'd been given a bath.

"Nothing except deposit him on the street and tell him what would happen if he bothered you again."

"You can't threaten everyone who gets angry with me, Chance."

"I fucking can, Aurora. And I will. Nobody gets to cuss you in public and say the things he said. Nobody disrespects you that way. Nobody accuses you of seeking attention, for fuck's sake, with a disease you didn't ask to have and don't deserve—"

She held up a hand, effectively stopping his tirade in its tracks. Anger simmered beneath the surface, but she worked to keep it under control. "Nobody deserves any disease, Chance. But it happens, and by God I won't be made to feel like I'm somehow less than because I have it. Not by you or anyone else. No I don't deserve it, but nobody does. Doesn't change the fact I have it. You are not allowed to feel sorry for me. That's the one thing I can't abide. I'm still *me* and I'm perfectly fine just the way I am. It'd be easier without diabetes, sure. But having it doesn't make me pitiable, you hear me?"

He was staring at her with wide eyes. They were already close because the conversation was private, but he leaned across the bar to bring them closer. "Jesus, Ror, I don't pity you. I've never met a less pitiable person in my life. The things that you deal with on a regular basis would take down anyone with less guts than you have. You have my admiration, not my pity. But I can't let anyone talk to you that way. It fucking hurts *me* when someone hurts you. I won't stand by and say nothing. I know you can fight your own battles, and do it all the time, but some battles I'm gonna armor up and take out the trash for you. Same as you'd do for me if the situation warranted it. You feel me?"

"I think so. And I'm not mad at you for throwing Jimmy out. He was out of line and deserved it, though yeah, I feel bad that I'm the one standing between him and the new life he wants, but I also suspect that's Ronnie Davis being a manipulative prick. He can build his massive development on four-hundred-and-sixty acres just as well as five-hundred. If he says he can't, then he's either lying or stupid."

"He's a rich man used to getting his way. It pisses him off that one small woman is going to stand between him and his vision. I don't think he's lying or stupid. He just wants his way, and he's willing to do anything to get it. Some people are shit like that, babe."

Rory dragged in a breath. Amber was walking over with an order. "I need to fill orders. We've still got an hour and a half 'til close."

"How you holding up? Glucose okay?"

She wasn't even mad that he asked. "I'm tired, but I'm fine. Glucose is fine. I ate earlier. If you're hanging around because you're worried about me, then don't. I'm good."

"I'm hanging around because I want to be near you. Put up the new cameras after work with the guys, locked up the chickens, and checked everything over. No reason for me to be there when I want to be here with you."

He leaned across the bar and pressed a kiss to her mouth. Second time tonight, though this one was less sizzling than before because tongues didn't get involved.

Probably a good thing since the fire between them had barely been contained the last time.

"Let me know if you need anything, baby," he growled in her ear. "I'll make sure it happens. Be thinking about what you need when we get home, because I'm gonna give you that, too. Until you can't walk or form a coherent sentence."

Chapter Thirty-Seven

Rory looked exhausted by the time she was done closing up for the night. If she was anyone else, she might not be as resistant to being told she needed to go home sooner, but after the way Jimmy had talked to her, Chance thought he had an idea why she was so insistent on doing things herself.

Still, when they went out the back door with the others, Chance steered her toward his truck. When he took her to the passenger side instead of the driver's, he could feel her starting to stiffen.

"Wait a minute. What about Clyde?"

Chance opened the door and waited for her to climb inside. She didn't, of course.

"Clyde'll be fine in the parking lot tonight."

"And what about tomorrow morning when you have to go to work?"

"Blaze can swing by and get me. Already talked to him about it."

"So you made plans without asking me?"

"Rory, you're dead on your feet. You're growing a human, for fuck's sake, not to mention working your ass off tonight with the reopen, so yeah, I made a plan. You gonna follow it or fight me?"

She frowned for a second. "Fine."

Chance closed the door behind her and went around to get behind the wheel. He had to wedge himself in, cussing, then press the memory button to get the seat to go back to his position.

"To be fair," Rory said, "I thought I was driving Chuck home again so I didn't put the seat back."

"Chuck? You named my truck Chuck? As in Chuck the Truck?"

She sighed. "No, you asshat. Chuck Norris the Truck. Because he's badass. Just like you."

"Thanks. I think."

"It's a compliment. How did you get Jimmy turned around so quickly without him throwing a punch? Because he looked like he wanted to."

Chance pressed the button to start the truck and the engine roared to life. "You want to know that, you gotta take a class out at the range. Proprietary information, babe."

"Seriously?"

He loved how outraged she sounded. "Nah, I'm fucking with you."

"For the record, I prefer the other kind of fucking."

His groin tightened. "Me too, kitten." He reversed out of the spot and hit the main street. "It's something they taught us in the Army. Whenever somebody's coming at you, you step into the swing, not away. You can deflect it and gain control by throwing them off balance. I simply moved before he had a chance to swing, because he was definitely planning on it."

"You anticipated his move and blocked it."

"Blocked and took control. He was emotional, too, so that didn't help him. I jammed his arm high on his back and he had no choice but to move where I wanted."

"I'm glad you didn't hit him." Rory was quiet for a moment. "I didn't want those *episodes*, as he called them, when I was a kid."

His throat tightened. "Of course you didn't."

"I was thirteen when I finally got diagnosed, but I had some problems before then. I'd be really thirsty and then I'd have to go to the bathroom a lot because I drank so much water. One time a teacher wouldn't give me a pass and I almost peed my pants. But I got so desperate I ran out of the classroom and down the hall to the bathroom. The teacher called my granny. She came to get me, and I slept for what felt like a week. I was irritable, moody, and sometimes I was so hungry I thought I'd never get enough to eat. I even wet the bed sometimes. That was horrible."

He reached over and took her hand. She squeezed his fingers. "After I was diagnosed, it wasn't any better in some ways. Some kids made fun of me because I had to get my glucose tested and I took shots. This was before I had the pump and monitor. Those things made life so much more normal, but I didn't get them right away. They were expensive, for one thing, and not as prevalent as they are now." She sighed. "I used to ask why me back then. I was angry and scared, but Granny told me that nobody asked to be sick, ever, and that there were degrees of sick. My sickness was controllable, so I needed to do everything I could to control it. So that's what I did. I've gotten really good at it, too, and that's why I get mad when people patronize me or think they know what's good for me better than I do. I don't feel helpless anymore. But when Jimmy said what he did about my *episodes*, it took me right back to middle school when I tried to be strong so the other kids wouldn't bully me. But I'd get weak, or I'd have a low-sugar event, and they'd say things about me being defective or they wouldn't want me near them in case it was catching. Stupid stuff like that."

"I'm sorry, honey."

"Thanks. Emma Grace never took part in any of it. She was always by my side. I think she wanted to be a doctor back then and I was kinda her first patient in a way. She looked after me like a hawk. My grandparents let me go to her house and go on vacations with her family because her dad was a doctor. I often wonder if he hadn't been, if I'd have been allowed to spend the night with anyone or go to the beach. I doubt it. My grandparents were already scarred from losing my parents, so I don't think they'd have trusted anyone else with me after my diagnosis."

"Understandable."

"It is. You know, you haven't asked if our kid's going to have diabetes because I do."

His heart squeezed. "I know there's a slightly higher risk because you have it, but that doesn't mean it'll happen. If it does, we'll handle it."

"I should have realized that one of the red flags with Mark was when he started asking me if I was worried our kids might be diabetic. I said I wasn't for the reason you said. Then he wanted to do genetic testing before we tried to get pregnant. But I already know I don't have any of the genes that can make you higher risk. I was tested when I was a kid. Don't remember why, though maybe my grandparents insisted. Anyway, he still wanted to do it, so I said I would. Then he ran off with Tammy and the point was moot. I always wondered if he made her get tested to see what kind of shit might be lurking in her genetics. Probably didn't since she didn't have any obvious defects. Unless you count being a back-stabber. But then he is too so they were made for each other."

He hated that people she trusted had hurt her. "Sorry you went through that, but think you dodged a bullet there, babe."

"It hurt like hell at the time, but I definitely did. I can't imagine he'd have been happy at the farm. He'd have had to commute to Decatur, which isn't far, but every time he drove across the bridge and through the historic district, he'd have wanted to move over there. If I'd gone with him, I'd be the one who was miserable." She shook her head. "Nope, I'm better off without him. But I'm still pissed I spent money on a wedding that never happened. At least I sold the dress on Marketplace and got some money out of it."

Of course she had. Rory was nothing if not practical.

They reached the farm and he turned into the driveway and

went up to the house. The lights were on, because she'd set her interior lights to come on at dusk now, and the motion light on the porch lit up as they crossed in front of it. He'd had alerts on his phone for the new cameras, but it hadn't been anything other than a few deer and one possum who went foraging near the barn.

They went inside and Chance left Rory to go and do his checks of the barn and outbuildings. Just because the cameras hadn't shown anything didn't mean he wasn't going to be thorough anyway. Just in case.

The chickens were quiet but a peek inside told him they were fine. The garden was still standing. The barn loomed, a dark shadow in the night. The moon would rise later tonight, but everything was dark until he crossed the motion sensors and the lights came on.

He walked through the center of the barn and toward the outbuildings. Something came to him on the slight breeze that stirred. A whiff of spent gasoline, like from a four-wheeler. Chance withdrew his gun and crept forward, scanning the area and wishing he had some night vision goggles right about now.

Everything was quiet, though. Nothing stirred except a startled deer. He looked for tire tracks and found none so he kept ranging toward the tree line. He stepped into the trees, following that scent that only teased at his nostrils. Whoever had been there was gone now. They'd probably left when he'd turned into the driveway.

Fucking hell, he was gonna have to put a trail cam in the woods. He hadn't done it because the woods were vast and he hadn't thought he'd need it with the others he'd already installed. Clearly did if somebody was planning to lurk in the woods instead of venturing out into the open.

A twig snapped and he stopped to listen. But a shuffling in the leaves on the forest floor told him it was an animal foraging. He started to move again, searching for tire tracks in the leaves. The forest path was free of tracks, which meant somebody had deliberately avoided it.

He'd been gliding through the woods a good ten minutes when a motor revved a few yards away before speeding into the night. The forest muffled sound and obscured the direction, but he calculated it was moving west, same as the last ATV that'd visited when the garden was destroyed.

Whoever it was, they were smart enough not to trigger the cameras or the lights. But they'd been lurking in the woods, planning something. It was only when he'd gotten too close that they'd sped away.

Chance clenched the grip of his Glock as anger swirled in his belly. Somebody was hell bent on harassing his woman and forcing her to sell her land.

The choices were obvious. Jimmy Turton. Carter Coombs, who'd yet to say a word to Rory about the potential sale. And Ronnie Davis.

Chance didn't know which of them it was, but he'd start with Jimmy since he'd been so utterly pissed tonight. Davis was sleazy, but he was the sort to throw money around instead of resorting to criminal activity. Junior was capable of it, but only if Daddy let him off the leash. Chance didn't think Ronnie would risk doing that. Too much as stake, and Junior was a classic hothead.

Chance scouted where the ATV had been hidden behind some brush, looking for any clues. There was nothing but tracks where the driver had gunned it.

He gave up and headed for the barn, intending to walk through one more time before going back to the house. His phone buzzed in his pocket and his heart squeezed with concern as he answered her call. "Everything okay, babe?"

"Yes," Rory said, sounding sleepy. "But I was worried. You've been gone a long time."

Thank God she wasn't having a problem with her blood sugars. "Just checking things out."

He could have told her the truth, but he didn't want to. He'd tell her tomorrow, when she was rested. Or maybe he wouldn't. He didn't want her storming over to the Turton farm or confronting Carter Coombs. Or, worse, tangling with the Davises again.

Because she would. Rory had taken enough shit from people during her life that she'd learned to fight back hard and fast.

That was his job now. Fighting for her. Protecting her. Loving her.

"When are you coming inside?" she asked.

"On my way now, kitten. Be there in five minutes."

"Good. I missed you. Can't sleep until you're here."

It wasn't a declaration of love, but he'd take it. "You already in bed?"

"Yes." He heard her yawn. "I'm gonna need a raincheck on that hot sex you promised me. Too tired tonight."

"There's always tomorrow, baby."

"You promise?"

"I promise."

She sighed. "If you leave me after all this, I'm going to be hella pissed. I might even buy a voodoo doll from Colleen and stick it with pins. Not that she sells those, but I bet she knows where I can get one."

"Kitten," he said softly, laughter and love mingling in his chest. "I'm not leaving you. I love you."

She didn't respond right away. When she did, her voice was softer than before. Wounded. "I've heard those words before. They didn't mean anything in the end."

Fucking loser ex-fiancé.

"Yeah, well I've never said them to anyone before you. I've made it thirty-five years of my life without falling for a woman. Until you. Think I know how deep and true those words are for me."

He thought she sniffled. "You make me want to believe."

"I want you to believe it, honey." He stepped onto the back porch and slipped his key—the spare—into the door, his eyes stinging with emotion. "Coming inside now, Rory. Then I'm gonna get ready for bed and hold you all night. We'll talk more tomorrow."

"Okay, Chancey Pants. But I… I like you. A lot."

"I like you, too, honey. So damn much."

"Hurry. I can hardly keep my eyes open."

Chance locked the door, set the alarm, and shed his clothes on the way to the bedroom. Less than a minute later, he was in bed beside his beautiful, sweet, prickly Rory, gathering her into his arms and kissing her forehead. She sighed and curled her fingers into fists against his chest.

She was asleep almost immediately. But he lay awake, thinking about the ATV in the woods. Wondering who'd been there and what they intended to do. Why had they waited? As soon as he and Rory had arrived, they should have gone.

Unless they'd been thinking about harming more than property this time.

Chapter Thirty-Eight

Morning light was streaming into the bedroom when Rory woke to the feel of a hard dick between her ass cheeks. Not literally, but Chance was wrapped around her, holding her close, and her ass was pressed to his groin. She shifted and pressed backward. She was rewarded with a sleepy groan.

Rory turned and pushed him onto his back, ripping her top off. She was smart enough not to wear bottoms to bed since she'd started having sex with Chance again. All he wore was those form-fitting boxer briefs, which she dragged down his hips with a little help from him.

"Whatcha got in mind, babe?" he asked, lying on the sheets in all his naked glory, his dick standing tall and ready for her.

"So many things," she purred, sliding down until she was between his legs. She grasped him in both hands and he groaned again.

"Rory."

"Chancey Pants."

She licked him from balls to tip and he stiffened. "Fuck, baby."

"That's the plan," she laughed before sucking him into her mouth as deep as she could. Which wasn't all that deep, but it was enough to make him swear and slide his hands into her hair to grip her head gently.

"You're gonna kill me," he groaned as she set up a rhythm of sucking his cock and squeezing his balls the way she knew he liked.

"Mmm," she said, swirling her tongue around the tip, catching that salty bead of moisture that appeared.

She loved looking at him while she sucked, loved the way his eyes gleamed, the strain of muscles in his abdomen as he watched her. The way his neck corded as he worked to keep his orgasm at bay, and the little sounds he made when she sucked a little harder or licked around the crown, or squeezed his balls just right. Every bit of it was intoxicating.

She didn't remember ever feeling this way before, but she told herself it was the pregnancy hormones. She was flooded with the kind of things that made her want to touch and be touched, to explode with pleasure and then do it all over again as soon as she caught her breath.

She'd been hot for Chance before but now it was almost painful the way she wanted him. The way she needed him.

He reached for her, dragging her away from her focus on his dick. Even as he did so, he was mindful of her pump and monitor. Chance never forgot, even when he had to be out of his mind with need, that she had them.

Rory climbed onto his chest and canted her hips until she could lower herself onto him. He raised his torso off the bed until he could suck her nipples, sending arrows of sensation into her core as he tended first one and then the other.

Rory sat for a minute, getting used to him, before she started to move. "Oh my God, it feels so good."

Chance lay back and glided his thumb over her clit. Then he rounded her body with his other hand and teased her back

Chance

entrance. She'd never been someone who thought of anal sex as something she wanted to try, but that little bit of a fingertip that invaded her with each thrust heightened every sensation.

And Chance knew it. He knew it so well that he stopped manipulating her clit and focused solely on her backside, tormenting and teasing as she rode him faster.

"You're so fucking sexy," he said. "I love watching you ride me, Aurora. If I died right this minute, I'd still be a happy man."

"Don't you dare die on me. Oh God, how did you know that would turn me on so much?" she said on a moan.

"I didn't. Not until the first time I did it. But you love that little tease, baby. Makes you wild."

It really did. Rory moved faster, dragging herself along the length of him, sinking deep, her body starting to shake with the sensations building to a crescendo inside.

The next time she sank down on his cock, Chance thrust his finger a little deeper into her ass—

And Rory exploded. She would have collapsed on him but he gripped her hips and kept thrusting, milking her body for everything she could give.

He came deep inside her, his body arching up into hers, her name a hoarse groan on his lips.

It was everything she'd ever wanted, and more. It was her romance novel sex come to life, though maybe not with horns or fangs, or five dicks all intent on pleasing her, but it was hot and sexy and so tender it made her chest ache.

Chance reached up and took her throat in one big hand, gently pulled her down to him, and kissed her. "Damn but I fucking love you, Aurora Harper. Never felt this way with anyone but you."

Rory folded onto his chest like an accordion. She wanted to tell him it was the same for her, that she'd never felt this way before. That she was pretty sure she'd broken all her rules and fallen in love with him, too.

But the words wouldn't come. They were stuck, dammed up behind a wall she'd erected a long time ago and didn't know how to breach.

Maybe it was safer. What happened if she said the words and then he left her anyway?

———

RORY FELT FANTASTIC FOR A CHANGE. After she woke Chance with hot morning sex, they'd had shower sex in her dinky shower, Chance sliding into her pussy from behind while she pressed her hands to the tiles and held on as best as possible while he fucked her into another shattering climax that left her breathless and boneless.

Once they were done, bodies dried off, he'd wrapped her in a towel and then dried her hair with another before combing it carefully until there were no tangles left. Then he left her to dress while he took care of the chickens, returning to make ham and cheese omelettes with toast for breakfast while she sat at the kitchen table and watched him work.

She felt loved, and it was confusing. She told herself not to rush into this, to let her feelings unfold naturally. To exercise caution.

But she didn't want to. She wanted to throw herself headlong into a life with Chance Hughes and this baby they'd made. Scary. Dangerous.

Tempting.

Her phone rang, interrupting her chaotic thoughts. She knew it was Emma Grace by the ringtone.

"What's up, Doc?"

"You will never get tired of that, will you?" Emma Grace asked.

"Nope. Too many Bugs Bunny reruns as a kid." She and Theo had watched them often because her grandmother had said they were her dad's favorite cartoons growing up. "You're calling about Jimmy Turton, am I right?"

Chance

Emma Grace blew out a noisy breath. "Yes. What was that asshat thinking anyway?"

Chance was at the counter, chopping ham into bits. Rory sighed at the sight of his fantastic posterior in those faded jeans. Already, she was getting a little prickle of arousal in the lady bits. Apparently, twice wasn't enough for her in the morning.

"I don't know," she said, dragging her attention back to her friend. "I think he's just desperate to get his mother to sell the property so he can have a different kind of life."

"I'm not sure how reliable this is, because I heard it in the bakery first thing, but Wendy said she heard that he called you a whore and then Chance beat his ass."

"Oh Lord. No, he didn't call me that. He asked Chance if I paid him in pussy to be my guard dog, which is probably where that came from. And Chance did *not* beat his ass, though he threw him out on his ass right after that."

Chance threw her a look. She mouthed "Emma Grace" just in case he hadn't figured it out. He nodded and went back to prepping breakfast.

"That's certainly a more reasonable version than what Wendy told me. I mean I know Jimmy's crass, but I don't think his mother would approve of him calling anyone a whore in public. Though I guess suggesting you pay someone in sexual favors is the same thing."

"Pretty much. He's mad, and I get it. It's not entirely his fault, though I'm not letting him off the hook for being a dick. The people to blame in this mess is D&B Properties. They told him they'll only buy all three parcels, not a single one. I guess I'm the holdout. I haven't heard from Carter that he's selling, but I have to assume so if Jimmy's haranguing me in public about being selfish."

"I spoke to Dolly Coombs yesterday. She said he wants to sell. He's ready to retire. I don't think it's what she wants him to do, though."

The ATV tracks from the garden had come from the direction of Coombs land a few days ago, but Rory didn't picture Carter climbing on a four-wheeler, riding through the woods, and destroying the garden in some wild plan to visit financial hardship on her and Theo. He was a quiet man in his sixties—not that sixty-somethings weren't capable of doing dumb things. But she just didn't see it. He and Dolly went to the First Baptist Church every Sunday, where he was a deacon, and he volunteered with the fire department after working all day on the farm. Carter and Dolly had four sons; a doctor, a lawyer, a diesel mechanic, and the youngest, Jack, who was still in high school. Jack helped his dad on the farm, but Rory didn't know if he wanted to take it over or not.

Gramps and Granny had liked the Coombses. They'd liked the Turtons, too. Called them salt of the earth people.

"I hate that the Davises are manipulating everyone this way. Just buy the two farms and build around me, for heaven's sake."

"If they really want this development to go forward, they will."

"I never thought I'd say this, but I hope you're right. I'll get used to seeing subdivisions where there used to be farmland. If it helps Carter and the Turtons to sell, then I hope Ronnie Davis stops being a jerk and buys both farms. He doesn't need my forty acres, too."

"Hopefully he'll come to that conclusion soon. Okay, gotta run, babe. My next patient is here. Just wanted to check in and learn the truth about last night. I'm glad Chance didn't beat Jimmy up. I have a feeling that wouldn't be an even match."

Rory winked at Chance as he slid a plate in front of her with a big omelette and toast glistening with butter. "You mean you think a ninja-assassin-warrior-monk-Navy-SEAL is too much for a redneck farm boy from Sutton's Creek?"

Emma Grace laughed. "I definitely think so. Jimmy is scrappy and strong, but he probably doesn't have the moves. Unless he took a self-defense class over at One Shot Tactical."

"I'm gonna doubt that."

"Me, too. Talk to you later, Ror."

Chance

"Later."

Chance poured more coffee and brought it to her, then sat across from her. "She wanted to know the truth about last night, huh?"

"Yep. Apparently Jimmy called me a whore and you beat him to a pulp."

Chance shook his head. "Gotta love the way a rumor grows as it makes its way around town. I'll be honest though and say beating his ass is exactly what I wanted to do."

Rory took a bite of her omelette. "Mmm, so good. Thanks."

"You're welcome."

"So why didn't you?" she asked after she scarfed another bite.

Chance sighed. "I didn't want to disappoint my guys. We're in this business together, and something like that would reflect poorly on all of us. But don't think that means I won't do whatever it takes to keep you safe, Rory, because I will. That situation didn't warrant violence so much as removing the offender from the premises."

Rory couldn't help but grin at him. "Listen to you. Not only a pretty face and hot body, but you've also got a brain in there. You're smart. Who knew?"

He snorted. "Smartass. Yeah, I've got a brain and I know how to use it."

"I'm relieved. Means our kid will get smarts from both parents instead of just one. I was worried, I gotta admit."

"You weren't," Chance said, grinning at her. "Brat."

"No, I wasn't." She sipped her coffee, enjoying herself more than she would have thought possible a few months ago. Back then they'd poked at each other for a reaction. "Listen to us sparring back and forth and not getting mad at each other."

"I haven't said Hotty Toddy yet."

"I don't think I care if you do. So long as I'm getting the big D on the regular, I can overlook your faults."

"You can have all the D you want, kitten. Does this mean you're gonna let me stay with you longer than it takes to deal with whoever's been sneaking around your property?"

Her heart squeezed. She'd told him it was temporary, just until he caught the asshole, but she wanted this. Mornings like this at the breakfast table. Nights together on the couch. Making love, eating food, sitting on the porch together. All of it.

She didn't want him to go back to the range to live. She wanted him here. Couldn't imagine waking up without him in bed beside her.

"You can stay for now, I guess. We'll see how it goes."

Because of course she couldn't let herself think it was permanent. Not yet. Maybe not ever.

He reached across the table and took her hand in his. "It's going to go better than you expect, kitten. I promise you that."

Her heart was hammering. "The jury's out, but so far you've been doing a pretty good job of cooking and taking care of business in the bedroom. Oh, and feeding the chickens, collecting eggs. You're a handy guy, Chancey Pants. Keep up the good work."

He laughed and slid his chair over next to hers. Then he kissed her temple while she took a bite of toast. Her entire body shivered at his touch.

"I love you, Aurora Harper. Like it or not. I'm gonna prove it to you, one way or the other."

"You can try."

"Intend to. I didn't tell you this last night because you were half-asleep, then we were a little busy this morning, but there was an ATV in the woods when I did my rounds. I don't know who it was or why they were there, but they took off when I got close."

The shiver of his nearness turned into a different kind of shiver. "Could have been Jimmy. He was mightily pissed off last night."

"He was. They went west again but that could be a ploy to make us think it's someone else. Could also be RJ, doing his dad's dirty work."

Chance

"Or somebody looking to steal tools or copper or you name it from Gramps's copious collections of junk."

"Do you really think that in light of everything else that's happened?"

Rory shook her head. "No. But I'm really tired of these jerk offs sneaking around and trying to scare me off the land. Makes me even more determined to stay."

"I know it does, babe. Need you to be careful though. Arm the system when you're here alone, and don't let anybody who'd benefit by a land sale into the house if they show up wanting to talk. Call me and I'll drop everything. Still working on that security overhaul in Huntsville so it'll take a little bit, but I'll send one of the guys until I can get here."

Fresh fear nipped at her but she was determined not to let him see it. She hadn't had an alarm system when Kyle Hollis walked into her house. Hadn't known she needed one, but she did now. She hated that she had to be suspicious of people, but she'd learned her lesson. She wouldn't let anyone in who she didn't trust.

"I'll call the police and then you."

He nodded. "That works. I'll still send one of the guys over, though." His phone dinged. He glanced at it and slid his chair back to stand. "Blaze is coming up the drive. I gotta get going."

She didn't want him to leave, but she bit the inside of her lip to keep from asking. Since when did she need a man around 24/7? She had Liza Jane and a phone. She could handle herself until it was time to go to the Dawg. And she wouldn't be here alone at night, which seemed to be when the cowards showed up anyway.

"You'll stop by the Dawg later?"

"I'm coming here first, see if anyone's hanging around in the woods but yeah, I'll be there."

Her pulse skipped. "Please be careful, Chance. I don't want anything to happen to you. I'm just starting to like you."

He laughed and tipped her chin up with a finger, pressed a quick kiss to her mouth. "Love that smart mouth, Aurora. You can use it on me later tonight."

"If you're lucky."

He winked and strode away. She heard him grab his range bag, heard the door open and shut. The lock engage.

She wanted to get up, run to the door and rip it open. Tell him she more than liked him.

But she didn't do it.

Instead, she cut into her omelette and daintily ate another bite.

Chapter Thirty-Nine

It was a long day at Griffin Research Labs, setting up new security protocols and training everyone to follow them religiously. Seth grumbled about the lack of information coming across his fancy hacker cables. Or, rather, there was plenty of information, but none of it was a smoking gun.

It was proprietary and important, what the engineers were working on, and it would take time to analyze the coding for flaws, but there weren't obvious red flags pointing to any single person in the lab.

Yet.

Seth remained convinced that Caroline Crowell—Callie to her coworkers—was the most likely suspect. Chance didn't disagree. The woman had spent time in Poland, spoke Polish and Russian, and had incentive to earn extra money. Maybe it was a stretch to think that she'd want to sell out her country to keep her sister in horses, but stranger things had certainly happened.

It was also possible they were barking up the wrong tree with the secure lab. There were others who had access to it even if they didn't work inside it all day. Could be one of them instead of someone actively programming.

By the time they were finished at the lab and heading back to Sutton's Creek, it was after seven. Chance texted Rory to let her know he'd be late. It took a few minutes, but she texted back that everything was fine, the Dawg was busy, and so was she. Then she texted a heart. Embarrassingly, he spent far more time than a grown man ought to spend trying to figure out what she meant by it.

He thought she felt more than she let on, but he couldn't be sure. Sex between them had been hot the first time they'd been together. It was still hot, but it seemed to have an emotional component now that hadn't been there before.

Or maybe it was just him reading too much into it. He certainly felt strong emotion when he was inside her, touching her, listening to the sounds she made and seeing the pleasure on her face. But what did she feel?

She said she liked him, a lot, and that was something. She also agreed that his stay with her was more than temporary. Yeah, he'd noticed that she'd added a caveat, but agreeing to it in the first place was huge for her.

Then there was the way she worried for his safety when he said he was heading to the farm tonight to check for the trespasser. Rory kept her feelings close, but she cracked them open from time to time. It was progress.

When he and the guys reached the range, Chance swung his bag into Clyde and fired him up. He wanted to go straight to town, park behind the Dawg, and walk inside to feast his eyes on his woman. The pull to do so was strong, but first he needed to head to the farm and poke around.

He decided to pull into the trees a little distant from the entrance and walk. Maybe he'd surprise somebody if they didn't hear him coming. He slid on his kevlar vest, checked his weapons, and jumped the split-rail fence. The house was lit up, the lights coming on at dusk now. Rory had said everyone knew she wasn't there, but he'd convinced her it was a good idea anyway. People who hadn't lived in Sutton's Creek their whole lives wouldn't know if she was home or not. They wouldn't know *who* was there, but they'd suspect someone was.

It was usually enough to deter opportunistic criminals anyway.

He slid through shadows, avoiding the motion sensor lights, and headed for the woods. There was no scent of spent gasoline in the air tonight. The woods were quiet, but he ranged deeper than he had last night, curious. The night birds stopped their noise when he passed beneath them, but the foragers only paused in their scraping of the forest floor.

There were black bears in this part of Alabama. Coyotes. Even now he could hear their yipping back and forth. There were bobcats and wild boars, too. And gators, but those were down in the wildlife refuge a good ten miles away.

None of them scared him. He knew how to avoid them, and how to get away if he needed to.

He found tracks from the ATV in an area where the ground was still wet after the last rain more than a week ago. The tracks were fresh, probably from last night. He followed the trail until he came to a place where they bent suddenly north. The trail was more obvious here, because there was a path through the woods that somebody would have likely rode at this point. They would have felt deep enough in the woods by now, and far enough away from Rory's place, to no longer have to hide.

They should have, but they hadn't because they'd thought they were safe by then. Idiot.

Chance followed the trail until it came out near a dirt road. He didn't know whose land he was on anymore, but the dirt was still damp enough to show tracks that turned sharply east. Turton land was east. Whoever had been in the woods rode a huge circular path to try and obscure their direction.

He was pretty sure last night's visitor was Jimmy. Maybe Jimmy'd been the one who'd destroyed the garden, too. If he'd done it, why had he done it? And was he the same man who'd crept up Rory's driveway in a car and disappeared toward the barn?

If so, what had he been up to that night? It didn't make a lot of sense, but maybe he'd decided to check things out before he came back to destroy the garden. He might have been casing the place, deciding. It was also possible he'd intended to do something then but lost his courage.

Chance wasn't sure how the Davises figured in yet, but he was positive they did. There was no way those two slime-balls weren't involved.

He growled in frustration as he stood on the dark road, looking in either direction, thinking about Jimmy Turton and the Davises. Then he spun around and headed through the forest, back to Clyde, back to town.

Back to Rory.

When he strode into the Dawg, she was behind the bar, pulling beers from the tap, laughing with customers, looking as beautiful as ever. Her blonde hair was in a ponytail, sleek and glossy, and she wore a black tank top beneath one of her plaid shirts with jeans and tennis shoes.

Rory was country, but country was perfect in his estimation. He hated that her ex had hurt her, but he was damned glad the man had stepped aside and left her for him to find.

He went over to the bar and waited. When she turned and saw him, the smile on her face lit him up inside. That feeling of home was there, stronger than ever. He wanted to walk around the bar, bend her over his arm, and kiss the fire out of her right there. Claim her in front of everyone. Leave no doubt who she belonged to.

"Hey, Chancey Pants," she said as she walked over to him. "What'll you have?"

He leaned toward her. "You, kitten."

She blushed a little. He liked it. "I mean to drink, mister."

"Oh, that. Gimme a Rebellion lager, please."

"I can do that." She grabbed a glass and put it under a tap. "How was work?"

"Good. I missed you."

She smiled again. "I missed you a little bit whenever I thought of you. Every once in a while."

He laughed. "Oh, that often, huh? I'm growing on you."

"Like a fungus," she said with a grin. "You want to order anything to eat? I can put it in for you."

"I don't think you have my first choice on the menu," he said with a wink. "For my second choice, I'll take a burger with fries. No cheese."

Rory tapped his order into the system, her skin pinker than usual. "Got it, big boy. Here's your beer. Now skedaddle so I can work."

"Yes, ma'am."

He carried the beer over to One Shot's usual table. Seth and Ethan were there. Ghost was playing pool with a hot brunette who seemed to be giggling a lot. Kane and Daphne were probably still looking at the car, and Blaze and Emma would probably be home doing whatever it was they did at this time of night.

"Find anything?" Seth asked when Chance dragged a chair out and sat.

"Tracks. They went west, then north, then finally east."

"Toward the Turton's farm."

"Yep." Chance sipped the beer. Damn but there were some mighty fine microbreweries in northern Alabama.

"We need to pay a visit to Jimmy?" Ethan looked as angry as Chance felt inside.

"Thinking about it. You hear anything more about Ronnie and Junior yet?" he asked Seth.

Seth shook his head. "Not yet. I can ping my contact again. I'll do it tonight."

"Thanks. Appreciate it. Think they can dig into Jimmy too?"

"I'll ask. Can't hurt."

Chance nodded and took a sip of the beer. "Sooner the better. Think I'll avoid Jimmy until then, unless he comes in here and makes another stink."

"Probably a good idea," Ethan replied, throwing a glance to where Ghost stood with pool cue in hand, concentrating on the table in front of him. "Don't need you going ninja assassin on his ass and giving the boss a heart attack."

Chance snorted. "Yeah, probably not."

He studied the crowd inside the Dawg. A few people glanced over at him but most minded their own business. No doubt they were wondering about him and Rory. Or wondering where he'd trained to be a warrior monk ninja assassin.

He seriously couldn't imagine what they were going to say when news of her pregnancy got out.

For now, it was a secret because Rory wanted it that way. The people who already knew—his team, Emma, Theo—wouldn't talk until they were given permission.

She couldn't hide it forever, but it was up to her when she wanted to tell the news. He wanted to put a ring on her finger before that happened, stake his claim publicly. Wasn't going to be easy, because Rory was adamant she would never get engaged again after the last time.

Since he couldn't actually plan a wedding yet, because of the mission, maybe she'd agree to a long engagement with no pressure to choose a date. And then, when Ghost Ops was done and he was free, he'd convince her that marrying him was the best decision she'd ever make.

One step at a time. That's how you planned a battle. And how you won a scarred woman's heart.

Chapter Forty

It was raining when the Dawg closed for the night. Rory was tired, but she miraculously found enough energy to throw herself at Chance as soon as they were inside the house. It was like lightning had been building beneath her skin all day and now she needed his touch to release it.

It stormed outside, but it was storming inside her body too. She needed to make the storm stop, and she only knew one way to do it.

"Baby," he said, his voice hoarse as he ripped his shirt off while she shoved his jeans down his hips. "I missed you."

She dropped to her knees and took him in her mouth, as deep as she could, her hands gripping his perfect ass as she started to suck. He tried to stop her when he got close, but she didn't let him. When he groaned and shot semen into the back of her throat, she drank him down while he stiffened and groaned her name along with a few cuss words.

She let him go, licked his balls for good measure, and got to her feet feeling very self-congratulatory. She loved making Chance lose control. It was one of her favorite things to do.

The lightning inside her still sizzled, but it was more stable now.

"Come here," he growled.

"Think I'm going to take a bath," she said, turning away. Teasing him. He caught her around the waist and she squeaked as he lifted her and carried her over to the couch. He tossed her down on it, stripped her naked, and buried his face between her legs while she giggled.

Well, she giggled until his tongue was on her pussy and then she moaned, her fingers tangling in his hair and holding him there while she pressed her hips against him, riding his tongue like she rode his cock. The lightning whipped and cracked as her body climbed higher.

"Yes, like that. Oh God, Chance, you know how to eat pussy right."

She knew he loved it when she talked dirty, but she loved it too. It was a release to say all the naughty things that crossed her mind. And there were plenty of them considering the books she read on the regular.

He teased her back entrance with a finger, then pressed the tip inside the way he knew she liked. He hadn't done that during oral sex yet, but it was enough to make her detonate with a hoarse scream.

She was still shuddering when he turned her over, lifted her ass in the air, and drove his cock into her wet core. His finger moved in rhythm with his body, entering her again and again while he fucked her. When his other hand strummed her clit, she was done for, coming hard, her body clenching around his almost to the point of pain.

He came a moment later, filling her, until they collapsed on the couch together, breathing hard.

"Wow," she said when she found the breath.

"Wow," he echoed, his mouth on her shoulder, his tongue grazing lightly until it reached her ear and tickled the shell.

Rory shivered. His weight was heavy, but he wasn't pressing her

Chance

into the couch completely. As always, he was conscious of her medical devices.

"I missed you, too," she admitted, her voice small. It was a lot for her to give him that, but her heart throbbed with feeling.

"Thank you. I know that wasn't easy to say."

And now there were tears pricking her eyes. Stupid hormones. Or maybe it was just him. Chance, being sensitive and beautiful.

"You're welcome."

He lifted himself and cool air wafted across her back. But then he gathered her in his arms and carried her to the bedroom. When they were tucked beneath the sheets, the sound of raindrops hitting the roof, she threw a leg over him and pressed her ear to his chest, listening to his heartbeat.

Her throat ached with unspoken words, and her eyes stung as she blinked back a fresh wave of tears. What the heck was wrong with her? Why did everyone else fall in love and get on with living, but she got caught in the what-ifs and the fear she'd get her heart broken again?

Emma Grace had dated a serial killer, without knowing it, who'd abused and gaslighted her. Then he'd stalked her to Alabama and set up an elaborate game to get revenge on her for leaving him. Meanwhile, with all that shit in her recent past, she'd managed to let Blaze Connolly into her life.

The best thing she'd done, clearly. He was good for her. Good to her. Emma Grace had found the strength to fall in love, even after what she'd been through. That love had saved her.

Chance skimmed his fingers down her back, up again. "What are you thinking about?"

She pressed a kiss to one gorgeous pec. "Life."

"Mm, pretty broad topic. Anything specific?"

"Not really. Just stuff."

He didn't say anything for a while. Then, "I need to tell you something."

Fear rolled down her spine, froze the walls around her heart.

Her breath stopped in her chest. This was it. The big reveal. The moment he told her something that he couldn't take back. She wanted to tell him not to do it, not to break her heart by revealing he was already married or something equally awful, but she didn't.

"Okay."

"I told you that my mom shot my dad because she thought he was having an affair. What I didn't tell you is that I was the one who confirmed it for her."

She pushed away until she could meet his gaze in the dim light coming from the air purifier. "Oh, baby. I'm so sorry."

"It's okay." He sucked in a breath. "I told you my mom was depressed, probably schizophrenic. She didn't seem like a real mom a lot of times and I got mad when she'd fail to do the things other moms did, like make lunches or pick me up from school. I wasn't even allowed to have sleepovers because she couldn't deal with it. Anyway, my dad was a lawyer. He saw a lot of clients for lunches and dinners, things like that. One day, when I was at the country club pool with friends, he went into the restaurant with a client. A beautiful woman I'd never seen before. A few days later, my mom asked me if I'd seen the woman. She had a photo. I said yes. I didn't even ask why. I just wanted to go to the pool with my friends."

She knew what'd happened next because he'd told her before, though without the picture of the woman. "Chance, it's not your fault."

"I know. Mostly. I struggled with it as a kid, had counseling. It's why I acted out, I think. I felt guilty. For so fucking long, I felt guilty."

His voice was tight. He was still struggling. Rory skimmed her palm up his arm, over his cheek, into his hair. Just touching, soothing. "What did the counselors say?"

"That it wasn't my fault. That I was a kid. That nothing I said made her do what she did. I didn't make my mom kill my dad. I didn't light the match. She was the one who was broken, not me. The bitch of it is, it wasn't an affair. The woman was seeking a

Chance

divorce and didn't want to talk to anyone in her town because she didn't want her husband to find out before he was served."

A tear slipped down her cheek. She ached for the child he'd been. Thinking he'd caused the incident that took his parents away from him. Being shuffled through the system, acting out, nobody loving him like he deserved.

"Do you hear me, Rory? Really hear me?" he asked, his voice gentler than before.

She sniffled and raised her gaze to his again. "Yes, Chance, I hear you. You know the counselors were right, don't you? That it wasn't your fault?"

"Yes. Even if I still struggle sometimes, I know they were right. She was the one who was broken. She made the choice. And baby, that's what I'm trying to tell you. The fact your asshat of a fiancé chose to screw your bridesmaid and run off has always been on him. It's nothing you did, or could do. He's the broken one. And at some point, you have to realize that never trusting anyone again, never being willing to risk your heart, is the same thing as me thinking I caused my mom to murder my dad and change my life forever. It's not you. It's not me. It's them. The broken ones."

She couldn't stop the tears that spilled over this time. "But what if I'm broken too? Have you thought of that? Because I am, Chance. I feel things deep inside and I do my best to squash them. I build walls. I'm too afraid of breaking any further that I have to protect what's left of me. Don't you get that?"

He gathered her to him again. She could feel his heart tapping a hard rhythm. She almost pushed him away, but she couldn't do it. Instead, she melted in his arms because it was where she felt safest.

"Rory, baby. I love you," he whispered in the darkness. "You aren't broken. You're scared. There's a difference. Feeling things is good. Building walls is normal. All I'm telling you is, once you realize you didn't cause Mark's betrayal, that it wasn't anything wrong with you, then maybe you'll realize you can let yourself love me without fear. Because the only thing taking me away from you is prison or death, you hear me?"

A chill shuddered over her. "What kind of talk is that? Prison or death?"

"It's just talk, kitten. Those are the two things that I can't fight when it comes down to it."

"Don't kill Jimmy, or either of those Davis assholes, and there'll be no prison. Right?"

He gave her a squeeze. "Right."

"You wouldn't, would you?"

He tipped her chin back to look into her eyes. "I would, but only if they hurt you. Then I don't care what happens to me."

The fierceness in his voice stunned her. "I care, Chance. A lot."

His teeth flashed in the darkness, cutting through the seriousness of the moment. "Think you just admitted a little something, honey."

She couldn't help but grin back, though she was still scared too. "Maybe I did. Don't let it go to your head."

"I won't."

She fell asleep in his arms, the rain slapping the roof harder now that the storm had picked up, the wind blowing through the trees outside. Her body was content, but her dreams were troubled.

Chapter Forty-One

CHANCE THREW ON A RAIN JACKET AND HEADED OUT TO FEED THE chickens. Rory was still in bed, sleeping, and the rain was still coming down, though not as much as last night. There was a flash flood warning for all the creeks and tributaries of the Tennessee River that ran in and around the land here like veins inside a body. In some ways they were veins, providing water to the crops that the original farmers had planted. They still provided water for farms and animals to this day.

Developers like Ronnie Davis ruined some of the smaller veins in the name of progress, redirecting them, hiding them underground with drainage systems while they built subdivisions and retail spaces on land that'd once provided food and cotton. Sutton's Creek had managed to avoid big developments for years but it was at their back door now, knocking insistently.

Chance opened the coop and scattered feed, collected eggs, and headed back to the house to remove his muddy boots and hang the rain jacket on the back porch. Today was Friday, the last day he, Seth, and Kane had to be at Griffin Research Labs for security training. They'd placed the cables, gotten the employee dossiers, and now they had to sit back and wait for someone to make a move.

The information on Caroline Crowell looked the way it should. Her background and security checks, her education. So far, it checked out. But Seth wasn't done yet, which meant they weren't dismissing her as their potential leak.

But at least it would be done from their office at the range instead of inside the company, which meant Chance would be closer to home for now. Until the threat to Rory was dealt with and Ronnie Davis either bought two farms instead of three, or gave up the idea altogether, he'd rather be a ten to twenty minute drive away rather than forty-five minutes to an hour in traffic.

Rory was at the kitchen table when he walked in, a cup of coffee in her hands. Warmth glowed in his chest at the sight of her. She centered him in a way that'd been unexpected at first. He wanted to do that for her, so badly, but there was no rushing Rory. She'd come to her senses when she came to them and not a moment before.

"Hey, Baby Daddy," she said with a sunny smile. "I poured your coffee."

"Thanks, honey. Baby Daddy, huh?"

"I'm trying out new nicknames. That one doesn't quite have the ring to it I'd hoped."

"It's clunky. Not to mention it gives away the secret, don't you think?"

She grinned. "Well, I wasn't planning to use it in public just yet."

He set the eggs on the counter. Over a dozen today. The bowl she kept them in was overflowing, but he expected she would take a bunch to Theo. They didn't do breakfast at the Dawg, but Theo needed eggs for some of the dishes he concocted. Anything he didn't need would go to Miss Mary or Wendy.

Chance hadn't realized you could keep eggs on the counter until Rory explained that so long as you didn't wash them first, eggs were perfectly fine staying out and would keep for a couple of weeks. Washing them thinned the membrane and meant immediate refrigeration. The things you learned on a farm.

"How do you feel this morning?" he asked.

"I feel good. Glucose is fine. Need to eat soon, though."

"You want scrambled or omelette today?"

"I think I want to cook for you this time. How about an egg sandwich with smoked gouda cheese and mayo?"

"Sounds delicious. What do you need me to do?"

She stood and grabbed his hand, tugged him over to the chair she'd vacated. "Sit, BD." She sighed. "Nope, that doesn't work either. Guess we're sticking with Chancey Pants."

He chuckled as he sat. She took her coffee and pulled his from across the table.

"Drink. Talk to me. I'll cook."

"Okay. What brought this on?"

She took out a pan, put butter in it, and turned on the gas. "I was making my own breakfast before you shoved your way in here, you know. Just thought it was my turn."

"Shoved my way in, huh?"

She waved the spatula around. "It wasn't my idea, if you'll recall. You see one random dude on the security cams and suddenly you're moving in. Then you're cooking breakfast, feeding chickens in the rain, and giving me orgasms. I feel obligated to do something nice for you."

"Kitten, I feel like you do something nice for me every time we're naked."

"Of course I do." She cracked eggs in the skillet and toasted the bread. "I can't believe I'm going to admit this, but I like having you around."

She didn't look at him as she said it. He knew it was another big admittance for her. He could tease her, lighten the moment. But he didn't. He told her the truth. "I like being around."

She finished the sandwiches and brought them to the table. When she put his in front of him, she bent and kissed his cheek. "I'm trying, Chance. I heard you, and I'm trying."

There was a knot in his throat. "I know, baby."

Chapter Forty-Two

Despite the gloomy day, Rory felt lighter than air. She hadn't had this kind of feeling in, well, she couldn't remember how long. She'd spent so much time worrying about the farm and the Dawg, her brother, her best friend, everyone she knew, really—was Miss Mary's sciatica acting up today? Did Wendy's daughter still have a fever? Was Mrs. Sutton really doing fine after her heart attack last year? Was Amber okay? How about Colleen? Was her obsession with demons and aliens a sign of dementia or did she just live in an alternative universe from the rest of Sutton's Creek?

Rory had always kept a running litany in her head of the people she knew and whether or not they were recovering from whatever minor ailments or setbacks had assailed them. Granny had been the same, though Granny made casseroles and took them to people. Rory just served them drinks or dinner and gave them discounts or freebies when things were really bad.

Maybe it was why she was a good bartender, always listening to people talk, offering opinions and sympathy or congratulations when necessary. But she'd carried the worries of the Dawg, and even her brother, for so long that it'd gotten heavier than she'd realized. Until Chance started looking out for her, really looking out for her, she hadn't known how heavy the burden of thinking about everything and everyone was.

She told everyone she was fine, that she could handle it, but sometimes you needed another person to be there and help you shoulder the load. Didn't make you weak or incompetent.

Things she'd always feared because of her disease. She'd been at such pains to prove she wasn't different from other people that she'd sometimes taken on too much.

And maybe she'd always have that tendency, but she was going to try and let others be there for her.

Starting with Chance, who'd tended to the chickens in the rain, cleaned up the breakfast dishes despite her telling him she could do it, and carried laundry downstairs for her before he'd had to leave for work. He'd kissed her before he left and told her to be careful bringing the laundry back up, but he hadn't been bossy about it.

He took Clyde because he insisted she needed the safety features of Chuck Norris in this weather. Rory smiled as she picked up the key and hit the remote start button. A luxury Clyde definitely didn't have.

Chance had moved Chuck near the porch for her, so she wouldn't have to walk across the ground in the rain to get inside.

Silly, beautiful man.

Really, she wasn't that fragile. She'd run through plenty of downpours in her life. And it *was* pouring. They'd had such a run of nice weather that it wasn't unexpected, but she knew this much rain all at once was going to create flooding. She kept getting notices on her phone about creeks and low-lying roadways. She knew better than to drive through a flood—*Turn around, don't drown*—and she had alternate routes planned if Cedar Creek had risen to cover the bridge she had to cross on her way to town.

At least it wasn't tornado weather. Not that they hadn't had plenty of that this spring. They always did, but fortunately Sutton's

Creek was still on the map. Had been for over a century, so maybe their luck would hold.

Rory checked all the locks, though she knew they were already on, checked her phone for motion alerts, made sure the stove was turned off (an obsessive behavior, yes), and grabbed her purse. With one last look around the living room, she disarmed the alarm so she could exit, rearmed it so it would be set to capture any interior motion or door or window breaching, and headed outside to lock the door behind her.

She still hated that she had to have an alarm system, but she understood why and was grateful for it. If the Davises bought the Coombs and Turton farms to build their developments around her, then she'd really be grateful for the alarm. Especially as more folks moved to the area and more stores went up to accommodate the expanding population.

Rory stood at the edge of the porch, unlocked Chuck, bounded down the steps and climbed up into his sleek interior. She was wet but not terribly as she wiped her hands along her jeans. She'd worn a ball cap to keep the rain from ruining her makeup, so at least she knew she wasn't sporting two black-streaked eyes right now.

Her throat tightened as she saw the profiles on the screen.

Profile one said Chance. Profile two said Kitten. He must have done that when he'd gotten in to move the truck for her.

She hit the button for Kitten. Chuck moved all the settings to her selections. Seat, mirrors, steering wheel.

"You adorable asshat," she said past the knot in her throat. She didn't even mind that he'd named the profile Kitten. Nobody had ever called her that before. She would have said nobody would have dared, but Chance had.

And she secretly loved it. Okay, maybe not so secretly since she never corrected him when he said it.

She sniffled and clipped her seatbelt in place. She was really going to have to get a vehicle with airbags and anti-lock brakes. Clyde would survive not going into town every day, and she'd keep him running, but she needed something safer. Chuck had taught her that with all his bells and whistles.

She and Chance could take slow Sunday drives in Clyde on beautiful days. She'd even let Chance drive if that would make him feel better about keeping her and the baby safe. But she didn't want Chance out there on rain-slick roads in Clyde any more than he wanted her there.

Rory blinked. Wow. She really had it bad, didn't she?

"You know you do," she muttered as she squeezed the gas and headed toward the road. "You're in love with the handsome, adorable, sexy-as-hell caveman. You're just afraid to say so."

She *was* afraid to say so. Like maybe if she didn't say the words, if she just let life keep on the way it was with him in her bed and her life, taking care of things and helping out, then maybe it would stay the same and he wouldn't get tired of her and want to leave. And if he did leave, well, she wouldn't have told him she loved him and he wouldn't know he was breaking her heart, right?

"Ridiculous logic, Aurora. You aren't going to tell the man you love him so he won't *know* your heart is broken if he leaves you?"

But it was *hard* to be vulnerable. She was already vulnerable with her diabetes, always having to make sure she kept a handle on her numbers and took care of herself. She was even more vulnerable now with the baby on the way.

If she let herself be vulnerable with him, and it didn't work out, then what?

She'd survive, that's what. Like people did when relationships ended. Like she already had once before.

She turned onto the main road. The wipers were automatic and they were beating frantically as the rain hammered down. Jeez, maybe she should have waited another half hour or so before she left home. But the house felt lonely without Chance in it and the sooner she was at the Dawg, the sooner work started. And then, in a few hours, he would be there, sending smoldering looks her way before they came home and she was wrapped up in his arms again.

Chance

Seemed logical at the time.

Rory typically loved to drive fast, but she wasn't about to in this weather. She took her time as she navigated the twists and turns of the country road that was as familiar to her as the back of her hand. Headlights appeared behind her after she'd gone a mile or so. The driver was impatient, riding up her ass, and she slowed further, hoping they'd go around. Any other time, she'd gun it and leave them in the dust.

But this was Chance's truck, the road was wet, and she had a baby to think about. The bridge over Cedar Creek was ahead. The water was high but there was still clearance beneath the bridge, though the ditches were filling quickly. Another hour of rain and the roadway might be flooded.

The driver behind her whipped into the oncoming lane, gunning his truck as if he planned to pass her.

Rory swore as the vehicle crowded her lane, slowing even more. She just wanted the asshole to go around and be on his way.

But the truck kept pace with her instead of passing. It was raining too hard, and the tint on the other truck's windows was too dark, for her to see a face.

She didn't need to see a face to know that what was happening was deliberate, though. It wasn't Jimmy's truck, or not one she'd seen before, and it wasn't the D&B Properties truck either. But there was no doubt whoever it was wanted to intimidate her.

She pressed the accelerator, hoping to surprise them with a burst of speed.

But the driver loomed in her lane, coming closer, and she had to jerk the wheel. The tires started slipping and then Chuck was sliding sideways toward the ditch. She tried to correct course, but the other driver wouldn't back off.

The last thing she heard before she lost control was the metallic crunch of metal.

Chapter Forty-Three

CHANCE WAS IN THE FRONT SEAT OF KANE'S YUKON, LISTENING TO the man talk about taking Daphne car shopping last night while Seth was in the back, mercifully without obligation to respond to Kane's list of complaints about the experience.

Daphne didn't care what color the car was, didn't care about horsepower, didn't give two shits about make or model so long as it was safe and reliable. She'd like air-conditioning and power windows, but she'd do without the latter if need be.

She didn't know what an anti-lock brake was, didn't understand that power steering hadn't always been an option, had no idea when a tire was worn and needed changing, and thought torque was something the Romans had worn.

Chance smirked at that one. He sincerely doubted Daphne thought the Romans had worn torques rather than togas. She was fucking with Kane because he annoyed her. Only Kane couldn't see it.

It was noon and they were on their way back to Sutton's Creek because they'd finished what they needed to do at Griffin Research Labs. The security team had their new protocols, the training was

Chance

complete, and they'd passed the test when Ethan showed up earlier and tried to talk his way in, similar to how Seth had done it last week.

This time security didn't fall for it. The One Shot guys would go back regularly to conduct more training sessions and go over security protocols, but they wouldn't be there every day like this week.

When Chance's phone rang, he was surprised to see it was Theo calling. His gut took a dive into the floor as he considered that maybe Rory had gotten sick or something had happened with the baby.

"What's up, Theo?"

Kane went instantly quiet.

"Rory said she was coming in early. She should have been here by now but she's not and she hasn't called. I checked the location of her phone. Last known location was near Cedar Creek but that was half an hour ago. I called the police, but they've got their hands full right now. All officers are out on calls because of the weather. Fuck," he finished. "This isn't like her, Chance. She knows better than to worry me."

Chance's body had gone cold, his blood icing in his veins. "I'm on the way, Theo. Text me a screenshot of her location and I'll head there first."

"Done. Call me as soon as you know something. Hell, just call me with updates even if you don't. I'll keep trying to call her."

The call ended and Chance looked over at Kane, feeling helpless. And scared out of his head.

"Tell me where I'm going," Kane said.

"Calling Ghost, Ethan, and Blaze," Seth said from the backseat.

Chance's phone pinged with a text. He opened the image and told Kane where to drive. Kane floored it as much as he was able with the slick roads. Thankfully they all knew how to drive in any condition. It was part of the training. But there was only so much you could do with the weather being what it was and the SUV not being a true all-terrain vehicle.

It took another twenty minutes, but they made it to the bridge from the Sutton's Creek side. The water was almost to the roadway, but the bridge still had a little bit of clearance beneath it. They were so busy concentrating on what the bridge looked like that it took a second to spot his truck. It was in the trees, the passenger side bent around a tree trunk. The ditch wasn't as deep there as it was just a few feet away, but the water was already around the wheel wells.

Kane slid to a stop and Chance was out of the Yukon, sprinting for his truck. He didn't care about the truck, only about Rory. What if she'd hit her head? What if she was unconscious, slumped over the center console.

It didn't compute that she couldn't be because the seatbelt and the slope of the bucket seats would keep her firmly in the driver's seat. All he knew was that Rory wasn't answering calls and hadn't shown up to work.

The water was up to his knees as he slogged toward the door. He yanked it open, ready to pull his woman to safety.

But she wasn't there. The cabin was empty. Rory was gone. Her purse was gone. Her phone, too.

He turned toward his guys, desperation nipping at his heels. Kane was behind him, standing on the side of the road, ready to assist. Seth was still in Kane's vehicle, his phone to his ear as he yelled something at someone on the other end.

Chance waded back to the road. "Talk to me," he said coldly when he reached the Yukon.

Seth looked troubled. "Ronnie Junior. He has a record of violent assaults, primarily against women, but also against anyone who has a run-in with him. He's assaulted law enforcement officers in the past, had weapons charges brought against him, one B&E, and he's been arrested for cruelty to animals. Nothing sticks because his daddy either pays somebody or knows somebody. The charges miraculously get reduced or suspended, and Junior walks. Every time."

Chance clenched his fists at his side. Rain poured down, soaking him to the bone. His jeans and boots were water-logged from wading in the ditch. His heart felt like a trapped animal ready to chew its own leg off to get free. His mind was blanking, but he knew there were things he had to do.

"Check your phone," Kane said. "See if there's been any activity at her place."

Chance fumbled his phone from his pocket as they climbed back into the Yukon. He should have known to check it but his brain was in panic mode. He needed to shut that shit down and *think*. He knew how this worked, knew what to do. He'd trained for it half his life.

The only alert was an indication the system was offline. Something that could only be done from his phone or Rory's. He hadn't gotten the alert when it happened, probably because they'd been in a dead zone with the weather. Then Theo called and he hadn't thought of anything except getting to the bridge and finding Rory.

He'd pictured her wrecked, passed out, maybe drowned. He hadn't considered that anyone could have taken her. It was the move of someone arrogant enough to think he'd get away with it because he always did. Chance initiated a reset of the system as Kane floored it across the bridge. Hopefully they'd get camera access again soon and be able to see where Junior had her so they could plan their attack. Because there was no doubt he'd taken her back to the farm.

But why? What was his end game?

"Ghost, Blaze, and Ethan are on the way," Seth said. He put a hand on Chance's shoulder, squeezed. "We'll get her back, Wraith. It's what we do."

None of them said the other thing they were thinking. The thing they had to consider with every mission they ever undertook.

That they might already be too late.

Chapter Forty-Four

Rory blinked awake. Her head hurt, and her body ached. Her first thought was the baby as she struggled to sit up. Was she in the hospital?

But no, though something was soft beneath her it was also scratchy. She blinked again and her surroundings came into focus. She was in her barn, lying on old hay that had gone musty, and it was still raining, the drops pounding down on the tin roof high above.

She'd been driving Chuck toward town, approaching the Cedar Creek bridge. Another driver had run her off the road. Her heart sank. She remembered the sickening crunch of metal, the slide toward the trees, the desperate bid to keep the truck on the pavement.

And then nothing.

Somebody kicked her leg. "Wake up, bitch."

"I don't like this, RJ. I don't want to be a part of this." It was a different voice from the one that'd told her to wake up.

"Shut the fuck up, dickweed," RJ growled. "Stick to the plan."

Rory moved her head and everything swam. Her stomach

lurched. A hand grabbed her arm and dragged her up until she was in a sitting position, her back against a wall. She cried out at the pain in her head. A moment later, nausea crawled up her throat and spilled out as she retched into the hay.

"Hurting her wasn't the plan. You said it wasn't the plan." He sounded panicky.

"It's called improvising."

"Jimmy?" Her voice was hoarse and small. She blinked again and he came into focus.

Jimmy Turton stood with his hands in his pockets, looking like he'd rather be anywhere else. Her gaze slewed to the other man. She already knew who she'd see. Jimmy had said his name, but it wasn't only that. It was the sound of pure evil in his voice and the memory of how he'd looked at her that day when he'd nearly pulled a gun on her. Her own fault for having Liza Jane, maybe, but the cold-blooded expression on his face when he'd started to reach for a weapon was something she wouldn't forget.

It was an expression he wore now, but intensified. Like any restraints he'd had on his behavior were gone.

She was unarmed, Chance was at work, and she was vulnerable. Jimmy was her only shot at survival. She knew it deep in her bones. Fear crawled up her throat, but she rammed it down again. She had to stay strong, had to fight. For her baby. For the man she loved and desperately wanted to see again.

"I'm sorry, Rory," Jimmy said. "I just need you to sign the papers, that's all. Once you do, then we can all get our money and everything will be great."

Rory wanted to throttle him. If he thought RJ was going to let her go after she signed papers, he was deluded. RJ was a man intent upon destruction and pain.

"How can you be involved in this? How?"

"It's not personal. I just need to get out. I don't want to run the farm anymore. I never wanted it. Opportunities like this don't come along every day in Sutton's Creek. We need to sell now, to people who have a vision, or God knows how long we'll wait for the next developer to come along."

"Jimmy, for pete's sake, there'll be another one in a few months. Have you seen those apartment buildings going up on the road between here and the interstate? Every day they get closer to Sutton's Creek. It's only a matter of time."

Jimmy looked unsure. RJ kicked her in the thigh and pain shot up her leg, stole her breath.

"Smart assed bitch. Listen to her, Jimbo. She's got the luxury of sitting back and doing nothing, slinging drinks at her little shit-hole in town, while you work hard every day to make ends meet. You ain't even got medical insurance. What happens if you break a leg falling off a tractor, huh? Bitch here can crow all she likes about options, but she's the only one who's got any."

"Sign the papers, Rory," Jimmy said, pulling a folded sheaf of paper from his back pocket. "Sell the land. You don't need it. You've got the Dawg."

Rory shot a look at RJ, who was smirking. Jimmy took a pen from his pocket and held everything out to her.

She had a decision to make. Sign the papers or tell Jimmy that whatever he had in his hand wasn't legit. You didn't sell land by simply signing an agreement. If that's the way it worked, then property would be changing hands through illegal means all the time. All somebody had to do was kidnap somebody, make them sign papers they'd drawn up, and that was it. Even signing over the deed had to go through legal channels in Alabama. It was *not* a simple process, and whatever he had in his hand wouldn't obligate her to shit.

Which RJ surely knew.

"Have you asked yourself what happens after I sign that? Do you think we're all just walking away from this like nothing happened? That I'll be over at the Dawg tonight, slinging those drinks, and you'll be planning how to spend your share of the money and applying for jobs at Polaris?"

Chance

Jimmy frowned. "Stop trying to stall, Rory. Just sign the goddamn papers and we'll get out of here."

He could not be that stupid. Except he clearly was.

Rory shot a look at RJ. "You going to tell him the truth or do I?"

RJ shrugged as he pulled a gun from behind his back. He aimed it at her and Rory swallowed a scream before it clawed its way free. She wouldn't give him the satisfaction.

"Wait, no, don't," Jimmy cried.

"Don't? Okay."

RJ turned the gun on Jimmy and squeezed the trigger.

The boom was deafening. Rory stared at Jimmy as blood blossomed on his shirt and his face went pale. A moment later, he dropped to the floor.

It took her a couple of tries to scramble over to him. She thought she was going to lose her cookies again, the barn spun sickeningly, but she made it. RJ had turned his back and walked away.

He didn't think she was a threat. And as much as she wanted to be, she needed to see if Jimmy was still breathing.

His eyes were wide and blinking as he turned his head toward her.

"Hang on, Jimmy. Don't leave me, you hear?" She glanced at the hole in his chest. It couldn't be his heart that was hit because he'd already be dead. She ripped her flannel shirt off and pressed it to the wound, not sure if she was doing the right thing or not.

"Sor-ry."

"Shh, you stupid asshole," she hissed as tears spilled down her cheeks. "You did a dumb thing but I'll forgive you if you don't die on me."

The odor of gasoline invaded her senses all at once. RJ had the gas cans for the mower and he was dumping them around the walls of the barn.

Jimmy lifted a hand blindly, feeling for her. Rory grabbed it and held on as he squeezed. "Scared," he whispered.

"I know. I won't leave you."

Except that fucking RJ was about to light a fire and she was going to have to try and escape and pull Jimmy with her. Assuming RJ didn't shoot her too. Or maybe he was counting on her being too dizzy to make it to the door, especially once he lit the match. The entire barn would go up in a matter of minutes, rain or not. Flames would hem her and Jimmy in from all sides. They would burn to death before anyone knew they were inside.

"What do you want?" Rory cried as RJ hummed a tune and shook gas all over the old wood of the barn walls.

"If you weren't puking, I'd make you suck my cock. But I guess I'll settle for a bonfire with you and Jimmy roasting inside."

Her stomach roiled. "You won't get away with this. They'll find you."

"Who? Your idiot boyfriend? I don't think so." He tossed the gas can aside and took a matchbook from his pocket. "The two of you are going to be ash before long. Who knows which one of you set the fire? Or why? But Jimmy there was the one who vandalized your property and bribed Carl Hoffman. Maybe you found out. Or maybe he came back over here on his four-wheeler today to perform another act of destruction. You caught him at it after wrecking your boyfriend's truck and walking home. And me, I'm out scouting locations with my dad. He'll swear to it, which means I wasn't here."

He backed toward the open barn doors. "Bet your brother will be happy to sell the land after you're gone. Poor Theo."

Rory growled. But there was no way she could make it to RJ in time. He was too far away, and he had all his faculties. She was dizzy and nauseous and couldn't stand up without getting sick.

Didn't mean she wouldn't try, though.

"I'm sorry, Jimmy," she whispered, placing his hand over the flannel shirt to hold it in place. Then she lurched toward RJ.

He laughed as he tore a match from the book and struck it.

Chapter Forty-Five

The barn was on fire. Flames licked up the sides of the building when Kane turned into the driveway. Chance's heart nearly stopped at the sight.

Kane sped down the drive. There was a hunter green truck with tinted windows sitting a few feet distant from the barn, and a four-wheeler parked beside it. The man who stood in the open door of the truck, watching the flames, turned at the sound of them barreling toward him.

Ronnie Junior dove into the driver's seat and slammed the door before fishtailing in a circle and flooring it. Kane swore as he sped past Junior, heading for the barn. He didn't have to ask where Chance wanted him to go.

Rory was in that barn. He knew it with every fiber, every cell, in his body. Junior hurt people. And animals. Leaving her to die in a burning barn was exactly the kind of evil thing he'd do. He was a sick fuck who hadn't yet paid the price for his crimes because his daddy fixed it every time.

Not this time. Chance didn't care that the man was on his way down the drive, intent on escape. He wouldn't get far.

Seth was already on the phone, barking a situation report at Ghost and the others. They would intercept Junior, or they'd make sure the cops did. Either way, he wasn't escaping this time.

All those thoughts flashed through Chance's mind in the space of a heartbeat. Because he could only think about getting to Rory. Was she still alive, or had Junior killed her before setting fire to the barn? Because if he had, if she died, Chance would stop at nothing to make sure the asshole didn't live to see another day.

No matter what happened to him for doing it.

Kane skidded to a stop in the mud. Chance was out the door and sprinting for the open barn doors while his teammates went for the hose that was used to water the garden.

The flames had engulfed the face of the barn, licking at the loft doors. The heat of the fire pressed him back, but love carried him forward. He couldn't get any wetter than he already was so he threw his arm across his face and ran through a wall of flame.

Inside, the smoke swirled, but it was drawn upward by the tall ceilings. He ran down the aisle, searching for signs of Rory.

"Chance," she yelled from one of the open stalls, and his knees nearly melted. "Over here!"

He rushed to her side, dropping into the hay and cupping her face to reassure himself she was really there and he wasn't hallucinating. There was no time to hold her or kiss her. He started to pick her up, but she yelled at him over the roar of the flames.

"We have to get Jimmy out!"

She pointed behind her. A body lay utterly still, blood soaking the hay beneath.

"You first," Chance said.

She shook her head. "No! He's going to die. He may already be dead, but I can't leave him. His mama deserves a body to mourn. Get him out and then come back for me. Please, Chance!"

"Stay here," he ordered before rushing to the body on the ground. There was a faint pulse as he scooped Jimmy Turton up and threw him over his shoulder. Then he returned to Rory. "Can you walk?"

"I'm really dizzy. Musta hit my head."

He reached down to yank her up and anchor her at his side. "I'll support you."

"I don't want to drag you down. I'm too much weight with Jimmy—"

"You won't," he growled. "We have to go now, kitten. There's no time to argue."

"Okay. I trust you, Chancey Pants."

Dear God, that she could call him a nickname at a time like this. Gave him hope that she was really okay.

He took off for the barn doors as fast as he could manage with Jimmy over his shoulder and dragging Rory along at his side. She wasn't quite the dead weight Jimmy was, but it was close. But Chance wasn't letting go of her for anything in this world. Not when she was his whole world.

He hesitated a moment when they reached the flaming entrance, trying to find the best path. Just as he was about to attempt to breach it, praying they didn't burn to a crisp, the flames climbed higher.

Then a jet of water shot through the fire and sizzled a big hole in it.

Chance rushed forward, barreling through the doors with Rory and Jimmy held tightly to his body. When he was well clear, he eased Jimmy to the ground. Rory let him go and sank to her knees to press her flannel shirt against Jimmy's chest while Chance fished his phone out and called for an ambulance. Kane and Seth kept spraying the water into the barn and across the façade, trying to keep the fire contained.

In the distance, sirens wailed. Chance gazed down at Rory's blond head, at her bare shoulders covered only by a tank top, and thanked God that she was still alive. Still his prickly, brave, beautiful Rory.

She looked up, met his gaze, and amazingly enough, despite the rain and the muck and everything that'd just happened, she smiled at him.

Home.

Chapter Forty-Six

"Stop fussing, I'm fine."

Rory was tucked up on the couch, pillows stacked behind her, a mug of tea on the end table, a book open in her lap, and the smells of Theo's chicken stew that he'd dropped by earlier wafting from the kitchen. It'd been three days since RJ had tried to kill her and Jimmy, and she was feeling perfectly healthy.

The baby's heartbeat had been strong and steady when they'd checked it at the hospital. She'd had a concussion from the accident, which had caused the new nausea and dizziness, but there'd been no trace of either for the past eighteen hours. She was ready to get up and start doing things, because sitting still was driving her crazy, but Chance was adamant she wasn't allowed to do anything until Emma Grace cleared her.

He'd been treating her like she was made of glass, and she was tired of it.

"I'm not fussing," her very handsome ninja assassin nurse said. "Just asking how you feel."

"And I told you," Rory said. "I'm tired of lying around like I'm sick when I'm not."

He was standing over her, hands in pockets, looking equal parts worried and hopeful. Chance hadn't left her side for more than a few minutes at a time since he'd pulled her from the burning barn. The firetrucks and ambulance had arrived soon after. She and Jimmy had been whisked to the hospital where Jimmy had undergone emergency surgery to repair the damage done by RJ's bullet.

Rory had been checked out thoroughly and released a few hours later with instructions to take it easy for a few days. Jimmy was still in ICU, still not out of the woods, but he had a strong chance of surviving. RJ was in custody and there were too many witnesses to everything he'd done for his daddy to fix it this time. She'd told Chief Vance what'd happened and then put it in writing and signed it. She would testify to it, too, and no amount of money was going to change her story.

It was a fact that RJ had shot Jimmy in cold blood and then tried to kill her and hide the evidence by setting the fire. He'd run her off the road and dragged her from Chuck as well, though that was small potatoes compared to what'd happened next.

Poor Chuck Norris. He was totaled, but Chance had shrugged it off like it was no big deal, telling her he could replace a truck but he could not replace her.

"Emma and Blaze will be here soon. Just hang in there, kitten. If she says it's okay, then you can dance around the room naked if you want."

"I'd rather get naked with you."

His eyes darkened. "Yeah, I want that too."

Rory swallowed. She hadn't yet worked up the courage to tell him she loved him. She wanted to, desperately, but it was like the words just clogged her throat whenever she tried. Plus she wanted it to be the right moment. When she'd been dirty and bedraggled from her ordeal hadn't been it. Kneeling beside Jimmy's body as she held her shirt to his wound hadn't been it either.

The hospital was a nope. Lying in bed beside Chance after they'd gotten home late was a good time, except it wasn't because she wanted to be able to make love with him when she said those words. She hadn't been able to for the past couple of days because of the random bouts of nausea and the fact he was adamant she wasn't doing anything like that until Emma Grace said so.

Sitting on the couch with him fussing over her wasn't the right time either.

Rory sighed. "Can they just get here already? I want my life normal again."

Chance perched beside her and put his palm on her cheek. She loved the feel of his hand there. It was softer than she'd expected the first time, but also rough in spots from handling and firing weapons all day.

"Being careful after a concussion *is* normal, babe. You aren't doing anything that I wouldn't do if it'd been me who'd hit my head and started puking."

She put her hand over his. He was so good for her. How was it possible to love a man so much? She'd thought she'd been in love with Mark but that feeling had paled compared to this one. "I know. Thank you."

"For what?"

"For knowing that feeling different is a trigger for me. For trying to make me realize that normal varies and I'm not abnormal for having to sit here like a spoiled princess and let you wait on me. It's hard for me to see it sometimes."

"I know it is, honey."

"But you still won't let me do anything until Emma Grace says so, huh?"

He grinned. "Nope. Sit there, princess, and read your book."

She glanced at the cover and frowned. "Actually, the book is part of the problem. I've reached the sexy parts. So many dicks at once. I just want one, but I can't even have that one yet."

He made a sound in his throat and then stood, shoving his hands in his pockets. "You'll get all the dick you want just as soon as

Emma Grace examines you and says you're ready to return to your usual activities."

"Like riding your cock?"

"Rory, for the love of God, stop saying anything that puts those images in my head."

She laughed because what else could she do? "Sorry, but you need to feel as desperate as I do."

"What makes you think I don't?"

"Fair point, sexy pants. Just so you know, the second I get the green light, I want you naked and hard and inside me."

He shook his head. "Maybe not the second you get it, though. I expect Emma wouldn't appreciate a live sex show."

Rory snickered. "Maybe not. Okay, you've got until she's out the door. Then I expect a performance to end all performances."

"I'll see what I can do," he said with a wink.

An hour later, Emma Grace breezed in with Blaze at her side. She went straight for the exam because she knew Rory wouldn't want to wait. When it was over and Rory was in the clear, the four of them sat down to lunch at the kitchen table because Rory asked them to stay.

Chance smirked at her, but she ignored him. Yeah, she wanted to climb him like a tree, but Granny had raised her better than to run her friends off without offering beverages or food. Not that she hadn't considered it, but with her luck Colleen would show up to deliver a blistering message from the beyond if she dared.

Maybe that wasn't the only reason she asked them to stay for lunch, though. Maybe she was a little scared of what being naked with Chance again meant.

There would be nothing stopping her from admitting her feelings. No more excuses. Fear swirled, but the cloud of it was much smaller than it used to be. She'd asked for time, and he'd given it. She didn't need more, but still the cloud persisted. Why?

"Have you heard anything about Jimmy yet?" Rory asked.

"Nothing new. He's stable, and that's good," Emma Grace said.

Rory nodded. "I'm mad at him, but I don't want him to die. I told him I'd forgive him if he didn't, so I hope I have to keep that promise."

Chance put a hand on her knee beneath the table and squeezed.

"He's alive because of you," Emma Grace went on. "If you hadn't tried to staunch the bleeding, he'd have lost too much blood before the ambulance arrived. He owes you his life."

"Well, that and the fact RJ was a poor shot."

"Honestly, unless you've had a lot of training—and by a lot I mean hours and hours a day for a very long time—nobody's that accurate, especially under pressure. Junior was filled with adrenaline and anger. His aim wasn't going to be what it would've been in the range under controlled conditions," Blaze said. "Considering where the bullet went in, he likely tips the gun down as he squeezes the trigger. That's how you miss the bullseye and land in the outer rings."

"Not the point, honey," Emma Grace told him, patting his arm.

"Sorry. Got carried away with explaining why his aim wasn't accurate."

He exchanged a look with Chance that seemed to say volumes and made her curious. It was like they knew things others did not. They'd known, somehow, that RJ had a record, though they'd only found it out the afternoon RJ had run her off the road and tried to turn her into crispy bacon. It wasn't as spectacular as knowing where to find her and Emma Grace when Kyle Hollis had abducted them a few months ago, but it was still interesting that they had the kind of information she'd thought only the police would know.

"Well, I'm glad y'all caught him before he got away."

"There was never any doubt," Chance said. "I just wish I could have been there when Alex, Blaze, and Ethan ran his ass off the road into Cedar Creek. I might not have dragged him out of his truck before he drowned, though."

"We debated it, gotta admit," Blaze said. "But Alex rightfully pointed out we needed answers. Plus the idea that his daddy wasn't going to get him out of trouble this time was kinda fun. Bet he's gonna make a fine piece of ass for some big Bubba in lockup."

Rory sipped her tea. "And I have to admit that's a thought that fills me with uncharitable glee. Granny would be horrified." She lifted her glass skyward. "Sorry, Granny."

"Sorry, Granny," everyone repeated, lifting their glasses as well.

"He deserves to be terrified though," Rory said, anger building in her belly. "I have no doubt Jimmy did what he did because RJ encouraged him and made him believe it was the only way to sell his farm."

RJ hadn't admitted to anything, and Jimmy wasn't able to tell his side yet, but Rory had no doubt RJ was the mastermind for all of it. He'd also very likely been the one trespassing on her property that first night when Chance had insisted on staying with her. Casing the place, making plans, and then roping Jimmy into helping do the job with the promise of success and riches.

The truth would come out, either when Jimmy recovered or when the police traced the money that'd been used to pay Carl for getting his hay elsewhere this year.

"All that effort and now his daddy isn't buying anybody's land," Chance said.

That was the other thing that'd happened. The development was on hold after several investors pulled out of the deal when Darryl Benson was indicted for fraud in Houston on Friday afternoon while RJ was going on a criminal spree of his own. Apparently Mr. Benson had been inflating company assets when seeking investors and it'd finally come back to bite him in the ass. Which meant D&B Properties wasn't buying anyone's land anytime soon. If ever.

When lunch was done and they'd exhausted the conversation, Emma Grace and Blaze rose to leave. Rory hugged her friend at the door, hugged Blaze, and then she and Chance walked out on the front porch to watch them get into Blaze's truck and leave. Rory's heart lurched at the sight of the barn. It hadn't been completely destroyed, but it would take a lot of work to rebuild the parts that had burned and make sure the entire structure was sound.

They'd had so much rain in the days before RJ set the fire that it'd helped save the barn from annihilation. It would have burned down without intervention, but the rain-soaked wood had slowed it enough to give the fire department a fighting chance.

Rory waved as Blaze and Emma Grace turned and headed down the drive. It wasn't until they turned onto the road that Rory did what she'd been dying to do. What she needed to do.

She threw herself at her man.

Chapter Forty-Seven

"Are you sure you feel up to this?" Chance asked as he carried Rory inside, her legs wrapped around his waist, her mouth on his neck, his jaw, then on his mouth again so that neither of them could speak for a long moment.

"Yes. Definitely," she whispered between kisses. "I need you, Chance."

He needed her, too, but he didn't want to hurt her. Not after what she'd been through. She'd been in a wreck, been scared for her life, watched a man get shot and tried to save him, then had to escape a burning building while dizzy and sick.

She'd had three days to rest, but was it enough? Emma said it was. He told himself Emma was right while Rory dragged his shirt over his head and dropped it on the floor.

"Slow down, kitten," he said when she went for his fly. "We've got all night."

"All night doesn't mean you take your time, Chancey Pants. It means you go for it like you might never have another shot. Then you do it again."

His heart squeezed hard. He took her hands in his and stopped her from ripping his jeans off. "Baby, it's not a race, and we aren't in danger."

He tugged her into his arms and held her against his chest. He could feel the tension in her body, the fear, and he hated it. He wanted to erase it and make her feel safe. Always.

He took his time, kissing her, caressing her, undressing her and worshipping every inch of her. The tension in her body leached away until they were finally locked together, limbs and breaths tangling as they made love in her four-poster bed with guitar music playing on the Bluetooth speaker.

She came first, crying out so sweetly as her orgasm rocked her. Chance was right behind her, pouring himself inside her as her walls gripped him, milking him for every last drop.

They lay together, breathing hard, happy and satisfied.

Rory propped herself on an elbow and gazed down at him. He tucked her hair behind her ear.

"I need to say something," she said, frowning.

His heart hitched. "You can say anything to me, kitten."

He meant it, too. Even if it hurt, he wanted to know.

"I spent some time on social media today. Looking at Mark and Tammy's profiles, their pictures."

"Okay."

"I don't know what I was looking for. Maybe somebody vague booking about being unhappy. I didn't see any of that, but there was something else I didn't see. Them looking happy. There are no family pictures that don't look staged. The kids are always perfectly groomed, the background is always just so. There was no mess, no joy that I could see. Not that people have to live their authentic lives on social media because of course they don't."

"Social media isn't real life, Rory."

"I know. I post about the Dawg all the time, because it's my job to market it, and I stage the hell out of the photos I share. But the Dawg is a business. My personal profile may go for weeks without an update. Not Tammy's. She's always posting. Like she's trying to convince herself as much as anyone."

She sighed. Chance didn't know where this was going, but he didn't want to interrupt her because he sensed she had a point that was important to her.

"Anyway, I wasn't unhappy or upset looking at her stuff. When I looked at Mark's pictures, I didn't feel any of that old hurt I used to feel. Which, honestly, I think has been more about my lack of control over life than about the event itself. Yes, I was hurt when he ditched me. But I think I spun that hurt into something it wasn't over the years. I built a brick wall around my heart and vowed it would never happen again. But you can't stop things from happening. You can't protect yourself from life."

"Baby—"

She put a hand over his mouth, stopping him from talking. He'd been about to tell her that she couldn't spend her life fearing people, that she didn't need to because she had him.

"I'm not done. I was scared to feel vulnerable and out of control ever again. And I still am because who wants to feel that way, huh? But I also know that if I don't share myself with someone, if I don't let myself feel the gift of love, then I'll only live half a life instead of the rich, full, messy life I'm supposed to live."

She dragged in a breath and let it out again. "What I'm saying here is that I love you, Chancey Pants. It scares me spitless but I do. I want you in my life for the rest of my life. I trust you to take care of my heart, and I trust you not to boss me around too much."

She took her hand off his mouth. She looked sweet and vulnerable at the same time, and he hurt for all the heartache she'd ever endured in her life. All he wanted was to make her endlessly happy.

"I love you too, Aurora Harper. So fucking much it hurts."

She grinned mischievously. "Say Roll Tide for me then."

He laughed. "Honey, it's no contest. I'll Roll Tide until the cows come home if it make you happy."

"Nah, just kiss me again."

He happily did.

A WEEK LATER, Chance bought a ring. It wasn't a big ring because Rory wouldn't want that according to Emma. She had to work at the bar and she wouldn't want to catch it on anything. Not to mention she was still a farm girl at heart. There were chickens and a garden to tend, a new master bath and laundry room to start building, and Clyde to maintain, though God knew Chance was going to do his best to keep her from doing any of it while she was pregnant.

Before he asked her for a long engagement, he was going to tell her about his job. His real job. Not the part about potential Armageddon, because that wasn't allowed, but he could tell her what he was doing was important and necessary.

He'd cleared it with Ghost, who'd sighed and put his head in his hands. "You know the drill, Wraith."

"I do, sir."

Just like being in HOT. Operators hadn't been allowed to tell their spouses what they were working on or where they were going when they deployed, but spouses knew their military person was a part of a special ops group. And that's what he had to tell Rory.

When the time came, he took Rory to the range after hours. The guys were all there. Emma was there too. Rory blinked in confusion when they walked in and she saw everyone waiting.

"I feel like I've walked into a secret meeting," she said with a laugh.

Chance squeezed her hand. "Kinda. I need to tell you something, kitten."

"I'm all ears, Chancey Pants," she said, taking a seat beside Emma.

"Uh, well, the six of us aren't quite what we seem," he began.

"No shit, Sherlock," his beautiful lady replied. "If you plan to tell me y'all are working undercover or something, no duh."

Chance blinked. Throats were cleared. Somebody coughed. Emma snorted. Ghost literally groaned.

"I didn't say anything," Chance blurted to his guys. "I never said a thing."

"I didn't either," Emma said. "But I could have told you Rory already worked out that y'all are up to something. She works in a bar, you adorable idiots. Talks to all kinds of people all the time. She observes and she's good at listening. She's exactly the sort of person who'd put two and two together if she spent any time with you guys. Which she has and did."

Rory shoulder bumped her friend. "Thanks, bestie. That's a lot of nice stuff you said."

"Well it's true." Emma folded her arms over her chest. "If they didn't want you to know there was something going on, Chance should have kept his pants on."

Which, coincidentally, was partly how Emma had guessed they were more than they seemed a few months ago. Because he'd had to take his pants off to show her his gunshot graze, not to mention the slice in his arm she'd had to sew up. And all of it in the middle of the night, which was totally not suspicious.

"Let's not be hasty," Rory said. "I like him with his pants off."

Chance wasn't the kind of guy to blush, but he could feel an uncharacteristic heat blooming inside. "No talking about my pants."

"It's what's under your pants that's interesting," Rory added. "But I'll quit now."

Thank God.

The guys were snickering. Chance took a moment to glare at them in turn. Once the snickering was under control, he told Rory what they agreed he could tell her. It was the same thing Emma knew, which is that they were a special ops team reporting to the highest levels of government. Secrecy was vital because it was their lives on the line if their mission was compromised.

She took it seriously, which he knew she would once the jokes had gotten out of the way. When he finished, she came to his side and put her arm around him, facing his friends.

"I would never—*never*—do anything that would endanger any of you. I love Chance, and I love Emma Grace because she's my bestie, and I'm seriously very fond of you guys. In fact, I probably low-key love you guys, too. Not like I love Chance, though there have been some books I've read where very interesting things have happened and—"

"Babe, no."

Emma had turned her face into Blaze's arm. She was shaking with laughter. Of course she was. She knew the kinds of books that Rory read.

"As I was saying before I was rudely interrupted, you saved me and Idgy from a psychopath, you were there to help fix the garden the instant Chance asked you, you helped put in the alarm system and cameras, and you showed up for me when I was about to turn into a slab of bacon. I owe you so much, but mostly I owe you for including Chancey Pants in your group when you moved here so I could meet him. He's changed my life and I'm grateful for it."

There was a knot in his throat. Chance fumbled in his pocket as he dropped to one knee. There was no better moment than when he had his family to witness his devotion to this woman.

When he brought the ring out, Rory slapped her hands to her mouth. He could see the tears glistening in her eyes.

"Aurora Harper, I love you. I want you to marry me at some undetermined date in the future, when you're ready, and I want to live with you for the rest of my life. We can have the world's longest engagement if that's what you want. You don't ever have to plan a wedding. And if you do, we can have it without bridesmaids if that makes you happy. Or we can just be engaged for the rest of our lives. I don't care, so long as I spend it with you."

Rory stretched one shaking hand toward the ring. When she held her hand still, he took that as his cue and slid it on her finger.

Then he dragged her into his arms and kissed the fire out of her right there.

"I love you, Aurora."

"I love you, too, Chancey Pants."

Epilogue

O<small>NE WEEK LATER</small>...

"I SEE you made the right choice."

Rory spun around to find Colleen sitting at the bar. She'd been restocking some bottles and hadn't heard the woman come in. It was still early and the Dawg wasn't busy yet. There were a few people at the tables, eating lunch, but nobody was sitting at the bar.

Until now.

"Oh, hi, Mrs. Wright. What will you have?"

Colleen put her hand over her chest. "I have to keep my mind and soul clear, hon. You never know when the other world is lurking, waiting for a way to breach the chasm."

"Oh, uh…."

"I'll have an iced coffee, dear."

"We don't fix coffee drinks, I'm sorry."

"You have coffee?"

"Yes."

"And ice?"

"Yes."

"Voila," Colleen said with a smile. "I'll have a cup of coffee and a glass of ice."

Sounded awful, but whatever. "Coming right up."

Rory poured the coffee, got the glass of ice, and put both in front of Colleen, who poured the hot coffee slowly over the ice. Then she picked up Rory's left hand with a callused one. "Like I said, you made the right choice."

"Getting engaged?"

She smiled. "No, dear. Choosing love. You did that before you got engaged, but this is a nice touch."

"Thank you."

Rory told herself there was no way the woman knew when she'd chosen love. She was guessing, but she was pretty good at it. Had to be to tell fortunes. Yet another mystical service she offered in her shop.

"You're welcome."

Colleen's phone rang and she pulled it out to flip it open. Then she started talking about an exorcism and a seance and Rory found a reason to busy herself at the other end of the bar.

Emma Grace came in a few minutes later sporting a huge smile.

"What?" Rory said.

"Jimmy Turton has been moved out of ICU. He's going to survive, Ror!"

"Oh my God, that's fantastic. His poor mother. She's been through the wringer."

"Yes, but he's doing well. And he's awake and talking. Mostly about RJ and about you. I'm told he doesn't remember being shot, which is quite common, or that you're the one who saved him. But believe me when I tell you he knows."

"It's okay if he doesn't remember. I didn't do it for praise."

"No, you didn't. But his testimony can help keep RJ locked up for a good long time. He did destroy the garden and give the money to Carl, but RJ was the one who broke into Theo's place and drilled the pipe. RJ also planned to bribe a health inspector, though I guess that didn't work out."

"Whoa. Asshole."

"Exactly."

"This is worthy of a celebratory drink," Rory said. "You want some champagne? A glass of wine?"

Emma Grace shook her head. "I'd love a celebratory drink. But first I have a confession to make."

"What did you do?"

Emma Grace leaned across the bar. "It's not what I did. It's what happened. I'm pregnant, Ror."

Rory felt her eyes bug out. Then she laughed and went around the bar to hug her friend. She had to pitch her voice low so Colleen didn't hear. But, really, wouldn't the woman know it anyway?

"Oh my God, you and me, having babies at the same time. Well, almost the same time. They'll grow up together. Like we did."

Emma Grace sniffled as they gazed at each other. "Like we did."

"Wait until your mother finds out," Rory whispered.

"Oh God, she's going to flip. Now she'll get to plan a double shower."

Which meant Ellen Sutton was going to be happier than a pig in mud.

"It'll be the event of the century. Until we get married."

"You realize we're about to scandalize Sutton's Creek by having babies before walking down the aisle."

"Eh, why not?" Emma Grace said. "At least we'll do it together."

Like so many other adventures they'd had growing up. Rory poured them both sparkling water and they toasted to the future while laughing and quietly making plans.

Emma Grace left a short while later, the Dawg started hopping, and Rory looked up to see her man stroll in after he was done with work. It wasn't until the Dawg closed that she could finally be alone with him, though. She hurried outside, knowing he was in the parking lot waiting for her.

He stood beside a big, blue, fancy truck when she'd expected Clyde. "What is that, Chancey Pants?"

"Meet Chuck Norris 2." He held out a set of keys. "He's our new truck, but if you don't like him, he goes back because I haven't finalized the paperwork yet."

Rory unlocked Chuck and got inside on the driver's side. "Oooh, fancy. I like him. Clyde will be jealous."

"Nah, Clyde's fine. I want you to drive Chuck to work. I'll take Clyde."

She caught his chin in her hand and kissed him. "Adorable man. I think it's time I went shopping for a new baby mama ride though. Something with traction control and air bags."

He grinned. "My thoughts exactly, kitten. You planning to drive us home?"

"Yep. Get in, sexy pants."

Chance went around to the passenger side and she put her foot on the brake and pressed the button to start the engine. It roared to life with a satisfying purr. "Before we go," she said, reaching for her phone. "Look at the new T-shirts I ordered for the Dawg today."

Chance peered at the screen. "Oh kitten, you didn't."

"Sure did."

"You think *'You Won't Gag'* sends the right message?"

"Theo thought it was hilarious."

"Of course he did."

"C'mon, BD, I have some things to show you and tell you when we get home."

"What kind of things?"

"Things that will make you shiver in delight and things that will make you happy."

He reached over and put a hand on her leg. "Everything with you makes me happy."

"Same, Chance. Same."

Chance

CALLIE STARED at the data on her screen. Something wasn't right, but she didn't know what. She'd been over the lines of code more than once, and it seemed fine. But there was a heaviness that weighed on her soul, as if she was missing something obvious.

She wasn't, though. The code was fine. So what else could it be?

There was a sound that startled her. She jerked her head up, gazing around the office. It was dark because she'd stayed late again, but she wasn't alone in the building. There were others in different labs, diligently doing their work.

Or so she thought. What if she was wrong and everyone was gone?

Silly. Security would still be there, watching over the building. She was not alone.

No, she didn't like the dark, but she stayed because she needed this to work. She needed the money this job brought. She didn't want to move again, couldn't afford to. She had to make a home for her and Nikki. Had to give her sister some stability.

Callie focused on the code again, went over it line by line. It should work, but it wasn't working. Why wasn't it working?

She didn't know how much time passed before she smelled smoke. She jerked her head up, glancing around like a wild animal about to be caught and killed by a predator bigger and stronger than she was.

A moment later the fire alarm sounded. She shot up from her chair, fear squeezing her heart as smoke poured into the lab. There was no time to waste. She slapped her terminal closed and bolted for the door.

But it wouldn't open. No matter how she tugged, how many times she swiped her card in the reader, the door didn't budge as the room filled with smoke.

She hadn't been willing to play the game.

And this was their answer.

LYNN RAYE HARRIS

———

THANKS FOR READING CHANCE! I absolutely loved bringing Chance and Rory to life! I hope you enjoyed their story as much as I did. Seth and Callie are next!

SCAN THE QR code to join my newsletter list! Get information on sales, new books, and free content.

Books by Lynn Raye Harris

Ghost Ops

Book 1: BLAZE - Blaze & Emma

Book 2: CHANCE - Chance & Rory

The Hostile Operations Team ® Books
Strike Team 2

Book 1: HOT ANGEL - Cade & Brooke

Book 2: HOT SECRETS - Sky & Bliss

Book 3: HOT JUSTICE - Wolf & Haylee

Book 4: HOT STORM - Mal & Scarlett

Book 5: HOT COURAGE - Noah & Jenna

Book 6: HOT SHADOWS - Gem & Everly

Book 7: HOT LIMIT ~ Ryder & Alaina

Book 8: HOT HONOR ~ Zane & Eden

―――

The Hostile Operations Team ® Books
Strike Team 1

Book 0: RECKLESS HEAT

Book 1: HOT PURSUIT - Matt & Evie

Book 2: HOT MESS - Sam & Georgie

Book 3: DANGEROUSLY HOT - Kev & Lucky

Book 4: HOT PACKAGE - Billy & Olivia

Book 5: HOT SHOT - Jack & Gina

Book 6: HOT REBEL - Nick & Victoria

Book 7: HOT ICE - Garrett & Grace

Book 8: HOT & BOTHERED - Ryan & Emily

Book 9: HOT PROTECTOR - Chase & Sophie

Book 10: HOT ADDICTION - Dex & Annabelle

Book 11: HOT VALOR - Mendez & Kat

Book 12: A HOT CHRISTMAS MIRACLE - Mendez & Kat

The HOT SEAL Team Books

Book 1: HOT SEAL - Dane & Ivy

Book 2: HOT SEAL Lover - Remy & Christina

Book 3: HOT SEAL Rescue - Cody & Miranda

Book 4: HOT SEAL BRIDE - Cash & Ella

Book 5: HOT SEAL REDEMPTION - Alex & Bailey

Book 6: HOT SEAL TARGET - Blade & Quinn

Book 7: HOT SEAL HERO - Ryan & Chloe

Book 8: HOT SEAL DEVOTION - Zach & Kayla

HOT Heroes for Hire: Mercenaries
Black's Bandits

Book 1: BLACK LIST - Jace & Maddy

Book 2: BLACK TIE - Brett & Tallie

Book 3: BLACK OUT - Colt & Angie

Book 4: BLACK KNIGHT - Jared & Libby

Book 5: BLACK HEART - Ian & Natasha

Book 6: BLACK MAIL - Tyler & Cassie

Book 7: BLACK VELVET - Dax & Roberta

The HOT Novella in Liliana Hart's MacKenzie Family Series

HOT WITNESS - Jake & Eva

---

7 Brides for 7 Soldiers

WYATT (Book 4) - Wyatt & Paige

7 Brides for 7 Blackthornes

ROSS (Book 3) - Ross & Holly

About the Author

Lynn Raye Harris is a Southern girl, military wife, wannabe cat lady, and horse lover. She's also the New York Times and USA Today bestselling author of the HOSTILE OPERATIONS TEAM ® SERIES of military romances, and 20 books about sexy billionaires for Harlequin.

A former finalist for the Romance Writers of America's Golden Heart Award and the National Readers Choice Award, Lynn lives in Alabama with her handsome former-military husband, one fluffy princess of a cat, and a very spoiled American Saddlebred horse who enjoys bucking at random in order to keep Lynn on her toes.

Lynn's books have been called "exceptional and emotional," "intense," and "sizzling" -- and have sold in excess of 4.5 million copies worldwide.

To connect with Lynn online:
www.LynnRayeHarris.com
Lynn@LynnRayeHarris.com